C.W. (Charles Wilkins) Webber

Tales of the southern border

C.W. (Charles Wilkins) Webber

Tales of the southern border

ISBN/EAN: 9783743463684

Manufactured in Europe, USA, Canada, Australia, Japa

Cover: Foto ©Andreas Hilbeck / pixelio.de

Manufactured and distributed by brebook publishing software (www.brebook.com)

C.W. (Charles Wilkins) Webber

Tales of the southern border

TALES

.

OF THE

SOUTHERN BORDER.

By C. W. WEBBER,

AUTHOR OF

"SHOT IN THE EYE," "OLD HICKS THE GUIDE," "CHARLES WINTERFIELD PAPERS,"
"GOLD-MINES OF THE GILA," ETC. ETC.

PHILADELPHIA:
J. B. LIPPINCOTT COMPANY.
1887.

PREFACE.

In presenting this series of Border Tales, there seems to be little more necessary to be said than that I have not only been to some pains in bringing together those of my fugitive sketches that have not heretofore been collected, but have also imbodied with them several somewhat lengthy stories, which have now first been completed, expressly with the view of rendering the collection more full and varied.

Many of these sketches have been taken off-hand, as the result of personal observation and experience, on the spot; and, even in those cases where I have not been an immediate personal actor, are drawn from such vivid memories as a frequent participation with, often, the very parties themselves, in scenes of nearly a similar spirit, would be likely to furnish. As delineations, therefore, they may reasonably be

3

supposed to convey, with something more than the fidelity of the mere romancer, the wild actualities of life on our most storied, yet least illustrated borders —those of the Great South-west and South.

I shall, some day, amuse myself by furnishing notes to this series of Border Tales, which will give the bare and literal outlines of historical reality upon which each sketch is based; and I am greatly mistaken in my estimate of those who shall have persisted in regarding me as having drawn exclusively upon my imagination for my facts, if they do not find, no little to their surprise, that I have in reality been more romanced against by their incredulity, than romancing.

CONTENTS.

A 2

JACK LONG;

OR,

THE SHOT IN THE EYE.

TALES OF THE SOUTHERN BORDER.

JACK LONG;

OR, THE SHOT IN THE EYE.

THE millions of copies of this story which have been circulated in this country through the daily and weekly press, have all been from a mutilated edition which was impudently pirated in an English periodical, under a new name. American editors, in copying, replaced a portion of the original title, to be sure, but took the text as they found it. I would, therefore, present it in book form for the first time, once for all pronouncing the following to be the only version author-

ized by me, of a narrative the facts of which are too nearly
historical to justify their having been wantonly handled.

It must be confessed that the man of high civilization will
find some difficulty in understanding how such a deed as I
am about to relate—requiring months to consummate—could
have been carried through in the open face of law and of the
local authorities—but he who has any knowledge of this
Texan frontier, will tell him that the rifle and the bowie
knife were, at the period of this narrative, all the law and
local authority recognized. Witness the answer President
Houston gave when application was first made to him for
his interposition with the civil force to quell the bloody
"Regulator Wars," which afterwards sprang up in this
very same county—"Fight it out among yourselves, and be
d—d to you!" A speech entirely characteristic of the man
and the country, as it then was!

It was the period of the first organization of the Regulators
to which our story refers. Shelby, in the latter part of —39,
was a frontier county, and bordering upon that region known
as the Red Lands, was the receptacle of all the vilest men
who had been driven across our borders, for crimes of every
degree! Horse thieves, and villains of every kind, congre-
gated in such numbers, that the open and bare-faced effort
had been made to convert it into a sort of "Alsatia" of the
West—a place of refuge for all outlaws, who understood
universally that it was only necessary to the most perfect
immunity in crime, that they should succeed in effecting an
escape to this neighborhood, where they would be publicly
protected and pursuit defied.

The extent to which this thing was carried may be conjectured, when it is known that bands of men, disguised as
Indians, would sally forth into the neighboring districts,
with the view of visiting some obnoxious person with their
vengeance—either in the shape of robbery or murder.
Returning with great speed, and driving the valuable stock

before them, till they were among their friends again, they
would re-brand the horses and mules, resume their usual
appearance, and laugh at retaliation. Even single men
would, in the face of day, commit the most daring crimes,
trusting to an escape to Shelby for protection. They
seemed determined, at any risk, to hold the county good
against the encroachments of all honest citizens; and this
came to be so notorious, that no man could move among
them with any citizen-like and proper motives, but at the
expense of his personal safety or his conscience—for the
crime of refusing to take part with them, was in itself
sufficient to subject all new comers to a series of persecutions, which soon brought them into terms, or resulted in
their extermination.

We do not wish to be understood that the whole population
of the county were avowedly horse thieves and cut-throats!
There was one different class of wealthy planters, and another
of the old stamp of restless migrating hunters, who first led
the tide of population over the Alleghanies. These two
classes made some pretensions to outward decorum, and in
various ways acted as restraints upon that of the worse
disposed; while they, with that utter intolerance of restraint,
which so unbounded license necessarily engenders, determined to submit to no presence which should in any way
rebuke or embarrass their deeds. Most of these bad men
were a kind of small land-holders, who only cultivated
patches of ground, dotting the spaces between the larger
plantations; but they kept very fine horses, and depended
more on their speed for acquiring plunder, than any
capacity of their own for labor.

They were finally wrought up to the last pitch of restlessness by this closing around of unmanageable persons, and
organized themselves into a band of Regulators, as they
termed themselves. They proclaimed that the county limits
needed purification, and that they felt themselves specially

called to the work. Accordingly, under the lead of a man, who was himself a brutal monster, named Hinch, they commenced operations. In this public-spirited and praiseworthy operation, they soon managed to reduce the county to the subjection of fear, if not to an affectionate recognition of the prerogatives they arrogated to themselves.

The richer Planters they compelled to pay a heavy black-mail rent, in fee simple of a right to enjoy their own property and lives, with the further understanding that they were to be protected in these immunities from all danger from without of a similar kind. The Planters, in return, were to wink upon any deeds, whose coloring might otherwise chance to be offensive to eyes polite.

The other class of simple-hearted sturdy men were goaded and tortured by the most aggravated annoyances, until, driven in despair to some act of retaliation, they furnished their tyrants with the shadow of an excuse, which even they felt to be needed, and were then either lynched with lashes and warned to leave the county in so many days, or shot if they persisted in remaining! So relentless and vindictive did these wretches show themselves in hunting down every one who dared to oppose himself to them in any way, that very soon their ascendency in the county was almost without any dispute. Indeed, there were very few left who from any cause could presume to do so. Among these few, and one of this last class of wandering hunters, was Jack Long.

Jack had come of a "wild turkey breed," as I have mentioned the phrase to be in the West for a family remarkable for its wandering propensities. He had already pushed ahead of two States and a Territory, and following the game still farther towards the south, had been pleased with the promise of an abundance of it in Shelby county, and stopped there, just as he would have stopped at the foot of the Rocky Mountains, had it been necessary to have gone so far; without troubling himself or caring to know who his neighbors were.

He had never thought it at all essential to ask leave of any
government as to how or where he should make himself a
home, or even to inquire what particular nation put in its
claim to any region that suited his purposes. His heritage
had been the young earth, with its skies, its waters, and its
winds, its huge primeval forests, and plains throwing out
their broad breasts to the sun—with all the sights and
sounds and living things that moved and were articulate
beneath God's eye—and what cared he for the authority of
men!

The first, indeed, that was known or heard of Jack, was
when he had already built him a snug log-cabin, on the
outskirts of the county, near the bank of a small stream—
stowed away his fair-faced young wife and two children
cosily into it, and was busily engaged in slaying the deer and
bear right and left.

He kept himself so much to himself, that for a long time,
little was thought or said of him. His passion for hunting
seemed so absorbing, he did nothing else but follow up
the game from morning till night, and it was so abundant,
that he had full opportunity for indulgence to his entire
content. Beyond this he seemed to have no pleasure, but in
that solitary hut, which, however rude, held associations dear
enough to fill that big heart, and quicken all the sluggish
veins of that ungainly body. Sometimes one of the Rangers
would come across him alone with his long rifle, amidst the
timber island of the plain, or in the deep woods; and he
always appeared to have been so successful, that the rumor
gradually got abroad that he was a splendid shot. This
attracted attention somewhat more to his apparently unsocial
and solitary habits. They had the curiosity to watch him,
and when they saw how devoted he was to his wife, the gibe
became general that he was a "hen-pecked husband, under
petticoat government," and other like gratifying expressions.
This, taken in connection with his lolling, awkward gait, and

B

rather excessive expression of simplicity and easy temper, disposed these harsh, rude men, very greatly to sneer at him as a soft fellow, who could be run over with impunity. They even bullied him with taunts—but Jack looked like such a formidable customer to be taken hold of, that no one of them felt disposed to push him too far, and risk being made, individually, the subject of a display of the strength indicated in the great size of his body and limbs. He was upward of six feet four in height, with shoulders like the butresses of a tower, a small head, and other proportions developed in fine symmetry. Indeed,—but for a slight inclination to corpulency, and that sluggishness of manner we have spoken of, which made him seem too lazy even to undertake the feat—he looked just the man who could take a buffalo bull by the horns amidst his bellowing peers, and bring him to the ground with all his shaggy bulk.

Finding they could not tempt him to a personal fray, they changed the note, and by every sort of cajolery endeavored to enlist the remarkable physical energy and skill he was conjectured to possess, in the service of their schemes of brutal violence. But Jack waived all sort of participation in them with a smiling and unvarying good-humor, which, although it enraged the baffled ruffians, gave them no possible excuse for provocation. They would not have regarded this, but there was still less invitation in that formidable person and long rifle; and somehow or other, they had an undefined sense that the man was not "at himself," as the phrase goes in the West—that he had not yet been roused to a consciousness of his own energies and capabilities, and they were, without acknowledging it, a little averse to waking him.

They finally gave him up, therefore, and Jack might have been left in peace to love Molly and the children as hard as he pleased, and indulge his passion for marksmanship only at the expense of the dumb, wild things around him, but that he was led to make an unfortunate display of it.

A few log huts near the centre, constituted the county town.   Here was the grocery, or store, as it was dignified— at which alone powder and lead and whiskey were to be obtained for many miles around.   Jack happened to get out of ammunition, and came into this place for a supply. Attracted by the whiskey, this was the head-quarters of the Regulators, and they were all collected for a grand shooting-match, and of course getting drunk as fast as possible, to steady their nerves.

When Jack arrived, he found them gathered in a group under a cluster of trees, several hundred yards from the house.   It had been some time since there had been any altercation between any of them and himself; and though he supposed it was all forgotten, yet he felt some little disinclination to joining them, and had resolved not to do it.   But as once, and again and again, that sharp report he loved so well to hear, would ring out, followed by the clamors, exclamations and eager grouping of the men around the target, to critically examine the result of each shot, his passion for the sport, and curiosity to see how others shot, overcame a half-defined feeling that he was going to do what, for Molly's sake, was an imprudent thing.

Hinch, the Regulator captain, had always been the unrivalled hero of such occasions; for, apart from the fact that he was really an admirable shot, he was known to b. so fierce, blustering and vindictive a bully, that nobody dared try very hard to beat him, since he would be sure to make a personal affair of it with whoever presumed to be so lucky or so skillful.   Now, everybody in the county was aware of this but Jack, and he was either not aware, or did not care for the matter, if he did know it.   He knew, though, that Hinch was a famous shot; and noticing that he was preparing to shoot, started to join them, determined to see for himself what they called good shooting.

He came swinging himself carelessly among them, with

long, heavy strides, as they were all vociferating in half-
drunken raptures over the glorious shot just made by Hinch,
—and he, in his customary manner, was swearing and raving
at every one around him, and taunting them with their
bungling, and defying them to try again.

Observing Jack, he jerked the target away, and with a
loud, grating laugh, thrust it, insultingly, close to his face.

"Hah! Jack Long-legs! they say you can shoot! Look
at that! look close, will you?" pushing it close to his eyes.
" Can you beat it?"

Jack stepped back, and looking deliberately at the target,
said very drily—

"Pshaw! the cross aint clean out! I shouldn't think I
was doin' any great things to beat such shootin' as that!"

"You shouldn't, shouldn't you?" roared Hinch, furious
at Jack's coolness. "You'll try it, wont you? I'd like to
see you! You must try it! You shall try it! We'll see
what sort of a swell you are!"

"Oh!" said Jack, altogether unruffled, "If I must, I must!
Put up his board thar, men. If you want to see me shoot
through every hole you can make, I'll do it for ye!"

And walking back to the " off-hand" stand at forty paces,
by the time the "markers" had placed the board against the
tree, he had wheeled, and, slowly swinging his long rifle
down from his shoulders to the level, fired as quick as
thought.

"It's fun of mine!" remarked he, nodding his head towards
Hinch, who stood near, while he was lowering his gun to the
position for reloading. "It's a trick I caught from always
shooting the varmints' eyes! I never takes 'em anywhar else!
It's a way I've got!"

At this moment the men standing near the target, who
had rushed instantly with great eagerness to see the result,
shouted, while one of the "markers" held it aloft—"He's

done it! His ball is the biggest—he's driv it through your hole and made it wider!"

Hinch turned pale. Rushing forward he tore the target away from the "marker," and examining it minutely, shouted hoarsely—

"It's an accident! He can't do it again! He's a humbug! I'll bet the ears of a buffalo calf agin his that he can't do it agin! He's afraid to shooot with me agin!"

"Oh!" said Jack, winking aside at the men, "If you mean by that bet, *your* ears against mine, I'll take it up! Boys, fit a new board up thar, with a nice cross in the centre, and I will show the Captain here, the clean thing in shootin'!"

As he said this he laughed good-humoredly, and the men could not help joining him.

Hinch, who was loading his gun, said nothing; but glared around with white compressed lips and a chafed look of stifled fury, which made those who knew the man shudder. The men, who were in reality puzzled to tell whether Jack's manner indicated contempt or unconscious simplicity, looked on the progress of this scene, and for the result of the coming trial, with intense curiosity.

The new board was now ready, and Hinch stepped forward with great parade to make his shot. After aiming a long time—he fired. The men were around the board in a moment, and instantly proclaimed a first-rate shot. And so it was. The edge of the ball had broken without touching the centre. Jack, with the same inexplicable coolness which marked his whole bearing, and without the slightest hesitation, shaking his head as he took his stand, remarked—

"'Twon't do yet—'taint plumb—'taint the clean thing yet, boys;" and throwing out his long rifle again in the same heedless style, fired before one could think. The men sprang forward and announced that the centre was cut out with the most exact and perfect nicety. At the same moment,

and greatly to the astonishment of every one, Jack walked
deliberately off towards the store, without waiting to hear
the announcement.

"Hah!" shouted Hinch furiously, after him, "I thought
you was a coward! Look at the sneak! Come back!" He
fairly roared, starting after him, "Come back, you can't
shoot as well before a muzzle."

Jack walked on without turning his head, while the Regulator, almost convulsed with fury, shouted, "Ha! ha! see,
the coward is running away to hide under his wife's petti-
coats!" and long and loud he pealed the harsh taunt after
Jack's retreat.

The men, who at first had been greatly astonished at the
rash daring which could thus have ventured to beard the
lion in his most formidable mood, and felt the instinctive
admiration with which such traits always inspire such breasts,
now, on seeing what appeared so palpable a "back-out,"
joined also in the laugh with Hinch.

They thought it was cowardice! A holy sentiment they
could not understand, kept watch and ward over the terrible
repose of passion. If they only could have seen how that
broad massive face was wrenched and grew white with the
deep inward spasm of pride struggling for the mastery, as
those gibes, so hard to be borne by a free hunter, rung upon
his ears, they would have taken warning to beware how they
farther molested that slumber of fierce energies.

The strong man in reality had never been waked. His
consciousness was aware only of a single passion, and that
controlled and curbed all others. The image of his wife
and children rose above the swelling tumult, which shook
his heavy frame. He saw them deserted and helpless, with
no protection in this wild and lawless region, should he fall
in a struggle with such fearful odds. For all these men were
the willing slaves, the abject tools, of the ferocious vices of
his brutal insulter; and it would have been a contest, not

with him alone, but with all of them. This was stronger
than pride with Jack, and he walked on.

But he had incurred the hate of Hinch—relentless and
unsparing. To be shorn in so unceremonious a manner of
the very reputation he prided himself most upon, in the
presence of his men; to be deprived of so fruitful a theme
of self-glorification and boasting, as the reputation of being
the foremost marksman the frontier afforded, was too much
for the pride of the thick-blooded, malignant savage; and
he swore to dog the inoffensive hunter to the death, or out
of the county.

From this time, the even tenor of Jack's simple, happy life
was destroyed, and indignity and outrage followed each other
fast.

Shortly after, a horse was stolen from a rich and powerful
Planter in the neighborhood of the town. The animal was a
fine one, and the Planter was greatly enraged at the loss;
for he was one of those who paid "black-mail" to the Regulators for protection from all such annoyances,—immunity
from depredations not only by themselves, but from any
other quarter. He now called upon them to hunt down the
thief, as they were bound under the contract to do, and
return the horse.

Hinch collected his band with great parade, and proceeded
to follow the trail, which was readily discoverable near the
planter's house.

Late in the evening he returned and answered, that after
tracing it with great difficulty through many devious windings,
evidently intended to puzzle pursuit, he had at last been led
directly to the near vicinity of Jack Long's hut. This created
much surprise, for no one had suspected Jack of bad habits.
But Hinch and his villains bruited far and wide all the
circumstances tending to criminate him. After making
these things as notorious as possible, attracting as great a
degree of public curiosity as he could to the further investi-

gation, which he professed to be carrying on for the purpose of fixing the hunter's guilt beyond a doubt, the horse was found tied with a lariat to a tree, in a dense bottom near Jack's hut.

This seemed to settle the question of his criminality, and a general outcry was raised against him on every side. For, though the majority of those most clamorous against him were horse thieves themselves, yet, according to the doctrine of "honor among thieves," there could be no greater or more unpardonable enormity committed, than that of stealing among themselves.

"He must be warned to quit the county," was in the mouth of every body, and accordingly he was privately warned. Jack, with great simplicity, gave them to understand, that he was not ready to go, and that when he was, he should leave at his leisure; but that if his convenience and theirs did not agree, they might make the most of it. This left no alternative but force; and yet no individual felt disposed to take the personal responsibility upon himself of a collision with so unpromising a person; and even Hinch, eager as he was, did not feel that the circumstances were quite strong enough to justify the extremes to which he intended pushing his vengeance.

Singular instances of the most vile and wanton spite now began to occur in various parts of the region around. At quick intervals, valuable horses and mules were found shot dead close to the dwellings of the Planters, as it seemed, without the slightest provocation for such unheard-of cruelty. The rumor soon got out that all these animals might be observed to belong to those persons who had made themselves most active in denouncing Jack Long. Then was noticed the curious fact, that all of them were shot through the eye! This was at once associated with the memorable remark of Jack, and his odd feat of firing through a bullet hole at the shooting-match. This seemed to designate him certainly as the guilty man; and as animal after animal continued to fall, every one of them slain in the same way, a perfect blaze of indignation burst out on all sides.

The whole country was roused, and the excitement became universal and intense. In the estimation of every body, hanging, drawing and quartering, burning, lynching, any thing was too good for such a monster. All this feeling was most industriously fomented by Hinch and his myrmidons, until things had reached the proper crisis. Then a county meeting was got up, at which one of the Planters presided, and resolutions were passed that Jack Long, as a bad citizen, should be lynched and driven from the county forthwith. Hinch, of course, dictated a resolution which he was to have the pleasure of carrying into effect.

In the meantime, Jack had given himself very little trouble about what was said of him. He had kept himself so entirely apart from everybody that he was nearly in perfect ignorance of what was going on. The deer fell before his unerring rifle in as great numbers as ever. The bear rendered up its shaggy coat, the panther its tawny hide, in as frequent trophies, to the unique skill of the hunter!

One evening he had returned, laden down as usual with the spoils, to his hut. It was a snug little lodge in the wilderness, that home of Jack's. It stood beneath the shade of an island grove, on a hill-side, overlooking a thicket which bordered a small stream. The gray, silvery moss hung its matchless drapery in long fringes from the old wide-armed oak above, and that mild, but most pervading odor, which the winds are skillful to steal from the breath of leaves, the young grass growing, and the panting languishment of delicate wild flowers, filled the whole atmosphere around. These were the perfumes and the sights the coy, exacting taste of a bold rover of the solitudes must have.

The fresh face of nature, and her breathing sweet as child-hood's, could alone satisfy the senses and the soul of one grown thus in love with the freedom of the wilderness.

The round, happy face of his wife greeted him with smiles from the door as he approached, while his little boy and girl, nut-brown and ruddy, strove, with emulous, short steps, pattering over the thick grass, to meet him first, and clinging to his fingers, prattled and shouted to tell their mother of his coming. He entered, and the precious rifle was carefully deposited on the accustomed "hooks" of buck's horns nailed against the wall. The smoking meal her tidy care had prepared was soon despatched, and the hunting adventures of the day told over.

Then he threw himself with his huge length along the buffalo robe on the floor, to rest and have a romp with the children. While they were climbing and scrambling in riotous joy about him, his wife spoke for some water for her domestic affairs. It was hard for the children to give up their frolic, but Molly's wish was a strong law with Jack. Bounding up, he seized a vessel and started for the stream, the little ones pouting wistfully as they looked after him from the door.

It was against Jack's religion to step outside the door without his rifle; but this time Molly was in a hurry for the water, there was no time to get the gun, and it was but a short distance to the stream.

He sprang gaily along the narrow path down the hill, and reached the brink. The water had been dipped up, and he was returning at a rapid pace through the thicket, when, where it was very high and bordered close upon the path, he suddenly felt something tap him on each shoulder, and his progress impeded strangely. At the same instant a number of men rushed from ambush on each side of him, several of them holding the end of the stout raw-hide lasso which they had thrown over him. He instantly put forth all his tremendous strength in a convulsive effort to get free; and so powerful was his frame, that he would have succeeded, but for the sure skill with which the lasso had been thrown, that bound him over either arm As it was, his remarkable vigor, nerved by desperation, was sufficient to drag the six strong men, who clung to the rope, after him. He heard the voice of Hinch shout eagerly, "Down with him! drag him down!" At that hateful sound a supernatural activity possessed him, and writhing with a quick spring that shook off those who clung about his limbs, he had almost succeeded in reaching his own door, when a heavy blow from behind felled him. The last objects which met his eye as he sunk down insensible, were the terror-stricken and agonized faces of his wife and children looking out upon him.

When he awoke to consciousness, it was to find himself nearly stripped, and lashed to the oak which spread above his hut. Hinch, with a look of devilish exultation, stood before him; his wife, wailing with piteous lamentations, clung about the monster's knees; the children, endeavoring to hide their faces in her dress, screamed in affright; while outside the group, eight or nine men, with guns in their hands, stood in a circle.

That was a fearful wakening to Jack Long; but it was to a new birth! His eye took in all the details of the scene at a glance. His enemy grinning in his face with wolfish triumph; the "quirt," with its long, heavy lash of knotted raw-hide, in his hand. He saw the brute spurn her violently with his foot, until she pitched against the wretches around; and he heard them shout with laughter.

A sharp, electric agony, like the riving of an oak, shivered along his nerves, passed out at his fingers and his feet, and left him rigid as marble; and when the blows of the hideous mocking devil before him fell upon his white flesh, making it welt in purple ridges, or spout dull black currents, he felt them no more than the dead lintel of his door would have

done; and the agony of that poor wife shrilling a frantic echo to every harsh, slashing sound, seemed to have no more effect upon his ear than it had upon the tree above them, which shook its green leaves to the self-same cadence they had held yesterday in the breeze.   His wide open eyes were glancing calmly and scrutinizingly into the faces of the men around—those features are never to be forgotten!—for while Hinch lays on the stripes with all his furious strength, blaspheming as they fell, that glance dwells on each face with a cold, keen, searching intensity, as if it marked them to be remembered forever! The man's air was awful—so concentrated—so still—so enduring! He never spoke, or groaned, or writhed—but those intense eyes of his!—the wretches couldn't stand them, and began to shuffle and get behind each other. But it was too late; he had them all— ten men! THEY WERE REGISTERED.

We will drop a curtain over this scene. It is enough to say that they left him for dead, lying in his blood, his wife swooning on the ground, with the children weeping plaintively over her; and silence and darkness fell around the desolate group as the sun went down, which had risen in smiles upon the innocent happiness of that simple family.

Nothing more was seen or heard of Jack Long. His hut was deserted, and his family had disappeared, nor did any one know or care what had become of them. For awhile there were various rumors, but the affair was soon forgotten amidst the frequent occurrence of similar scenes.

It was about four months after this affair, that in company with a friend, I was traversing Western Texas. Our objects were to see this portion of the country, and amuse ourselves in hunting for a time over any district we found well adapted for a particular sport—as for bear hunting, deer hunting, buffalo hunting, &c. Prairie, timber and water were better distributed in Shelby than any Western county we had passed through—the timber predominating over the prairie, though interlaid by it in every direction. This diversity of surface attracted a greater variety of game, as well as afforded more perfect facilities to the sportsman. Indeed, it struck us as a perfect Hunter's Paradise; and my friend remembering a man of some wealth, who had moved from his native State, and settled, as he had understood, in Shelby, we inquired for him, and very readily found him.

We were most hospitably received, and horses, servants, guns, dogs, and whatever else was necessary to ensure our
C

enjoyment of the sports of the country, as well as the time of our host himself, were forthwith at our disposal, and we were soon, to our hearts' content, engaged in every character of exciting chase.

One day several of the neighbors were invited to join us, and all our force was mustered for a grand "Deer Drive." In this sport dogs are used, and under the charge of the "Driver" they are taken into the wood for the purpose of rousing and driving out the deer, who have a habit of always passing out from one line of timber to another, at or near the same place, and these spots are either known to the hunters from experience or observation of the nature of the ground. At these "crossing places" the "standers" are stationed with their rifles, to watch for the coming out of the deer, who are shot as they go by. On getting to the ground, we divided into two parties, each flanking up the opposite edge of a line of timber, over a mile in width, while the "Driver" penetrated it with the dogs.

On our side, the sport was unusually good, till, wearied with slaughter, we returned late in the afternoon towards the planter's house, to partake of a dinner of game with him before the party should separate. It was near sundown when we dismounted. Soon after we were seated, it was announced that dinner was ready. All had come in except my friend, whose name was Henrie, and a man named Stoner. We sat down, and were doing undoubted justice to the fare—when Henrie, who was an impulsive, voluble soul, came bustling into the room with something of unusual flurry in his manner, beginning to talk by the time he got his head into the door—

"I say, Squire! what sort of a country is this of yours? Catamounts, buffalos, horned frogs, centipedes, one would think were strange creatures enough for a single country; but, by George! I met something to-day which lays them all in the shade."

"What was it? What was it like?"

Without noticing these questions, he continued, addressing our host in the same excited tone—

"Have you no cages for madmen? Do you let them run wild through the woods with rifle in hand? Or, does your confounded Texas breed ghosts amongst other curious creatures?"

"Not that I know of," said the Squire, smilingly interposing, as the young fellow stopped to catch his breath; "But you look flurried enough to have seen a ghost. What's happened?"

"Yes, what is it?" "Out with it?" "Have you seen the Old Harry?" Such exclamations as this, accompanied by laughter, ran around the table, while Henrie drew a long breath, wiped his forehead, and threw himself into a chair. Our curiosity was irresistibly excited, and as Henrie commenced, the whole company leant forward eagerly.

"You know, when we parted, that Stoner and myself went up the right flank of the timber. Stoner was to take me to my stand, and then pass on to his own, some miles further down the stream. He accordingly left me, and I have not seen him since. By the way, I perceive that he is not here," he exclaimed, looking sharply around the room.

"Oh, he'll be here directly," said several. "Go on!"

"I hope so," he replied, in rather an undertone. "Well, I was pretty thoroughly tired of waiting before I heard the dogs, but that music, you know, stirs the blood, and one forgets to be tired. In a few minutes a fine buck came bounding by, and I fired. He pitched forward on his knees at the shot, but recovered and made off. I knew he must be badly hit, and sprang upon my horse to follow him."

"Rather a verdant act, that of yours," interrupted the Squire.

"Yes; I found it to be so. After a pursuit of some twenty minutes, at full speed, it occurred to me that I might

get lost among the motts, and reined up. But it was too
late. I was lost already. How I cursed that deer as his
white tail disappeared in the distance between two bushes.
I had common sense enough left not to go very far in any
one direction, but kept widening my circles about the place
where I halted, in the hope of finding the traces of some one
of the party; at last, to my great relief, I came upon an old
disused wagon trail, which, though the winding way it held
promised to lead to nowhere in particular, yet went to show
that I could not be very far from some habitation.

"I was following it through a high, tangled thicket, which
rose close on either hand; and stooping over my horse's
neck, was looking closely at the ground, when the violent
shying of my horse, made me raise my eyes—and, by heaven,
it was enough to have *stampeded* a regiment of horse!

"Just before me on the right hand, with one foot advanced,
as if it had paused in the act of stepping across the road,
stood a tall, gaunt, skeleton-like figure, dressed in skins, with
the hair out—a confounded long beard—and such eyes! It
is impossible to imagine them. They didn't move at all in
the shaggy hollow sockets, more than if they were frozen in
them; and the glare that streamed out from them was so
cold and freezing! It startled my nerves so strangely, that
I came near dropping my gun, though he was just swinging
a long rifle down to the level, bearing on me."

"Why didn't you shoot?"

"Ay! why didn't I? I did not think of self-defence, but
of those eyes. The rifle was suspended, but they fairly clung
upon my features till I conceived I could feel the ice-spots
curdle beneath my skin as they crept slowly along each
lineament. The fact is, I caught myself shuddering—it
was so ghostly! After regarding me in this way about
ten seconds, he seemed to be satisfied; the rifle was slowly
thrown back on the shoulder, and with an impatient twitch

at his long grisly beard with his bony fingers, and a single stride which carried him across the road, he plunged into the bushes without a word.

"I started in vexation at my stupidity, and shouted. He did not turn his head. I was now enraged, and spurred my horse after him into the thicket, as far as we could penetrate, but lost sight of him in a moment. I felt as if I had seen the devil sure enough, and actually went back to see if he had left any tracks behind."

Everybody drew a long breath. "I warrant you found 'em cloven!" said one. "Didn't you smell sul—"

"Never mind what I smelt—I found a very long moccasined track, or I should have been convinced I had seen something supernatural. I think he must be some maniac wild man."

"He's a strange animal, any how." "Singular affair," was buzzed around the table.

"Hear me out!" said Henrie. "After this incident, I continued to follow the devious windings of this road, which seemed to turn towards each of the cardinal points in the hour, until my patience was nearly exhausted; and it was not till after sunset that it finally led me out into the prairie, the features of which I thought I recognized. I stopped and looked around for the purpose of satisfying myself, when suddenly a horse burst from the thicket behind me, and went tearing off over the plain, with every indication of excessive fright, snorting furiously, his head turned back, and stirrups flying in the air."

"What sort of a horse?" "What color was he?" several broke in, with breathless impatience.

"He was too far off for me to tell in the dusk, more than that he was a dark horse,—say the color of mine."

"Stoner's horse was a dark brown!" some one said, in a low voice, while the party moved uneasily on their chairs, and looked at each other.

C 2

There was a pause. The Squire got up, and walked with a fidgetty manner towards the window to look out, and turning with a serious face to Henrie, remarked—

"This is a very curious story of yours, and if I did not know you too well, I should suspect that you were quizzing. Did you hear a gun after you parted from this lank-sided fellow you describe?"

"I thought I did once, but the sound was so distant, that I was too uncertain about its being a gun, to risk getting lost again in going to find it."

"Was it about a quarter of an hour by sun?" (that is, before sundown,) interrupted the "driver."

"Yes."

'Well, I hearn a gun about that time on your side, but thought it was some of yourn."

"It may be that this madman, or whatever he is, has danger in him," continued the Squire. "I can explain about the winding of that road which puzzled you so. It is a trail I had cut to a number of board trees we had rived on the ground. They were scattered about a good deal, but none of them far from any given place, where you would strike the road, so that you were no great distance at any time, from where this meeting occurred. We must turn out and look for this creature, boys."

"I expected to find the horse; he—he came on in this direction," said Henrie.

"No," said the Squire, "Stoner's house is beyond here."

Henrie now seated himself at the table; and great as was the uncertainty attending the fate of Stoner, these men were too much accustomed to the vicissitudes and accidents in the life of the frontier hunter, to be affected by it for more than a few moments, and the joke and the laugh very soon went round as carelessly and pleasantly as if nothing had occurred at all unusual.

In the midst of this the rapid tramp of a horse at full

gallop was heard approaching. The Squire rose hastily and went out, while the room grew oppressively still. In a few moments he returned, with contracted brows, and quite pale

"Stoner's negro has been sent over by his wife to let us know that his horse has returned, with his reins on his neck and blood on the saddle. He has been shot, gentlemen."

We all rose involuntarily at this, and stood with blank, white faces, looking into each other's eyes.

"The madman!" said one, speaking in subdued tones, breaking the oppressive silence.

"Henrie's bearded ghost," said another.

"Yes," exclaimed several, "devil or ghost, that's the way it has happened."

"I tell you what, Henrie," said the Squire, "it has occurred to me ever since you finished your story, that this singular being has been on the look-out for Stoner, and while you rode with your head down, thought that you were he, for there are several points of resemblance, such as size, color of your horses, &c., but that in the long look he took at your face he discovered his mistake; and, after leaving you, passed over to the left, and met Stoner returning, and has shot him. He is one of the Regulators, though, and Hinch is a very blood-hound. I shall send for him to be here in the morning with the boys, and they will trail him up, if he is the devil in earnest, and have vengeance before sundown to-morrow."

This seemed the most reasonable solution of some of the inexplicable features of the affair; and, as it was too dark to think of accomplishing anything that night, we had to content ourselves with a sound sleep preparatory for action on the morrow.

Soon after day-break, we were awakened by the sound of loud blustering voices about the house. I felt sure that this must be Hinch's party; and on looking out of my window, saw them dismounted and grouped about the yard. I recognized the voice of our host in sharp, decisive altercation with some one, whose harsh, overbearing tones convinced me that it must be Hinch. I listened anxiously, and heard him swear in round terms, that Henrie's story was all gammon, an "old woman's tale," that he didn't believe a word of it; but if Stoner was murdered, Henrie was the man who did it. I could only distinguish that the Planter's tone was angry and decided, when they moved on out of hearing. How he managed to quiet him I cannot conjecture, (Henrie, fortunately, heard nothing of it,) but when we joined them, Hinch greeted us with a gruff sort of civility. He was a thick-set, broad-shouldered, ruffianly looking fellow; wearing the palpable marks of the debauchee in his bloated person and red visage.

We were soon under way. A ride of nearly half the day through the scenes of yesterday's adventures elicited nothing, and we were all getting impatient, when fortunately Henrie's search, undertaken at my earnest suggestion, was successful in recognizing the place where he witnessed the curious apparition of the evening before. On close examination, the moccasined tracks were discovered, and with wonderful skill the Regulators traced them for several miles, till, finally, in an open glade, among the thickets, we found the fragments of a man who had been torn to pieces by the wolves, numbers of which, with buzzards and ravens, were hanging about the place. The bones had been picked so clean, that it would have been out of the question to hope to identify them, but for the fact that a gun was lying near, which was instantly known to be Stoner's.

I observed that there was a round fracture, like a bullet hole, in the back of the skull; but it was too unpleasant an object for more minute examination. We gathered up the bones to take them home to his family—but before we left the ground a discovery was made which startled every one. It was the distinct trail of a *shod horse*.

Now, there was hardly a horse in Shelby County that wore shoes, for where there were no stones, shoes were not necessary; certainly there was not a horse in our company that had them on. This must be the horse of the murderer! Of course, Henrie was freed, even from the suspicions of these brutes. They believed that this trail could be easily followed, and felt sure that now they should soon come upon some results. They set off with great confidence, trailing the shod horse till nearly night, when in spite of all their ingenuity, they lost it; and though they camped near the place till morning, and tried it again, could not find it. They were compelled to give up in despair, and scattered for their several homes.

The very next day after their breaking up, followed the astounding report that the horse of a second one of their number had galloped up to his master's door with an empty saddle. The Regulators assembled again, and after a long search, the body was found, or the fragments of it rather, bare, and dismembered by the wolves. The rumor was that, as in Stoner's case, the man had been shot in the back of the head, but that the skull had been greatly disfigured.

These two murders occurring within three days, (for the man must have been shot on the day the Regulators disbanded, and while on his way home,) created immense sensation throughout the country. The story of Henrie, which afforded the only possible clue to the perpetrator, and the singularity of all the incidents, completely aroused public emotions. What could be the motive, or who was this invisible assassin, (for the last effort at trailing him had been equally unavailing,) remained an utter mystery.

Hinch and his band fumed and raved like madmen. They swept the country in all directions, arresting and lynching what they called suspicious persons, which meant any and every one who had rendered himself in the slightest degree obnoxious to them. It was a glorious opportunity for

3

spreading far and wide a wholesome terror of their power, and of wreaking a dastardly hoarded vengeance in many quarters where they had not dared before to strike openly.

Public sentiments justified extreme measures, for the general safety seemed to demand that the perpetrator of these secret murders should be brought to light, and great as was the license under which he acted, Hinch yet felt the necessity of being backed by some shadow of approval growing out of the case. He, and the miscreants under his command, enjoyed now for several days, unchecked by any laws of God or ·man, a perfect saturnalia of riotous violence. Outrages too disgustingly hideous in their details to bear recital, were committed in every part of the county. Inoffensive men were caught up from the midst of their families, hung to the limbs of trees in their own yards till life was nearly extinct, and then cut down. This process being repeated four or five times, till they were left for dead, and all to make them confess their connection with the murders! I will not further particularize.

One evening, after a deed of this kind, which had afforded them the opportunity of displaying such unusual resource of ingenuity in torture, that they were glutted to exultation, they were returning to the grocery with the determination of holding a drunken revel in honor of the event. As they rode on, with shouts of laughter and curses, one of the number, named Winter, noticed that a portion of his horse's equipment was gone. He remembered having seen it in its place a mile or so back, and told them to ride on and he would go back and get it, and rejoin them by the time the frolic had commenced. He left them, but never came back.

They went on to the store, and commencing their orgies, at once forgot, or did not notice his absence, till the next day, when his family, alarmed by the return of his horse with an empty saddle, sent to inquire about him. They were instantly sobered by this announcement, which had grown to be particularly significant of late.

They immediately mounted their horses and went back on their trail. They were not long kept in suspense. The buzzards and wolves, gathered in numbers about the edge of a thicket which bordered the prairie ahead of them, soon designated the whereabouts of the object of their search. The unclean beasts and birds scattered as they galloped up, and there lay the torn and bloody fragments of their comrade!

Hard as these men were, they shuddered, and the cold drops started from their ghastly and bloated faces. It was stunning. The third of their number consigned to this horrible fate—eaten up by the wolves—all within a week! Were they doomed? What shadowy, inscrutable foe was this who always struck when least expected, and with such fearful certainty, yet left no trace behind? Was it, indeed, some supernatural agent of judgment, visited upon their enormities? Awed and panic-stricken beyond all that may be conceived of guilty fear, without any examination of the neighborhood or of the bones, they wheeled and galloped back, carrying the alarm on foaming horses in every direction.

The whole country shared in their consternation. I never witnessed such a tumult of wild excitement. It was the association of ghostly attributes, derived from Henrie's story, with the probable author of these unaccountable assassinations, which so much roused all classes; and this effect was not a little heightened when the report got out that this man had been shot in the same way as the others—through the back of the head. Hundreds of persons went out to bring in the bones, making, as they said, the strictest search on every side for traces of the murderer, without being able to discover the slightest.

These things struck me as so peculiar and difficult to be reasoned upon, that I felt no little sympathy with the popular sentiment, which assigned to them something of a supernatural

origin. But Henrie laughed at the idea, and insisted that
it must be a maniac. In confirmation of this opinion, he
related many instances, given by half-romancing medical
writers, of the remarkable cunning of such patients in
avoiding detection and baffling pursuit in the accomplishment of some purpose on which their bewildered energies
had strangely been concentrated. This was the opinion
most favored among the more intelligent planters; but the
popular rumors assigned him the most egregious and fantastic features.

The Bearded Ghost, as he was now generally named from
Henrie's description, had been seen by this, that, and the
other person; now striding rapidly, like a tall thin spectre,
across some open glade between two thickets, and disappearing before the affrighted observer could summon courage to
address it—now standing beneath some old tree by the road
side, still as its shadow, the keen, sepulchral eyes shining
steadily through the gloom, but melting bodily away if a
word was spoken; now he was to be seen mounted, careering
like a form of vapor past the dark trunks of the forest aisles,
or hurrying swiftly away like a rain-cloud before the wind
across the wide prairie, always hair-clad and gaunt, with a
streaming beard, and the long heavy rifle on his shoulder.

I soon began to note that it was only men of a particular
class who pretended to say that they had actually seen with
their own eyes these wonderful sights, and they were those
Emigrant Hunters who had particularly suffered from the
persecutions of the Regulators. I observed, too, that they
always located these mysterious appearances in the close
vicinity of some one of the houses of the Regulators.

It at once struck me that it was a profoundly subtle
conspiracy of this class—headed by some man of remarkable
personalities and skill, with the deliberate and stern purpose
of exterminating the Regulators, or driving them from the
country.

It seems the cunning mind of Hinch caught at the same conclusion. He observed the peculiar eagerness of these men in circulating wild reports, and exaggerating as highly as possible the popular conception of this mysterious being. His savage nature seized upon it with a thrill of unutterable exultation. Now he could make open war upon the whole hateful class, rid the country of them entirely, and reach this fearful enemy through his coadjutors, even if he still managed to elude vengeance personally.

He denounced them with great clamor; and as the people had become very much alarmed, and felt universally the necessity of sifting this dangerous secret to the bottom, many of them volunteered to assist—and for a week four or five parties were scouring in every direction. Thus doubly reinforced, Hinch rushed into excesses, in comparison to which, all heretofore committed were mild. Several men were horribly mutilated with the lash—others compelled to take to the thickets, through which they were hunted like wolves. At last Hinch went so far as to hang one poor fellow till he was dead.

During all the time when these active and violent demonstrations were being made, and the whole population astir and on the alert, nothing further was heard of the Bearded Madman. Not even faint glimpses of him were obtained, and Hinch and his party, while returning from the hanging mentioned above, were congratulating themselves upon the result of his sagacity, which, as they boisterously affirmed, had been no less than the routing of this formidable conspiracy and frightening of this crazy phantom from the field. They felt so sure of being rid of him now, that they disbanded at the grocery to return home.

One of their number named Rees, almost as bad and brutal a man as Hinch himself, was going home alone late that evening. As he rode past a thicket in full view of his own door, his wife, who was standing in it, watching his approach,

D

saw him suddenly stop his horse and turn his head with a
quick movement toward the thicket—in the next moment
blue smoke rose up from it, and the ring of a rifle shocked
upon her ear. She saw her husband pitch forward out of
the saddle upon his face, and thought she could distinguish
a tall figure stalking rapidly off through the open wood
beyond, with a rifle upon his shoulder. She screamed the
alarm, and with the negroes around her, ran to him. They
found him entirely dead, *shot through the eye*, the ball
passing out at the back of the head.

A perfect blaze of universal frenzy burst out at the first
news of this fourth murder; but when the curious circumstances noted above followed after it, very different effects,
and great changes in the character of the excitement, were
produced.

When Hinch was told that Rees had been shot through
the eye, and that from the course of the ball in the other
cases, it was probable all the others had been shot in the
same way, he turned livid as the dead of yesterday—his
knees smote together—and with a horrid blasphemy he
roared out, "Jack Long! Jack Long!" then sinking his
voice to a mutter—" or his ghost come back for vengeance!"

Other citizens, not connected with the Regulators, felt
greatly relieved, now that this impenetrable affair was to some
degree explained. They remembered at once the peculiar
circumstances of Jack's noted mark, and the lynching he
had received; though many still persisted in the belief that
it was Jack's ghost, for they said—" How could it be anything
else, when the Regulators left him for dead?"

But, ghost or no ghost, it was universally believed that
Jack Long and his rifle were identified somehow with the
actor in these deeds. The disfiguration of the skull, in the
other instances, had prevented the discovery until now; but
everybody breathed more freely since it had been made. It
was the painfully embarrassing uncertainty as to the object

of these assassinations—whether any individual in the county might not be the next victim, and the propensity for murder indiscriminate—which had caused such deep excitement, and induced the people to aid the Regulators.

But now that this uncertainty was fixed upon the shoulders of the "bloody band," and their own freed of the unpleasant burden, they were greatly disposed to enjoy the thing, and, instead of assisting them any further, to wish Jack success from the bottom of their hearts. They felt that every one of these wretches deserved to die a thousand times; at all events, whether it was really Jack, his ghost, or the devil, it was a single issue between him and the Regulators, and no one felt the slightest inclination to interfere.

Those who professed to be very logical in solving the question as to what he really was, reasoned that it must be Jack in the body, beyond a doubt; but that it was equally certain that the injuries he had received must have deranged his mind, and that it was from the fever of insanity he derived the wonderful skill and sternness of purpose which he displayed. They could not understand how a nature so easy and simple as Jack's was reported to have been, could be roused by any natural energies of slumbering passion to such terrific deeds.

Those of Jack's own class who had escaped the exterminating violence of Hinch's hate, now began to look up and come forth from their hiding-places. They laughed at all these versions of opinion about Jack, and insinuated that he was as calm as a May morning, and that his head was as clear as a bell. One testy old fellow broke loose with something more than insinuation, to a crowd of men at the store, who were discussing the matter.

"You're all a parcel of fools, to talk about his being a ghost or a crazy man. I tell you he's as alive as a snake's tongue all over, and a leetle venomouser. As for bein' cracked in the bore, he talks it out jest as clean as his long

rifle whar's been doin' all this work. I let you know Jack
come of a Tory-hatin', Injun-fighten' gineration, and that's a
blood whar's hard to cool when it gits riz.   Them stripes
has sot his bristles up, and it'll take *some* blood to slick 'em
down agin."

Hinch heard of this bold talk, and, half maddened between
rage and fear, made one more desperate effort to get the
remainder of his company together. They were now afraid
to ride singly; and those who were nearest neighbors collected
the night before, under an escort of their negroes, and started
for the rendezvous at the grocery next morning, in groups
of two and three.

Two of them, named Davis and Nixon, were riding in
together, prying, with great trepidation, behind every tree,
and into every clump and thicket they came across, large
enough to hide a man. They had to pass a small stream
which ran along the bottom of a deep, narrow gulley, the
banks of which were fringed along the tops by bushes about
six feet high. This was within half a mile of the town; and
as they had seen nothing yet to rouse their suspicions, they
began to think they should get in unmolested.

While they stopped to let their horses drink for a moment,
and were leaning over their necks, the animals suddenly
raised their heads, snorting, towards the top of the bank.
The men were startled, too, and looked up. The dreaded
enemy! A grisly head and shoulders, above the bushes, and
the heavy rifle laid along their tops, bearing full, with its
dark tube, into their faces!

The shudder which thrilled through the frame of Nixon
was prolonged into the death. The black muzzle gushed
with flame, and the wretched man pitched head-foremost into
the stream. Almost immediately the frightened companion
heard the heavy tramp of a horse's feet.

Leaving his companion in the water—one crushed eye-ball,
and the other glaring glassily at the sky—Davis urged his

horse up against the ascent, and saw from the top of the bank, a gaunt outline of a receding figure, just losing itself through the trees, among which the horse was speeding with wonderful rapidity.

Davis galloped into town with the news on his white lips. The Regulators dispersed in inconceivable dismay, and never got together again. They shut themselves up in their houses, and for two weeks not one of them dared to put his eyes outside of his own door.

Jack was now sometimes seen for a time, publicly, and was regarded with great curiosity and awe; for, with all he had already done, it was known that his mission was not yet finished. Everybody watched with intense interest the progress of the work, especially the hunters, who began now to express their satisfaction openly.

At last, one of the Regulators, a poor scamp, named White, who was greatly addicted to drink, grew impatient of abstinence, and determined to risk Jack's rifle rather than do without liquor any longer. He set off in a covered wagon for the grocery, to get him a barrel, lying on the bottom of the wagon, while one of his negroes drove. The liquor had been obtained, and he had nearly reached the entrance of a lane, which led up to his house, on his return, without even lifting his head so far as to expose it, when the wagon run over a large chunk of wood, which had been placed across the track, just where it ran close to the thicket.

The jolt was so severe as to roll the barrel over on him. He forgot his prudence, and put his head out of the cover to swear at the boy for his carelessness. The negro heard him say, "There he is at last!" cutting short the exclamation with a torrent of oaths, when a rifle-shot whistled from the thicket. His master fell back heavily in the wagon, and he saw a tall, "hairy man," as he called him, stalking off through the woods with a gun on his shoulder. It was observable that White, also, was *shot through the eye.*

D 2

A week after this, another of them, named Garnet, who had kept himself a close prisoner, got up one morning at sunrise, and threw open the door of his house to let in the fresh air. Stepping from behind a large tree in the yard, stood forth the Avenger, with that long rifle levelled, and that cold eye fixed upon his face, waiting for a recognition, as he did in every case, before he fired. The man attempted to step back—too late! The sun was in his eye, but, winged with darkness and oblivion, the quick messenger burst through, shattering nerve and sense, and the seventh miserable victim fell heavily across his own threshold.

But, by an ingenious elaboration of vengeance, the most terrible torture of all had been reserved for Hinch. His imagination became his hell. He died, through it, a thousand deaths. He had been passed by, to see his comrades one by one fall from around him, with the consciousness that the relentless hate and marvelous skill which struck them down, was strung with ten-fold sternness against himself. One, two, three, four, five, six, seven! He had counted them all many times. They had all gone down under his eye, and as each one fell, came the question, Shall it be my turn next?

From the certainty that it would come, there was no escaping. He had put forth all the malignant ferocity of cunning and brutal passion in vain; and as successively he missed his minions from his side, the dark circle grew narrower and narrower, closing in terrible gloom about him, till he stood almost singly in the light, the only target for that pitiless aim. Ay! the very spot where the ball should strike him was distinctly marked by seven several instances! And the wretch clasped his hands before his eyes and shivered in every fibre, as he felt the keen shock strike in blackness, through tissues so sensitive, that even a hair touching them now was agony.

Such a consciousness of coming doom was too much to be

endured. Within a few weeks, he shrank like a rank weed, from above which the sheltering boughs had been cleft, and the strong sun let in upon its bare stems. His bloated face became wrinkled and pallid. He became so nervous, that the tap of a crisp leaf, driven by the winds against the window, made him shudder and glare his eyes around, expecting that dark tube to grow through upon him from some crevice of his log house.

There were yet two other men besides himself, Davis and Williams; but they were young men, much the youngest of the band. They sold their property, and one night were *permitted* to escape. Hinch caught at this incident with the frantic hope of despair. They succeeded in getting off, and why not he ? He managed very secretly to procure one of the best horses in the country, and set forth one dark night for the Red River.

The news that he was off created a strong sensation through the county. However rude and primitive may be the structure of any society, there is yet beneath its surface a certain sense of the fitness of things, or, in other words, an intuitive sentiment of justice which requires to be satisfied; and there was a feeling, not very clearly defined, of the want of this satisfaction, left in the minds of men through this whole region. They had recognized at once the appropriateness and savage sublimity of the retribution which had been visited upon these abominable men; but in Hinch's escape, the consummation was altogether wanting. Vengeance was only half complete.

Hinch reached Red River after a desperate ride. He sprang from his foaming horse at the top of the bank, and the poor animal fell lifeless from exhaustion as his feet touched the ground. He did not pause for a single glance of pity at the noble and faithful brute which had borne him so far and so gallantly; but glancing his eye around with a

furtive expression of a thief in fear of pursuit, he descended
the sloping bank to the river's edge, and threw himself upon
the grass, to wait the coming of a boat.

In two hours he heard one puffing down the stream, and
saw the white wreaths of steam curling up behind the trees.
How his heart bounded! Freedom, hope, and life!—once
more sprung through his shrivelled veins and to his lips.
He signalled the vessel; she rounded to and lowered her
yawl. His pulse bounded high, and he gazed with absorbing
eagerness at the crew as they pulled lustily towards the
shore.

A click—behind him! He turned with a shudder,
and *there he was!* That long rifle was bearing straight
upon him—those cold eyes dwelt steadily on his for a
moment—and, crash! all was forever blackness to Hinch
the Regulator! The men who witnessed this singular scene
landed, and found him *shot through the eye!* and saw the
murderer galloping swiftly away over the plain stretching
out from the top of the bank! And so the vengeance was
consummated, and the stern hunter had wiped out with much
blood the stain of stripes on his free limbs; and could now
do, what I was told he had never done since the night of
those fatal and fatally expiated stripes, look his wife again
in the eyes, and receive her form to rest again upon his
bosom.

Powerful elements sometimes slumber in the breasts of
quiet men; and there is in uncultured breasts a wild sense
of justice, which, if it often carry retribution to the extremest
limits of vengeance, is none the less implanted by Him who
gave the passions to repose within us—

> "Like war's swart powder in a castle's vault
> Until the lin-stock of occasion light it."

THE BORDER CHASE:

A FIRST DAY WITH THE RANGERS.

THE BORDER CHASE:

A FIRST DAY WITH THE RANGERS.

It is not to be expected that an attempt at preserving the chronological order of events is to constitute a very determined feature of this series. Indeed, I must beg to assert the autorial privilege of dovetailing my material—whenever there is no immediate connection between the parts—where it will best suit my own and my publisher's convenience.

The reader must remember that he now accompanies me back to the extreme frontier of Texas, more than twelve years since, and that portion of it, too, nearest Mexico and the Indians, amid a population of whites, Spaniards, mongrels, and Peones, and living in a state of perpetual feud, in which the knife and rifle were the sole arbitrators; in short, where all the stable elements and organization of society which afford protection in the decorous observances and staid proprieties of civilized life, are totally wanting.

Strong men and unregulated passions exhibit their worst and best extremes, in this atmosphere of license. History scarcely affords an analogy to the fierceness of the guerilla warfare constantly raging between the three races; yet fragments of them all, under one pretence and another, amalgamated in the society of San Antonio.

The Mexicans, who were greatly in the majority, were

most of them refugees from the other side of the Rio Grande, for political or criminal offences.

The Indians were wretched fragments of once powerful tribes, which had been cut to pieces in their contests with the other two parties, and now cowered between them, begging protection of both, and patiently biding their time for secret revenge upon either.

The whites were hardy and reckless men of every stamp, to whom the excitement of adventure—of complicated and incessant peril—had become a necessary moral aliment.

This morbid passion certainly found abundant gratification here, for with the constant liability of attack from without, they were for ever surrounded within the town by natural foes, the most faithless and malignant.

When it is remembered, besides, that they only numbered fifteen in all, and attempted to domineer with a high hand over as many hundreds of the other two races at home, and, in addition, defend a line of several hundred miles of frontier against the invasion of predatory bands from beyond the Rio Grande, or from the mountains of the Indian country; and furthermore, were compelled to guard against and baffle the treachery of spies lurking round their very doors, it may well be conjectured they had their hands full.

Of course, to effect all this, a very thorough organization was necessary, and a troop of Rangers, numbering generally about ten men, grew out of this necessity.

It is the period of my first connection with these gay and daring fellows at which I design to open my note-book of daily incidents.

A few words, in general explanation of the circumstances of my arrival in San Antonio :—

Determined to make myself familiar with all the phases of life in this curious country, I had traversed the greater part of it alone. But at that time (the latter part of February, 1839,) the journey to San Antonio was too perilous to be undertaken singly; so happening to meet with an old acquaintance from my native state, who was, like myself, anxious to make the trip, I joined him, and we undertook it together.

He was a Brazos planter, and owned, of course, a number of slaves. One of these, in the effort to make his escape to Mexico, had succeeded in reaching the neighbourhood of San Antonio, where he was arrested by the vigilant Rangers, thrown into chains, and his owner advertised of the fact by a special messenger. The particular object of my friend Taney was to recover this boy.

Escaping to Mexico is a favourite scheme of the slaves of Texas, and numbers of them annually attempt, and some few effect it. They have the impression that their condition is very greatly bettered by the change. Indeed, the more spirited of them acquire, by contact with the whites, habits of thought and action which elevate them to decided superiority over the average Mexican population; and if they succeed in reaching that country, they are generally more than a match for the imbecile natives.

Several notorious instances of these runaways acquiring in a short time, position and rank, added to the fact that the Mexican population of Texas had always exhibited a warm sympathy for them, and never failed to assist them in getting off by every means in their power, contributed of late to greatly increase the frequency of these attempts, and, in the same ratio, the vigilance of the planters and Rangers to counteract them. The San Antonio route was the only practicable one across the desert plains to the Rio Grande, so that such refugees were all compelled to pass through it.

In a word, Bahai is the gate of that frontier.

After a journey full of fatigue and danger, we were approaching it on the night of the 25th: news that the Indians were down and ravaging the country, had compelled us to

E   4

travel after dark, with a view of lessening the probabilities
of a meeting with them.

It was a very clear night, brilliant as only Texan moonlight can be, and I felt strongly impressed by the majestic
breadth of the plain upon which we had lately emerged from
the broken and wooded ground, and which lay sheeted in
the vast circumference of a becalmed and silvery ocean
around us.

These primeval solitudes—with all the grandeur on, and
solemn silence that they wore when first God said, "Let
there be Light!" and that shining negation burst upon Old
Chaos, revealing all forms in its annihilation—are wonderfully imposing.

With the high arch above me, its glittering fretwork niched
with "golden candlesticks," and resting upon this broad level
base, which reflected their bold radiance in misty softness, I
felt as if we crept with our slow pace along the plumb-line
of the universe, under the full gaze of the infinite host of
heaven, with their cold keen eyes searchingly upon us.

The awe one feels upon these sky-bound prairies is positively oppressive. If you do not realize eternity and God's
being and omnipresence in such a scene, then you were born
without a soul, or else it has died within you.

After a ride of several hours, during which neither of us
spoke, we observed the monotonous profile of the horizon
before us broken by several objects. As we approached,
they gradually crept up from the darkness, and we could
distinguish the square outline of Mexican houses—very soon
we were among them—clustered irregularly along the bank
of the San Antonio River, the gleam and ripple of which now
struck upon our senses. These houses were square stone
pens, thatched with bulrushes, and, as we passed them, looked
desolate and dark enough, for it was very late.

To some distance, above and below the ford, they were
dotted along without any appearance of regularity, while on

the opposite side, the confusion of black angular masses defined against the sky, indicated the location of the main town.

The river, which leaps forth with a sudden birth, from a cave a few miles above, rushes roaring clamorously over the wide rocky bed which constitutes the ford.

It seemed, as it really is, a hazardous experiment to cross it during the night; but, however, our venturesome impatience was more fortunate than skilful in effecting a passage. The bank is by no means steep, and we found ourselves, in a few paces from the water, amidst the low stone and thatched houses, in a narrow street of the suburbs: this, after a while, led us into a broader one, in which the houses on either side grew gradually from mere huts to the dignity of one, two, and three stories of massive stone.

One of these, standing somewhat singular and taller than the rest, my friend paused before and announced that, according to the topographical description of our whereabouts, with which he had been furnished, this must be the house of the merchant who had cashed the reward offered for the apprehension of the boy, and held him in charge. There was a light glimmering through the door-chinks and key-hole; we dismounted, and thumped lustily and long for admittance; and at last a man in his shirt-sleeves thrust his head cautiously through the half-open door, and demanded who we were.

The night was very cold, and Taney had some difficulty, from the chattering of his teeth, in making himself understood. He succeeded finally in satisfying the cautious merchant, and the door was thrown open.

When our eyes had recovered from the broad dazzle of a large fire, we saw that there were a number of men sleeping on cots and buffalo-robes, along the whole length of an extended and narrow room; near the head of each man lay a Mexican saddle, gleaming with silver mounting, and a gaudy-coloured "serape," or Mexican blanket, thrown either over it or the person of the sleeper.

But the object which at once arrested my gaze was the figure of the negro boy, curled up upon the hearth, and, as he rose to a sitting posture from his sleep, the clank and glitter of heavy manacles upon his arms and legs struck me most unpleasantly.

He was a young, stout, athletic-looking fellow, and after rubbing his eyes in astonishment, received the quiet and scornful greeting of his master, with that stolid, heavy look of insensibility, which always has enraged and made me, for the moment, forget any sympathy for negroes.

In a moment afterward, I was listening and inquiring of the merchant, with full as much interest as Taney exhibited, concerning all the details of his capture, and the present circumstances which insured his safe durance till my friend should call for him in the morning.

The arrangements for his close keeping seemed, at a glance, so perfectly secure, that there was no probability of his escaping. His chains were of the heaviest cast, and he had worn them for months, under the eye of the merchant; he was sleeping in the same room with half a dozen men— the room lit by the blaze of a large fire—its two doors massive and well secured by bolt and bar.

What occasion was there to doubt of his safe keeping? We could see no possibility of any, and, inquiring for the locality of the American tavern, which we had understood was kept in the town, we took leave.

This street led us into a large square. Precisely in its centre towered a massive cathedral, in the usual century-defying style of Jesuit architecture all over the world. Lights in the windows of a long, low, stone building, which faced the square, designated the place of which we were in search.

We dismounted, and entered a well-lighted apartment, furnished very much as American bar-rooms usually are, and, late as it was, fully tenanted. My first impression was that we had entered among a crowd of Mexicans, but I quickly saw that their complexions were not at all consistent with their costumes.

Eight or ten very young-looking persons, evidently Americans or Europeans, were promenading the room, back and forth, puffing away, every man of them, earnestly at Mexican "cigarittas," and all dressed in a costume singularly composite in Mexican and American tastes. Most of them wore the "sombrero," or Mexican hat, and the many-hued "serape," thrown carelessly over the characteristic suit of "foxed" cloth, or of buckskin entire.

The sombrero is a high, sugar-loaf crowned and broad-brimmed hat, generally decorated with a wide band of parti-coloured beads, while the serape is a thick blanket, curiously interwoven with angular zigzag figures, having a hole in the centre, through which the head is thrust. This, falling down to the waist, over the ordinary American dress, and exhibiting the gleam of pistols and knife in the belt underneath, made up a very picturesque costume.

Our arrival was noticed with nothing like the ill-bred and hard-staring manner common in American villages; but we were greeted with a manly and straight-forward courtesy, that at once placed us at ease with ourselves and with them.

Indeed, I was at once irresistibly impressed by the perfect *bon-homme*, yet man-of-the-world expression, which characterized the bearing of these persons. There was nothing of familiarity, but rather a degree of touch-me-not-ism, which it would be difficult to give an idea of in words, tempering the almost boyish and boisterous frankness with which we were questioned and bantered upon the incidents of our journey, precisely as though we had been old familiar friends since time began.

This pleasant cordiality I have noticed is very apt to be a trait of our frontiersmen of any grade, but it was especially

E 2

agreeable coming from these men, with a certain touch of
polish and good taste in it, which reminded one strongly of
the wild blades and eccentrics of college life. Indeed, if by
any magic one could have dropped suddenly into the circle
without the attendant and explanatory circumstances, it would
have been the first impression that it was a party of merry-
making collegiates.

These are the sort of men who are never taken by surprise
at any thing. Though young, their experience embraces
the whole round of the passions. They are prepared for all
that can come. Their personal familiarity with "imminent
perils" of every stamp, and with all the exigencies and excesses to which the life of humanity is liable, gives to their
port, and regard of all circumstances alike, an air of coolness
and indifference, as if—however startling they might be—
they came as matters of course, which were to be expected,
and certainly not wondered at.

This same familiarity with danger gives to their appreciation of the social, or rather the convivial virtues, a high
tone—though the habit of self-reliance, engendered in scenes
of solitary daring, infuses a tinge of individual reserve which
characterizes their open good-fellowship.

I was particularly struck with the youthful appearance of
the whole party; my impression on glancing around was,
that there was not a man in the room over twenty-two.

There was not a single commonplace physiognomy among
them all—all was decidedly expressive, one way or another;
but I was greatly amused afterwards, in recollecting how in-
congruous my first hasty conceptions were, with what I afterwards ascertained to be the character of each; my faith in
my own sagacity was no little diminished!

The personage who earliest arrested my notice was the
most boyish looking of them all. His figure, though scarce
the average height, was stout, and moulded with remarkable
symmetry—his hands and feet were womanishly delicate,

while his Grecian features were almost severely beautiful in their classic chiseling. The rich brunette complexion and sharp black eye, indicative of Italian blood, would have made the fortune of a city belle. The softness of his voice, and his caressing manner, increased the attraction of his appearance; and, but for a certain cold flash from those brilliant eyes, I should have been entirely in love with him at once.

I thought him some wild and petted scapegrace from a Southern family, who had run away from his friends, and fallen upon such a locality and such society by accident. Yet, as I afterwards learned, this man, of all others in the room, was reputed most dangerous. The quick, unscrupulous vindictiveness of his passions had become proverbial, and the *sobriquet* of "the Bravo" had been universally applied to him.

The man on whom he seemed to lavish most attention, and who, indeed, appeared to be regarded with particular deference by all, was a slight, raw-boned figure, with a lean but bold Roman face, and an expression of modest simplicity that struck me as peculiar; there was something absolutely shrinking and hoydenish in his bearing, and I remember feeling some surprise that so unsophisticated, easy, good-natured looking a personage should be treated with so much respect by men necessarily of so hardy cast as those around.

Yet this individual was the celebrated Captain, now Colonel Hays, the leader and foremost spirit of the Rangers, a mere youth; though more distinguished for tempered skill and gallantry in the Mexican and Indian wars, than any man who had yet figured in the history of that frontier.

There was still another person who specially deceived my preconceptions of his character. This was a tall, heavy-boned, heavy-featured, gawky Irishman, who was lolling about with rather an excessive expression of *abandon* and jollity I took him at first for a decided " flat," but I soon observed a deep rich current of the quaintest and most spicy humour conceivable, under the surface of this careless mannerism.

Indeed, young Fitzgerald, the brother of the unfortunate Santa Fe prisoner, was the finest impersonation of the best and most racy traits of Irish wit and Irish gallantry that I had yet met with.

The remainder of the party looked like men of severe, or at least of decided tempers.

But such as they were, these were the Rangers, and these were my first impressions of them.

I announced my wish to Captain Hays to become one of them, and share the rough and tumble as well as their jollities with them—the risks as well as pleasures. I was welcomed with frank cordiality into the ranks, and called for a number of bottles of "noyau" at the bar, to commemorate and seal our fellowship. These were drunk merrily enough, Fitzgerald giving a bantering toast before we separated:—

"Here's to old Kentuck! May he get the green out of his eyes, and eat his salad as soon as possible, in preparation for the close shooting and tough chawing we, the free Brotherhood of Rangers, indulge in!"

The last phrase I did not fully understand until my after experience in dried or "jerked beef" enlightened me.

It was past two o'clock before we parted for bed, and with a brain dizzied by the excitements of the day, the novelty and originality of the scenes and characters I had fallen upon, it was some time before I got to sleep. It seemed to me that the sleep had lasted only a few minutes, when a loud thumping at the door of the hostelry awakened me.

It was a messenger from the merchant, post haste, announcing to Taney that his boy had escaped. We rose hastily, and found that day was just breaking.

The messenger said the negro had got off clear, and had taken with him a quantity of valuable property; that his chains had been left upon the hearth, the back door open, and a splendid horse—the very finest in the country—gone; along with a fine silver-mounted saddle; that the picket fence of the back yard, which was deep set with very heavy posts, had been torn up to afford him passage; that, in addition to the horse and saddle, he had appropriated several costly "serapes," a brace of pistols, and a fine rifle, and that the direction of his trail, so far as they had taken time to trace it, rendered it most evident that he had made for the Rio Grande.

This was stirring news, and created for a while no little confusion, as the Rangers were all forthwith astir. Taney and myself hurried to the house of the merchant, to ascertain for ourselves if these statements could possibly be true.

Whatever had been the causeless and petulent prejudices I had indulged myself in towards this boy, on the night before, for his stupid looks, they gave way now to almost the opposite extreme of admiration for the cunning and resolute skill he had displayed in the manner of effecting his escape.

It appeared that he must have had his chains filed some time before, in accomplishing which we ascertained that he had been assisted by a Mexican blacksmith, whose shop bordered upon the back yard, the liberty of which had been granted him.

But the prudent daring of his measures had been so consummate as to elicit expressions of astonishment from every body. He had managed to conceal the fact of his chains being filed from the vigilance of the merchant, and had patiently bided his time, till the arrival of his master, who would take him in charge the next morning, rendered it necessary that decisive steps should be taken at once.

He had then—after we left him, and a sufficient time had elapsed for the inmates of the room to get to sleep again—quietly divested his limbs of the chains, which he left upon the hearth; and noiselessly possessing himself of the holsters, rifle, and saddle, (which last article was plated with two hundred dollars' worth of silver,) belonging to one of the sleepers, he unfastened the back door and passed out to the stable.

This stable was inside the yard, and enclosed by a high picket fence. By a wonderful exertion of strength, he had torn up a number of the posts, sufficient to afford a passage for himself and the splendid horse he had selected from among a number of others, and thus reached the street by a back lane.

In addition, he had provided himself with a valise of clothing and provisions for several days. All of these items belonged to the same person—a rich trader who had lately arrived from the Rio Grande. The rage and astonishment of this individual, on waking in the morning and finding himself *minus* to such an extent, may be better conceived than told.

After ascertaining these details for ourselves, by personal observation, in company with the restless and excited merchant we returned to the front door, where, greatly to my astonishment, we found Hays and several of his Rangers already collected—two of them mounted on swift horses, and armed for the pursuit, waiting for us in the street. We were too inexperienced of course to have thought, in our hurry and confusion, of this prompt preparation, and as there was no time to be lost, could not accompany them at once. One of these mounted men, I observed, was the "Bravo;" the other was a swarthy complexioned, handsome-looking young fellow, named Littell. He was mounted on the horse of Hays, the most fleet and best-trained animal in the company. All the speed that could be brought to bear was obviously necessary for overtaking the boy, as well mounted as he was, and with such a start as he had gained. The horse of the "Bravo" was also a very game animal.

"Fifty dollars for the boy!" shouted Taney to them, and just as they were bending forward to apply the "quirt" and spur, the hoarse voice of the enraged trader rang out from over our shoulders—

"And fifty dollars more for the horse and saddle!"

They were off at full speed, clattering over the stone pavement, while sparks flew from the iron shoes of their receding animals. It would be a severe chase, every one was aware, and the possibility of recapturing the boy seemed most problematical. I could not help hoping in my own heart, that what seemed so unlikely, might not by any accident be brought about; for, apart from all abstractions, the coolness and daring the fellow exhibited showed him worthy to be a freeman.

The day opened bright and pleasantly. About ten o'clock that morning we were all collected, grouped in the sunshine, in front of "Johnson's," on the square, when pistol-shooting became the accidental topic, growing out of the inspection of my beautiful rifle-barrels. Hays was said to be a wonderful shot, and gave us a proof that the report did justice to his skill.

He held one of my pistols in his hand, when he observed a chicken-cock some thirty paces off in the square, which was just straightening its neck to crow.

"Boys, I'll cut that saucy fellow short," he observed, as he levelled and fired quickly at it, and, sure enough, the half-announced clarion note of chanticleer was lost in the explosion, and it fluttered over dead with a ball through its head. Our exclamations of astonishment and admiration were interrupted by the voice of one of the party:

"Hays! yonder come your horse and Littell full-tilt up the street!"

"Yes," observed another, "he rides very stiff. He looks like a dead man!"

At the same moment the panting animal dashed up among us, and stopped by the side of his master.

Never in my life did I look upon a more terrible object than his rider!

With both hands clasped convulsively around the high pummel of the Mexican saddle, his eyes closed, his face ashy and rigid, a clotted tide of gore issuing from his side and streaming down the yellow skirt of his buckskin hunting-shirt, his reins on the neck of the horse, his gun missing, his whole figure stiffened and erect—he looked, indeed, a spectre horseman! a riding corpse!

"He's warm yet," said Hays, as he placed his hand upon his chalky fingers; "let's take him down. He may not be dead for all."

We sprang to his assistance, and the body at the first effort fell over into our arms. I shuddered at the cold earthy weight, and that horrid smell of fresh and bloody death which, once experienced, can never be forgotten. We bore him into the bar-room and laid him upon a bench.

I observed, on examination, that his pulse was still beating faintly, and on the application of strong restoratives, it began, after a short interval of suspense, to rise.

We now proceeded to strip him, and on doing so, ascertained that he had received a large musket-ball just above the lower rib; and on tracing the blue line its track had left half round the body to the opposite side, we were induced to hope that it had glanced under the flesh and not penetrated the chest. Gradually his pulse continued to heighten, until we saw the colour returning to his pallid face.

"Boys, saddle up! The Bravo is in danger! This is the work of the cursed Mexicans, you know," exclaimed Hays, as soon as our suspense had been relieved by the appearance of these favourable symptoms.

"Yes, Mexicans, of course!" muttered Fitzgerald. "That's a Mexican ball, or it wouldn't have been so bunglingly placed. We'll show 'em the clean thing, boys, with our rifles!"

We left Littell in charge of the tavern-keeper. We were

mounted in a very short time, and collected before the door of the tavern, ready to start, when Johnson came out bareheaded to tell us that the wounded man had so far recovered as to be able to speak a few words. His utterance was yet so feeble, that he had only been able to hear so much of what he said as conveyed the idea that the Bravo had been in advance of him when he received the ball from a thicket.

This, at any rate, gave us a faint clue as to how the affair had happened, and we immediately set off on the pursuit at the full speed of our horses. It was clear enough that either the negro himself, or some of his Mexican friends for him, had made this murderous attempt to arrest pursuit, from ambuscade; and whether the Bravo had not fallen a positive victim, we were left in painful uncertainty to conjecture.

It appeared the more probable that the hand of the Mexicans was in the affair, from the fact that the ball received by Littell was too large to fit the rifle the boy had taken with him, and apparently could only have been sent from the wide muzzle of a clumsy escopet. I observed, as we swept through the town, that groups of Mexicans, with their heads buried in their closely-folded serapes, were leering at us with a grinning interest, which, to say the least of it, was any thing but comforting. Those unpleasantly cheerful looks haunted me through the early part of the chase.

We soon reached the wide level of the plain on which the town stands, and for several hours galloped along its vast monotonous expanse. After we had become thoroughly fatigued by this objectless sameness, relief came in a dark dim line which began to loom on the horizon before us, and which, as we approached it, opened into broken, irregular masses of timber, some of them heavy and tall, stretching for miles, others low, brushy, and dense, ranged like black-shaded islands of ragged and angular outlines, on either side of the old Spanish trail we followed.

Just where it led us within a few paces of the edge of one

F

of these motts or islands, we saw a rifle lying upon the ground. It was Littell's, and had the appearance of having been dropped suddenly on receiving the shot from the chapparal or thicket, which was an unusually dense one, of stiff, thorny bush.

We separated to ride around it and look for the trail of the assassin. On coming together again, Hays announced that he had found both the trampled spot where a horse had stood hitched for some time and the single trail of the flight, leading off in the direction of the Rio Grande. After following this for a quarter of a mile, another trail of a single horse, leading from the main track, was observed running parallel with the first. This was that of a shod horse, and Hays exclaimed, as soon as he saw it:

"Ha! the Bravo is safe yet, boys, and after the fellow, too! We'll have him yet. Bravo had got past before Littell was shot, and must have caught sight of the scoundrel making off."

The sharp, experienced eyes of these men at once recognised the trail of their comrade as well as the main features of the occurrence. We followed these two trails for a long time without difficulty, at the same headlong pace we had held since starting. Though they continued to hold the same general course with the old beaten trace we had left, yet they did not lead into it again, but, diverging in an irregular manner, dodged around among the motts, leaving every proof that the chase must be a desperate one. The skill with which the Rangers unerringly traced this devious way, although we were going at a swift run, was very surprising.

This hard riding had of course very greatly fagged both ourselves and horses, and we were beginning to fear that the night would overtake us and prevent the prosecution of the pursuit to any advantage, when we came upon a wide and seemingly interminable plain, the bare undulating surface of which afforded us little of either pleasure or encouragement.

Suddenly, however, and most unexpectedly, one of the men in front shouted, while he pointed with his gun over to the right:

"Look! that must be the Bravo. He's got him!"

We turned our heads, and the figures of two horsemen were just rising into view over the ridge of an undulation far away across the plains.

The figure of a man heaving in sight amidst these wild solitudes, always causes a startle and thrill of expectation and doubt similar to the feeling produced by the announcement of "a strange sail ahead" on shipboard, during a long voyage.

The eye glances with careless indifference over great herds of deer, buffaloes, or mustangs, dotted in the distance; but a glimpse of any shape, even remotely resembling a brother man, makes the pulse leap fast and sharp, and the blood rush back to the heart; for in this lawless region it is impossible to conjecture whether, what would naturally be an auspicious event may not result in a mortal struggle, and death to one party or the other.

This distorted condition of things causes strange emotions, for it does seem most *outre* and unnatural, that the outlines which of all others ought to be the most agreeable should be productive of the most unpleasant excitement—while we can look upon thousands and multiplied thousands of brutes with a negative feeling, if not one of pleasant companionship. I have been particularly struck with this while travelling alone, when any thing the imagination could conjure into a resemblance of the human form would produce the most uncomfortable sensations.

There is nothing to fear from the animals, but from that likeness to yourself every thing of hate and treachery is to be dreaded.

We instantly headed our horses towards these distant riders, who seemed to be jogging on very sociably at a leisurely gait in the direction of San Antonio. As we neared them, every moment made it more probable that the man's first conjecture was right.

They soon observed us, and stopped with some flurry and hesitation of manner, but after a long and deliberate survey they started to meet us.

I had thought at first that they intended to wheel and make off, but the assured recognition was simultaneous, and with a loud cheer we increased our speed.

The Bravo waved his sombrero in the air and answered us. In a little while more we crowded around him and his prisoner, eagerly asking a multitude of questions.

The man was tied with a lariat about his feet, which was passed under the belly of his horse. His hands were also tied behind him, and their appearance of sociability at the distance was fully explained when we saw that the Bravo was leading his horse by another lariat. He was a Mexican of spare figure, with a lean Roman face, sharp black eyes, and a vivid expression of bold knavery, not at all cowed by our numbers and wrathful looks. His whole appearance was altogether unlike the usual downward-eyed, sneaking, wolfish look, common to Mexicans in circumstances of peril such as those surrounding him. The audacity of the fellow's bearing at once attracted comment.

"Why, Bravo," said Fitzgerald, "what the deuse are you doing with that saucy-looking fellow alive? You are the last man I should have suspected of having the 'vice of mercy' in you!"

"Ha, ha!" laughed he, "the best of the joke is, that I kept him alive simply because he gave me so much trouble in catching him. He's a regular curiosity; and I wanted to show you a live Mexican, who was good pluck to the very back-bone—the only specimen of the kind that I conjecture any of you ever saw."

"The scoundrel," said Hays, "I don't see that it required

any great bravery to shoot a man from the bush. We'll take him off your hands—I'll have him disposed of."

"That's just what I wanted, Jack," (so Hays was familiarly called,) "I spared the rascal once, because he made me laugh by his bold impudence, just as I was in the act of pulling trigger upon him for the second time, and I don't feel disposed to kill him now, though I want you all to do it, for he deserves it a hundred times. Don't you remember him ?"

"I think I have seen him before," said Hays, "but where or when I can't recollect. It doesn't matter, though : we'll relieve you of him."

"You have not forgotten Gonzaleze, the dexterous thief, who stole your sorrel horse, last summer, and ran him off across the Rio Grande ?"

"Ha ! this is the same fellow : well, we'll pay him off all scores this time."

"He understands perfectly what you say. By the way, have you seen or heard any thing of Littell ? He went off in a singular style. I thought he was shot."

Hays explained to him the circumstances the reader is already in possession of; and while we rode slowly towards a distant line of timber, indicating a stream on which we meant to camp for the night, the Bravo related his story of the day's events to us.

"After leaving you in the street this morning, we continued at the best speed of our horses on the old Rio Grande trail: for though we saw nothing of the boy's trail upon it at first, I felt convinced we should find it after a while, for I knew he must have taken this route. Sure enough, within about five miles of town, we saw where it came in along with another horse. I suspected at once that this was the Mexican who was guiding and assisting him.

"We kept on very rapidly, and Littell had fallen several hundred yards behind me, when, after passing that point of timber some moments, I heard a gun behind me, and, turning my head very quickly, I saw your horse just shying from the smoke, and wheeling on the back track, while the rifle of Littell dropped from his hands.

"I saw from his manner, that he was hit, and expected to see him fall. The horse appeared to be greatly frightened, and was clearly running without any control. It at once occurred to me that the man who fired would attempt to escape from the other side of the mott, and thinking more of vengeance than any thing else, as soon as I could rein up and turn my horse, I galloped round it.

"I saw this fellow already in the saddle, making across the prairie, and instantly took after him. He had the start of me, and kept it for nearly two hours, through the hottest and hardest chase that ever I had. I thought at one time the scamp would beat me and get away; but the staunch bottom of my horse proved too much for his. Such doubles, and turns, and twists as he made among the motts you never saw in your life."

"Yes," interrupted Fitz, "we have had a very perfect idea of them: haven't we been worried enough in following your trail?"

"As his horse began to fail," continued the Bravo, "he doubled like a fox in the effort to lose me among the islands; but I had no notion of being thrown off, and after a while began to close rapidly upon him.

"When he became convinced that there was no chance for his escape, very greatly to my astonishment, he turned suddenly in the saddle, levelling a large pistol at me: I bent forward over my horse's neck, and the ball whizzed above me; as I straightened up, I also fired, but missed, and at the same instant my horse came full tilt against his, and we went down together.

"I was on my feet first, and, with my second pistol against his prostrate body, was in the act of firing into him, when, with the most cool and comical expression conceivable, he exclaimed, as he looked up, grinning in my face—

"'You missed and I missed—we are even!'

"I burst into a laugh, and threw down my pistol, while the fellow rose and shook himself, and began to kick and curse his prostrate horse.

"'Garracho! you nasty brute, if I hadn't thought you were better bottom, I should not have gone to the trouble to steal you;' and turning to me, he observed, 'but he pushed you some, any how. I shall have to steal your bay next.'

"I was so tickled at this unprecedented impudence, that I fairly roared, while the knave, finding he had got the right side of me, continued in the same strain—

"'I let you pass, but it was an old grudge I had against Littell. He had me whipped in Matamoras, last spring, and I promised to be even with him before the year was out; and you see I have been as good as my word. I hope he's done for.'

"There was something so funny and original in the rascal's saucy self-possession, that it was some little time before I could restrain my laughter sufficiently to address him.

"'You can't expect any mercy from us, you scamp,' said I.

"'Oh! no, I suppose you are going to have me shot. *Muy bueno*—I think I've worked for it. I have stolen some half-dozen horses from you Rangers.'

"'Ha! you are Gonzaleze?'

"'Yes.'

"'Well, I pity you if Hays or any of the boys get hold of you. I mean to tie you and take you into town.'

"'Bueno,' he said, holding out his hands readily, and I tied them, and here he is. You may shoot the fellow if you can, but I'll be sworn I neither can, nor will have a hand in it. He's such an odd genius, that I think it would be a sin almost to shoot him ; though it ought, undoubtedly, to be done, and I wish you all would do it."

" Oh !" said Hays, dryly, " never fear, Bravo, we'll relieve you on that score very shortly.   But here's the water—we'll draw lots for the six who shall shoot him, as soon as we get ready for camping."

I could not help feeling enlisted in the Bravo's sympathy for the man, who, during this conversation—every word of which he understood—had maintained the same bearing of reckless and defiant coolness.

We dismounted by the side of a clear, rapid stream, under the narrow fringe of timber which bordered it, and after tying the Mexican to a tree, proceeded to strip our horses, stake them out to grass, kindle a fire, and make all the usual preparations for camping.   This was all done in perfect silence, for the stern resolve which was about to be executed left, under any view of it, no room for frivolity of feeling.

The Bravo had instantly, on dismounting, and in entire forgetfulness of his faithful horse, stretched himself on the grass in front of Gonzaleze, and continued to regard his face—which maintained unblenchingly its expression of calm indifference—with a gaze of intensely curious interest.

Indeed, it was an awful trial his hardy nerve was subjected to—looking upon the silent progress of a preparation, the consummation of which he well knew was to close his account with men and the world.   There was to me something positively terrible in the mute activity of our men, and the sharp, fixed alertness of the regard of the prisoner.

When every thing had been arranged, we gathered around the fire, in speechless awe—feeling that the crisis had come, yet dreading its action.

Not a word was spoken, till Hays said, in a low voice, as he pulled a pencil and some paper from his pocket :—

" The six men of the eleven, who draw the lowest numbers, will shoot him !"

He then proceeded to write them down, and handed them round to us in his hat.

I drew my number with a degree of nervousness that surprised me; for, independent of my natural and invincible horror of a cold-blooded execution such as this, I had partaken of the Bravo's liking for the singular and piquant traits this fellow had exhibited, and was very loath to be made an instrument of his death!

My gratification was extreme, when I saw that my number was so high as to place me out of danger. Those who drew the low numbers, seemed to feel the most perfect indifference about the affair, and ranged themselves in front of Gonzaleze with precisely the same air that would have characterized them had it been a wooden target they were going to shoot at, instead of a fellow being.

The row of dark tubes was levelled at him, and Hays was opening his lips to enunciate the fatal word "fire," when the man, in a clear, petulant voice, said—

"Garracho! don't aim so low, you clumsy sapheads!"

The Bravo, springing to his feet, exclaimed—

"Jack, hear that! don't shoot this fellow! spare him for my sake!"

Hays waved his hand, and the guns, greatly to my gratification, were lowered, and in another moment, the Bravo had cut the thongs which bound the limbs of the Mexican, and he stood before us a free man.

With the same unmoved self-collection and frankness which had characterized his whole bearing, he proceeded to explain to us his connection with the negro's escape.

He told us that, attracted by a human sympathy for the boy, whom he had accidentally met in the shop of the blacksmith, with his heavy chains on, he had furnished him with a file to cut them, and advised him to the utmost as to the manner of his escape, and guided and accompanied him in his flight to the thicket, where he had concealed himself while the boy went on, and, recognising the Bravo, had let him go by; but the features of his old and sworn enemy had proved too much for his prudence, and he shot at him, with the results we have seen.

Such as it was, this was my first day with the "Rangers," and we were soon afterwards sound asleep on the grass. It is hardly necessary to add, that the boy made good his escape across the Rio Grande, with all his plunder.

GONZALEZE AGAIN;

OR,

THE BRAVO'S STRATAGEM.

GONZALEZE AGAIN;

OR, THE BRAVO'S STRATAGEM.

It must be confessed that our Rangers held a somewhat nominal allegiance to the President of Texas, though their commissions were in his name. That august official had far too many hungry pap-suckers clinging to the lean bosom of the home Treasury to spare one generous drop even, for the nourishment of this distant frontier; so that the bold spirits who ventured there had glory to any amount meted out for their subsistence by his prodigal hand, and if they found any thing less sublimated and more substantial necessary, they were told with a superb hauteur, that "honour was the dearest gift of princes;" and that, as to these grosser matters, they might shift for themselves!

The consequence was, as "necessity knows no law," that these young gentlemen could not at any rate be expected to trouble themselves with framing an original code for it, under such circumstances; indeed, their veneration of a custom so antiquated as that "the memory of man runneth not to the contrary," would have forbidden it, if nothing else; and in this classical taste they were necessarily highly prejudiced in favour of the primeval axiom, "Might is right," which was adopted as their creed, moral and political!

The fifteen hundred Mexicans, who made up the remaining

G 73

population of the town, as well as the swarms along the distant banks of the Rio Grande, were made to appreciate very fully the practical results of this creed, which was carried out at their expense in sundry unceremonious contributions, levied by these adventurous zealots with a faithfulness which would have secured the seventh heaven to followers of Mohammed.

Captain Hays, as we have mentioned, was the master-spirit of this band, and ranking next to him was the hero of our adventure, whom we have already introduced as a young gentleman whose very feminine and delicate features contrasted remarkably with the traits of remorseless hardihood which had gained him the soubriquet of "the Bravo."

There was no desperate enterprise in which the Bravo did not of choice lead the forlorn hope; there was nothing too madly daring and too near impossible for him to undertake, if he once took the whim into his head that he would accomplish it. Hays was the more powerful character, and like

> "Hector in his blaze of wrath subscribed
> To tender objects; but *he*, in heat of action,
> Was more vindictive than jealous love."

And not in the heat of action only, but under all possible contingencies where the blood of the hated Mexicans of the Rio Grande was at issue, he was pitiless as winter!

Antonio Navarro, a Mexican of Hidalgo descent, who had joined the Texans in their revolt, and fought shoulder to shoulder with them throughout the revolution, was very popular and much respected by the Americans of Bahai, who had given him their votes as Mayor, and were ready to stand by him under all circumstances. Navarro was rich, and carried on, through agents who were not altogether so obnoxious to the Mexican government as himself, quite an extensive and lucrative trade with the villages beyond the Rio Grande.

It happened just at this crisis that he was in a serious quandary.

His last trading venture, which had been a heavy one, had been successfully converted into silver; but his faithful agent had sent him word that he dared not budge a foot with his precious charge, two or three mule loads of which he was guarding night and day at the rancho of Navarro's old friend, Don Jose, on the Texan bank of the Rio Grande. For he feared that his old friend, tempted by the richness of the prize, had proved unfaithful, and had given the renowned and formidable outlaw, Agatone, a hint of the intended transfer, that he might intercept it on the way across those sterile plains which stretch between that river and Bahai.

It was very certain, at least, that he was beleaguered by the spies of the bandit captain; that a detachment of his troops were hanging round the rancho, waiting for the treasure to be started, with the intention of attacking those having it in charge, on the prairies; that Agatone, who was the mortal enemy of Navarro, had sworn that his money should never reach Bahai; and the agent, in sore distress, begged him to send a formidable escort, sufficiently strong to defy the whole force of Agatone, for without this it would be madness to leave the walls of the rancho; and he was not even sure, by any means, it was safe there, for that the conduct of Don Jose savoured very strongly of treachery.

Poor Navarro was sadly taken aback by this news. But he went instantly to work and equipped a troop of the vagabond braggadocio Mexicans about Bahai, and started it off under the command of a trusted servant, to bring in his silver, and frighten Agatone's cut-throats. He sent private instructions through to his agent having charge of the money, not to trust it to these fellows unless he had ascertained whether they would stand fire or not, for on this point he nad some shrewd doubts, growing out of his intimate knowledge of his fellow-citizens. The agent was first to send them with a great parade of sacks, stuffed with moss and gravel, a day or two's journey on the return trail.

In this time the attack of Agatone would probably be made, and if they should prove able to cope with him and show any game, the agent might then go back and fill his sacks in earnest, with some prospect of reaching home with their contents.

This wary stratagem was carried out to the letter, and the result proved it to have been a wise precaution, for the cowardly ragamuffins scarcely waited Agatone's first charge before they were scattered, flying helter-skelter in every direction over the plains; and nearly all of them killed their horses by running, and came straggling into Bahai on foot, with an awful tale of robbery, blood, and devoted courage on their part, each man vowing as he arrived, that he had fought until all those yet left behind him were killed; and not a little laughter did it create among the Americans, as one after another the ghosts of these heroes thus unceremoniously consigned to the gory bed of honour, would come dropping in, apparelled in the old-fashioned garb of flesh and blood.

The truth was, that Agatone had not pursued them at all, but stopping at the money bags, eagerly ripped them open with his dagger, that he might gloat his hungry vision upon the shining contents. The rage of the baffled ruffian may be better conceived than told, when a stream of shells and pebbles followed through the rent; he swore all sorts of dire oaths as he thrust his damaged dagger back into the sheath.

But the faithful agent, whose name was Alvarez, had taken care to keep out of harm's way, and, with the most trustworthy of his men, was securely housed in Don Jose's rancho, guarding the treasure like a sleepless gryphon, and in despite of the treachery of his host, who dared not take ground openly, he managed to keep the infuriated Agatone at bay.

Navarro of course needed no telegraphing to be made

aware of what had occurred; but he was now fairly at his wit's end, for it was clear enough he would never get his money if he trusted to Mexican valour to bring it to him; and besides, no possible inducement would have operated in organizing another expedition composed solely of Mexicans, for it would take them a month or two to recover from this fright; and were he even to send double the number, they would all run at the first sight of Agatone.

The jealousies between the Mexican and American citizens had prevented his asking assistance of Hays and his company, for he knew that they scorned his cowardly countrymen too entirely to participate with them in any enterprise; and now that he had endeavoured to get along without them, and being so signally defeated, he feared it would sadly injure his popularity should he employ the Americans, and give them another opportunity, by contrasting the successful issue of their adventure with the disgraceful one of the Mexicans, to taunt and crow over them, which spirit they had already carried to sufficiently galling extremes to endanger the public peace.

He knew that if he applied to the Americans now, they would only assist him in view of this very triumph, and be sure to make the most of it; so that between the fear of losing his popularity, and of losing his money, he was fairly half-demented; how both were to be secured, he could not by any possibility conceive.

He had been chafing and foaming over the matter for several days, without seeing his way any more clearly out of the difficulty; and, to cap the climax, had just received another message from Alvarez, urging him, as he valued his silver, to hurry on some one to his relief, for he was almost worn down by watching, and the aspect of affairs was becoming every hour more unpromising; but that there was a solitary glimmering of hope left, for he had received information from a sure quarter that Agatone had gone for a re

G 2

inforcement, and was to be absent several days, but that
when he returned he intended storming the rancho, and had
sworn to cut all their throats for the trick they had played
on him, and have his revenge and his money any how.

He prayed Navarro to take advantage of this absence of
his enemy—who had left his troops in command of a lieutenant—and slip in and get him out of this scrape, and the
money in before Agatone returned. That he must try to
effect this by stratagem, if not by force.

This was a strong appeal. The worthy merchant and
mayor, already near the last gasp of desperation, was almost
floored by it. But those self-same venerable laconics which
have asserted that "necessity knows no law," have also
christened it the "mother of invention;" and Navarro, in
this mortal extremity, suddenly bethought him of the "Bravo,"—of the violent passion he had been seized with to possess a certain coal-black and magnificent steed which Navarro
had taken from a Camanche chief.

It was by far the finest animal ever seen on that frontier,
and the Bravo had tried often and over, in all sorts of ways,
to obtain him. But although Navarro valued him immensely,
yet the estimate did not quite overbalance his silver bags,
and he knew the Bravo would risk his life a hundred times
to get possession of him.

Delighted by the sudden illumination of this thought, he
sent for the Bravo at once, proposed the expedition to him,
and the coveted steed as the reward.

The eyes of the young adventurer glistened; for of all
things he could conceive of just then, that horse he valued
the most. Money was nothing in the scale against him, for
no Arab had ever greater cause for regarding the mettle of
his horse as quite as important, in the sort of life he led, as
that of his dirk or his pistol; and what was more, he had
not been in a single fight for a week or two: the Camanches
had become so distressingly shy, and the Mexicans so uncom-

fortably quiet, that he was almost bored to death by the vapid and tiresome monotony of peace; and his blood was fairly seething for a small affair of some sort or other; so that nothing could have been more apropos than the proposition of Navarro, even leaving the horse out of the question; but with the prospect of getting "the black," and killing a few of Agatone's rascals to boot, he was supremely and perfectly beatified.

He forthwith closed with Navarro's offer, adding as conditions, that he was to have the horse to ride, and to manage the whole affair in his own way, without any questioning on the part of any one; that he should select five men who were to be equipped to accompany him: and great was the astonishment of Navarro when he announced that these five men were to be Mexicans, and the most roguish, worthless vagabonds in the town, at that.

He had expected, of course, that the Bravo would take with him his own countrymen, and it was upon their combined boldness and ingenuity he had counted for success; and at this unexpected proposition he was grievously disturbed, for the inevitable result seemed to promise the loss of both horse and money. In vain he remonstrated. The Bravo would make no explanation of his plans, but insisted upon his terms, or refused to have any thing to do with the matter.

Navarro went to Hays, and begged him to use his influence in persuading the Bravo to change his plans, and take Americans. Hays went to him, and offered to accompany him with his whole troop; but he refused the proffer, and Hays turned off, saying very coolly to Navarro—

"O never disturb yourself about the Bravo! he'll do it! He's got a plan of his own—let him alone!"

So, as it was the only hope, Navarro was compelled to equip the five Mexicans designated, and let him have his own way.

But it was with a heavy heart he saw him start the next day, curvetting over the prairie on the black steed, and he drew a long sigh as his favourite horse disappeared beyond the undulations; for he never expected to hear from him or his money again.

In truth, it appeared to every one, Mexicans as well as Americans, the most fantastically impossible scheme that ever entered the brain of desperado;—the effort, in the teeth of all Agatone's banditti, to bring off a large sum in silver across a hundred miles of desert plains, with only five cowardly Mexicans for escort, any one of whom would sell his life for a plug of tobacco! It looked like the collapse stage of the dare-devil mania! But the Bravo had done so many improbable things, there was no telling what might be the result now.

So everybody waited, with the most intense curiosity and anxiety, the issue. With permission of our readers, we will accompany the mad-cap through this promising undertaking.

He travelled with great speed, making long stages, and only stopping to refresh his horse, and seeming to be utterly regardless of the five Mexicans, leaving them to keep up or not, as they could. They, poor rascals, were frightened at the idea of being left behind to shift for themselves, in case they should meet Camanches, and took very good care to keep in sight, at least; though to accomplish this on their inferior horses was a very serious business; so that by the time he reached the rancho of Don Jose, their animals were pretty well used up.

The Bravo had purposely selected these fellows from among the most notoriously drunken and faithless villains of Bexar! Honest Alvarez, who was on the watch, instantly opened the gates to the Bravo.

Don Jose happened not to be at hand when this was done; but when he returned and found the single American insolently ordering his people about, and acting in all respects as if he were lord of the rancho, he became furiously enraged, and ordered the Bravo to clear out, and threatened to tie him up and give him a *quirt* on his bare back.

It never occurred to him for a moment that a solitary American, with only a river between him and Mexico, and with several hundred Mexicans about him, would dare to offer resistance! The Bravo paid no attention to his threats, but in an imperious tone demanded of him the surrender of the silver.

To Don Jose this seemed capping the climax of presumption. He ordered his peones to seize and strip him. But this was more easily said than done.

While they hesitated a moment without obeying, the Bravo very coolly drew a pistol, and stepping up to Don Jose, who was surrounded by his peones, twisted his hand into his hair, and drawing down his head, placed the cold iron muzzle of the pistol against his temple. At the same instant, as the peones were in the act of rushing on him, some one shouted from the crowd—

"It's the Bravo! It's the Bravo! Look out!"

At this formidable name the menial herd scattered as if a torpedo had fallen among them, and poor Don Jose was left to his fate.

Such was the terror the singular hardihood of this man had inspired the border Mexicans with, that they had as soon undertake to encounter a regiment of devils as brave the prowess of his single arm. He held the shivering Don Jose in this pleasant position until he made him kiss the cross and swear to be true—this is the only form of oath at all binding with a Mexican.

With a magnanimous air he then told him he would spare his life, and released him. He ordered him to get the key, and show him the most secure room in the rancho, which having been done, he compelled him to assist Alvarez and himself to remove the silver into it. Then speaking a few

6

words in a low tone to Alvarez, he entered the room alone,
closed the door, locked it on the inside, and throwing himself down with the bags for a pillow, was sound asleep in a
few moments.

Great was the rejoicing among the Mexicans that this
scourge of the borders was at last entrapped—had in his
over-daring recklessness thrown himself alone amidst swarms
of enemies; and though they submitted to his insolence in
the rancho, and dare not attack him openly, they revelled in
anticipative gibes over his carcass riddled with balls, as they
intended it should be. How was it possible for him to
escape? The faith of the villains he had brought along with
him had given way at the first assault—for they had been
forthwith surrounded by the emissaries of Agatone, and for
a few pounds of tobacco apiece, had agreed, every man of
them, to join the plot for his assassination.

The lieutenant of Agatone had seen his approach, and
might have set upon him then, with all his men, and killed
him, but he chose rather to wait till he started on his return
with the money, and thus secure both objects at once. As
for poor Alvarez and his two honest followers, they were of
course to be exterminated along with him!

And then, this carelessness of his, in throwing himself
down to sleep without taking any precautions to see that his
men were not tampered with, showed that he neither feared
nor suspected any thing; and they fairly danced for joy, as
they saw every thing so propitious for a certain revenge of
all the high-handed indignities and murders he had committed upon their countrymen. Alvarez seemed to be in a
wonderfully fine humour, highly elated at the prospects of
escaping, and paid no attention to the whisperings and plot-
tings that were going on around him.

He bought several gallons of nouya, and, with one of the
Mexicans who had accompanied the Bravo, called Juan, and
who was the most proverbial scoundrel among them, he

seemed determined to make a regular drunken frolic in honour of his deliverance. The rest, having settled their plans with Agatone's spies, who departed, were soon drawn into the carouse, which they kept up regularly until day. Had a sober man looked on, he would have perceived that Alvarez and Juan were not quite so drunk as they wished to appear.

When morning came, the Bravo chimed in with the convivial spirit of his followers, and at starting, filled all their water-gourds with nouya for them. Don Jose was very officious in furnishing the Bravo with spirits, and chuckled heartily as he saw him so much disposed to drink freely, for this was making assurance doubly sure of the success of the plot, which he knew was to be carried into effect that night.

He rubbed his fingers with glee at the thought of the coin they were soon to be counting, for he was of course to go shares in the plunder. Indeed, the avarice of the traitor became so thoroughly roused by the thought of certain success to all his schemes, that he began to think of the many "slips betwixt the cup and the lips," and to remember that Agatone's banditti had never been remarkable for good faith, and that it would be the surest course for him to be on the ground in person when the money was seized, and attend to securing his share; so that his heart suddenly overflowed with courtesy, and, mounting his horse, he insisted upon having the honour of accompanying the Bravo the first day's journey on his return. The Bravo, seeming to be thoroughly mollified by the generous liquor, heartily responded to the politeness.

So off they started, merry as a wedding party, the doomed Bravo and Alvarez more boisterously jovial than any of them, and taking great pains to make the money-bags conspicuous, "for the benefit"—as the apparently half-drunken Bravo swaggered—"of the spying whelps of that wolf-cur

Agatone, that are sneaking along after us through that line
of timber !''

As he said this, he pointed directly to where Don Jose
knew the spies of the banditti were hid. He was somewhat
startled at this for an instant; but the Bravo was so evidently under the influence of the nouya, that he forgot it
directly, supposing that it was an accident that he pointed so
truly, and merely such a boast as was natural for a half-
intoxicated man.

It seemed to Don Jose that his victims were perfectly infatuated, for during the whole day the Bravo and Alvarez
did not permit the carouse to flag ; and in this they found an
able coadjutor in Juan, for the knave seemed as thirsty as a
sand-bank. We should mention, by the way, that it is an ·
almost invariable habit on this frontier, particularly when
Americans are of the party, to spend the first night in camp
in a carouse, when a long or perilous expedition is undertaken; so that all this conduct of the Bravo, however stupid
and reckless it might seem, was in perfect keeping with
usage.

They camped at night on a spot designated by Don Jose
as most admirably adapted for the purpose. The Bravo appeared to place unbounded confidence in the judgment of the
courteous ranchero, and agreed to his selection without hesitation. The spot was most excellently well chosen for a
night surprise. It was a small open space on the bank of a
stream, surrounded on all sides by a dense thicket. The
Bravo was not so far gone that he did not take wonderfully
good care of the black steed ; and Alvarez managed, with all
his staggering, to secure the pack of mules, and one or two
horses, remarkably well under the circumstances.

The supper of dried beef and tortillas over, the Bravo suddenly grew excessively cautious, and would not permit a fire
to be built, for fear, he said—

" The blaze or smoke might betray us to Agatone's fel-

lows; for," he continued, with a loud laugh, "I rather think
I've thrown the cowardly sheep-thieves off the trail this
time."

Don Jose assented most heartily to this, though he laughed
in his sleeve as he said to himself—

"The drunken fool! a blind man couldn't miss the trail
he's made, even if I hadn't seen the spies following us all
day!"

The drinking now commenced again, and it was soon an
nounced that the gourds had been emptied. The fellows,
who had become very drunk and insolent, were clamorous
for more. The Bravo, at last, and seemingly with great reluctance, brought a special private bottle of his own, that,
he said, was filled with choice brandy, which he had obtained
at Bahai, and brought along for contingencies.

Don Jose, who had been very wary, and had drunk nothing
heretofore, thought he might certainly now indulge himself
a little, as matters were in such glorious train; so he took a
stiff draught of the Bravo's superfine brandy, and, passing
the bottle round, it was very soon emptied.

One of the Mexicans shouted, laughingly, that Juan was
shirking, and didn't drink his; but Juan played his swallow
so vehemently, that the fellow jerked the bottle out of his
hand, and drank himself, but was too much stupefied to notice that Juan had not lessened it a drop.

In a very few minutes after this, each man had thrown
himself back with his head upon his saddle for a pillow, and
seemed to be sleeping soundly. Don Jose had followed the
example of the rest, so far as position was concerned, but
had not the slightest idea of going to sleep. He lay thinking
over the occurrences of the day; every thing had worked
right; it was impossible the Bravo could have any suspicion,
for all his Mexicans had been bribed; and even supposing
they had only pretended to be so, he had watched them

H

closely since daybreak, and it was impossible that any inti-
mation of the plot could have been conveyed by them to the
Bravo without his witnessing it, though it had struck his
crafty mind as singular that the Bravo should be so reckless as to get drunk when he knew he was surrounded by
deadly enemies, yet it seemed so evident that he really was
so, that his suspicions were entirely lulled.

He felt an unaccountable propensity for sleeping, which
he could not overcome, and, consoling himself with the re-
flection that as his friends were not to come till daybreak,
there was plenty of time to take a short nap, he gave way
to the invincible inclination, intending to wake again in an
hour or so.

A profound silence now reigned over the camp and the
still snoring figures for an hour or so, and the wolves—for
there was no sentinel out—were sneaking round the death-
like sleepers, and smelling cautiously at their noses to see if
they were yet breathing; but when one of them happened
to try this experiment on the Bravo, it suddenly bounded
wildly off, shaking its head. The Bravo rose quickly, and
gazed after it as it dashed through the moonlight, at every
leap clawing with its fore-paw at the stump of an ear that
had been sliced off by his bowie.

He turned with a sardonic grin, and muttered, "Ah
ha! my fine fellow, you will not be the only one that is bitten
to-night!" Alvarez and Juan were standing erect and wide
awake by his side.

"Come, boys, let's be quick!"

They soon had the money upon the pack-saddles, and their
horses equipped, all but saddling the steed of the Bravo.

"Shoot the man with his head on the silver-mounted saddle,
is it?" he chuckled, as he took up the rich saddle his own
head had been resting upon, and replaced the saddle which
Juan had softly taken from under the head of Don Jose,
with it.

"But that the joke is too good to lose, I couldn't afford to leave my fine saddle, and forego the pleasure of splitting the rascal's gizzard myself!"

He laughed as he threw the saddle of Don Jose upon the "black," and leaped into it.

"Keep close under the bank, boys, and hurry!" he said, as they started the pack-mules, with their precious freight, down the hill into the bed of the stream on which they were camped.

"Stop! stop!" said Alvarez, as they got into the water, "we have forgotten my two men who stood by me so faithfully! Wo must not leave them to be shot, when the fellows find out the trick, for revenge!"

"Go back, then," said the Bravo, carelessly, "and drag them by the heels into the thicket, and hide them; you needn't be afraid they will wake, for they took a heavy dose of that *superfine brandy* of mine!"

Alvarez obeyed, and said, when he and Juan returned, after an absence of a few minutes—

"I've hid 'em where they'll be out of harm's way when they wake!"

"That's more than those jolly 'yellow bellies' will ever do! Come, let's be off!" said the Bravo.

It is impossible for us of the misty North to realize the clear brilliancy of moonlight on the elevated prairies of Western Texas.

The atmosphere is so wonderfully lucid and dry, that all our preconceptions of distance are annihilated. A deer, a tree, or any object, is as distinctly defined on the retina, a half-mile off, as it would be in our medium at eighty paces. The broad radiant face of a full moon hung almost, it seemed, in reach of the tree tops, pouring such floods of mellow light upon the scene, as brought in perfect relief even the thin fibres of the grass, the white thorns of the broadleafed cactus, and the slim stems of the frail flowers.

Faint pencillings of a stronger light were just beginning
to struggle dimly through the forest-shaded rim of the
eastern horizon, when a party of about sixty men might have
been seen, slowly and cautiously creeping towards the camp,
on the side opposite to that on which the Bravo and his
friends had left it.

These men were evidently Mexicans, as could be seen from
the broad-brimmed, sugar-loaf sombreros, which shaded their
tawny and moustached faces; and as they stooped and
crawled, and skulked among the bushes, their small black
eyes gleaming with a strong animal light, they looked the
very ideal of cowardly and traitorous assassination. They
soon reached a point from which the sleeping figures were
discernible. They raised themselves quietly amongst the
bushes, and looking over them, could clearly distinguish the
group.

"How!" whispered the man nearest the lieutenant, whose
quick eye had detected that all were not there who had made
up the party during the day.

"How! they are not all there! Where are the rest?"

"All there," said the lieutenant, "that are to be shot!
The rest are in the bushes, out of the way. See! there is
the silver-mounted saddle!"

"Remember, men," said he, elevating his voice as he
turned to his company, while his finger pointed at Don Jose,
"you are to shoot all! but be *sure* you shoot the man with
his head on the silver-mounted saddle! Fire!"

There was the long, rolling fire of the platoon, and they
all sprang forward.

"Garracho! we have killed Don Jose, and the Bravo and
the money are gone!" roared the lieutenant.

"There's nothing here but the filthy carcasses of those
curs of Bahai for our pains!"

Two nights after these occurrences, the young Americans
of Bahai met for a grand carouse, in honour of the safe re-

turn of the Bravo with the money of Navarro. The Bravo had just finished the relation of the incidents we have narrated up to the time of his leaving the camp, and the hearty bursts of laughter which had followed the Bravo's affectionate leave-taking, of "Pleasant dreams to the honest Don Jose!" had somewhat subsided, when Hays remarked—

"But, Bravo, I don't understand how you have managed to make so useful and faithful a servant out of that notorious drunkard, thief, and villain—Juan!"

"Oh! the simplest thing in the world! Even a Mexican is capable of gratitude! Juan is not the fellow's name! Have you forgotten that famous knave, Gonzaleze, you ordered to be shot one morning, about two years ago, for shooting Littell and stealing your favourite sorrel, and whose life I took a fancy to save, because he made an impudent face at us, while we were levelling our guns to fire at him?"

"Yes. Is it possible this is the same?"

"This is Gonzaleze, and he's given his soul to me. I took the other four along for the express purpose of getting them killed. As they are out of the way now, may be my black horse will be safe. I knew I should not be able to keep him three weeks while those thieving scoundrels were alive!"

"Good! Bravo, you deserve a vote of thanks from us all. Under the shadow of *your* black steed, *our* horses will now be safe!"

The vote of thanks was formally drawn up and presented; and along with it came a splendid silver-mounted saddle, that did honour to the glossy back of even "the coal-black steed."

H 2

ADAM BAKER, THE RENEGADE.

ADAM BAKER, THE RENEGADE.

THE mania for travel and adventure has always been with me unconquerable. I sometimes think that there are men in the world born with quicksilver in their bones where the marrow ought to be—who cannot be still—one incessant fever of restlessness burning to the core, and only endurable under the diversion of a stronger excitement in perilous action—and that I must be one of these unfortunates. For, possessed by the mobility of the quicksilver, the "spirit of unrest," or some other "blue spirit or gray," of vagabond propensities, I have done little else than rove all my life long.

You may well conjecture that this errant humour has got me into not a few scrapes, and thrown me into some singular juxtapositions; and that these "accidents," if you choose to call them so, have made to me some strange revelations of humanity, and proved to me, too, that all its singular phases are not confined to cities, called "the great hot-beds of distorted vice."

No—out on the frontiers of civilization is the soil for genuine monstrosities; there they grow, like the rank vines or the bottom cotton woods,

> "And nothing know
> Of stipulations, duties, reverences,"

to "cabin and crib" their legitimate proportions. Tall and huge they grow in that rank alluvion of license—ill birds nestle in their boughs, and under their thick shadows grow

deadly plants where reptiles suck their poison, and all the
air is mortal round them; and there—the daughters of the
free winds and the sun, with glorious colours on them, dis-
tilled in dew-drops from the sky into their warm veins—
grow gentle flowers that *will* be fair, and smile in fragrance,
for all the deadly breaths about them!

Toward the conclusion of very extended peregrinations
which had embraced the wildest portions of Northern Mexico
and Western Texas, I found myself approaching the outskirts
of settlement on the upper Brazos.   I had been thoroughly
starved on "jerked beef" for a month or so, and as I came
in sight of a large plantation on the edge of the prairie, the
nasals of my imagination were busy enough snuffing hot
coffee and pig on the inodorous winds.

There is the dim white sheen resting upon the dark line
of the forest, which lies like a huge shadowy snake stretching
its winding length across the wide prairie.   That white shimmer is the play of the sunlight upon the gable—that thin,
blue column, too; ah, who does not know the honest curl of
a chimney smoke?   All the pleasant odours from the family
boil and roast wasted, for there is not even the man o' the
moon above there in the empty arch to inhale it!

Come, my good steed, we'll make a run the rest of the
way.   Gramercy! but it's a thumping big plantation!
Here we are, in the lane at last.   Here's the gate!   Hilloa!
Frame house, long and low—piazza in front—wide passage
through the middle—as I live! we can see the long dinner-
table—they have just laid the cloth and knives and forks!
Halloo!   "Yes, sir!"   There he comes down the steps—
man of the house, I suppose—a very slight, delicate-looking
body for a frontier's man.

" How do you do, sir?   Get down!   Our landlord is not
at home—no matter, though—these Cherokee planters are
all hospitable.   Leave your horse there—we'll have him
taken care of.   Any news?"

".Nothing special! I am just across from Bexar—heard of the Camanches doing some of their old jobs—they speared two Mexicans just out of town !"

"Ha! ha! ha! they do that trick beautifully—but sit down—dinner will be ready directly, and I see yonder's Sewene returning. He's just coming in from camp—the four or five neighbours he has within twenty miles have all come together for a mustang drive—they've been at it four days, and I suppose the herd are pretty well run down by this time. You were lost when you stumbled here, warnt you?"

"Yes, rather! I only had an indefinite idea that I was approaching settlements, but what the character of them was I had no conception. This is the plantation of a Cherokee, you mentioned—that's a new idea to me."

" Oh, some of these Cherokees are very wealthy. Sewene inherited a large fortune in Georgia, and when the old cock happened to get killed off in a fray with some white men, he sold out every thing, put the money in his pocket, and like a wise man picked the two fellows off from ' the bush' and came to Texas, married a white woman, brought her off here, and settled this plantation. Ha! Sewene! back already? Got the wire-edge off of them fellows yet—willing to be cultivated—to listen to reason ?"

"Yah! yah! they be dam draggle-tail—git lazy—nꞇ switch flies so quick now."

"A stranger, Sewene! across from Bexar—lost—stopped awhile to rest."

"Ver' good! Stay—see mustang—this evenin' make 'em go—fifteen—to pen."

With a careless shake of the hand he passed on into the house. He was a tall, portly man, with a handsome Roman face, and a complexion rather a dark, healthy olive than copper, showing the presence of a foreign tinge—the French —which language he spoke with some elegance, though he made a lame sort of English.

The little man who first received me, and who seemed to
De a great fidget, continued walking with a rapid, restless
step to and fro before me, talking with wonderful volubility
about any thing and every thing—jerking and twitching
with a sort of convulsive action of legs, arms, fingers, and
muscles of the face at each articulation. His figure and step
had in them an elasticity which left one altogether in doubt
what might *not* be the amount of activity and endurance
they indicated. His tread had the quick, soft rebound of
a wild-cat's, and his limbs, though small, were wonderfully
lithe and supple: his features, except his mouth, were sharp
and small, perhaps owing to their great emaciation, which
was so peculiar that, with the exceeding fineness of texture
in his skin, the effect was produced of exhibiting as under a
transparency the minutest play of the smallest tendon and
muscle in the whole bust, as far as it was exposed by tho
open collar.

His forehead was very white and broad, and finely developed, and upon it fell in careless and wavy clusters, that
seemed to cling there from clammy damps, light chestnut
hair of almost gossamer texture, and very thin: his mouth
was wide, with thin, colourless lips, and a constant ripple
about the corners even when closed, which rendered it impossible to catch the expression, for all expressions were
there in one moment; his eyes were the most peculiar feature—they were far apart and very protruded—they were
pale blue, and there seemed to be always a tear ready to
brim over the lids.

His voice was soft and low. The only particular I could
detect in his manner that I did not fancy, was its excessive
uncertainty, never dwelling on one thing long, but seeming
to rush into all themes with equal enthusiasm, and leaving
them all with equal coldness.

I pass over the dinner, welcome as it was. As soon as I
had time to look up from my plate, I glanced round upon

the company at table; there were six or eight—among them a tall, slender personage, with florid complexion, curly hair, red whiskers, and a man-of-the-world air about him; something that indicated polish in the very manner of lifting a plate. I heard him addressed by the pale little man, whom he called Williams, as Morgan. They seemed to be on very familiar terms. Our hostess was a fat, ruddy, and not unhandsome matron, with a large, bold, black eye.

But what made me forget appetite, dinner, and every thing else—fortunately she had glided in without my observing her before—was a young girl at the side of the matron, of almost startling beauty. She was evidently a daughter of the two races—of Sewene and his American wife—but to tell how the asperities of both were softened into the exquisite finish, the wild graceful tenderness of her *ensemble*, is more than I shall venture upon at once.

It is enough for you to know that splendid profile—the vaulting arch of that bold forehead—just a summer evening's tinge of orange on it, enough to make it warm under the intense black of that glossy mass of hair—then the free curve of that classic nose, and the curl of the upper lip, that, with a saucy coyness, brooded over the rich swell of its ambitious twin—and then the burning ebon depths of those large eyes —the shadow of the long, dark lashes seemed to be over them in mercy—for what the full blaze thereof might be, imagination could not compass; then her neck was long, with a set like a listening fawn's.

Oh! she was as beautiful as day, with the delicate tinge of the mingled blood flushing almost into chestnut on her cheek, as she caught the burning joy and wonder of my gaze fixed upon her. Heavens! what a revelation in this rude land. My blood was fairly burning—my fork and knife had dropped upon my just replenished plate—my third cup of coffee was half out, but appetite was gone.

I saw she had noticed and was confused by the intensity

I   7

of my look, which brought me to my senses; and, sipping away with my tea-spoon through the rest of the meal, I had formed the doughty resolution, by the time it was over, that if no other excuse offered for my stay the next day, my horse should fall suddenly lame!

And what added to the fixedness of this resolve, was a something like assiduity in the table courtesies of Morgan. I found myself cursing his infernal suavity from between my teeth, wondering what right he had to take such airs. I hated the man forthwith, and the more heartily that I could not help acknowledging there was a "winning way" about him, and that she recognised it, too, with a subdued grace that was perfectly bewitching.

I was not a little enraged, when the horses were brought out for a ride over to the mustang drive, to find that Morgan did not go. But I could find no excuse for staying—go I must! Sewene had ordered a horse of his own to be brought out for me, so to get rid of my impatience I proposed that we should try the gait of his horse in a canter.

This suited all parties, so away we went, Williams keeping alongside of me, seeming determined to avail himself of a new hearer, until finding that listen I must, and warmed, too, by the motion of the animal, I found myself strangely interested in this man. A more remarkable command of language I never heard, but it was accompanied by a cold recklessness of satire, glancing equally over all things, icy always and always pitiless. He could be eloquent in enunciating generous thought, and laugh at the interest he had excited.

Our brisk gait soon brought us to the camp, where we found three white men lying on the grass, their horses saddled near them, and evidently waiting for us. They received us with a blunt cordiality, told us that the rest of the party were in pursuit of the mustangs, and they thought them tired enough by this time to try them at the pens.

On inquiry I found that the plan had been for half the party, at a time, to follow the mustangs just near enough to keep them always in motion, and give them no opportunity for stopping to drink or graze, night or day. It is a silly instinct of the animals to keep within their habitual range, which is generally some ten or fifteen miles in circumference, and pursue them as long as you may, they will still be found near the same place once or twice in the twenty-four hours.

Taking advantage of one of these places for a camp, the hunters in pursuit, when they or their horses become fatigued, give warning by a horn as they approach to the relay, who are thoroughly rested and fresh, and these catch up their horses and put in to the relief of their friends, who in turn take possession of their camp and refreshments. In this way a party of six or eight men will keep the poor mustangs travelling incessantly four or five days without food or water, until they are thoroughly jaded and worn out.

The hunters have previously prepared the pen somewhere in the range, in this way :—They select a piece of prairie ground, bordered on one side by a dense, unbroken thicket— for mustangs have an invincible horror of the bush, and cannot be forced to take it unless there is an opening which they can see through. This line of thicket is to serve for one wing of the pen; the other, stretching out a mile into the prairie at a right angle, is made of posts driven into the ground. These posts are eight or ten feet apart, with a stiff bush woven into the intervals to the height of six or eight feet.

The wing being finished, the pen is now made at the point where the two lines meet; the entrance is about ten feet wide and the same height, with a sliding gate, over which a man is placed to let it down. The pen itself is an area of several hundred yards, fenced in with a strong stockading of heavy posts. When the mustangs are to some degree subdued by fatigue and the starving process, the hunters make a general rally of all the forces they can muster, and a rush is made to hurry them down the wings and through the gate.

This was the work we had before us. We were promptly under way, and a brisk gallop across the prairie soon brought us within hearing of the division in pursuit. We let our horses out to full speed, and soon closed with them. They were going at a slow canter, keeping within about a quarter of a mile of the little drove of mustangs, which evidently dragged themselves along at a very heavy gait.

In the few rapid words which passed, I understood that we were about half a mile from the opening of the wings, and that the crisis was close at hand. We were directed to form in line about a hundred yards from each other, to gradually increase our pace as we neared them, and when the mustangs were once fairly in, to "rush" the animals at the gate before they had time to suspect the danger.

This was all done very successfully, and now commenced the barbarous process of breaking the animals to the rope. This was positively revolting. A Mexican, (who always makes one on such hunts,) after the gate had been firmly secured, and we had stationed ourselves there to prevent the horses making a rush at it, jumped down into the pen, his coiled lariat in hand, and following at a run the half-frantic creatures round the pen, threw the noose at one of them. It fell round its neck, and in an instant the wretched animal was dragged by the neck out of the huddled and hurrying crowd of its fellows, and literally choked down.

The instant it was fairly stretched, the Mexican jumped with his feet upon its free and glossy neck, and held it thus ignominiously in the dust, while others of the party tied the feet together. It was painful to me to see that silken coat all defaced, those strong, graceful limbs tethered, and the beautiful animal that was but a little while since so gay and proud and buoyant, now trampled and bound by these coarse men, to be made a slave for ever.

One after another they were all subjected to this treatment, until the whole fifteen were stretched upon their sides, floundering and struggling to get free; then, after tying the other end of the stout lariat on their necks to posts set in the open space of the pen, they let up four at a time, which, as soon as they felt themselves on their feet again, would dash off at full speed, till reaching the end of the rope, they would be brought up on their backs. They sometimes break their necks in this way.

After tremendous efforts to break loose, during which they are choked to the ground half a dozen times, they begin to "get the hang of the thing," and to fear and obey the rope. They are then untied, let outside, and fastened to stakes driven into the ground very deep, while the others are let up in their turn.

Until now there had been so much excitement and bustle that no man had any time to notice his neighbour; but now we were gathered into little groups, looking at the captured animals—Williams, the Cherokee and myself standing somewhat apart, admiring a beautiful horse which our host had selected for himself, when our attention was attracted by the loud, angry voice of a man.

On turning, I instantly recognised him—a swarthy, powerful fellow, who was leading the party in pursuit of the mustangs—I remembered having observed him exhibit great excitement when our party joined them, staring with intense fierceness at Williams, and muttering a hasty oath between his teeth.

I turned to see if Williams had noticed it, but he seeming to be perfectly calm, the circumstance had almost passed from my mind in the rapid action that followed; but now the man and the incident were instantly associated as I saw him furious, with one hand upon his belt-pistol, the other pointing toward us, struggling to get away from his friends, who

I 2

seemed to be remonstrating with him.   I heard him shout at
the top of his voice—

"It is he! the d——d traitor! it is he!   I'll shoot him
like a wolf!"

The hunters ran to him, grouping eagerly around him, and
for a moment we could not hear what they said.

These vehement words sent an icy thrill through me, for
there was terrible meaning in them for some of us.   Was it
Williams?   I looked round; his pale face was livid, and in
an instant it had undergone a remarkable change : that
incessant muscular vibration had ceased as if struck by the
hand of death, and his features were cold and still as marble.
There was not even a quiver about his lips.

"What does this mean?" I said to him.

He made no answer, merely shaking his head and gazing
with a sort of stare at the crowd, which now began to advance
toward us—the big fellow, whose name was Roach, still endeavouring to break away from the midst of them.   They
were all talking at once, in angry, excited tones, and I could
only distinguish the words "guest," and "Sewene."

When they had nearly reached us, Roach, by a furious
effort, broke from his friends, and, springing forward, waved
them back with his hand, and with a large pistol cocked and
presented, stopped about five paces in front of Williams.
His friends fell back, and there was a dead pause.

I had half drawn my pistol, and so had Sewene, but the
singular gesture of Williams held all in suspense.   He simply
and deliberately folded his arms upon his breast, and drawing
a very long breath that seemed to break a heavy trance,
with a quiet smile looked eloquent inquiry into Roach's eyes.
The savage felt his manner, and though his voice was still
harsh with rage, it was not so tempestuous as I expected.

"You are 'Adam Baker,' the murdering renegade!   Deny
it if you dare!"

"I do dare."

"You lie!" Roach screamed—"you lie, you bloody villain! would you make me doubt my own eyes? Did I not see you at Chihuahua for weeks with my comrade Clark? Ha! you know me now, don't you?"

The man's rigid face had twitched slightly at this.

"Clark was murdered for his money, and you did it, you cowardly cut-throat! I shall always believe you did it. You escaped that time, but I've got you now, and you shall die for it—yes, die like a dog!"

Roach raised his pistol again. Williams, or Baker, still in the same position, smilingly remarked, in a low, soft voice—

"You call yourself a brave man, my friend, and you are six feet two inches in height, and strong in proportion—yet you've got a long, nine-inch barrel pistol, loaded to the muzzle, to blow into shivers a little atom of a man like me, not stronger than a woman, and unarmed to boot, and all because I happen to look like somebody you suppose murdered your friend: you'd feel very foolish to find you'd killed the wrong man; it will be cowardly in you to shoot me unarmed—I am not Baker, and you are going to play the fool!"

Roach seemed to be confounded by this cool speech for an instant. He raised himself upon his feet, and bringing down his arm with a fierce imprecation, exclaimed—

"You lie, you oily traitor! you sha'n't escape me with your cool impudence—didn't we drink together all the evening before Clark left town with you and never came back, in Callistro's tavern? You had been running your horse that day, and we had all won money and were on a spree, and you got Clark drunk, and took him off and murdered him—ay, and this is not the only murder you have done. I don't care if you are unarmed. If you had arms, you wouldn't use them—you never strike but in the dark. You shall die

here on this ground, if the last drop of my heart's blood pay
for it."

He levelled his pistol this time with deliberation.

During this scene we had all gradually closed up round
them—I sprang forward just in time to knock the weapon
from its deadly level before it exploded. I looked at Williams; he was standing in exactly the same position, the
blood slowly trickling down his bare white neck, but the
smile was still upon his ghastly face. There had been a
general rush to seize him, but they all recoiled awe-struck
from the singular being—I could stand it no longer. Sewene
and myself, as by one impulse, rushed with our weapons in
hand in front of Williams.

"Gentlemen, you are going too far; if this man be a
murderer, he's already wounded—give him a fair trial—he
denies that he is Baker."

"Sacre Roach!" cried Sewene, " he no Baker—my friend
—dam—take that."

Sewene fired—Roach staggered and pitched forward on
his face. Sewene's fire was instantly returned, the shot
striking my arm instead of him.

"You are all a pack of fools!" shouted Williams, throwing
himself as quick as thought into the midst of Roach's friends,
and catching at their pistols. "Fools! d——d fools! You
are shooting at each other because that blockhead made a
mistake! Are you going to kill one another because he was
a jackass! I tell you I am not Baker! Hold! hold! listen
to common sense a moment. The fellow got just what he
deserved ; he shot me unarmed, and an inoffensive stranger,
because he took a stupid fancy I was like somebody he called
Baker. Didn't Sewene, your own neighbour, tell you I was
not he? Do you blame him for shooting the fellow who was
going to murder a friend and a guest ? And may be he has
done it, for, curse him, he hit me in the neck. Are you men,
and would see a man slaughtered in cold blood, making no

resistance? Pretty Texans, you! Mexicans might do this! I am ashamed of you!"

I saw they were impressed by this logic, and felt in an instant that my wound was but a trifle, though it had paralyzed my arm and prevented my returning the fire at the moment. I saw, too, that Williams's policy was the only one, for they were double our number, and well armed; and following it up, I said, holding up my bleeding arm—

"You see one of your shot has struck me—I have not returned the fire, because you are all crazy! Is there a man with a soul among you, that would not have done as Sewene did? Come, let's be at quits—Roach got what you know he deserved—he was going to kill this man in cold blood, who may not be Baker; and if he is, you'll find him at Sewene's whenever you can prove his identity."

"Yes, by heaven! you will find me there for the next two weeks, come when you may. Prove me to be this Baker. Be sure it's the dog that killed the sheep before you hang him."

"Yes," said one of the hunters, "that's fair, boys. I thought Roach was hasty—poor fellow, he was a brave man, but he always was so."

"D—n you!" said another one, "we'll hang you with a dead dog at your heels if you should turn out to be Baker."

"Thank you for your polite intentions! I hope I shall be able to reciprocate compliments with you some day by ourselves, out on the prairie. Is the man dead?"

"No."

"Pity, Sewene, you hadn't planted it better—he fell well!"

"Look you! I believe you're the devil, if you are not Adam Baker. You'd better take yourself off from here— you and that young fellow there, and Sewene—you'd all better make tracks."

"The fellow's advice is good," said Baker; "come, Sewene —Kentuck, let's be off!"

We turned and were leaving, when the hunter who spoke last shouted after us—

"Sewene, look out for yourself anyhow! Roach has got a brother, you know—and you, you starved whelp, who call' yourself Williams, murder is not the only count we have against that man Baker—he's a traitor to Texas, and wants to sell our blood for Mexican gold. He's come in to look at the state of the frontier, and report to Santa Anna. Tell him, if he's a friend of yours, that there are men not far from here who do know him; and we mean to watch you, my dear, night and day, so that you don't get away—sleep on how a hemp tie will feel—you, my' young fellow, look out, you are in bad company!"

This was timely and, consolatory advice; my bleeding arm bore testimony that my chance association had at least been unfortunate, and from all I could see ahead, it was likely to be more so now. But the daughter of Sewene! Could I think of personal consequences with her entrancing beauty in the question—and she in the midst of such ruffianly scenes —such wretches as these around her? No, I rather blessed my wound—perhaps her own "flower soft hands" would dress it. I should have an excuse for staying; should be near her in the desperate scenes which I foresaw must follow this day's work—might save her!

During the process of this very prudent and sensible argumentation with myself, we had been advancing to where our horses were standing, and had stopped there to examine Williams's wound.

"It's a glancer," he said; "thanks to you, Kentuck, the rascal has only phlebotomized me a little—haven't got much of the claret to spare, though—tie my handkerchief around it—not quite so bad, that, as the hempen one that loud-talking fellow gave me, as a Yankee at a country wedding gives a piece of gingerbread to his gal, to dream upon. Ha! ha! Kind of him, that! but let's go, or those cursed bears will scratch their sore ears and snuff blood there until they get furious again.''

Sewene tied up my arm, and we were on horseback and off. We had gone but a few paces when the Mexican, of lariat memory, who had not been seen since the commencement of the affair, suddenly stepped out of the thicket, and caught the bridle of Williams's horse.

With an oath Williams struck at his hand and spurred his horse—the horse sprang violently forward, almost jerking the Mexican on his face, breaking his hold; but the man had spoken some eager words in his native tongue which I was too far ahead to understand, but which seemed to produce a tremendous effect upon Williams.

Reining up his horse, he wheeled and was instantly at the side of the Mexican, and stooping from his saddle, close to the man's face, with intense eagerness of manner, seemed to be using his utmost eloquence in persuasion; he would pat him rapidly on the shoulder, then point to where his horse was standing, then at Sewene, but the man drew himself back and shook his head with an air of stolid obstinacy.

Williams, without straightening himself, suddenly spurred his horse, and with a single plunge, placed himself between the man and the bushes, and in the same instant I saw the gleam of a long knife in his hand. The Mexican shrank back cowering—another quick gesture—Williams had drawn a purse from his pocket, and in trembling haste emptied a handful of silver coin from it, and motioned it toward the man, who instantly, with a grin upon his face, jerked his "sombrero" from his head and caught it in the crown. The chink of the metal acted like a charm, and as Williams held toward him the handle of his poignard, which was a silver cross, he stepped forward without hesitation, and making the sign with his finger on his forehead, kissed it, then turning, ran at full speed toward his horse.

Williams watched him until he was in the saddle, and

coming in a gallop to join us; he then rode leisurely to us, his face wearing an expression of devilish glee, such as I never saw on human countenance before—still holding the weapon in one hand, tossing the purse in the air, and catching it with the other.

The Mexican had now closed up behind us—Sewene, turning in the saddle, looked at him inquiringly, and said to Williams, "He know too much—must be took care. Yah! yah! git him home! will be safe as wolf neck in de big steel trap."

"Yes, Sewene, you know what's good for his health: the bush and the river are very close."

We were here interrupted by a loud yell from the hunters, above which I could distinguish "Antone," the name of the Mexican. Looking around, we saw part of them mounting "in hot haste," while the others were tearing a passage through the bush fence.

"Sewene, they smell the rat; there'll be hell to play if they catch us. Go it for your lives, and take the fence as soon as it gets low enough."

We were off in an instant. The Mexican hesitated, and looked back timidly. Williams reined back, with the knife raised, and a muttered oath. The man's indecision was cured—he bent forward, plunged spurs into his horse, and was at his best speed. We were inside the wings, and the men, by breaking through, would get the start of us on the direct route to Sewene's plantation—this was the peril.

"This fellow was a servant of Roach's," shouted Williams, with a slight tremor of voice—"they've just missed him. They'll kill their horses to get him. Steady, there, Sewene. Can we clear it?"

"No."

"Steady, then. Don't blow the horses till we are over the fence." He looked back—"Hell! they've nearly got it down! Take it any how, Sewene! It's a half mile to the end yet."

"Sacre! damn! yes!"

He checked up slightly, and breasted his horse at a part of the fence which his quick eye had detected as lowest. His horse was true and cleared it, taking off part of the top brush as he went through. This made it less difficult for the rest of us—one after the other we followed him, Williams coming last—preferring to see the Mexican over—and, from a loud grunt the fellow gave, and blood I saw on his shoulder afterward, I supposed he had pricked his courage for him; and never did I see *quirt** and spur plied with such faithful earnestness as were those of the poor wretch afterward, for he saw death in the eye of Williams in the event of our being hard pressed.

The case was urgent enough for all of us, for on looking up the outside of the fence, I saw the party just emerging from it, and with a fierce howl, like wild beasts, make for the point of timber about three miles off, which they knew our escape depended upon our reaching first. Had we been compelled to go round to the end of the wing, there would have been no chance, but the bold manœuvre of leaping it had somewhat equalized our distances from the timber.

All depended now upon the speed of our horses, and the skill with which it was used; if they overtook us, a bloody and desperate fight, of course; if we reached the timber first, we had them so much at advantage they would hardly pursue us farther.

Williams, or rather Adam Baker, as I now felt convinced he was, (else why this anxiety to get in his power this servant of Roach's, who had probably been with his master in Chihuahua?) said to us, hastily—

"The fools are tearing it down like mad; they will soon

---

* A short, heavy, Mexican whip, made of plaited raw-hide.

K

break their horses' wind—it's three miles—they can't hold
that gait through it—steady! steady! Sewene—we must let
them think they are going to beat us—that will make them
rush the harder; their horses are tired already by the mustang chase—ours are fresher—the last mile we will let it
down in earnest—ours won't be much blown then, and we'll
beat 'em half the distance."

I saw he was right, and the hunters fell into the trap.
We could soon tell, from their louder shouts and the more
rapid play of their arms, that the *quirts* were coming down
still hotter, and in their frantic eagerness they were over-
tasking their horses under the impression that they were
closing upon us.

The interest of the scene was now wrought up to painful
intensity—the party were within three hundred yards of us;
we could hear the heavy thump of their horses' feet, and
their savage oaths. I looked over my shoulder, and could
see them already disengaging their pistols for the mortal
onset, but their horses were evidently doing their best. We
played out a little, to ascertain whether we could lead off at
ease, and, satisfied with this experiment, merely kept the
same distance between us through the next mile. The trunks
of the trees at the point were now becoming more distinct.

With yells that were becoming hoarser, and strokes of the
whip that fell more heavily upon our ears, they seemed throwing the infuriate energy of their own passion into the action
of their horses for one last desperate effort; and though we
too were now plying the *quirt* and the spur, the distance was
lessening between us.

For the next half mile both parties, with steady speed,
were driving on at their utmost. The rumble of the pursuers' tread was growing more and more fearfully distinct—
the poor Mexican, his legs and arms going with frantic rapidity, his face collapsed and ashy with terror, his blue lips
drawn tight and apart, like those of a corpse that had died in

a strong agony, showed his white, set teeth, his eyes glaring wildly back at Baker, watching that long dirk, when suddenly there was a break in the full tide of yells behind us—one of the party was down, man and horse!

"Ha!" shouted Baker, "their horses are giving out; good! Now for it, boys, we shall beat 'em! Just as I said —they've overdone it. The rest of them will go down if they don't hold up—steady! we shall beat them easy enough and have the half mile to spare."

The yells were less frequent now, and, as he prophesied, we rapidly left them. We saw two others of their horses go down—the trick had been perfectly successful: in their head-long fury they had overdone their already fatigued horses by rushing them too hard at first, and in another moment we were sweeping across the friendly shadows of the heavy forest—their last howl of disappointed rage reverberating through its columned aisles.

Baker and myself, after the excitement of this chase, found ourselves suffering greatly from the loss of blood, and by the time we had reached Sewene's we were almost used up. The Mexican seemed to be suffering a sort of paralysis from terror, and had almost to be dragged into the house, which was done in very unceremonious style by two stout negroes. In obedience to Sewene's orders, given in a low tone, they hurried him into a back out-house, and I heard the rattle of bolts and chains. Morgan met us in the passage, with some agitation upon his smooth face as he saw the blood on our persons.

"Hell is let loose upon us, Morgan! It's all up—we shall have to travel!"

"Are you much hurt?—what's to pay?"

"Death and the devil—Roach, you know, was of that party, and I, like an idiot, didn't notice him. He would have done for me but for Kentuck here: Sewene pilled him."

"I hope he stopped his mouth. You are hurt, too, sir! You must have had a rough-and-tumble of it!"

"Regular rough work—we shall have to leave, Morgan—too hot here! Sewene, where's the brandy?"

"Father! father! what have you been doing?" The daughter of Sewene, pale as death, was among us. "Blood! oh, God, are you hurt? Another of these dreadful scenes! Oh, my father! my father!"

She threw her arms about his neck, her long lashes drooping with tears, and gazing through the sparkling mist into his eyes for an instant, she said—

"Must this be always so? Let us go! please! please let us go to the States. That fearful man! father, he will get you killed: mother will go crazy. I! I! what will become of me?" She shuddered, and in a low voice, clinging more closely to him, as she pleaded, "Do! you say you love your child—you call me sweet Nimqua when you kiss me!"

With a convulsive shiver she sank into a chair, covering her face with her hands.

"Oh, I shall go wild, my father, I shall go wild, if I cannot get away from such scenes!"

Sewene stood gazing down at his weeping child for an instant, with a stricken and sorrowful look; then quickly, in a startlingly abrupt tone, he said—

"Sacre! no! no! no blood on my pale flower! stain like these!" stretching out his tawney hands. "Mother—you—shall go—New Orleans!"

"Sewene," said Morgan, who had been eagerly watching this scene, "you are right; this is noble of you. This savage frontier is no place for your wife and daughter. It was cruelly selfish of you to bring her here after an education in the seclusion and refinement of a nunnery. Send them to New Orleans; you are wealthy, and establish them there in a style worthy of your daughter's accomplishments and beauty. Let them start early in the morning, at once—you can trust your overseer—every thing will blow over in a short time, if we all get out of the way. You can then come back yourself, when you get tired of the city, and leave them there until this frontier becomes more settled. Baker and myself will accompany you all the way, and this gentleman," bowing to me, " will, no doubt, so far as there is any danger."

I merely nodded, scarcely conscious of what was said, for the ice-bolt had entered my soul from another quarter.

During this speech I had been watching Nimqua. At the first sound of Morgan's voice she had started slightly, but as he went on, her drooping figure had regained all its elastic grace, and with neck slightly curved, her rich lips a little parted, and those dark, open eyes flooding the liquid light of love and gratitude in beams that lived and glowed upon the air, she gazed into his face as one entranced.

I looked up—so intensely had I been absorbed by the scene just described, that I had not noticed, nor had any one until now, the remarkable silence of Baker since he had asked for the brandy. Nimqua was standing, her delicate hands raised and shivering with terror, staring aghast upon what was indeed a terrible object.

There, upon a bench outside of our group, lay Baker stretched upon his back, his head resting upon a Mexican saddle, placed there accidentally, the ashy hue of death upon his face, his jaw fallen, his lips blue, with flecks of red foam upon the corners, his large eyes protruding and dim, fixed in that rigid, frozen stare, that once seen is for ever unmistakeable. Nimqua broke the heavy silence.

"Dead! dead! that dreadful man!" she gasped, and sank back. I sprang forward to catch her, but Morgan was before me—I caught myself in the very act of striking him, as with a calm bow to me he lifted her in his arms, and bore her into the next room.

Sewene had rushed out to look for restoratives—I was left alone with Baker—I lifted his hand, still clenching the cross-hafted dagger; it was damp and cold, and fell heavily like lead upon his side. Strange man! the wound had been more desperate than we dreamed. I opened his bosom ; he wore a mail shirt next his skin, and masses of clotted blood showed that he had been bleeding most profusely. He had sunk down with that last reckless speech upon his lips, and died without a groan.

The restoratives availed nothing—life was utterly extinct. Sewene's manner became more and more confident as this certainty became fixed ; his step became more buoyant ; his whole air was that of a man who felt himself relieved from some heavy impending curse—some incubus that had stagnated the currents of his life.

Sewene was a fiercely passionate, strong man, but very much of the animal ; and the subtle intellectuality of Baker had enslaved him, and turned these passions often into the wrong ; and now that his better nature had been stirred by the pleadings of his fair child, he felt that to be relieved from that devilish influence was like a respite for his soul from a black doom ; and he ordered the preparations for our journey by daybreak, with the eagerness of a prisoner about to have the bolts turned that were to let him out into the glad sunshine again.

And what seemed strangely righteous to me, (for it was the retribution of his crimes,) from the moment when it was certain that he was dead, nobody approached or touched the body of Baker ; and when I retired to catch a few hours' rest, by the dim light of a single candle, I saw it lying in the same position—the foam still upon his lips, and the stony eyes glaring out into the darkness—alone with the silence and his bad name we left him—while the owls hooted and the hoarse wolves chorussed a fitting requiem.

I had slept most profoundly for several hours, when I was awakened by the heavy trampling of many feet in the passage where the body lay, and the hoarse, subdued sound of many voices. I was on my feet in an instant, arms in hand, when I heard the voice of Morgan in loud, clear tones—"You see he is dead, my friends! It matters not what his crimes were, he is out of the reach of your vengeance."

"But we will drag his cursed carcass to the tail of a mustang," said a coarse voice. I opened my door and looked out: there were ten or fifteen rude men grouped about the body—the faint light just sufficient to show the somewhat awed but stern purpose on their features, and the gleam of their long rifles.

Unarmed and half dressed, Morgan was standing in the door of his room; one of the men stepped forward suddenly, and, seizing an arm, shook the body violently—

"I am afraid the cunning little devil isn't dead sure enough!"

The body was rigid, and the red foam bubbled over from the lips; the man drew back—

"God! I guess there's no mistake in that!"

"Yes, Jack, he's done for, certain! Roach is revenged!"

"But Sewene did it—let's have him!"

"Gentlemen," said Morgan, "in the first place you will have a desperate fight for that—we are prepared for you. Sewene, the negroes, his overseer, myself, and the Kentuckian are well armed, and ready to protect the females in this house and our own lives, so that it will be no child's play—in the next place, Baker, the man you want, is dead, and you surely are not going to be brutes enough to put that threat into execution—in the next place, you are interfering in a matter that rests entirely between the brother of Roach and Sewene. You will always find Sewene ready to account to him, blood for blood. I appeal to you as men to leave quietly, and not frighten these poor women—we will fight to the death rather than permit it—here is his young daughter. in the house, and his wife. It will be unmanly in you! You know Sewene is not a man to shrink from responsibility!"

"Well! well! that's sensible, boys, and if you haven't killed that Mexican, we will go."

"The Mexican is not dead—here's the key—he is in that house; take him, and leave quietly!"

He tossed the key to one of them: the man caught it, and said—

"Come, boys, let's go! leave that rotten lump there—we won't have a row, for the sake of the women—Jim Roach will be here to-morrow, and we will all come with him, and see that he has a fair fight out of Sewene. Let's be off—we won't hurt Sewene's little girl. It's bad luck, you know, to blood a 'white fawn.'"

The party moved off, and I was astonished to see these ruffianly men pass out on tiptoe, cautiously as if they were creeping on an enemy, for fear they might disturb the "white fawn." This was a generous trait that all-conquering beauty and innocence will call up, in hearts however savage and brutalized.

I heard them unlock the door, and in a low, stern voice, command silence of the Mexican, who had commenced a sort of wail—thinking, no doubt, that his time was come—and in a little while the sound of their horses' feet died away in the distance. Much to my amazement, Sewene, with thirty negroes, fully armed, and the overseer, came forward out of the shade, where they had been standing in the yard, waiting the result of this scene.

It was nearly day, and all was now rapid preparation for setting off. I threw myself on the bed again, and when they summoned me to start, I noticed, as I passed out, that the body of Baker was gone. I made no inquiries what had become of it; and, after a hearty meal, we got under way, Sewene, Morgan, and myself, with three negroes leading pack-mules.

Our trip was a pleasant one. I found my companions very agreeable, and many a strange revelation Morgan (whom I learned to like exceedingly) made to me of his own wild career and connexion with that remarkable being, Baker.

Fifteen days after, we arrived in the crescent city. And it was a gay wedding that I attended, a few days after—a little splenetic I could not help feeling as the bridal kiss was given; and Nimqua, the "White Fawn," illustrated on her happy face "the silent war of lilies and of roses."

THE TEXAN VIRAGO

AND

THE TAILOR OF GOTHAM.

THE TEXAN VIRAGO AND THE TAILOR
OF GOTHAM.

AUNT BECK was a character such as could have flourished only in Texas or Australia. She was a tall and large-framed woman, who, having come of Scotch and Irish parents, bore, in her rounded, yet iron-jawed face, a singular union of that mischievous humour and stolid will which are the characteristics of the two races.

We think it was evident enough when you met her eye, that Aunt Beck had never been born to exhibit, under any possible circumstances in this troublesome life, a very saintly degree of patience—for, find her in howsoever placid mood you might, there was still a certain sharpness in the twinkle of her humour which made your nerves creep.

This may be an uncharitable conjecture of ours, since Texas (a few years after the Revolution) was by no means a hot-bed of the godly virtues; and, from all accounts, there had been little in the fortunes which had befallen Aunt Beck to sweeten her temper, or cultivate in her great devoutness of resignation.

A partial and plausible theory asserts that circumstances make men—and women, too, we suppose!—but we incline to

L

the belief that such women as Aunt Beck make their own circumstances—or, rather, *find* such as are most congenial to their tempers.

She was one of those born to be despots—to rule with a tyrannous will whatever persons and conditions she might come in contact with; and though her fate had been a cruel one, yet misfortune had as little hardened her generous impulses as it had softened her domineering temper. But she stood the best sponsor of her own character; for, though a "lone woman in the world," she was known to be so remarkably well able to answer for herself, that no heaven-daring ruffian of the wild frontier on which she lived ever presumed to cross questions with her in a way to risk provoking an experiment of her hair-splitting skill with the pistol, a brace of which she carried where housewives usually carry the bunch of keys.

For her log hut in the old town of Goliad—of bloody memory—was at this time the only tavern, and she found pistols more useful than keys in protecting her property, and keeping her rough customers in order.

Indeed, it was perfectly understood that she ruled, with an iron hand, all who claimed the hospitalities of her roof-tree, and that from her despotic fiat there could be no appeal; for if the resort was to force, her ready hand and savage temper were nothing loath to meet it; if the tongue was to be the weapon, then hers was, beyond all possible competition, the bitterest and most abusive that ever wagged!

Whatever of misfortune really had occurred, Aunt Beck's was a "silent sorrow;" for she never spoke of her past life in connection with any of its affections; and that she had ever known those which are common to her sex at all, you could only discover in occasional and unconscious outbreaks of a tender impulse, which revealed the woman through the desperado.

But though she herself was sternly silent at all times upon

such themes, there were plenty of others who volunteered to talk for her, and it was a gloomy tale of utter desolation at which these whispering rumour-bearers hinted, in connection with her career in Texas.

It was said that her husband was one of the early colonists with Austin, and that they had brought with them from the mountains of Pennsylvania a lusty family of sons—six stout and manly-looking fellows as ever drew "a bead" or slung an axe. She never had a daughter—but her seventh and youngest boy was very feminine and delicate—unlike his six rough brothers as contrast could make him, both in appearance and in temper. Her mother's heart clung to this boy before all the rest, while her husband, who was a fierce and rude old ruffian, regarded him with contempt, and finally even a pitiless aversion as womanly and feeble. .

Until the birth of this unfortunate child the pair had got along together with as little difficulty and as few serious collisions as could be expected from natures which were mutually strong, tenacious, and unyielding—that is, they had quarrelled now and then pretty savagely; but as they really loved and respected each other heartily, they had soon come together again, with a renewal of the affection which had only generated something of warmth in the separation. But now his slight form, and fair, pretty, girlish face, came between the contending powers, not as the angel of peace, but of discord.

They lived amid perilous scenes, and the ruder virtues of brute strength and courage were more highly valued than all others, and while the old man rejoiced in the prowess and daring of his six stalwart boys, who were in every sense so useful and congenial in his lawless pursuits, the youngest became an eye-sore and a shame to him in their midst. Not that the boy had really shown himself to be deficient in manly spirit by any overt act as he grew up, but mainly because he seemed to have no sympathy with their cherished moods of feeling and habitual deeds; for this the elder sons hated him, and aided to nourish the father's hate.

The old man was a cattle-driver, or "cow-boy," as those men are and were termed who drove in the cattle of the Mexican rancheros of the Rio Grande border, either by stealth, or after plundering or murdering the herdsmen! They were, in short, considered as banditti before the revolution, and have been properly considered so since. This term "cow-boy" was even then—and still more emphatically, later—one name for many crimes; since those engaged in it were mostly outlaws confessedly, and if not so at the beginning, were always driven into outlawry by the harsh and stern contingencies of their pursuit, which, as it was in violation of all law, compelled them frequently into the most heinous crimes, to protect themselves against entailed consequences.

The predatory excursions of this man and his six boys had furnished one of the earliest occasions for the harsh measures of the central government toward the new colony of Texas, which led to the first collisions between them.

The son, who was then sixteen years of age, had always refused to accompany his father and brothers on these excursions, and, although he said little, had, in spite of their united taunts and insults, persisted in remaining by the side of his mother. She had heretofore taken his part, and shielded him indirectly from these persecutions as quietly as possible for her impetuous nature. But now a crisis had arrived. He was old enough to go with them and share in the hardships, as well as dangers and crimes of their expeditions; and the old man scornfully demanded that "the white-faced gal" should go along to cook for them, if he had not the spirit to do any thing else!

The boy, it seems, was of a delicate and poetical nature, and shrank, now more than ever, from the harsh and uncongenial association of his father and brothers; for the dreams of a calmer and nobler life, which had been nourished in him by the constant study of some few books which his mother had brought along with her, had now begun to take the warm complexion of reality; and, with an inherited firmness of will, they had become as laws and a fixed purpose to him.

He refused positively to go, or to hold any thing in common with his father and brothers, and that with a resolution and tenacity which both surprised and astounded the old man, who had heretofore left him to himself and his mother with a contemptuous disregard, never dreaming, of course, that he would have the insolence at any time to assert his life as his own. The reaction of his surprise was furious anger. He loosened upon the poor child's head the vials of his hoarded wrath, in words of the bitterest, the most brutal and savage denunciation. This was in the presence of all the six brothers and the mother.

The boy stood among them, white and firm: not a nerve quivered while he looked his father steadily in the eye. This only enraged the old ruffian the more. He taunted him with the most merciless and even ferocious malignity—the boy's face merely grew whiter and more rigid. The brute now roared with anger, and cursed him in dreadful curses, and swore finally, with a hideous imprecation, that if the boy did not start with them the next morning, he would tie him up to a tree and lash his naked back with a quirt while he could stand, or there was life in him.

"You will have it to do," said the child, calmly. "I won't go with you, old man! I will stay with mother!"

"You won't!—won't you?" roared the old wretch, springing forward. "Take that! and go to her then!"

He struck him in the ungovernable paroxysm of his rage—struck him on his fair and delicate temple a blow that would have felled an ox. The brave boy sank without a moan, the blood gushing from his eyes, nose, and mouth.

The mother had stood by during the scene without offering
L 2

to interfere; she sprang forward, as she saw the blow about
to be struck, to arrest her husband's arm; but it was too late.
Her darling—the child of her heart—lay at her feet dead,
the red blood streaming over his white face. The woman was
gone—a raving tigress was in her place—an unnatural monster! She sprang upon her husband, and before the sons
could interfere, she had snatched the bowie knife from his
own belt and cut him with a dozen mortal strokes; and then
charging like a demon of blind retribution upon her elder
sons, had scattered them with the bloody knife far and wide,
several of them badly wounded before they had time to
realize all the horror of the awful and unnatural scene.

They never dared go near her again. While pursuing
them with the knife, she had screamed in their ears, in the
broken language of her demoniac fury, that *they* had been
the cause of the boy's death—that they had set their father
on from the first, and might have prevented him from striking now if they had tried—that they had hated the boy because he was better than themselves! They knew her too
well ever to venture into her presence again, and, bad as
they were, the horror of that event made them worse and
more desperate than ever; so that in a few years they were
all killed off either in foray or fray along the border.

Who shall speak the dark, unutterable wo of this fierce
woman, thus left alone with the bodies of the slain, and her
own exhausted, reacting passion? She lived far away from
any neighbours, and for several days nobody came to intrude
upon her mournfully fearful solitude. When at last some of
the neighbours gathered in—having heard the report of her
sons—they found her busied about her house as usual, and
when they asked her for her child and husband, she pointed
in stern silence to their graves, and harshly bade them go
about their business.

One of the party, a little more pertinacious or officious
than the rest, insisted that something should be done in the

case, and that she should go in with them to Brazoria to be tried. The woman stepped back into her cabin, and bringing forward two guns, leaned one against the side of the door, while, with a grim relentless scowl upon her ghastly face, she ordered them to start, at the same time presenting the other gun at them.

They were all armed of course, but they did not choose to bide the issue of such a contest, and that with a woman, too; so they left, and nobody ever dared to mention the event to her again. For more than a year it was believed no white person went near her house, and that she did not see a living soul, except the wild Indians, perhaps, who are said to have been frequently repulsed by her single hand, in attempts upon her property.

Her house was then on an old trail which led into the Rio Grande border, somewhere in the neighbourhood of Mier. It had formerly been traversed by the tobacco smugglers from the Sabine or the coast; but of late years it had been disused, for fear of the cow-boy depredations. Her husband and sons were said to have frequently robbed and murdered the companies of *traders* as they called themselves—but really smugglers—along this trail; and now that they had disappeared, the bands of these equally lawless men began to make their appearance again along the trail, with their long trains of mules laden with bales of tobacco.

These men were the earliest intruders upon her solitude, and a rough reception it was they met with at first. But these men are a merry and dare-devil class, and the laughing recklessness with which they braved her savageness at last won upon her to a certain degree, and she sullenly permitted them a sort of take-care-of-themselves hospitality. They represented her appearance, when they first intruded upon her, as awfully hideous.

She had been a fat and ruddy dame, with hair slightly grizzled, one year before; now she seemed tall and gaunt,

and her chalky skin was shrivelled to her bones. Her hair
was a mass of creamy, unnatural-looking white, and her
sunken eyes burned with a sultry sullenness that was appalling. After the first uncontrollable shudder, these men were
either too brutal or too careless to pay any further regard to
these appearances, and they knew her reputation rather too
well to venture to speak of them in her presence.

Their rude and boisterous mirth seemed to have an immediate effect in rousing her life from the deadly lethargy into
which it was sinking. They first awakened her anger furiously, and then, as that was permitted to exhaust itself in
harmless vituperation upon them, her kindlier feelings became gradually aroused through the strongly-inherited mirth-
fulness of her Irish descent. They say that when she finally
broke out of a sudden in their midst into a loud laugh, they
were frightened—that it had an unearthly sound, like the
dry chatter of a skeleton's laugh. She checked herself suddenly, and glared around her in a fury; but they all looked
so really startled and affrighted, that she burst again into a
roar of spasmodic mirth, which continued, peal upon peal,
until she sank hysterically upon the earth; and after weeping for a long while there, she arose to her feet a changed
being. The spell was broken!

She resumed a partial cheerfulness before they left, and
when the party returned, they found her greatly altered in
appearance, as she was in temper and bearing. She looked
like a human being now, and met their rough greetings with
something like good humour, though when they ventured
upon some rude bantering, the savage tartness of her retorts
warned them to keep in due bounds. As time progressed,
this class of outlaws became great favourites with her, and
her house came to be a sort of frontier rendezvous for them.

 The year after she heard of the death of the last of her
sons, she undertook a pilgrimage to the Rio Grande, for the
purpose of confession, penance, and absolution, at the great

cathedral of Monterey. She had been educated a Catholic, but, until the events of late years, had entirely forgotten her religion. The journey was a very perilous one, but she made it in company with one of those smuggling bands so far as the neighbourhood of Mier.

On parting with them she crossed the river above Mier, and reported herself to the Padre there, who, believing her account of the object of her journey, gave her a permit to travel, which he obtained from the Alcalde, and forwarded the pious pilgrim, with a strong escort, to his superior at Monterey—she, of course, leaving behind a heavy remembrance for his blessing. Returning with a conscience now entirely at ease, and a purse nearly as light, she rejoined the smugglers, and from that time until the revolution she was openly engaged herself in the smuggling trade, and even led her own little band of men and mules in person. Her journey to the confessional had given her all the advantages of information she desired, and she availed herself of them in her own adventurous manner. She spoke Mexican admirably, and as she now had the reputation of possessing a long purse, and, of course, great piety, it was easy enough for her, on pretence of relieving her sensitive conscience, to cross into any of the border towns, and, after feeing the priest heavily, obtain through him an interview with the Alcalde, who had to be feed again yet more heavily for the privilege of introducing her tobacco into the town during the night, concealed beneath carts of hay or other produce for the market.

The permit or understanding being obtained, she would send back a trusty Mexican servant to the camp—on the other side of the Rio Grande, in which she had left her company concealed—with directions where to cross, and at what hour. She would then meet them, having previously, with the zealous aid of her coadjutor, the worthy Alcalde, sent her smuggling convoy of carts or mules to the same point by many different routes. The tobacco being transferred to these, they scattered again, and came in by the different routes, mingled in with other market-carts or mules coming in from the country.

The Alcalde was, of course, on hand, in the zealous discharge of his duty, which was, in part, to see that the revenue-laws were duly respected within the limits of his jurisdiction. The great man was unusually condescending that morning, and if he had not chosen to take his officer—whose duty it was to inspect all loads and packs—into confidence, and go shares of the plunder with him, he would so overwhelm that functionary by his astonishing and loquacious condescension, as to completely distract his attention from his duty, and thus permit the tobacco to pass in safely. Usually, however, there was no necessity for all this trouble. The Alcalde had only to send for his officer and get him drunk over night, and the tobacco would be safely enough housed before he awoke; or else, if he was a person he could entirely trust, he would merely convey the intelligence to him that he had a little speculation on foot, and desired that officer would wear his brown spectacles next morning, and this hint would, of course, be understood; and when the tobacco was fairly out of harm's way, this obliging functionary was to be remembered by a third heavy disbursement.

In spite of the entailed necessity for all these heavy outlays—and these are only the direct and legitimate ones, under the easiest possible conditions—the trade was occasionally so very lucrative, that the smuggler dared every thing rather than give it up, though it was quite as common for him to lose *all* as to make these enormous percentages. As, for instance, the Alcalde might be attacked with a sudden fit of indigestion, and, of course, of virtue and patriotic zeal—then his unpurchasable honour was dangerous, though by no means rash. He would take the purse of the tamperer with smothered indignation—assist him with well-dissembled activity to cross his tobacco—nay, even get it into the town, and then, in a sudden fit of abstraction, inform his officer, privately, that the prey was in the net, and he would draw the strings at once. Consequence—forfeiture of the whole—seizure and imprisonment of the smuggler at the pleasure of the Alcalde.

It was the duty of this virtuous person to forward such prisoners to Mexico, and of course account to the government for the forfeited property; but as his fit of indigestion would have passed off by this time, his ears were mercifully open to propositions for *ransom* from the friends of the captive, and when a few thousand dollars more had been forthcoming, he would permit his benevolent heart the gratification of freeing the poor prisoner, without a shirt to his back, while the government remained nothing the wiser of such good deeds on the part of its distant servants. Sometimes it happened that the unfortunate adventurer never saw the light again, having been disposed of in some mysterious way; and as there was nobody who dared come to inquire after him, nobody of course was any the wiser for his fate but the sleek Alcalde and his tractable ministers.

Hard as were such contingencies, the smuggler no sooner escaped from the consequences of one than he risked another without fail. There seems to be a something of charm in the wild and perilous exigencies of such a life, which holds with it a strange power over those who have once felt its spell; no sort of danger, suffering, or defeat can deter them from a renewal of the attractive risks. Strange as it is that this should be so with men, it is yet more remarkable to find a lone woman persevering through years of perilous vicissitude in this traffic.

She is represented to have passed through nearly every difficult strait to which the life of the tobacco-smuggler is liable, and indeed to have personally faced a greater amount and variety of dangerous extremes than any of the most noted leaders of the other sex along the whole border

There may have been some romancing in this statement, as
is natural from the unusual character of the circumstance
that a woman should be engaged in such a traffic at all; but
these few facts are known to be absolutely certain, namely:
that she was for a period of five or six years on horseback
for three-fourths of her time, riding like a man, with pistols
in her holsters before her, and at her belt—she never carried
a gun—and passing between her own house and the towns
of the Rio Grande; that she usually had five or six men with
her, one of whom was her Mexican servant, and a dozen or
more pack-mules loaded with tobacco going out, and some
with specie coming in; that during this time she was frequently taken prisoner, and her men came straggling in
without a mule or a penny; that she always came in alone
on these occasions, and frequently made narrow escapes
from, and had desperate fights with the Indians; that she
never hesitated to go anywhere she chose, Indians or no Indians, and did not seem to regard their being in her path at
all, &c. &c.

Such facts as these were notorious; and it was further
whispered that she owed her frequent escapes to the powerful intercession, or rather interference, of the Padres down
along the valley from Monterey, who, it is said, held her in
high regard for her piety, or rather her liberality to the
church. It was also said that she was both feared and hated
by the majority of the men whom she employed; but that
she always had one or two about her who were faithful.

On several occasions when they were returning, the men
have attempted a mutiny, to get possession of the specie, by
taking her life. She has always discovered the plot in time,
and permitting it to come to a head, has killed, often with
her own hands, the ringleaders. At such times she was always as profusely liberal to the faithful few as she was pitiless in her vengeance upon the traitorous majority.

There are very many extraordinary stories told of her

daring, her cunning, her vindictiveness, and her humour; but it is a marked and curious fact, which I have noted often with great interest, that amidst all these tales, in the mouths of very many different grades of lawless men, we never yet, in one instance, heard any thing like an insinuation directed against her fair fame and honour. She was by no means so old a person that such charges would not have been thought of and greedily circulated about her; but that there was a certain grave, stern, and reserved austerity, which made itself so frequently apparent in her looks and bearing, in spite of her humour and recklessness, that such thoughts were utterly rebuked, even in the minds of the most obscene blackguards. She is said, on one occasion, when near the Rio Grande, on her way out with tobacco, to have slit the ears of such a fellow, who said something in her presence offensive to her delicacy, and then driven him from her camp, without food or a gun, to find his way back as best he might. This was a lesson that lasted ever afterwards, whenever she was present among men, of whatever stamp; for such an incident as this has always wide circulation.

At the time the revolution broke out, she was thought to be quite wealthy, and was engaged in smuggling, on a more extensive scale than any one else in Texas. She had not much visible property, but her wealth was said to be all in gold and silver. Be this as it may, that event broke up her smuggling operations entirely, and she remained quiet at home, taking sides with neither party.

But neutrality at such a time was out of the question, and her house was surrounded suddenly and pillaged by the blood-thirsty and brutal Cos. It is said that he carried off a large sum in specie, which he found concealed under the floor of her rancho. From that time she became a fierce and deadly foe of Mexico and Mexicans; and it turned out, that although Cos was said to have carried off all her money, she still had a great deal left to spare to the cause of Texas.

M

She never did any thing by halves, and so, by the time the war was over, she found herself nearly penniless, and was compelled to begin the world anew. She had been hanging around the army, sometimes taking a hand, on a pinch, with her pistols, and at others cooking for the officers and attending the wounded.

But when the army was finally disbanded, she went back to her old life of solitude again, but soon found that she could not live upon air; all her money was gone and her stock scattered to the four winds. She would not condescend to trouble the new government for repayment of the sums she had advanced; but, with characteristic recklessness and energy, got together some few of the remaining men formerly in her employ, and then, making a sudden descent upon the distracted borders of Mexico, drove back a herd of five hundred head of cattle;—in a word, became a female " Cowboy," as her husband and elder sons had been ! On reaching the settlements, the cattle were rapidly converted into money, although she did not appear in the business, but acted through an agent.

Having received the money, she is said to have declared her determination to alter her mode of life—quit adventuring, and settle down in quiet for the rest of her life. That her ideas of quiet were decidedly comparative, will be perceived, when it is known that the deserted site of Goliad, of bloody memory, was the location of her new and *quiet* home. It was then the extreme frontier of settlement west. The whites had been driven from Bahai, and the little settlement at Victoria was scattered; the country was filled with outlaws—stragglers from both armies—the ravens of spoil and slaughter, that were starving now for want of their unclean food.

The Indians, taking advantage of the general confusion, were driving the settlers steadily back and back towards the San Bernard, and were constantly scouring the country back and forth in small predatory bands. It was in the midst of such a condition of things that our wearied and saintly hermitess, sighing for the calm delights of peaceful seclusion, away from the harsh strife and wicked turmoil of an evil world, threw herself for the remainder of her days. She was the pioneer of resettlement, and took things as they came with a most philosophical resignation. If the Indians troubled her stock, she sallied out and gave them a drubbing—if renegades and horse-thieves annoyed her, she dealt with them in an equally summary manner, and soon made her neighbourhood respected to such a degree, that two or three adventurers from the settlements plucked up courage, and came to live in deserted tenements of the old town. If any one came who did not suit her, she soon drove him off with a flea in his ear.

Thus several years had passed, and though there were still not more than a half dozen others in the town, yet the Old Trail to Bahai had begun to be travelled now and then, and the little settlement at Victoria had begun to gather in again, and Aunt Beck was not unfrequently called upon by land-hunters, travellers, speculators, and so forth, for food and lodging—so she concluded, as the thing became inevitable, to give in and "keep tavern" at once.

About this time my friend Dick Hord, a wild and gallant young Virginian, went to Texas to seek his fortune. He was reckless as exuberant life and a mirthful and dare-devil spirit could make him; but yet he had a sober purpose before him—that is, he protests that he had—but we have always thought that he obtained the commission of surveyor of Goliad county rather as an excuse for running himself into all sorts of scrapes and hair-breadth ventures, rather than with the thrifty view of locating the best lands for himself, and thereby laying the foundation for a fortune. Be this as it may, the best proof of his being a sad scamp is to be found in the incidents we are about to relate.

He made Goliad the centre of his operations, and of course his head-quarters could be nowhere but at Aunt Beck's tavern. Dick and she got along surprisingly together; for there was something in the cool matter-of-fact way in which he pushed his surveying or hunting expeditions right into known Indian territory without the slightest regard to their numbers or formidable fame—which quite won Aunt Beck's heart—because it was so much after her own habitual mode of procedure.

Dick had been living this wandering and adventurous life for over a year, when the monotony of its seclusion began to be somewhat relieved. Young men were flooding into Texas from every State in the Union—their pockets stuffed with "land scrip," the most of which was located on some imaginary grant on the remote frontier. The mania for speculation, which was the first reaction from the depressing times of the revolution, had scattered this worthless paper far and wide, and many a clever, warm-hearted fellow had been gulled by the oily-tongued agents of those irresponsible companies into giving up a valuable certainty at home to chase the wild goose that was to lay him golden eggs over those desolate and dangerous plains.

These verdant and eager adventurers had begun to push their way as far as Goliad; and sometimes when Dick came in he would find a party waiting his arrival at Aunt Beck's tavern, to go with them and survey these " promised lands." On the occasion to which we shall particularly refer, he found two young men who had just arrived from "the States," and were anxiously awaiting him. One of them, named Allen, was a plainly dressed, bright-eyed youth, who said he was a farmer's son from Tennessee; while the other was a heroic tailor of Gotham, who had dropped one goose to chase another.

The usual frank and rough greeting of the frontier being over, these men, together with Dick and his two chain-carriers, were soon seated at dinner around an old pine dry-goods box, which served them for a table. In the centre of this stood a large wooden bowl, filled with a boiling hotch-potch of beef and potatoes. A tin pint cup flanked the pewter plate which was in front of each man. There was no sign of spoons, and the two strangers looked with a puzzled and hungry curiosity at the contents of the bowl, when Dick laughingly drew his hunting-knife and commenced spearing vigorously at the potatoes and fragments of meat which were bobbing about in the hot and muddy-looking pool.

They took the hint and followed suit, while Aunt Beck—her strong features flaming from the heat of the fire—walked round behind them, filling each cup with coffee from a great black tin boiler. Aunt Beck was usually sulky or tart when strangers came; but for a miracle she was in a rare good-humour this evening.

"There! there!"—as she was running his cup over in her generosity—"you mean I shall have enough this evening, Aunty?"

"Sure and yes, hinney! ye should be afther ateing enough while ye've the convaniences and the bowels!"

"But Aunty, I say!—though I may not always have just such luxurious conveniences at hand as you furnish here, yet I don't know what's to spoil my appetite."

"Ah, chiel Dicky! Chiel Dicky, ye'r ower brash! Them long-hair'd britherin o' Satan will spile ye'r stomach for ye yet!"

"Who? the Camanches?"

"What!" interrupted young Allen, quickly, while his eyes glared a little, "are the Camanches about?"

"Camanches aboun! saft craythurs ye are, not to be smellin' the wasp-nest ye'r pokin' ye'r noses in! Sure, mon, they'r thick as thrae in a bed, on these pararies: This hare-'em scare-'em Dicky, here, has aven been plading and inthrating of 'em to ase him of his wool for moonths and

M 2

moonths; but I'm a thinkin' they won't hae it because it's
sun-burnt and frizzled. They likes fresh, slick, ilely hair,
like yourn, best, hinnies."

This was said with demure solemnity, and a side wink at
Dick.

" I hope they won't take a fancy for mine !" said the Tennessee boy, very innocently smoothing down his shining
black locks.

"By blood!" said the knight of the scissors, with a
hoarsely savage intonation, stroking rapidly, at the same
time, a huge moustache, "if they get mine, they'll have to
fight for it, by G—d!"

Aunt Beck stared at him with round, opening eyes for an
instant; then, lifting her hands as if in pious adjuration—

"Lord help us !—a lone creetur !—how fierce he is ! Sae
they will, mon, nae doubt. Sorry the day ye didn't run a
baker's dizen of 'em to look at ye ! The puir divils are
awful 'fraid of the brush; and by the sainted snake-killer !—
barrin' your nose and eyes—but ye'r got the maist cantan-
kerous brush-heap on ye'r shoulders thar, that has travelled
since the day o' guid King Macbeth !"

"I—I cultivated them expressly !" said the sappy hero,
half closing his eyes with an excessively devil-may-care air,
and plucking and stroking yet more affectionately the rough,
reddish thicket which covered alike his throat, face, and
head.

"Och ! deary ! and ye should ha' been more mercifuller—
to be scarin' the ignorant salvages into duck-fits so ! Bonny,
aisy Dicky, there, thinks physikin' 'em wi' lead pills is bad
enough, but ye are o'er cruel craythurs wha coom fra the
States ! Wait till ye get to know 'em better, my darlin', and
ye'r heart will be tenderer to 'em !"

"Oh, I am quite tender-hearted, as to that," said he of
the whiskers, shaking his head to one side, and putting on a
ferocious scowl, which clearly contradicted his words.

"Bless your sowl, deary, and so you are. The dugs o' the mither that nursed ye ain't safter! Did she gi' ye the suck-bottle to bring along, hinney?"

This was too rich. Dick and his chain-bearers, who had been nearly bursting with smothered merriment since this conversation began, now exploded in the most uproarious peals of laughter as they jumped from their seats and tumbled convulsed about the room. Young Allen, who had begun to smell the rat, joined the laugh, but with more moderation; for he had not seen enough of life, and such life especially, to exactly understand the characters about him.

The astonished tailor drew himself up to his full height; then opening his big white eyes in a wild stare around him for a moment, assumed a lofty air of sneering indignation as he threw out his right arm towards the offenders grandly, and hissed from between his teeth—

"Ye—s—es, old woman! Do you just show Hector Napoleon Smith one of those bloody Camanches you seem to be so 'fraid of, if you want to see whether he is done with his suck-bottle or no!"

"Dicky! Dicky, dear!" screamed the old woman, "where's your pet Camancha? Let's show it to my darlin'."

"You mean in the cigar-box? There it is on the shelf, outside the door."

Aunt Beck bounced out of the door, and in an instant was back, holding a cigar-box in her hands, with narrow strips tacked on the front. She pushed it towards the face of Hector Napoleon Smith.

"There, deary! Don't faint, now. That's a Camancha! Wouldn't you like to eat him without salt?"

Hector Napoleon sprang back amidst reiterated peals of laughter. He looked frightened—no wonder!—for it was one of those famously hideous and loathsome creatures of the southern prairies called horned frogs, and which she had named her pet Camancha.

"What is it?" he gasped. "Take it away, woman!"

But Aunt Beck still followed his retreating steps, pushing the box under his nose until it touched his face. He struck the frog-cage aside, and pushed her rudely from him, as he roared out furiously—

"Get away, you d——d old hag!"

"D——d old hag, is it?—you moon-eyed spalpeen! Take that! and that!" Heavy and fast she rained the blows upon his head with the cigar-box, until it split into a thousand fragments, while she continued to repeat "D——d old hag, is it?" every time her heavy hand came down; and then—"The mither that suckled a calf sha'n't ken ye!"

Her quick eye detected the poor frog attempting to escape along the floor of the cabin. Springing after it with wonderful activity, she seized it in her fingers, turned, and advanced upon the poor tailor with the exclamation—

"By the ghost of St. Patrick, he shall ate the Camancha!"

But Hector Napoleon Smith had availed himself of the short respite to seize a heavy stool by the leg, and throw himself upon the defensive, with his weapon upraised to strike. The expression of the old woman, which had been merely that of mischievous deviltry before, changed now to one of pitiless fierceness: she put her hand beneath her apron and whipped out a pistol quickly; then, laughing harshly as she presented it at his head—

"Down with it! ye terrier-faced cummudgeon! In my ain house, too!"

The arm of the affrighted fellow dropped to his side, and the stool fell to the floor. Looking somewhat mollified by this prompt obedience, she approached as he shrunk cowering back into a corner, with a most ludicrously gracious and winning leer upon her face—

"Aisy, my dear, aisy! Sae bluid-thirsty a chiel as ye shall ha' it to say he's ate a Camancha without salt!" and she pushed the frog nearer his mouth, which he endeavoured to shield by throwing his arms pitifully across his face.

"Hut! tut! nae scringin', my bonnie pet! Bite awa bravely! Bite awa!" pushing it up still closer to his mouth.

"Good God!" groaned the agonized tailor, rolling his eyes about him, with a wild look of forlorn, imploring despair—for the filthy reptile almost touched his lips, and the muzzle of the pistol gaped like a cannon's mouth before his swimming vision.

"Ye'll ha' it to do!" said the inexorable old creature, still following his shrinking face with the frog.

But the joke had gone far enough, and Dick, who by this time had sufficiently recovered from his convulsions, came to the poor wretch's rescue, and snatched the pistol from the old woman's hand, as he pushed her suddenly back. Thus was the horrified tailor relieved, though the experiment might have cost any other man a pistol-ball; but Dick was her favourite, and after abusing him a little, she joined good-humouredly in the continued laughter, saying, as she turned off about her housework—

"Sure, I'm a thinkin the dear chiel will na forget his first taste o' Camanches soon!"

They now resumed their seats, to finish the meal that had been so farsically interrupted. Hector Napoleon looked considerably chop-fallen for awhile. But Dick, who now suddenly conceived a warm interest for him, consoled him by exclaiming, in an emphatic whisper—

"Pshaw! never mind it! she's nothing but a woman! What man could help himself?—you were obliged to stand it, or strike a woman!"

Perceiving that this sort of consolation took admirably, 'e proceeded to launch out for quantity with a string of direful stories, illustrating, in highly-imaginative colouring, the desperate and blood-thirsty traits of the Camanches. This sort of rigmarole romancing was addressed to the tailor in a low, confidential voice, as a man of tried valour, to whom such scenes were matters of course. Now and then, in winding up some story in which cowardice had lost the day, he would exclaim, in the most confident and enthusiastic manner—

"Ah! that affair would have ended very differently, had *you* and myself been only there! wouldn't it?" and soon he had the satisfaction of seeing his victim caress the moustache as affectionately as ever, and nod his head threateningly in the affirmative, as he would drawl out, with the most irresistibly imposing nonchalance—"I ra-a-a-ther think it would."

This was exquisitely rich to Dick's palate; for not having the slightest idea of seeing Camanches really, he had determined to amuse himself, in crossing the prairies to-morrow, by playing upon the vain-glorious valour and ignorance of the tailor. He accordingly followed up the "stuffing" game, until, before they took to their blankets for the night, Hector Napoleon Smith was panting for the battle-field—for deeds of gory heroism and immortal daring, to be perpetrated at the expense of the dusky skins of the poor Camanches.

It seemed that the tailor and the young Tennessecan had come together by accident, both being on their way to Goliad on the same errand—namely, to get lands surveyed, for which they had bought scrip purporting to be located there. Dick found the scrip of young Allen really of value, though he had some doubts of that of the tailor. He started next morning, soon after sunrise, to survey Allen's land. Hector Napoleon, of course, accompanied them; and as they were mounting to start, Aunt Beck came to the door and screamed after him—

"Arrah, hinney! and had'nt ye better take some salt along, to-day, to put on their tails! Camanches is hard to catch—they're a wee bit wild on the prairies, dear!"

The tailor, who did not seem to think there was any great savour of the attic in this sort of wit, merely muttered something about a "d——d old she-bear!" and started off into a gallop.

Dick continued the game of last night, and amused himself by stimulating, with approving flattery, the surplus valour of Smith. When he would get up a false alarm now and then, he would praise the firm bearing of the valorous tailor, and hint how fiercely he knew he would have charged into them, had they turned out to be Indians.

He thus worked the fellow up until he became more and more bombastically heroic, as they progressed with impunity, and would now and then let off steam by dashing his horse ahead of the party, jerking his gun to his face, and eyeing along the barrel at imaginary Camanches. Indeed, to all appearances, he was "crazy for a fight."

Dick, who was a good-hearted fellow, wished from his very core that the enthusiastic young gentleman might be gratified; but as there seemed to him to be no prospect of this, he soon grew tired, chuckling at the effects of his own mischievous wit.

It was time for business, for they were now in sight of the line of timber in which the land lay. He now, for the first time, turned his attention to it; and on looking at his compass, found, to his great mortification, that an indispensable screw of the instrument was missing. There was nothing left but to gallop back to the cabin and get it, where he supposed he must have left it. He pointed out a bend in the line of timber to the young men, as the place where the land lay, and told them either to go back with him, or proceed themselves to the land and ride over it until his return.

The chain-carriers had not come out, for the young men were to carry the chain themselves. The tailor looked a little wild at this proposition to go on there alone with Allen; but the young Western man, who had become wonderfully cool and self-possessed by this time, said at once—

"Certainly, Mr. Hord! I will ride on and take a good

look at the land, while you go back!" and without waiting to hear from the tailor, rode on as a matter of course.

They proceeded quite leisurely. The hero was in a very fidgety, restless mood, talking incessantly, while Allen paid little attention to him, but regarded with great curiosity the beautiful scenery they were approaching. They were now skirting up the timber towards the sharp elbow, or bend in the stream, which it bordered. Like all the small streams of Texas, this was a deep and narrow cut. Immediately on its brink the timber was small and brushy, but farther out into the prairie it grew larger and more scattering, until there was only here and there a great live-oak to dot its surface.

They turned the sharp bend, which it happened was a point of thicker woods, and found themselves entering a lovely nook of meadow, with these old live-oaks scattered at intervals over it. Two horses, with lariats about their necks, were quietly grazing among the trees, a short distance from them. They stopped in astonishment, which was not a little increased when two Indians, who had evidently been lying upon the grass near the horses, asleep, sprang suddenly to their feet with a hoarse ejaculation of surprise.

They were the dreaded Camanches! The young men were nearly between them and their horses. This, together with the sudden awaking, seemed to confuse the warriors for a moment. It was but for a moment, when one of them darted for the cover of a tree which was nearer the horses, while the other glided behind that beneath which they were sleeping.

Both parties were too much surprised, at first, to think of using weapons, though, with the prompt instinct of his Western blood, young Allen's rifle was up to his face very quickly, but just in time to be too late for the quick Indians. Seeing the advantage they had gained, he immediately dismounted and took the nearest tree himself; for on looking behind, he had perceived at a glance that there was nothing to hope from the tailor in charging them.

That heroic person, in the meantime, was sitting stock-still and erect upon his horse, with mouth and eyes stretched to their utmost capacity of extension—staring before him in blank, stupid astonishment. One of the warriors waked him from his stupor very suddenly with an arrow, which glided through the hairy thicket about his throat, and ripped up the flesh considerably. With a quick sound, something between a yelp and a roar, the fellow fell from his horse into the grass, and commenced rolling over and over until he reached the tree behind which Allen was sheltered.

He paid no attention, but fired. The keen ring of his rifle echoed through the woods on the stream. The reply to it was an Indian whoop from the same quarter. The Indian he had fired at fell, but at the same moment the other sprang to a tree still nearer to the horses, and answered the whoop from the woods.

The horses of the young men had by this time joined those of the Indians, and the rustling in the woods near, and the whistle and patter of arrows around him, told Allen that re-inforcements had arrived. Things began to look serious, but the young man only became more cool.

He nudged the tailor with his elbow, while he was loading his rifle, and told him to keep a sharp eye upon those fellows in the bush, and fire at the first he saw; but he would pay no attention to him, and lay upon the ground moaning about the scratch in the neck he had received. There was no time to be lost, and Allen, utterly out of patience, drew one of his pistols, and rapping the terrified noodle sharply over the head, muttered a threat to give him the ball instantly if he did not raise himself and watch those Indians in the bush behind them.

The doubly terrified fellow now rose on his elbow, and as five or six Indians boldly showed themselves above the bank,

N   10

he shut his eyes and fired. It chanced that the shot told, and they jumped down again. Allen, in the mean time, had drawn himself round the tree, somewhat out of the range of those fellows behind, and had given his whole attention to watching the warrior in front of him, who was determined to get to the horses.

Allen and the warrior were warily watching each other, when, his attention being slightly attracted to see the effect of the tailor's fire, the warrior took advantage of this to reach another tree, which placed him within a few paces of the horses. Allen immediately shifted his ground, too, and was wounded in doing so by those behind. But the wound was slight, and he could now cover perfectly the space yet to be passed by his subtle foe.

All was now as still as death for a few moments. The tailor had forgotten the other barrel of his gun, and crouched panting at the foot of the tree, in overwhelming terror at finding himself thus left alone. The Indians behind the bank had changed their tactics, and proceeding farther down under the shelter of the bank, took to the trees in the meadows; and the frightened booby saw ten or twelve dusky figures gliding from tree to tree, and rapidly closing around him.

Remembering, in his despair, that he had a second barrel, he fired it wildly towards them, and then throwing his gun away, made with frantic speed for the stream they had just left. With half a dozen arrows sticking in his body, he tumbled headlong over the bank into the water, and this was the last seen of Hector Napoleon Smith, the heroic tailor—on this occasion at least; for if the arrows did not finish him, he probably sank in the quicksands of the stream.

The Indians, when they saw this extraordinary manœuvre, rushed forward towards Allen and the horses with a yell of triumph, which, however, was cut short by the crack of his rifle and the death-shriek of the warrior in front, who tumbled over among the horses.

Allen's load was out, and they rushed at him again, thinking they had him now for a surety; but he ran as hard as he could for the horses, and succeeded in mounting into his own saddle while they were yet thirty paces behind him. He might now have made his escape with ease, but the Indian-fighting blood of the gallant youth was up, and he determined to carry off the horses too. He shot down the foremost Indian with his pistol, and while the rest retreated behind trees, he started off the three best horses into a gallop.

It seems that there was a large party of Camanches camped on the other side of the stream, which, like many others of the country, was impassable, except at particular points, on account of the quicksands through which it passed. The crossing-place was a mile above where the collision had occurred, and those who had shown themselves after it had commenced, had left their horses on the other side, and crossed to the assistance of their companions, on a log, while a larger party had gallopped up to the crossing-place, and they now made their appearance, thundering down upon Allen at full speed, yelling their hoarse war-whoop, and clattering their lances against their shields.

This was a sight one would think formidable enough to shake the cast-iron nerves of a veteran Indian-fighter. But, no! Allen had sworn to carry off those horses with him as trophies. He had got a taste of Indian-fighting, and found it to suit him; so he coolly took his measures to accomplish his purpose, in the face of all these foes. It was too late to run now, at all events!

Reining up his horse a little to finish loading his gun, he then let them have his other pistol so soon as they came in range, and as that set a warrior to reeling in his saddle, it somewhat checked their headlong career. He now threw down his pistol, and drew his gun deliberately to his face.

Quick as thought they stooped until they disappeared behind the bodies of their wheeling horses, and, sending a shower of arrows at him from under their necks as they passed, were soon out of reach of his rifle.

They now commenced riding round him in a rapid circle, so as to confuse his aim, but closing up closer with every round, so as to get, imperceptibly, within reach of him for their arrows. Though this was his first fight, he had yet listened with such strict attention to Dick's stories, that he had a pretty clear idea of the Camanche mode of fighting, and how experienced frontiersmen managed them at odds.

He had learned that they never close upon a man so long as they know his rifle is loaded; so he started on his three horses, and whenever they had closed up closer than he liked, he would pause, and bring his rifle slowly to his face. They would instantly dive behind their horses, and wheeling, scatter out of reach of the ball. Then he would push on again for a little distance, when the manœuvre would be repeated on both sides.

His object was to drive the horse into a mott, or island of timber, he saw about a mile before him on the prairie. All the timber near him was in possession of the Indians on foot; and he thought, as the mott was small, that he would be able to make good his stand in it until Dick returned. But they saw his object, and the Indians on foot left the timber and made for the mott to cut him off; while those on horseback redoubled desperately their efforts to confuse him and draw his fire harmlessly.

They broke up their line, and commenced dashing, with marvellous rapidity and the most hideous yells, back and forth, here and there, before and behind him, and would even sweep past him—though going like the wind—close enough to hit either his horses or himself. This maddened his horses, and they grew unruly.

Poor Allen himself now began to grow confused and dizzied by the infernal maze of those flying figures rapidly weaving in and out before his eyes. The arrows had begun to come faster and faster, as they grew emboldened by the success of the new manœuvre, and now they flew thick as hail-stones about, and a number of them struck him, but came from too great a distance to be fatal.

Their movements were so swift, that by the time he had concluded upon firing at a particular Indian, he would have passed out of reach, or else an arrow from behind would tap him and distract his aim. His horse was deeply wounded. He saw, at last, that there was no hope of getting to the mott alive, and desperately threw himself from the tottering animal, determined to make a breastwork of its body, and sell his life as dearly as possible.

The Indians swooped at him like hawks upon the stoop, and were nearly upon him when his feet touched the ground. There was no time for parleying now! He fired steadily, and brought down the foremost warrior. At the crack of the rifle they swerved back a little, but it was only for an instant—they rushed at him with ferocious yells; for now they were sure of him with his empty gun.

The gallant boy was panting from loss of blood; but with set teeth he clubbed his gun desperately for one more blow before he died, when suddenly there rang upon his fading senses—bang! bang! bang!—a number of guns—a tremendous shouting and trampling—when he sank to the ground insensible.

The Indians, who were in the very act of plunging a dozen lances in his body, were scattered as if a hurricane had struck them, and Aunt Beck, with Dick and the chain-carriers, their horses foaming with speed, leaped over him as they swept on in pursuit of the flying Camanches.

All was oblivion with young Allen now, and until some time after, when a sudden sense of cold water in his face revived him. The men were standing in a group around him

N 2

as he opened his eyes; and Aunt Beck stooped over him to
bathe his temples from a water-gourd.

"By the ghost of St. Patrick, the little bantam is only
stunned!" said she, as he opened his eyes. "Sure it's cock-
a-doodle-doo ye may now, my bonny game-chick; for it's
bravely ye'r fleshed your spurs to-day!" she continued, as
she patted him affectionately on the cheek with her rough
powder-stained hands.

We took Allen to Aunt Beck's tavern, where she nursed
him as tenderly as she knew how; for the little Tennessee
bantam had completely won her heart. Indeed, during the
weary and almost desperate illness which followed, the character of Aunt Beck appeared in a new light.

She watched by the bed of this youth with all the eager
and yearning watchfulness of the most affectionate mother;
for a long-silent chord appeared to have been once more
touched in her rude bosom, and her youngest—her fair boy—
the child of her heart, seemed to be replaced by this young
stranger, and the hard and fierce virago was subdued once
more into the woman.

She clung to young Allen ever afterwards with such extraordinary and boundless affection, that he could never bring
himself to leave her. His parents were no longer alive; and
she adopted him, and, relinquishing entirely her masculine
pursuits, settled down into the *comparatively* mild, certainly
superlatively pains-taking and careful housewife, and all for
the sake of her little Tennessee bantam, as she sometimes
called him ever after.

Allen recovered the money she had loaned the Texas
government, and she gave it to him; whereupon he prospered
greatly, and is now a distinguished man in the new State.
Dick and he continue warm friends to this day.

Several days after the fight, a haggard, ghastly wretch—
who, as Aunt Beck said, "looked like a ghost playing boo-
peep through a hole in a bear-skin!"—came crawling up to

the door of "The Tavern," and begged a morsel of food in God's name. After some difficulty they recognised the poor rascal Smith.

He had, it seemed, sunk in the quicksand, but had managed to sustain himself by a drooping limb or twig; and then, after all was quiet, had dragged himself out by its aid. Starvation, and the long cold bath he was compelled to take, had prevented his wounds from killing him. How he managed to get back in his weakened condition nobody can tell, not even himself. The old woman, at the solicitation of Dick, took care of him until he recovered his strength.

But Hector Napoleon Smith was "a done-over tailor!" His two experiences of Camanches quite sufficed him; and with a very humble opinion of himself, Texas in general, and Aunt Beck's tongue in particular, he mounted his horse one fine morning with the intention of putting as much earth and water as possible between himself and such "dem'd peculiar doing!"

Aunt Beck screamed after him—

"Arrah, darlin'! and the naixt time ye gang Camancha-hunting, ye'll na forgie the salt to pat on their tails?"

DEATH OF LITTLE RED-HEAD.

DEATH OF LITTLE RED-HEAD.

THE time of Secret Societies is not yet passed—at all events, we believe that many of them still continue to exert a wide and powerful influence, little realized in our common-place world. It is too much the outward manner of the times to sneer at the power of confederacies, though they are feared—nay, dreaded—with a peculiar sort of vehemence, and frequently even with superstition.

We mean to assert nothing disrespectful of such institu-tions in general, and of their results in particular; for we do believe that, in spite of the Inquisition, they have been most important agents and means of progress. The deepest truths must come out of the heart of the world, whence they are worked up by the pale and begrimed miners of thought, towards the surface, until the ruddy children of the sun can grasp them, and they become, in their robust hands, REALITIES!

So with the principle of these Societies generally. The object to be attained is most usually what is called a romantic or impracticable one, and, of course, not strictly orthodox—therefore, secrecy may be required to prevent controversy. In a word, we do not undertake to defend such organizations, but simply to assert their existence in much greater numbers and power than men are generally disposed to believe; and, whether for evil or for good, their tremendous influence upon the times.

Most of the pretended revelations with regard to them have been proven to be false, and, of course, from the very theory of their principle, we can only really know of them by their effects. It is exclusively from such a point of view that we would presume to speak. Such Societies have existed, and do exist among us, and, as elsewhere, have exerted, and do exert a most extended influence. The distance and division between North and South have been more felt than expressed through such organizations than otherwise—therefore, it is with effects that we propose to deal in this narrative, rather than causes, which we must beg leave to have in a great measure inferred!

Years ago, before Texas was known as more than a wild province of Mexico, there existed an extensive and powerful association within the limits of our own territory, the operations of which were extended to a greater distance than was dreamed of by many of the most able and shrewd men of the day. It is unnecessary to particularize further the motives and methods of such an institution, than to say that it was founded in a grasping, stern, but deep intelligence, and had for its objects what, at that time, would have been considered merely vague and wildly impossible schemes of territorial acquisition, which, having been suggested by the most boldly unprincipled man our country has produced, have been perpetuated by some of its most able, since, to a dazzling consummation. We cannot reveal more than glimpses of the methods pursued, and that rather by implication than by explanation.

It suffices to say, that young men were in some demand by them—but that they were young men of peculiar character. Agents, everywhere in the principal cities, such as New York and New Orleans particularly, kept their treacherous eyes secretly upon the movements of such young men as made themselves conspicuous for spirit, and were known to be of good families and education. The more dissolute the

better, so they were truly courageous. There was use for
such men towards the South, and many such were redeemed
from gambling hells or dragged from the stews by a power
of which they knew nothing but its munificence and its imperious dictation.

Mark Catesby was a man capable of much that was both
good and evil, as are all those who are capable of any thing
worth mentioning. His family was good; his father, a
wealthy Englishman, had brought over his property to this
country, along with his prejudices and habits. He had settled in New York, as metropolitan, and lived in lordly style.
He was munificent as he was haughty, and had one vice
which soon told upon a large estate.

He gambled desperately, and died with the reputation of
great wealth, leaving his son to inherit both his vices and his
insolvency.

The son inherited both his vices and his virtues; but a
poor sister was all that was left now to love. He became
more reckless than before, after the last blow that took from
the two their only surviving relation on the continent, and,
in the heat of wine, made a heavy bet that ruined him utterly.
His sister was an accomplished artist, and surveyed with
comparative calmness the wreck of every thing, and bravely
struggled to uphold the brother who was so dear to her.

He was a reckless young man, haughty to excess, and
filled with a blind family pride. When the great misfortune
had been fully realized by them both, it was finally determined, amidst his despair, through the advice of their old
family lawyer, that the young man should commence the
practice of a profession he had studied with effect—the law.
The brave young sister persuaded him too, after a long
struggle, to permit her to trust her own support to her
pencil.

Such were the determinations on all sides, when a mysterious intervention came to give a new direction to events. A

O

duel, attended with shocking and fatal results, occurred. It had grown out of the gambling debts of Mark, and of course left the already gloomy condition of things involved in still greater gloom. He was not a party, but the cause; and as neither party survived, he alone was left to bear the blame.

To take the most reasonable view of the case, as Mark was the only person left, immediately accessory to the fact, all the public indignation and regrets were visited upon his devoted head. He was denounced in every way, and shamefully persecuted by the press, until his frank and sagacious friend, the old family lawyer, advised him, by all means, to go from the city, and commence a career somewhere else, under more favourable auspices. Although the good old man was willing to do any thing in his power, or within the limit of his means, to assist the son of his formerly munificent patron, yet the truth was, that his own benevolent habits had so straitened his resources, that he could do little more than advise.

It was under these circumstances that Mark one day received, to his great astonishment, a letter containing a draft for a considerable sum. The letter bore the city post-mark, and gave no explanation, further than the words:—

"Go to New Orleans; a good practice awaits you. Be silent, and you shall hear again."

The sum was sufficient to rescue him from his embarrassments, and to leave his sister in comfort; but yet this mysterious donation both shocked his pride and roused his anger. What could it mean? Who should dare insult a Catesby by the offer of such a gift? He was not yet so poor as that! and he threw down the letter in a burst of rage and rushed out of the house. His sister heard his hurried exit, and, entering his room, picked up the letter and draft from the floor. The moment she saw the signature, which was only

"Regulus," her face blanched, her eyes shot fire, and she sank upon an ottoman. A shudder ran through her frame, her lids drooped, and for several hours she sat motionless, with her hands clasped before her, while tear after tear coursed each other down her cheeks.

But now the silent struggle was over. She rose with a deep sigh, as her brother's hurried ring was heard, and, taking up the papers, met him in the parlour. He was much flushed, and deeply excited. She took his hand calmly, and led him to the sofa, still holding the papers in her hand.

What was the purport of the long and earnest conversation of these two young persons, we are not prepared at present to reveal. The result was, that the draft was cashed—the sister established as an artist in neat rooms on Broadway—and one week from that time the brother was on his way to New Orleans.

*   *   *   *   *   *

It was the early spring of this year, but one of those rare days, when the sun, tired of his icy bondage, bursts upon the earth with a sudden warmth of glory that startles all nature out of her chill repose into a soft dreamy state, half waking and half sleeping. Bird, insect, the open blossom, air, cloud, and water, responded lovingly to the call of their mother, thus awakened, and for her sang in chorus songs of sweetest harmony.

Filled with the exquisite loveliness of the day, Catesby lingered upon his accustomed evening ride, falling unconsciously into a sympathy with the hazy dreaminess around him. Lost in the one delightful sense of living, of breathing the fresh luxurious air, he wandered along the river's bank, utterly unheeding the danger by his side. He rode along the crumbling *levee*, and although a tremendous flood was rising, hurled down from an icy home far back on the mountains of the west, so much was he absorbed as not to notice that the slight embankment along which he rode was trem

bling beneath his horse's feet. Living and being were
enough for him; for Mark had been fortunate lately! and
rode with the consciousness of a man well to do in the world.
Business had been urged upon him in such an astonishing
way, that he could not but regard New Orleans as a real El
Dorado to spirited young lawyers. Although it had usually
taken the old-fashioned men of his profession more than half
a lifetime to get into a good practice, Mark had found his
youthful talent appreciated in so extraordinary a degree,
that he had almost come to regard the talent of these "old
fogies" of the bar with sovereign contempt. In fact, business
had flowed in upon him in a greater than usual proportion,
and although he could not help an occasional feeling of distrust and anxiety, in regarding the strange and unsolicited
commissions sent to him from unexpected quarters, yet who
is really angry with prosperity, in the worldly sense? He
congratulated himself upon his own merit and legal skill, and
was supremely satisfied that a Catesby could not know want.
The fact was, that Mark possessed a great deal of cleverness
in his profession, and though his success was rather mysterious
and extraordinary for so young a man, and one living, too,
in a strange and almost foreign city, yet it was deserved, for
the sake of his sister, if not entirely and in strict justice for
his own.

It was the year of a tremendous freshet, and the planters,
with that sharpened experience which a long series of losses
gives, had, for a week past, detected the symptoms of the
coming flood, and had been at work with all their force in
strengthening the weak places of the levee, in dread of the
formidable "*crevasse.*" The timbers, ropes, &c., extending
over the furious current, were therefore frequent along the
bank; but Mark was too much absorbed to notice what was
indicated by these signs. His thoughts were in other scenes,
and that fair sister that he loved filled all his heart. The
young man had never loved with passion. She alone oc-

cupied his thoughts as yet, and he had hardly realized that there was a stronger tie on earth. His life had yet been unsettled, though not profligate, in this respect; and as he worshipped that dear sister, so he invested other women with a sacred and delicious veneration, becoming to a nature purely chivalrous.

He looked down into the dark and swollen flood, comparing its onward course to his own wild life. It was still with him the spring-time. The summer that could cálm those mighty waters into a smooth and placid current had not yet overtaken him.

He had now come in sight of the old and well-known convent. He looked at the curious and familiar building, examining its walls, its windows, its gates, with a sort of dim, prophetic feeling, that somehow with it his own destiny was strangely mingled.

Suddenly the small gateway opened, and a single female came out from the sacred precincts. His heart throbbed, though he could not have told why!

That she was young, he saw by her free, graceful carriage. That she was beautiful, he felt by an admonition stronger than reason. An irrepressible desire to see her, which he probably mistook for natural gallantry, grew within him. He urged his horse onward, and as she was walking in a direction parallel with him, he was soon gratified by the sight of one of the most exquisitely lovely faces that had ever shone upon him this side of dreamland.

And like a dream it vanished; for of a sudden the levee, or raised bank, crumbled beneath his horse's feet, and horse and rider were precipitated into the mad waters.

The current was fearfully swift, and the young man was hurled with stunning violence against some beams that extended beyond the levee over the stream, and which had been used in repairing the damages of the freshet. There were a number of ropes strewed about. The girl, who turned

her head at the splash, rushed immediately to the rescue, and
screamed at the same time an alarm to some labourers a
short distance below. Without waiting, however, for their
arrival, she promptly threw a rope to Mark, who, although
considerably stunned, had consciousness enough left to grasp
it.   His horse, snorting and struggling desperately, was
swept past, and went down the torrent. The frail girl leaned
her body against a post which had been sunk as a sort of
pivot into the levee for the arms of the rest of the machinery
to work upon, and giving the rope a turn about it, was
enabled to hold on, even with her small hands, until the labourers came to her aid.

They drew poor Mark up, more dead than alive; for the
force of the current had bruised him terribly against the
very obstacle that saved him. When he recovered consciousness, he was in a convent, and a fair watcher, with dark
lustrous eyes, was bending over him.

Days passed, and Mark Catesby would have scorned to
call himself any thing but strong and well, had he been in
the tent—were the field before him; but it was so beautiful
to be an invalid with so gentle a nurse to minister to him,
his strength would not come! With ever so cunning skill
let his tonics be prepared by the wise men of medicine, still
lingered his strength back in the chamber of sickness.

But this could not last always. He had to get well—poor
sinner!—at last—and about this time old Garcia, the father
of this sentimental young lady, made his appearance in New
Orleans, and on the same day, at the convent. He had a
long interview with his daughter, the result of which was
rather a significant one. She was immediately removed
from the convent.

Love has strange instincts! Mark was not wrong in obeying the mysterious letter he received about this time, (and,
indeed, immediately after the disappearance of this beautiful
and tender-seeming hourie, who had haunted his bedside,)

which ordered him immediately to the frontier-town of a country then little known, except through vague report.

All that he knew of his love was, that she was a Spaniard —or of Spanish descent. As she was undoubtedly of this race on one side or other, and most probably of an exiled Mexican family, he had a faint hope that he might meet her in the direction indicated by this despotic missive, which he had, by the way, learned to venerate in a singular manner. Commands had come to him by this one formidable signature—

"Regulus!"

He had tried to disobey. He dared not—and the reason he could not have told, for his life. He did obey. He surrendered his practice—he gave up every thing. *In a word, he went to Texas!*

Our story is here too sadly—we might say, madly true— so far as we can remember the incidents as detailed to us by one of the mutilated survivors of this extraordinary affair.

Our narrator was a member of a distinguished family of the District of Columbia, and had formerly held the rank of lieutenant in the United States navy. An ungovernable lust for wild adventure, fired by the vague and bewildering romance which was just beginning to invest all the details we could then obtain of the life upon this dangerous frontier, had induced him to throw up his commission and repair thither, accompanied by a few young adventurers like himself.

They reached San Antonio de Bahai, through great perils, for at that time nearly the whole route was infested by bands of various Indian tribes, that have since been reduced to complete subjection, or entirely exterminated.

They found the old Spanish town, of nearly three thousand inhabitants, very coolly domineered over by a little squad of eight or ten Americans, who, as military traders, adventurers, and desperadoes in general, carried things, with a

high hand, pretty much in their own way. They ostensibly
recognised the city government, as well as that of Mexico;
but as they did not hesitate to shoot or bully any one of the
officers of either who might venture to make himself too
officious, these valorous gentlemen were very glad to wink at
any misdemeanours they could not avoid seeing. Though
hated by all classes of the Mexicans with a deadly hatred,
these adventurers knew too well their own value to labour
under any very serious apprehensions of any outbreak of
this feeling, further than an occasional fray in a gambling-
hell or pulque-shop.

They had to look out, to be sure, in passing dark door-
ways or rounding corners, not to hug either too close, for the
assassin's blade is the only one the Mexican wields with
effect. But this made little difference with these reckless
men, who scorned the apprehension of danger in any form at
a Mexican's hand, though they took good care to keep their
eyes open, nevertheless.

The true secret of their power lay far enough beyond the
civic limits, for the Mexican inhabitants dreaded more than
any thing else on this earth—or in purgatory, even—the
annual descents of the Camanche tribes from their impenetrable mountains. These audacious plunderers had never
yet received a single salutary check upon this frontier until
the appearance of a few North Americans in Bahai; and
though they had received from these some severe lessons, yet
they had not yet been entirely sufficient to inspire them with
that remarkably wholesome respect for the rifle which they
have since exhibited; yet these had nevertheless made them
somewhat shy, as the matter between them had finally come
to be settled by a sort of tacit arrangement of—" You let me
alone—I let you alone."

We cannot say that this agreement had at any time been
too strictly kept on either side; but as the bickerings and
animosities between the adventurers and the Mexicans had

become, day by day, more and more deadly on one side, and ferociously contemptuous on the other, they had at last come to regard the outrages of their natural enemies upon this malignant and treacherous population with a jeering indifference, and enjoyment, even, that was terribly galling.

As they now pretty much confined themselves to looking out for their own interests and keeping neutral, the Camanches soon took the hint, and did not disturb them or their property, unless on occasion when the temptation thrown in their way proved too strong, and then I suppose they thought the fault lay most at the door of the Americans —who, knowing their weakness, should not have subjected them to so severe a trial : though the result usually was, a sound drubbing the first time they could be caught. Yet as no very serious disparity in accounts had arisen in the long run, both parties were willing to be content in not exacting too strict a settlement *every* time they met.

Matters had been standing in this position for some time, and the Mexicans were becoming rapidly impressed with the profoundest conviction that they had been unduly thankless for the goods the gods had sent them in the person of the redoubtable borderer, Captain Red, or "Little Red-head," as the Indians had christened him, from the fiery colour of his hair, and his formidable band of riflemen : they were accordingly of late fawningly endeavouring to propitiate them, and make every amends for the past.

But no ! The sturdy and reckless adventurers treated them with more galling mockery, which they bore with only increased servility. No creature on earth is so pitifully subservient as the Mexican when the "time of his fear cometh." They well knew this trait, and greatly amused themselves in drawing out these servile and unconscious traits, which, of course, became more and more ludicrous to the Americans at the usual time—the spring—when the time of the Camanches' descent approached. They heaped indignity after indignity upon

them, and though many a furious eye glared from beneath
the shadow of a slouched sombrero upon them as they passed,
the hand that clutched the assassin's knife dared not strike a
blow—they feared them—they hated them—but they needed
them !

The disasters of the last two years had cowed them; but
well the Americans knew that, once released from their in-
cumbent fear, these treacherous slaves would turn upon them
with redoubled vindictiveness, and therefore scorned their
fawning, as well as their malignity.

Matters were in about the above position when our informant, with his three comrades, arrived. They were welcomed with that reckless and bantering good-fellowship, which
is usually so remarkable towards countrymen, among men
placed habitually in circumstances of great danger.

They were forthwith taken in hand, and with a boisterous
civility, shown round all the lions of the place—monte tables
—pulque-shops—cock-pits—the great cathedral—not forgetting, you may rest assured, the dark-eyed and voluptuous
Senoritas.

These preliminaries over, the parties proceeded to business,
though in a manner precisely as informal as every thing
else.

Somebody proposed, that as they were now strong enough
to whip all Mexico, with the Camanche nation thrown in,
" we do hereby organize for the above purpose !"

As this was received with tremendous applause, and as
nobody was of course thought of as leader but Captain Red,
the next question was, " What shall our name be ?"   Several
rather romantic names having been proposed by the younger
members, and which did not prove entirely satisfactory to the
rest of the company, at last the captain arose. He was a
man below the average height, with a head most resembling
that of a Scotch terrier, with its wiry, bristling hair on fire,
except that the bushy, freckled face, and round, quick eyes,

were dignified by a broad, yet low forehead, of almost snowy whiteness, while the stiff, heavy eyebrows fairly blazed in contrast along its rim.

This singularly-looking person merely remarked in a sharp, quick voice—

"Boys! it's no use with that nonsense! We're going to take care of a pretty big range around here, and why shouldn't we call ourselves *Rangers ?*"

"Good!" "Good!" "That's the figure!" "That's the name for us!" " Hurrah !—Three cheers for Captain Red !" "Now three for the Texas Rangers!" was uproariously shouted from as many different voices, and the matter was settled.

This celebrated order, thus originating upon this frontier, lost precious little time in discussing the "articles of war," either on that occasion, or on many a one since, in which they have made themselves felt withal, and that "with a vengeance !"

They now set themselves to work in serious earnest, each man equipping himself at his own expense, to regulate the affairs of the Border. The country, when not scoured by savage tribes, was suffering terribly from the maraudings of cut-throat bands of robbers from the valley of the Rio Grande. These wretches, ferocious as they were cowardly, committed the most horrible outrages upon the feeble and almost defenceless rancheros on the northern side of the Rio Grande, and along the river San Antonio, the Coleto, the Gaudaloupe, and upon the white settlements even of the Colorado, and along the Brazos to the neighbourhood of where Houston now stands, on the north, and down the whole length of the Nueces on the south. Whenever this daring little band could hear of such depredations in reasonable time for pursuit of the perpetrators, the cry was instantly "to horse!" and away, on their swift and hardy steeds, in the true spirit of the ancient chivalry, they rushed "to the rescue!" It

mattered not to them who were the parties—ranchero or
white man, so they did not belong to San Antonio—they
perilled life and limb to avenge their wrongs, and many a
wild deed of fierce and summary retribution did they wreak
upon those dastardly plunderers, under the valiant lead of
the stern and chivalric "Red," whose name grew still more
a word of terror to robber or Camanche.

"Los Indios! Los Indios! Garracho! Los Indios!"
The dreaded cry of alarm, mingled with screams and wails
and yells of terror, suddenly arose in the quiet, sunny square
of San Antonio de Bahai, one fine morning in the early
spring. In a moment, above all these sounds, rang out in
hoarse, unearthly screeches, the wooh! woo! woo! woo!
wooh! of the Camanche war-whoop—while, driven pell-mell
before the long, lithe lances of the marauders—men, women,
and children, mingled with cattle, horses, mules, pigs, and
poultry, were tumbled headlong over each other through the
narrow streets into the wide square.

A party of Americans, on a carouse in a long, low stone
house that fronted the square on the northern side, arose
quite deliberately from the table, and, with glasses in hand,
stepped, with no very steady gait, to the doors and windows,
to see the "sport," as they facetiously called it—for they
understood the meaning of such sounds well enough.

Sport for devils it was, with a vengeance! The frightened
Mexicans, bewildered by the suddenness of the thing—for
this descent was unexpectedly early—and by their terrors
together, were running confusedly here and there about the
square—while the dark, fantastically bedizened warriors were
plunging to and fro upon their swift and active horses,
trampling the panic-stricken mass, driving their bloody
lances through the nearest victims, of whatever sex, age, or

condition, and howling like starved wild beasts with their white-fanged jaws amidst a helpless prey.

The scene was sufficiently horrifying to have appalled the most ferocious spirit of ruffianism; but our jollificating Americans,

"Albeit not used to the melting mood,"

seemed rather to enjoy it most decidedly.

Some poor wretches rushed towards the door where these drunken madmen stood; one or two pushed them back with their feet,—"No, no! you infernal Greasers! you can't get in here! you've got to take it as it comes!" But, to the credit of human nature, Captain Red rushed forward, pushed these brutes aside, and said—"No! hold! shame, boys! let them in."

He was obeyed, but with evident reluctance by some. This humane act first attracted the attention of the Camanches to them, for they had been too busy to observe their presence before. The warriors in pursuit of the fugitives galloped almost up to the door, when, recognising at a glance the dreaded form of Little Red-head, they set up a yell of surprise, and drew back.

In a moment the news spread, and the shouts of the chiefs soon drew together the scattered warriors. Collected on the opposite side of the square, the Rangers saw, to their no little surprise, what they had not suspected during the confusion, that this was one of the most formidable body of Indians any one of them had ever seen together. What the precise number might be, no one could do more than make conjectures, and such passed hurriedly through the room, rating them at from three to five, six, and eight hundred.

To say that these men were any more than surprised, would be absurd, as the sequel will show. They were in a moment or two more boisterous in their hilarity than before, and crowded about the door, drinking, and laughing at the forlorn appearance of the killed and wounded Mexicans strewed

P

about the square, and occasionally shouting some half-drunken jibe across the square at the Camanches.

In the mean time, the clatter of hoofs—the neighing and bellowing of their frightened owners—had died away through the different streets into which they had made their escape; the crowded fugitives, with their cries of pain, had disappeared together into the houses around and nearest to the square, and only the laughter and shouts of the Americans rose occasionally above the momentary lull, of which the groans from the wounded made a sort of silence.

The Camanches gathered together in a close squad, and seemed to be holding a council of war for a few moments, by gestures, and in such low terms that nothing could be heard from them; when suddenly, like a flock of swallows diving from an old tree-top, they broke up, scattering in all directions, to come together again in the middle of the square as suddenly—hooting, yelling, and shaking their lances in the faces, almost, of the Rangers, as they darted past the door of their quarters.

As this was merely bravado, they took no further notice of it than to jeer at them in the most insulting manner: not condescending, even, to step back into the room to fetch their rifles.

But when this insolent challenge to a fight had been repeated several times, and at each with some more insulting demonstration, the majority of the party began to become incensed. They grasped their rifles, and were rushing to the door and windows to resent these indignities, when Captain Red again restrained them. This impunity only increased the insolence of the savages, whose object was clearly to provoke a sally on the part of the fiery Americans; but, if some of the men were not, their captain was, cool enough to understand this very well, and to prevent it, especially as he could clearly perceive their exultation at the thought of having him at such overwhelming advantage.

Such an infernal babel of whooping, screeches, howls, and yells, as now filled that square, was probably never heard before from the same number of human throats. They dared not—or rather it is against one of the fixed usages of their warfare—to charge upon a building or enclosure of any kind, and therefore, when they found they were not coming forth, they changed their tactics essentially, for this seemed too good a chance to entrap their hated foe.

The main body drew back to the other side of the square, and dismounting, laid their bows and lances down at their feet, and then stood with folded arms at the heads of their horses, to signify that they would be contemptuous lookers on, while a party of only twenty picked warriors rode forward at a gallop, and when immediately in front of the door, a fellow among them, who spoke a little Spanish, dared them to come forth and meet them in equal combat, calling them cowards, women, dogs, and every possible obscene epithet, and pointing back to the large body of warriors behind, told them that brave men scorned to fight such white-faced cowards at disadvantage of numbers, and that these would not move from where they were if that great coward chief, Little Red-head, dared to come out and prove that he was not a feeble woman, &c. &c.

The Rangers, who had now recovered their good-humour, only greeted this ludicrous farce with loud shouts of laughter, and twirled their fingers at them ludicrously.

The savages, rendered furious at this failure of their—as they supposed—profound stratagem, wheeled their horses suddenly, and slapped their breech-clouts at them as they galloped off. At this, the last indignity an Indian can offer to a foe, and which no frontiersman can or will endure, by one simultaneous movement the Rangers sprang to their rifles, and let drive a terrible volley among them, which tumbled nearly a dozen of the rash vaunters from their saddles.

This unexpected retaliation very suddenly awaked the Camanches up from the delusion of impunity, and brought back rather emphatically to their memories the kind of persons they were dealing with—for this kind of conclusion had been no part of their calculations. Their object had been to taunt the Rangers forth to meet them on their own, that is, open ground, where they would have all the advantage of numbers and of their peculiar modes of warfare. They had thought that a brave so noted for fierce courage as was the Little Red-head, would not stop to consider numbers, when grossly insulted after the manner in which we have seen, and, when invited to come out for an equal fight, but would rush forth with all his men to meet the challenge; when they would have him in their power, as it would only take an instant to regain their arms, leap into their saddles, and be upon him before he could possibly regain shelter. Now, when they saw some of their most noted braves tumbling from their horses as the fruits of their foolish mistake, their rage knew no bounds but that of usage, which prevented them from storming a fortress of any kind, and they rushed forward with the horrid cries of infuriated demons; and, in face of another galling fire from the house, they bore off the bodies of the slain, by this time considerably increased in number, and shaking their lances behind them with diabolical gestures of menace, they passed clattering through the town towards the open plains on the west, while the taunting laugh of the Rangers was shouted in their ears.

They continued for an hour or so to gallop to and fro in swift troops, like flocks of plovers, over the plain, making insulting gestures and uttering cries of defiance in renewed invitation to the Rangers to come forth. Some of the parties, again emboldened by their quiet, re-entered the town, and committed some most infernal outrages upon the poor Mexicans, which were every now and then reported to the Rangers by some breathless messenger—even carrying off a number of handsome Mexican girls. These cool gentry heard all this with the greatest unconcern, and continued their carouse amid shouts of laughter at the expense of the poor Camanches.

Suddenly the Little Red-head, whose blood was now up, as he had tasted battle, sprang to his feet as the shrieks of some poor Mexican women, who were being dragged into hateful and hideous captivity, were wafted to his ears—

"Boys, I can't stand this! Let's drive these scoundrels back to their own mountains."

The words were scarcely spoken, when every man jumped to his feet as by one electric impulse, and sprang for his rifle amid cries of approval.

"We can whip the whole!"

"That's you, captain! We're your boys! We'll fan 'em out, the filthy thieves, if they are a thousand."

"Hurrah for our captain! He's *some* in a brier-patch!"

"We'll teach these dirty copper-heads to come into Bahai while Rangers own it! Whoop! whoop! hurrah, boys! One more glass, before we part to get our horses!" said Captain Red, as he filled his to the brim. The rest followed suit, and in another moment, amid the sounds of social uproar, these men separated to get their horses for a ride on one of the maddest dare-devil chases ever ridden by men before.

It took them but a little while to mount, for a Ranger's horse is always ready at a moment's warning, as well as his arms; and with one wild whoop, which made the terrified Mexicans tremble and slink closer in their corners, they dashed out of town at full speed, in the pursuit.

When they emerged from the streets of the town and its thin, straggling suburb of dobey huts, they came abruptly upon the broad plain of the prairie, which, after a short distance, became gradually dotted, at wide intervals, with small islands of timber, called "motts." They saw, to their no small surprise, only a single predatory party, such as we have spoken of: and this seemed to have just issued from the

P 2

town, and to be encumbered with plunder and prisoners. The hurried supposition was, that the other parties who had so lately been in sight, must have crossed the San Antonio River above, and be entering the town on the other side.

Be that as it may, had it been one party or the whole body of the enemy, it would have been all the same to the Rangers; so they dashed at the one in view, and, come what might, they meant to overhaul it at any rate.

The race soon became exciting, since, as the flying party were encumbered heavily, the Americans gained rapidly upon them, and were beginning to yell, in anticipated triumph, when they reached the larger motts, which are several miles out from the town. Here the fugitives were suddenly joined by another party, which glided out from behind one of them, and seemed to take a portion of the embarrassing burdens upon themselves—by which movement the pace of the first was wonderfully accelerated.

The sight of this accession only increased the enthusiasm of the Americans, who urged the race with yet greater eagerness; for the Indians were just about three to one now, and that would afford them some sport. The distance between the two parties was at once considerably increased,— for these Indians have a wonderful faculty of getting work out of their tough mountain horses—so much so, indeed, that they usually escape from American horsemen, even when the latter are better mounted.

When the chase had continued for several miles, the Camanches either really were, or appeared to be, losing ground. Their horses flagged in speed considerably, and when this was noticed, Little Red-head bent forward in his saddle, and, yelling like a madman, lashed his horse until the blood flew at each whacking blow, and shouting hoarsely, "They're ours! Come on!" darted ahead. His party, as much excited as himself, responded until the welkin fairly rang again with their fierce cries.

On ! on ! sweeps the clattering race, hurled headlong over the shaking plain—now beginning to change its character—which, heretofore, had been only diversified by "motts" of timber, scattered promiscuously over the surface; but now they were approaching a long line of thick timber, fenced along its edges by a low chaparral of dense and thorny growth, which was utterly impenetrable to horses, and which the naked Camanches would rather die than attempt to ride through, if it had been possible for horses.

This the Rangers well knew, and they had almost held their breaths as they watched—bending over their horses' heads, with parted lips and straining eyes, to see whether the Indians would head in that direction, where they were as securely cornered as if they had run against a stone wall. The moment it became certain that this was the direction they were taking, there was a universal burst of jeering laughter, rendered savagely hysterical by the excited passions of these wild men.

"Ha! ha! We've got you now!" was almost hissed, in a smothered voice, from between the set teeth of Little Red-head, as they closed rapidly upon the flying savages, who, exhibiting every sign of terror, began to look back, and drop articles of plunder.

"Ha! peeling—disgorging—are you? I'll ease your stomachs for you!" muttered the leader, as he looked to his rifle, which lay across the saddle before him.

"Let out another link, boys!"

He shouted in a deep tone, as they neared the wood, and were now within rifle-shot. The eager men were beginning to handle their rifles.

"Hold on! Keep your horses to the work! Time enough when we're among them! They can't escape!" was the prompt command.

At this moment the Indians reached the timber, and, one after another, their dark forms disappeared within its seem-

ingly impenetrable bosom—like a great black serpent, gliding
into its shadowy den.   To describe the yell of infuriated astonishment—the blank, pale look of surprise, which the
Rangers exchanged during one brief instant of uncertainty,
would be impossible.   But the stern leader shouted quickly—
" On, boys!—if they're going below, we'll follow them!"
   The men cheered, and they swept after them into the
wood.   One short minute beneath the shadows—a little time
of darkened, breathless speed, and they burst into the sunlight of a prairie beyond.   Their eyes were dazzled!   Their
senses stunned!   It was but for an instant.   The harsh and
stunning howl that greeted them into this dazzling light,
they had heard before—those dusky, hideous forms, rush
upon them from every side—but they had seen their long
lances and feathered crowns shake and toss in fight before—
and though they came like a torrent closing round them,
these brave men were not unnerved!
   The ring of their rifles rose in deadly lullaby over the
triumphing howls of successful strategy—recoiling the overwhelming waves in silence for a moment, while the smoke
arose—but then the recoil was stayed by the tremendous
rush from the circles without—for they were in the very
middle of a camp—or rather ambush—of over three hundred
Camanches, and only those nearest could reach them, of
course; but then this rush drove on those before, upon them,
trampling the bodies of their own slain that had fallen by
the first fire, and in spite of the terrible execution done by
the pistols of the Rangers, the roaring tide hurled these
inward circles on.   The Camanches were wild with ferocious
exultation—for here they had, at last, entrapped their formidable and most audacious foe, the Little Red-head, whose
fiery scalp was worth the feathered coronet of a chief to any
one of them.   Terribly these barbaric billows swayed and
rolled before the murderous fire of fifteen hemmed and desperate men.

Pistols soon became useless. Recoil after recoil of the Indians had been driven in, yet the relentless thirst for vengeance and that fiery scalp grew more and more unappeasable; and though lance grated against lance in the bodies of Ranger after Ranger, and arrows flew like hail, still this strange and furious fight went on. The Rangers had drawn their heavy bowie-knives, and were laying about them with desperate strength, clipping off the lance-heads like carrot-tops, as they were frequently crossed above them in the tumultuous struggle.

It was a volcanic chaos of fringed buckskins—breech-clouts—streaming feathers—rifles—lances—pistols—arrows —horses—oaths—knives—death-groans—screams—yells and whoops, boiling and tumbling wild beneath the smiling sun of God's own blessed, gentle spring.

Ah, it was horrible enough!

It would seem as if this presumptuous squad should have been borne down at once, and utterly exterminated by this tremendous pressure; but it should be kept in view, that the Camanches had at that time little knowledge of firearms beyond the effects from which they had suffered, or been witnesses of, and therefore greatly amplified them, and indeed held them in a sort of superstitious awe.

Be this as it may, perhaps the world never witnessed—on a small scale, to be sure—a more remarkable instance of an agile, fierce, relentless struggle, than this between these few men and the comparative host by whom they were surrounded. Think of it!—fifteen to over three hundred!—taken by surprise, too!

There was one young man in this doomed party, who had acted wildly since they set off on this fatal chase. He it was who had whispered hurriedly in the ear of Little Red-head something that, in addition to the shrieks of women they were carrying off, caused his sudden and unexpected proposition to follow the Camanches. He had been one of

12

those who came out in the party with the lieutenant whom I
have mentioned as my informant. His real name had not
been given. He had been the most eager and rash of the
Rangers, and had fought with almost superhuman fierceness.
Since the moment of their falling into this ambush, his object had seemed to be to cut his way through the overwhelming mass in the direction of a group of warriors at a
little distance, that took no part in what was going on, but
were evidently in charge of the prisoners. He had even
taken the lead of his captain, and by his frantic efforts had
succeeded in carving a bloody lane through the Indians to
this point. They had evidently been impressed with a sort
of panic by his incredible fury, and gave way before a desperation which seemed to bear a charmed life. Now was the
time to escape, if ever!

But his eager eye had sought for one form among the
prisoners. There were but three. The glance was quick as
lightning, but seemed to be sufficient.

"Oh, God! she is not there!"

He rather shrieked these words than spoke them, turned
ashy pale, and without a word more, or a single groan,
pitched forward over the head of his horse, among the
trampling hoofs. Little Red-head was at his side when he
thus fell, without a wound; for, strangely enough, he had as
yet entirely escaped. With a strange, sorrowful cry, he
reigned in his horse, and the last that was seen of Little
Red-head, twenty lances were meeting through his unresisting body; and as the two young men who escaped burst free
upon the open ground again, and made off, bleeding with
many wounds, the demoniac yells of triumph from the Camanches echoed horribly in their ears. There was little
attempt made to overtake them, and they got in safe—the
lieutenant with the loss of the finger and thumb of one hand,
together with half a dozen body-wounds, and his friend reeling in the saddle from the loss of blood from as many more.

Thus ended this horrible and strange affair, which, perhaps, has hardly a parallel in any annals. But not the least singular part of it was revealed afterwards.

From papers discovered among the effects of Little Red-head, it appeared that this young man was Mark Catesby, and that Red was his natural brother—an illegitimate son of old Catesby!

A paper of instructions with regard to Mark was found, too, containing the mysterious signature "Regulus," and which was worded in the imperious language of entire despotism. What became of the young girl Juliet Garcia, we may yet hear. That she was snatched up on the street, and carried off by the Camanches, is all we can say at present.

GABRIELLE:

THE WHITE MARE OF CHIHUAHUA.

Q

GABRIELLE:

CHAPTER I.

THE remarkable valley of Encinnillas, which extends for a long distance north of the city of Chihuahua, on the route to Paso del Norte, is noted for its three great haciendas, and for the contrasts in colours maintained in its immense herds of more than half-wild cattle. The greatest of them, the Hacienda Encinnillas, at the head of the valley, contained many thousand head of a dark-brown, shaggy breed, resembling the buffalo somewhat in appearance, and still more in fierceness. The next, Hacienda Sauz, contained a less but still very great number of a heavier-built variety, the coats of which were, with the occasional exception of a few small mottles, as white as the bull Europa rode; while the third, Hacienda Torrean, was covered with herds of a tall, slim, active animal, possessed of enormous horns, and a colour varying little from uniform jet-black, with sometimes a few white marks. To a stranger moving down this picturesque valley, these marked and consistent contrasts would seem very curious; but by a provincial, they would only be regarded with connoisseuring interest.

The prevalence of this sort of fancies among the privileged and hereditary owners of these great estates, and the singu-

183

lar extent to which emulation would carry them in preserving
the integrity of their favourite colours throughout the whole
of their uncounted herds, were matters not only of severe
criticism, but of sympathetic interest, among all grades of
their countrymen.

Some years since, an old and proud Spaniard of the hidalgo blood, called Don Carlos Gonzalcze, was governor of
the province of Chihuahua, in Northern Mexico.

This venerable soldier owned the great Hacienda Encinnillas, situated as above described, between ninety and a
hundred miles north of the city of Chihuahua, on a small
tributary of the Rio Conchas. His mansion, which was
about in the middle of the estate, was a very extraordinary
looking building in some respects, though in others it was
only peculiar to the country, or rather to Mexico, both north
and south. As you approach along the winding bank of the
small, clear stream which descends to meet you, swift,
bright, and cold, from out the dark fastnesses of the huge
sierra, looming vaguely in the immeasurable distance toward
the west, you obtain the first glimpse of it, and that while
entering from a wide, undulating prairie, sodded with crisp-
curling grama grass, and covered with herds of cattle and
mottled horses, beneath the low shadows of a great forest
of live-oak trees. These oaks, although scattered over
the surface something in the proportion of a dozen to an
acre, shroud the pale sward beneath by the prodigious
stretchings of their low, long arms, hung from the nearest to
the outermost twigs with the drooping and pensile drapery
of a gray and shining moss, in a sort of swinging, slow and
nearly funereal gloom ; but the moss seems almost too much
alive, as it waves with a mild shine in the breeze, and, with
the hardy glisten of the evergreen live-oak leaves, makes a
sort of reflex twilight on the dainty sward.

The walls of the hacienda glitter strangely beneath the
sun in the distance, and visions of the miraculous creations

of Aladdin's lamp are suggested; but as you approach, the illusion is dispelled, for you perceive them to be built of a light-gray pudding-stone, of volcanic origin, peculiar to this province, and which holds in it a large proportion of shining quartz. It is a beautiful and singular stone for building, and is susceptible of the highest polish, which in this instance it had received.

The singular appearance of this building is not a little heightened by the great size and number of its windows, of diminutive laminæ of mica, which on three sides, as you approach, reach from near the eaves of the single story to within two feet of the ground, and are separated by intervals of less than three feet. This gives to this portion of the mansion a shiny, glistering appearance, which is grimly enough contrasted with the long continuation of solid masonry beyond, which grins with small port-holes only, and looks massive enough to defy a strong cannonade. You are thus forcibly reminded that though this be a sunny land of the orange and the vine, it is also one of blood.

Indeed, the fortress-like appearance of the rear of the house is amply enough compensated by the gay and lightsome air of the front; for all the great windows of this quaint conservatory are clustered about with sweet-scented shrubs bearing delicate blooms, and filled with the magnificent flowers of the tropics, or festooned across the intervals with the polished leaves and gorgeous trumpets of evergreen creepers, and wild vines of the native grape, with their dark-purple clusters.

As might be expected in such a scene, the sweet voice of a woman is heard. It is a low, mellow warble, swelling fitfully upon the perfume-burdened air, with drowsy pauses, as if some sleeping song-bird twittered in a dream. Through one of those low great windows, and between the clustering flowers and vines, a young Spanish cavalier was peering cautiously, as if to obtain a sight of the warbler, himself unseen.

Q 2

He was very young, and a very handsome fellow, too. His
long, black, wavy hair fell down his shoulders, over the rich
colours of his splendid serape. His trousers of buckskin,
beautifully dressed to resemble black velvet, with two rows
of silver buttons and links down the side, showed, through
the wide slash, the delicate pink silk of the drawers beneath,
while a long, black plume fell back over the wide brim of
his gay and bead-wrought sombrero. His slight, downy
moustache shaded a delicate but sensuous lip ; his nose had
the proud vault of the Roman, and his large black eyes
literally glittered with eager delight, as he gazed into that
great airy room. And of a truth, the object he saw there
was such as to justify him fully in his curious eagerness, for
in clear view, the delicate, voluptuous, and superlatively
lovely form of the beauty of the whole province, the daughter
of the old governor, reclined upon a sofa in all the graceful
abandon of unconsciousness, singing herself drowsily into
the siesta in which all Spanish maidens are proverbial for
indulging.

It was a glorious picture the young man stood bending
forward in breathless rapture to enjoy. She was " beautiful
exceedingly," that dark-eyed senorita, with her long, black
lashes, that fell like feathery clouds over the pale-tinted olive
of her glowing cheeks. The very lids seemed burdened with
their dark, shining weight, as they struggled heavily to rise,
in sleepy cadence with the sultry monody she sang. But
those dim peepers flew open widely enough, like a burst of
starlight through the darkness, when, with a sudden movement, the young man sprang through the window, which he
had thrown up, into her room ; and, with a low cry, half of
fright and half of joyful surprise, she leaped into his arms,
and there suddenly rang upon the air that crisp, mysterious
sound with which young lovers are familiar. Without regarding the poor guitar which had been leaning against her lap,
and now fell with a crash upon the floor, the young lovers

clung to each other as if this were to be the last moment of their earthly meeting.

Indeed, it was a shocking pity to serve the frail guitar so, for, like every other article in the great room, it was singularly slight and delicate, and seemed as if it might have made the music for Titania's court; while the harp which stood near looked an æolian thing, just fitted for the fingers of young Zephyrus.

It was a fair and pleasant vision, that of the meeting of these young and tender lovers, both so beautiful and fresh, both so fond and so trusting, the halcyon life just dawning upon them. Surely, it would never know the shadow of change! From the intimate endearments and familiarity of bearing and language toward each other, it was apparent that this was no sudden love-affair, but that they had known each other long, even for life. In fact, the pair were neighbours, and had seldom, since early childhood, been separated long at a time. They had been unconsciously betrothed since childhood by their parents, who had witnessed, with many a secret chuckle of no small delight, the progress of their favourite scheme. They had been too judicious to disclose the intended purpose to either party until within a very short time, when the intended pair had come to them with fear and trembling, to obtain that sanction to their love and proposed marriage which the old governor and his chief friend and supporter, his near neighbour, the old General Jose Espartero, were so well prepared to grant in advance.

There had been a small pretence of stern questioning, particularly on the part of the veteran general, the most anxious of the two, and then, of course, a delighted assent had been given; for, as the estates of the old governor were far more extensive and valuable than his own, he was something the gainer by the bargain, though the convenient contiguity of the Hacienda Sauz reconciled that person fully to the disparity, especially since the general was his most powerful political supporter.

The young people had been thrown much, indeed, and almost incessantly together. They had shared the same amusements and studies, had travelled together to the city of Chihuahua in the same coach of state, had danced together at the fandangos of the governor's court, had gossipped together, and though we do not pretend to say exactly that they took their siestas together, yet we do assert that they took them at the same time, and in much the same fashion; and, however shocking it may appear to American readers, we further assert that they took their afternoon baths together, without fail, when the last cigaretta of the siesta had burned up to their lips.

Thus it will be perceived they had at least been moderately intimate for a long time; and, as they were altogether the handsomest and richest couple in the whole province, what could be more natural than that they should have gradually become inseparable; and, although they might have had— with the fortune of all other lovers, for whom "the course of true love never did run smooth"—an occasional bickering or small lovers' quarrel, yet, on the whole, imagined that it was mutually impossible to live without each other. They had latterly, indeed, become so thoroughly convinced of this self-evident truth, that the fear of death had become alarmingly present with them, and the determination to dodge for the present this "inevitable end" so remarkably warm, that they were beseeching the old dons to set fire with the torch of hymen to the whole quiverful of the arrows of that venerable archer, death. The old dons were nothing loath in special, but for the present, as they saw there was no need for hurry, were amusing themselves by torturing the ardour of their mutual heirs, in putting off the hour of bliss by pretended serious excuses about age, settlements, &c. &c.

This, by the way, a dangerous sport in any climate, is

especially so in a country so near the sun as Mexico; and if
much further protracted, what the result of these long, clinging caresses we have witnessed already might have been,
"we can better conjecture than describe !" And, indeed, they
are not usually very particular in inquiring about these things,
either of the future or of the past, in any part of Mexico;
and we do not see why we should trouble ourselves to do so
here, especially as our future must show for itself.

We would convey no shadow of imputation against the prudence of the fair Senorita Gabrielle, any more than against
the unsullied purity of that modest Adonis of handsome young
cavaliers, Don Juan Espartero; but we do mean to convey
to fond and mischievous old "*governors*" in general, a protest
and injunction against the perils of such dangerous sport,
especially, as we remarked, in warm climates, where the
"young people" are surrounded by blazing flowers, that pant
"with their love-laden" fiery breaths upon the sultry air, as
we have seen this handsome couple.

However, as providentially nothing more came of it in this instance than quite a serious expenditure of warm and still more
fragrant breaths than those of the amorous flowers, breathed
in certain mysterious explosives, at which we have hinted,
and quite as large a proportion in quick yearning sighs, we
may safely venture to relate what *did* follow, namely, ciga-
rettos ! the bath ! &c. &c.; but one thing at a time.

The first greetings over, (we don't say how long this took,)
off came the gay sombrero of the young don, and from it came
forth the most delicately-fibred leaves of the husk envelope of
the ear of the Indian corn; then his keen, jewel-hilted stil-
letto flashed in his jewelled-hand, as with a quick and graceful
movement he cuts the leaf transversely; and then opening his
gold tobacco-box, filled with the dark, fat tobacco of the
northern barbarians, which had been chopped up quite fine,
he proceeds to strew a smart pinch of this along the shuck-
leaf he has cut; and then, by an inconceivably rapid manipu-

lation, rolled it up, and presented the little tube to the senorita with a low bow. It was accepted playfully, and she
gabbled in the prettiest conceivable coquettish way to him
while watching the process of manufacturing a similar,
though stronger one, for himself. This completed, out
comes the elegant silver box, in which is carried the ever-
lasting flint, steel, and tinder of the Mexican and Spaniard.
Another flash and sparkle : the burning "punk" is handed
to her : the cigaretta lighted, and those rich, dainty lips
become at once the breathing crater of a blue, curling aroma.
The "punk" returned to him, his own is rapidly ignited,
and they are quickly enveloped in the slowly-lifted cloud of
sleepy fumes.

Now the loving clatter of their gentle voices gradually
subsides into fragmentary inquiries, with answers in slow
pantomime from opposite sofas, while their endearing glances
sleepily grow dim beneath the brooding soporific.

A few minutes and they breathe in harmonious concert,
gentle as two young eastern nightingales within a bush of
poppy ; the cigaretta, in the mean time, slowly subsiding toward their compressed lips, until at last, in half an hour, it
had burned down into an uncomfortable neighbourhood to
those red-ripe "nectaries of bliss"—where, as might reasonably be expected, symptoms of wakeful return to their sub-
lunary relations might readily be detected, and soon, with a
small start, caused by the fire that had burned down, they
again woke to paradise in each other's eyes.

The gentle Gabrielle sprang quickly to the neglected
guitar, which had lain upon the floor like some fairy toy
neglected, and with swift, practised fingers, beat upon its
taut and unmarred strings a tinkling reveillie in some wild
gipsy air of Andalusia, that made her young lover bound
with a joyous laugh to his feet, improvising the movement,
accompanying the air in a dance as wild and graceful as its
rollicking cadences.

Soon the guitar is thrown down, and with arm linked in arm, they go dancing through the long sunny room, toward that gloomy continuation of the mansion, concerning which we have spoken. They passed through a wide, strong door, like the gate of a fortress, from this frail summer-house of glass, into the dark shadows of the fortified court beyond. Here they entered upon a square of some three or four hundred feet on each side, upon which the low but massive houses of the Peones of the hacienda faced, by narrow entrances at short distances, and these entrances descending, by an easy and pebbly path from each, to the narrow bed of the small, clear mountain stream which we have mentioned, and which passed through the centre over its natural bed, and then, by a short wind, came out so as to pass exactly at the proper picturesque distance, before the front of the massive palace and ice-like parlours of the mansion.

They descended through the wider door of the interior, and on both sides there was a small alcove, hung with drapery to the ground. Into the two the lovers separately retired. There a quick transfer of the garments habitually worn was effected, and they came forth in the thinnest and slightest possible costume, it must be confessed; but still it *was* a costume, comparatively.

Hand in hand they descended into the clear, swift stream, with such a shudder as any one who has been once introduced to an ice-bath may well conceive; but the shudder was soon forgotten in the fun! Such a splashing as there was! The bed of the small stream spread and deepened here into a beautiful basin, extending nearly the whole length of the court. This was the hour for general bathing, and the pool was swarming with young girls, the daughters of the Peone inmates of the court. These were entirely nude; for nothing is more common in any part of Mexico than to see females of this class in such condition, bathing publicly in the rivers, when they will return the wondering and curious stare of the

North American passer-by with interest, and then coolly
proceed with their sports. It is a very cheerful and en-
livening scene, and of course peculiarly attractive to the
habitual connoisseur of feminine graces. We shall not undertake categorically, and with a grave technical minute-
ness, to name, classify, and describe the genuine and specific
character of the charms thus frankly exposed. We can only
specify that their figures, from the youngest girls up to the
developed women, were remarkable for symmetry and a voluptuousness of outline peculiar to those southern races which
possess any mixture of Spanish blood. Their dark limbs
glowed beneath the pellucid water with a round, bewitching
grace that defies description; while they stood still, in
abashed and half-awed silence, at the moment when their
young mistress and expected master were descending to the
water. For this little space of time they seemed, beneath
the veils of their long dark hair, which many of them had
thrown back with both hands upraised, most like a group of
startled Naiads, who stand listening, while " Triton winds
his hollow shell" to announce the sudden coming of old
Neptune!

But very soon, with gradual accession, the hubbub rises to
be quite as great again, and all the court is ringing with the
merriment of sweet but reckless clamours. They kept at
first at a rather respectful distance from the young senorita
and don; but as these cheerful persons seemed to be utterly
fearless of any undue encroachments upon their rank, or
rather unconscious of any such thing as etiquette to defend,
it was not long before they were in the midst of the screaming throng, being splashed, and splashing water upon them in
turn, and participating as noisily as the rest in the exhila-
rating sports of the bath.

But all pleasant scenes must have an end, and so had the
bath; and the two, with their thin robes clinging to dripping
forms, retired to the curtained alcoves to dress—a process

which occupied surprisingly little time on either side; when they came bounding forth at once, and hand in hand, with merry voices and buoyant steps, they returned through the dark passage-way to the airy summer-room beyond.

With a cry of endearment, the joyous Gabrielle sprang upon the neck of a swarthy and strikingly venerable-looking man, who met them at the large door or gateway of this room. He greeted the fond child with a parental salute, while he extended his hand with a familiar cordiality to the young don. This was a beautiful picture; the fine head of the old governor, its long, white hair mingled sparsely with threads of the intensest black, towered like some iron-gray rock beside a magnolia-tree, to which the flowering vine that clasped its rough pinnacles stretched out its gentler arms.

The appearance of Don Carlos Gonzaleze was very noble and careworn. It was such as you meet a thousand times in Italy, Spain, and everywhere in Mexico where the Spanish blood prevails. Even among the lazaroni and leperoes of these ancient races, you are constantly struck by meeting with those majestic heads which could only have been born amid the associations of that pride which lives in the story of ancient greatness, of those images and objects which are the relics of a glorious art, and those sounds which are the prolonged echoes of a classic lyre. It is a well-known joke that many of the possessors of these noble heads make a good trade of sitting to the young pilgrims of modern art who visit Rome, and that their remarkable lineaments are thus diffused over the four quarters of the civilized world as veritable portraits of saint, apostle, hero, priest, and king whose name is associated with the illustrious memories of the Eternal City.

For our own part, though this fact may seem matter of gibe and jest to others, it has always conveyed an impression of deep sadness to us; for in no other is the incurably "downward tendency" of these once so magnanimous and

R   13

glorious races to be seen so forcibly. I have often met such persons among Mexican population in the most unexpectedly ignoble positions, frequently with not enough of rags to hide the fine lines of forms possessed of those perfect symmetries which are never one of the "accidents of birth," but which must come from a long line of gentle descent and ennobling deeds. We could never see them without the same feeling with which the passionate lover of ancient art regards the exhumed fragment of some buried era of peculiar grandeur. We could never treat such persons, however much degraded as they frequently are, though always with a proud and conscious bearing even in degradation, otherwise than with consideration. They seem to me the sculptured imbodiments of faded glories, done in flesh by Time, and left on his way-sides to perish miserably because of a perfection too high to be heeded in degenerate conditions and by an emasculated race.

The old Don Carlos possessed such a face; but, as is the case with many others of this stamp, those noble features expressed rather the "hollow promise" of characteristics formed from any age of loftiness and noble virtues, than conveyed any substantial reality. He seemed to have been born more in the servilities of such an era and of such virtues than with the robust possession of them at any period in their vigorous health. He was proud, as might be expected; ambitious, as a matter of course; brave, as something not quite so consequential. He was pompous, too, and sadly lacked executive energy, in his old age at least, though he was said to have been possessed of most commanding power at one time, in Spain. He was vain, pompous, and avaricious; audaciously unscrupulous, as such persons usually are; and his very best trait, in a word, was the most extravagant and yearning affection for his daughter. She was the apple of his eye, for whom he would have sold, without hesitation, life, honour, and fortune.

The old Don, incorrigibly pompous as he usually was, always melted into an earnest and benign manner in the presence of his daughter and her approved lover: then there was something remarkably attractive about him, his bearing possessed a gracious, pleasing loftiness, which was finely mingled of the patriarch and ancient Castilian knight.

At such times you could quite forget that the heroic blood of his descent was thinned not alone by his own individual age, but as well by the age of his race; which, like all noble strains of animals, had been degenerated by the breeding "in and in"—as it is termed among farmers—to which it had for so many centuries been studiously insulated by the jealous exclusiveness of grandee pride. You perceived, too, that although the general *morale* and habits of the modern Spaniard had in addition contributed much to this declension of the more manly virtues, yet manner, that "last best gift" of gentle descent, had not yet passed away, along with the chastened beauty of person to which we have so often alluded. Indeed, it seems that not alone "the pregnant hinges of the knee," but as well every other "joint and motive" of the body, must be cultivated through generations, amid the graceful flections of courtly scenes, before they can attain once more to the true expressions of natural politeness which have been so coarsely degenerating since Adam, through our debasing vices! When the manners of civilization become polite once more, we may look for Eden scenes returning!

CHAPTER II.

THE group turned from the great gate, and hand to hand they promenaded the long room to the slow stately step of the old knight, whose tawny and deep-seamed face shone with delight as he listened to the lively and artless prattle of his daughter. Sometimes they would pause for a moment before one of her flower-pots, or rather great marble vases, in which they grew—ranged along beneath the frequent windows of the room, while Gabrielle, loosing her hold of the two hands which held hers, would bound away to bend over her pet, like some guardian sprite, to inspect its condition or caress it with her dainty lips; then springing back to her place between her emulous admirers with a light, coquettish movement and ringing laugh, they would pass on.

The old Castilian seemed supremely happy, and to have laid aside the cares of state in earnest for the time, while the gallant Juan, as might be conjectured, realized the promised beatitudes of the seventh heaven in the flesh, with the reality of a dark-eyed Hourie for his guide.

The time for the evening ride had now come, and two stout Peones were seen leading the horses to the door. Darting away through the great gate into the interior for a moment, the Senorita Gabrielle appeared equipped for the saddle. A light pink jacket of silk, jingling with many rows of small silver buttons and tiny links, had been put on over the boddice of the white gauze robe she wore; the "rebesos," or vail for the head, without which no Mexican maiden goes into the open air, was clasped beneath the chin with a delicate emerald brooch. Over the rebesos, which was of the lightest gossamer texture, and is considered more particularly as appertaining to the walking costume, she wore a light "gipsy hat," which only differed from that with us, in having the conical-shaped crown belonging to the "sombrero" of the men, and in being somewhat differently ornamented, with a broad band of fantastically grouped and coloured beads. Her small yet voluptuously rounded figure was admirably set off by this picturesque costume.

The horses of the two were held with difficulty as they approached. Hers was a beautiful little mare of the Mustang or wild Arab race, peculiar to the continent since Cortez introduced it here. It was white as the driven snow, with the exception of a small spot of red bay on each ear; and as is always the case with white horses of the true Arab breed, its skin was white also, though showing through the close hair a rich creamy deepening of colour. The head was thin and small, with nostrils of vast width showing red within; and though somewhat long and angular in its outlines, the ears were most delicately diminutive and tapering, the large blue vivacious eyes stood out prominently as those of a startled antelope, while the voluminous and wavy veil of the mane which flooded the forehead and fell like a cataract of dazzling white from the delicate arch of the neck nearly to the ground, was only rivalled by the full and flowing splendour of the tail. The unshod hoof of unusual roundness was almost shrouded by the graceful length of the fetlocks. The legs, which appeared as you approached in front to be slim almost as those of the deer, presented, as you saw them from the side, a broad bone with sinews swelling like whip-cord, but seeming taut as steel, and as if they would make metallic twangings as she bounded. The shoulder was thin but broad and high, and the long hamstrings reminded you of those of that miracle of speed, the great-eared rabbit of the plains. She had something of the ragged outline of the Arab in the hind-quarters, which were high, and would have been too angular for beauty had she been low in flesh; but, high conditioned now in her glistening coat, there was nothing to detract from that closest approach to absolute symmetry of which this blood, without at all diminishing its wonderful endurance and speed, is capable. She looked, with her short ears, fiercely gentle eye, her quick-arched neck, her thin and mighty bones, her steel-like cords, her chest of the female panther, her small, flat iron hoofs and wide-flowing mane and tail, most like some hair-winged creature of a genei's spell, summoned to chase his truant winds upon; and now that she had been tamed to human ken, the bright Gabrielle, with her

R 2

sylph-like form and most etherial voluptuousness, looked the best framed to mount the wizard palfrey.

The horse of Juan was, of course, larger than this mare, and it is sufficient to say was a very fine animal of the same stock, though it was worthy of more particular notice for a peculiarity of colours, which is always emulated by the young men of Mexico, whether of high or low degree. They all pride themselves upon the strangeness and variety of the markings of their favourite steeds. They are crossed with great care, with the view of obtaining the strongest possible contrast of colours in the motless blotches and spots of the skin. Many of them are very curious and beautiful. Such was the case with this animal, which was covered upon a white ground with deep reddish-black or dark umber spots, of small, but irregular size and shape, with a long, white mane, and tail as snowy, except that, curiously enough, a large tuft of coal-black hair burst streaming from its centre down to the extreme.

They were gayly caparisoned in the semi-barbaric style peculiar to Mexico, the dress-saddles being plated before and behind with a great quantity of silver, and the grotesque and peculiar ornament of the *coraza*, or seat-cover, being likewise embossed with silvery thread upon fine leather, while the *cola de pato*, or housings, of the same material and make, covered the haunches; and the bridles, with their heavy bits of solid silver, jingled with rows of little bells of the same metal. The head-pieces and reins were decked with bunches of horse-hair dyed with the scarlet cochineal of the country. The *armas de pelo*, formed of the long and silken fleece of the Rocky Mountain goat, dyed of the same colour, and richly bordered with embossed leather, hung down from the high pommel of the saddle, and formed an occasional covering for the leg of the rider when mounted.

The fairy senorita sprang lightly to her seat with little assistance from her lover, who was quickly at her side, jingling his enormous spurs of solid silver as he mounted, and the horses keeping time with their silver bells, as they dashed off merrily; and now the rumbling of heavy wheels was heard, and the chariot of the old governor rolled heavily through the great gate of the court. It was driven by a smoke-dried peone seated in front, and drawn by four pale-dun mules, very tall, with slim and well-proportioned bodies, while their fine round limbs were striped with small black marks, which seemed continuations of the larger stripe which traversed the back to the tail, down even which it was faintly continued. The chariot was a very clumsy and primitive affair, though there had been considerable effort at a rude sort of decoration, much in keeping with that of the horse-furniture I have described. The spirited team moved in a very brisk trot, and soon the parties were in motion together, the two young people, at a slow gallop, keeping alongside the window of the chariot, to exchange a word now and then with the old governor.

As its blood warmed by the motion, the fiery little palfrey of Gabrielle, becoming impatient of such slow procedure, darted ahead, with ears laid back, like a frolicsome pantheress, while she, looking behind, waved a laughing farewell to her father, and resigned herself fearlessly to the mood of her spoiled and petted favourite. Juan joined her, and away they went, like two glad wild birds together, singing on the wing, while the old governor looked wistfully after them, as they swiftly disappeared around a turn of the road, and then settled himself in his chariot with a smile of benignant and happy complacency. As he thus threw himself back upon the moss-stuffed cushions, he gave himself up to well-satisfied speculations concerning the precise value of his neighbour's estate, about to be thus ceded to his own, and to splendid visions of a green and honoured old age, surrounded with all the power of great wealth and influence, and with lovely grandchildren added to fill up the measure of his bliss.

This was a delicious evening, unusually so even for the equable and mild temperature of this climate. The sun was near to setting, and its mellow rays fell in long, slanting lines through the huge arms of the moss-draped live-oaks, and touched now and then the venerable head within, through the open windows of the coach, with a golden salutation and a soft farewell, that spoke of peace and hope. The sounds of the evening, which are very few here, and these exceedingly sweet and low, had just commenced to fill the air with a slumberous lullaby, which, with its charming drowse, soothed the old man to a half sleep, filled with pleasant images, while the coach rolled smoothly, as along a floor, over the level road.

The monody of nature, which was creeping upon his ear, seemed to him the musical receding of the dear voice of his daughter, fading as she went; and as the sleepy choir of evening rose in higher strains, it seemed to him that loved sound returning again in merry mood to meet him. But the old man opened his eyes quickly, and with a convulsive start, as the driver, in a shrill pipe, screamed into his horrified ear, "*Los Indios! los Indios! los Apache!*" and without waiting for any order, wheeled his team of mules, and with frantic eagerness commenced lashing them into full speed down the road toward the mansion.

The stricken old man, as the coach was turning, caught one glimpse of a sight that, with his knowledge of that country, was enough. It was that of the horse of Juan, with head tossed on high, and streaming mane, rushing after them riderless, and wild with fright. The horse soon passed in its panic-stricken speed, and as it went by, the horrified old man saw blood upon the splendid saddle, and that it was wounded by several arrows, which still remained sticking in its body.

About the meaning of these appalling signs there could be no mistake, and the frightened driver lashed his mules

still more desperately, and yelled with a yet more ear-
splitting energy of fright.   And of a truth there seemed
to be good cause for his alarm.   The dreadful war-whoop
was sounding in his ears, and the clatter of pursuing hoofs
grew more distinct each instant.   There was no time for
looking back; none for any thing, indeed, but the most
headlong speed.   Now the mansion is in sight.   If the
great gate be not thrown open in time, they are lost.
On! on! rushed the goaded team.   The headway is too
great; they cannot pause.   Arrows begin to whistle past
the ears of the screaming and despairing Peone.   Ha! it
is but a few paces farther to the gate—mules and chariot
will be dashed to pieces.   The yelling as of ten thousand
maddened fiends deafens them from close behind.   The
gate swings suddenly back; they are safe; and, as the
gate is slammed, with a baffled howl the dark warriors
swerve past like a flight of hawks that have missed their
quarry on the swoop.   The old man springs to the ground
in the court, and rushing through it with all the energy
of youth, calls his people to arms.   He passes through
into the summer-room, to look after the retiring foe.   They
are just passing out of view beneath the great oaks; and
he sees among their dusky forms the flutter of white
drapery, and rearing furiously in the effort to escape,
he recognises a snow-white palfrey, with long, flowing
mane and tail.   The poor old man falls heavily to the
marble floor.

CHAPTER III.

THE country called Northern Mexico is in many respects peculiar, but in no other is it more entirely anomalous than in its general topographical features. It really seems to be all at sixes and sevens with the rest of the continent. Its rivers, instead of running east, west, or south, as is the case with our other rivers, coolly turn tail upon them all, and very independently rush away toward the north. Whether this is the result of a hauteur of temper which scorns the company of "common folk," we cannot tell, though sure it is they have nothing in particular to brag of, except this and a few other eccentricities.

But there are some odd fashions these have, which are, if any thing, still more unaccountable. There is the little Rio Grande of Durango, the Rio Nazos, and the Rio Patos, which, with the most unusual and extraordinary originality, start out upon their own hook, from the bowels of the rude Sierra Madre, and after flashing in foam-lightning with zigzag leaping down the steep bare rocks, and rumbling through the deep cañons beneath, subside within a hundred miles or so into beautiful lakes, of comparatively small size, and having no apparent outlets.

What the meaning of all this fussy parade is, we leave it for sages to determine; but if we were left to conjecture, it would be that it was got up simply for the sake of making a fuss for the pure love of it; for those sombre old mountains have quick ears, we tell you! while they stand listening silently, up in the blue, crisp air, to the glad, glittering, tinkling dash of the merry waters, giddy with the joy of freedom and the light, as they go tinily shouting down their rugged sides; and then, when the morning comes, haloing with the aurora their white frosty brows, they, with commendable vanity, love to see themselves looking at the best, and, on tiptoe, seem to lean and peer at the giant reflexes those small bright lakes give forth. Ha! ha! the jolly old boys! what a toilet is theirs, when their hair of knotty laurels and the rough mesquit has just been combed by the hurricane, and all their white powder whirled off glistening into the thin air! When they look down into the mirrors at their feet they are amazed, you may rest assured, to see themselves looking so young, and, like punctilious, old-fashioned gentlemen, as they are, sadly taken aback at the idea of appearing at court before the sun, without the complement of hair-powder which etiquette requires! But the fitful winds that make their toilet will soon be along; and not the down of cygnets is so soft and white as those fleecy clouds they bring, and no footfall of minister of air so dimly musical as their flakes while they fall!

We mentioned at the beginning, that the Hacienda Encinnillas was situated on a tributary of the Conchas: we should have qualified this assertion somewhat, by saying that it was rather conjectured to be a tributary than known to be so; for, as the mysterious Lake Patos, in which this little river lost itself, had no visible outlets, it is natural to suppose that it must have an invisible one, or else, as it is no miracle in point of size, it might be reasonably expected to run over some day. As this "some day" has never come yet, it was quite as natural to suppose that it never would; and considering it was near the Conchas, which, as it was the largest, was certainly the most self-willed, proportionably, of all the droll rivers in this droll country, why might it not have something to do in the affair? "Why," it might be pertinently asked, "since the Conchas, like another great river, the Nile, in the 'far countrie,' has taken the fancy to

run north, while all the rest of the world runs South, should
it not as well be a pipe-laying politician, and have under-
ground tributaries which would darkly and secretly work to
swell its importance?" The thing seems plain. However,
whether right or wrong, the Patos River and Lake are
pretty generally considered as underhand contributors to the
rather turbulent importance of the Conchas !

On the morning after the occurrences we have related, the
shores of this little Lake Patos were thronged with a strange
assemblage. On the southern side, where its shores were
stupendously abrupt, with the exception of a narrow beach
at the foot of the cliffs, this curious mass was rushing along
the sand, and stretched like a rabble army nearly a mile in
length. Such bellowing and pushing as there was in that
great herd of brown, black, and white cattle, all mingled, who,
urged by the sharp lances of their Indian captors, gored,
roared, and butted, throwing out their heels, pitching, tumbling, and trampling each other in the wildest panic of pain
and rage ! Their fierce captors, as they passed the fallen, re-
lentlessly lanced and left them writhing on the ground.
Then came a thousand mules, and nearly as many horses,
rearing, plunging, biting, snorting, leaping, and kicking, in
a sort of pent-up stampede, for they could not break
through the heavy and compact masses before them, nor
could they get by without rushing into the lake. Then came
a curious jumble of Indians mixed up with their Mexican
prisoners, and hundreds of mules laden with plunder of every
kind—articles of which were strewing the sands at nearly
every stride they made. Then came the main body of the
robbers, half a mile in the rear, and consisting of over two
hundred warriors, darker than any of the southern tribes,
naked to the clout, and wearing horse-tail cues attached to
their long hair, and streaming on the wind behind. Their
lances were ornamented with horse-hair, as also their bridles,
which were plaited and tufted with it; and their rawhide quirts

had the same appendages.   To increase the spirit, if not the spirituality of the scene, these wild devils were yelling like a herd of wolves with the staggering prey in view, only that the voice of the human monster was more terrifically hoarse and alarming.

Suddenly the lead of this headlong mass diverged toward the lake, and such a splashing!   The hundreds of "browns" were followed by the hundreds of "blacks," and then the hundreds of "whites" capped, like horned foam, the waves of the startled lake.   Then came the mules and horses, and even some animals, bearing the Mexican prisoners, rushed in with their screaming burdens.   So strong is the propensity among beasts of all grades to follow the lead!

It was now rather a peculiar sight, it must be confessed, that placid lake, that seemed ever to have slept beneath the eyes of stars and shadows of great rocks, suddenly invoked by this wild tumult of heads and horns, of snorts and sneezes, bellowings, plunges, rearing, shrieking, winding up with horrid yells as the rear-guard of warriors came up and boldly plunged their horses into the lake, and, urging them through the now tumultuous water, struck out to drive back the refractory drove.

Many were drowned, but it was not long before the great body were turned in toward the shore, and were seen meekly wading back through the near shallows, and showing themselves tame as drowned rats.

It is not to be supposed that these audacious warriors had been urging this mad rout because they were afraid of pursuit or of their pursuers, by any means.   How that is, you will probably perceive soon; but you may rest assured this whole affair was entirely a matter of common usage and deliberate calculation with them.   They knew well that the wild and frightened animals they had thus unceremoniously appropriated would be unruly customers to manage in driving as they were, and that it was necessary to teach
s

them some manners at the outset; so they cunningly chose
this long beach, where they knew it was impossible for them
to break but in one direction, and that one the best calculated to cool off their surplus vehemence—into the lake !

When once on the beach there was no escape: they had
either to be goaded in the manner we have described, through
the whole tedious length of some fifteen miles, when they
would be thoroughly used up, or else they must take to the
water, either of which alternatives would have, as they well
knew, the desired effect !

Now by the time the swimming warriors reached the sands,
all dripping as they were, they marshalled their humble and
drooping victims into double herds, which walked meekly on,
not needing the goad of lance or frightening yell.

But amid all the noise and confusion attendant upon
such an event as this we have just witnessed, there was one
party of four warriors which stood fast, immovably watching
the scene. They bore between them, as they sat upon their
horses, a rude kind of litter, composed of a buffalo-robe
stretched between two lances, and another above thrown over
the arches formed by two withes of green boughs lashed
across to each of the lances, and at both ends. What was
held in this curious litter was not so apparent, although the
flutter of a white garment occasionally, within, might have
rendered it suspicious that we had seen or heard of the
owner before ; and more especially, since you discovered, in
the thickest and most tumultuous part of the throng, a small,
and snow-white mare, with flowing mane and tail, which was
kicking, biting, and leaping here and there like an enraged
pantheress, thus managing to add no little spirit to her part
of the scene, and give some trouble at least to the youthful,
but comely young warrior who bestrode her, side-saddle and
all ! She seemed wild with furious indignation, and snorted
her wrath and neighed her scorn at the filthy barbarians
that were presuming to profane her silken hide with their

vulgar touch, and lashed out her heels with savage emphasis, and without distinction, at all who presumed to approach her. She had already bitten several warriors or their horses, and lance after lance had been levelled at her side, but as her bold young rider always assumed the attitude of defence for his prize, their owners had finally concluded to give her a wide berth and let her alone.   When they plunged into the lake, she came very near taking her rider "out to sea," for she clenched the bit in her teeth, and started out across the water for the other shore, four miles distant; and when the young warrior attempted to check her up, she plunged and went under very deep with the most vixenish desperation, as if determined to drown him off, or drown herself, and thus get rid of her ignominy.   But he was not to be baffled, and, with wonderful coolness, (his bath had made him cool, if he had not been so otherwise,) he held her head above water, and, in spite of her struggles, urged her toward the shore. When arrived there, instead of being tempered down as the other animals were, she commenced rearing and plunging among the disordered crowd, even more ungovernable than before.   She made her way through the throng of cattle, by leaping over the backs of some with most astonishing bounds, that would have unseated any other rider than a Southern Indian or an Arab, and by dashing out most furiously, or biting them, until she had carried her rider, "whether-or-no," through the divisions of the white and black, and reached that of the shaggy browns.   Here she began to behave better; and the young warrior, who had been absolutely sweating with his exertions to "keep her on the wind," began apparently to console himself that the trouble was all over, when, to his great astonishment and discomfiture, she all at once lifted her head, and, with a wild shrill neigh, cleared in swift successive bounds the backs of three or four of these great shaggy brutes, and then, with head down and nose before, nearly dragging the poor warrior off, she rushed

through the crowding herd; and then, with a strange, eager
cry as they got through, leaped over the back of a burden
mule, and stopped so suddenly as to pitch the unfortunate
young fellow violently forward and nearly over her neck,
with his head thrust into the opening of that unique litter of
buffalo-robes, concerning which we have spoken.

The scream of terror that followed, and his look of grinning delight as he regained his reins and seat, were not far
from comical, to say the least; but what was absolutely so,
was the whinnying ecstasy with which the little mare thrust
her fine head into the same place, though more gently, and
begged a recognition from her lawful mistress; and, furthermore, it was not a little comical to see the unavailing efforts
of the laughing young warrior to get her away from that immediate vicinity, after her fair mistress, who had been somewhat reassured by the appearance of that familiar nose, had
stroked and kissed it, and spoken some familiar words of endearment. The young warrior, after various desperate efforts,
finding it was of no avail to try to get away from that litter,
seemed to resign himself to his fate, and now rode quietly
along in its rear.

Thus it pressed on, this wild, tumultuous mass. Lake after
lake was passed, whose sunlines roughly broken by the wild
invasion, set all the solemn mountain-tops dancing in their
bosoms, like colossal shadows in fantastic wake above the
death of ancient solitude. They tossed their hairy arms
about in many a measured wave, nodding their white heads
seriously and slow, while far beneath their huge limbs
flashed in quick and zigzag antics, that seemed strangely
limber for such grave and stiff-kneed watchers of the storms.
Perhaps their stout, unbending natures had yielded their
venerable proprieties to grief, that the deep bosom of this
quiet they so long had guarded was thus being robbed of its
informing presence—of its fairest incarnation—the lightsome,
joyous, and gentle Gabrielle, whose delicate spirit had

humanized them all, and whose regal will had bound them
as her servitors, held by the imperious etiquette of her majestic court to breathe not over loud themselves, nor let the
uncivil winds dare more than whisper on their pipes a drowsy
undertone—that all the rocks and waters of that wreck-
piled, caverned earth, might hear the mellowest ripple of her
silvery laugh, and soothe their bristling horrors into the ver-
nal smiles of a perpetual peace.

Alas, alas, ye cold-nosed mountains! well may the slow
teardrops, now trickling from many an eyelid spring adown
your rugged points, freeze in funereal pendence, glistening
aloft in that icy, desert air, the which the soft radiance of
her spring-like smiles may never soothe and thaw again!
She has been reft from thee—she is departing! Are not
thy moveless pinnacles all tottering with the weight of sorrow
even now? In thy wild wrath, may they not be hurled beneath, upon the doomed war-crest of that black and savage
herd, that would thus ravage all thy joy away?

Thou troubled lakes, whose crystal quiet has been thus
profaned, deep in the cavernous chambers of thy mystery,
hast thou no pent-up floods to loosen overwhelming on this
sacrilegious rout, that ye may bear her on the white mare,
triumphing on the unsoiled crest of your white-foaming
strength?

Alas, alas, the flinty heart of mountains and the torpid
power of those dumb lakes, they are yet unmoved! May
the genii of those baffled storms possess them both hereafter
with wildest throes. The angel of their old-time peace has
vanished! Gabrielle, the fair Gabrielle, has passed away!
She has been torn from their midst, their guardian arms all
unresisting!

Though deserted by her natal guardians, the power of
lake and wood, rock and stream, the fair Gabrielle retained
at least one fast and faithful friend in the beautiful white
mare of Chihuahua; who, having by this time taught her

swarthy captors that *her* will was to be law, now, with her
nose close against the litter, followed demurely with drooping ears, and large eyes melancholy-moist, seeming to respond
from her deep chest in sighs to every sob of the frail prisoner within, who, forgetful of aught else, strove, yet in vain,
through closed lids, to shut out some gory spectacle that
would rise up, bearing the form, scalpless and torn, of her
own gallant Juan.

Poor child! poor child! She thought not of her dreadful future. The past brought darkness and horror enough
to her faint heart.

Still it rushed on—that ruthless herd, and roar and yell,
and clang of lance and shield yet mingled in dull and dreadful monody upon her listless ear. Still the white mare clung
close beside her—still the young chief had failed to move her
wilful, dogged faith—still those white ears dropped—still
that deep chest heaved with mute and pent-up wrath, and
the funereal trail of her white mane and tail swept the curt
brown sod.

Night came—and still the troubled mass rolled on beneath
the pitiless stars and the cold, staring moon—no pause, no
rest was there.

The bellowings of the goaded herds were only now and
then rendered less distinct by the shrill shrieks and outcries
that told how the ferocious robbers had turned aside to strike
some new hacienda near their path, or sweep fresh victims
from the pillaged suburbs of defenceless villages, to hurl
them onward in the turbid rush of the dark flood they urged
before them to their mountain home.

The morning came—and a more general wail uprose from
all the shaking land they trampled, and a great concourse of
prisoners—weeping as she wept, and for many another scalped
and gory Juan, too—swelled the long, mournful train of
fairest Gabrielle.

Suddenly, as with a great shock, all this bewildered tumult

now was stilled. The insolent marauders had paused before
the very gates of the city of Chihuahua—and leaving a few
of their number to guard their prisoners and plunder, charged,
howling their fierce war-whoops, rattling their shields and
lances against each other, upon a force of some five hundred
regulars, constituting the garrison of the city, which was
issuing from the open gates with characteristic pomp and
bluster to punish the aggressors. These flaunting, ferocious
champions of New Mexican honour, scarcely awaited the
charge of less than three hundred half-naked savages, but,
breaking instantly, were driven back in panic-struck confusion
to the wide-open gates of their city, their dreaded foes entering pell-mell with them.

The lieutenant-colonel to whom the gallant old Governor
Gonzaleze had intrusted the sole command during his retire-
ment at his hacienda, had been first to lead forth his tinselled
troops to meet this wild band; and, with equal promptness
and activity, had proved the first to enter, not only the gates
of the city, in this shameful retreat, but the first as well to
reach the shelter of the citadel.

Fortunately, their foes held the environment of walls in
deep aversion, and did not venture to penetrate so far as the
citadel, of which, no doubt, they might have possessed themselves with equal ease, in the panic.

At the sound of the escopets, which a few stragglers had
nervously fired into the air in their retreat, the white mare
of Chihuahua had pricked her ears, and darting forward with
a shrill snort, had succeeded, by the suddenness of her movement, in unseating her tenacious rider, and then, with the
speed of an arrow from the bow, her wild hair singing in the
wind, she had darted with fierce neighings through the
crowded gate, and held her way, trampling and overturning
every thing opposed, direct to the citadel, into the accustomed
courts of which she rushed, plunging and foaming like some
wizard, wild thing, broken loose.

Nothing could restrain her furious neighings, and as the gates were now closed, the gallant colonel was soon made aware of her presence.

The cheek of the chivalrous Don Diez turned yet a shade paler, and his long, silken moustache quivered still more palpably, as he recognised the favourite palfrey of Senorita Gabrielle, yet fully caparisoned, showing full plainly that evil had come to her whom he well knew to be as more than the apple of the eye to his indulgent master, the old Governor Gonzaleze.

She must be a prisoner to this wild horde—and now a double disgrace stared upon him like a death's head, should he do nothing to rescue her. No excuse could save him now, no lying bombast of reported prodigies of valour could avail him now. No swaggering bulletins from imaginary fields of blood would divert that old father's heart from the stern questioning which would demand her—his life—his child!—the child of his old age—at his hands.

The recreant felt that indeed something must be done to save appearances; and instantly, with loud gasconading, he ordered the white palfrey to be equipped for him—for his own warrior seat—that upon it alone he would lead them forth to die a thousand deaths, or to the rescue of their mistress.

The Apaches had now left the town, and for hours and hours the chivalrous knight galloped hither and yon about the city, collecting his scattered heroes, thus managing to waste the precious time within, which it might safely be conjectured that the foe, he was thus ferociously bent upon exterminating, could have reached a security beyond the possibility of pursuit, within the fastnesses of the neighbouring Anahuac mountains.

But his swarthy foe, meanwhile, proved to be in no hurry to gain this desirable shelter; and after loitering for some time plundering the suburbs and insultingly challenging the garrison to come forth and fight them upon open ground, they at length leisurely moved on with their encumbered train, sending forth many a bitter taunt and defiance to pursue.

When they were at length safely out of sight, and even miles away, the gallant Lieutenant-colonel Diez came forth, all renewed in burnished splendour, leading his valorous force of green and gold-laced chivalry. The white palfrey that he rode seemed verily snorting flames, so eager was she chafing to plunge away at once upon the wild pursuit.

And now the drama hastens to a close. Hours have passed, and it nears evening. The listless Apaches, who are gorged at last with rapine and with blood, are slowly moving, in a long, straggling, careless line, toward the entrance of the first defile into the sheltering mountains.

Some, half asleep, bend forward, resting with their shields upon the brooding necks of their jaded steeds. Others, in reckless attitudes, gossip in groups as they walk lounging beside their horses. A deep and tangled chaparral stretches on either side, from the mouth of the defile out into the plain. The advance-guard of warriors has already entered the pass, while behind them, stretching for more than a mile, follows the scattered train of stolen herds, and after these the loose phalanx of their prisoners, tied upon horses and mules, or straggling on foot—the precious litter of which we have spoken, alone being guarded, on the extremest rear. Then came the lounging rear-guard of some fifty apathetic warriors, when, as they were about entering the defile, a thumping and irregular discharge of escopets, from the chaparral on either side, told of an ambush—when the listless warriors, like drowsy wild-hawks to the clash of coming wings, are on the instant wide enough awake, and bending for the stoop, glance fiercely round them for the coming foe.

Shot after shot burst dully, thumping round them; and yet no harm seems done, no warrior falls, nor even starts with sudden wound—when suddenly, with a loud, derisive

laugh, they wheeled and darted back, to turn the chaparral
on either side, and rout the foe their scorn had so surely
recognised.

It was but a moment, and the chivalrous knights of Mexico
were seen scurrying, in sad disarray, hither and yon across
the open plain, back for Chihuahua, far faster than they came.

But see! yon gayly plumed knight, who leads the frantic
rout, has suddenly wheeled from out the press, and is darting
back alone, upon his snow-white steed, as if in shame and
scorn he left the coward rabble, to expiate with his own gentle
blood this foul blot upon the high chivalry of Spain, or with
his own puissant arm singly to rescue the fair prisoner in
yon guarded litter.

It is the gallant Diez! Who but he? Mark what a falcon
flight he flies! How direct is that fell swoop he makes!
Shall his swarthy foes stand up before him? Dare they
abide his fearful coming? See, he is upon them! Their
warrior ranks are opened. Hark as he passes! was that a
wild yell of derision? That furious neigh of his fiery steed,
—those tremendous vaultings! Hah! Lieutenant-colonel
Diez is unseated by his snowy steed—his foot drags in the
stirrup—fiercely lashing his prostrate form with her heel,
the white mare of Chihuahua drags his lifeless body over
the plain, through, around, and amid the jeering warriors,
who will not deign to honour all that fallen chivalry with one
good, honest weapon-thrust. And so this fierce knight died
without one warrior wound. Alas! alas!

The rout now disappeared within the deep defile, and the
fair Gabrielle and her milk-white wizard palfrey have
passed from before our vision! It may be for ever—we
shall see!

WILD GIRL OF THE NEBRASKA.

TALES OF THE SOUTHERN BORDER.

THE WILD GIRL OF THE NEBRASKA.

CHAPTER I.

THE WANDERING HUNTERS.

WE aré off! and, far through the illimitable evening, are

"Flying an eagle's flight—bold and forth on!"

Swiftly the cities of men are left behind our daring way, and then, as we swing, flapping with tireless pinions through the mid-air—brushing fleecy edges of clouds away—the towns seem lessening into villages, and these are sown broadcast now, dotting the hill or river side, the forest, valley and plain. Now the little farms are scattered widely, and here and there a "settlement" flecks the unbroken wild, at broad intervals, with openings that let in the sun.

On! on! The forests darken—the hills, the river, and the prairies look more solemn. Here and there a hunter's lodge seems to crouch from loneliness beneath their shadows, and then the thin blue column of a camp-fire smoke soars upward.

Now there is a wide interval of dark and unrelieved repose. The shadows look as if they never had been crossed, so still are they upon the smoothly-gliding surface of wide, swift rivers—so still are they upon the rippling edges of broad, ocean-like prairies, whose green, flowery surfaces are bowed and lifted, wave-like, as the winds go by—so still are they,

T   217 flung down from abrupt cliffs into the dim, hushed valleys—so still are they, laid across the brows of grim and time-stained rocks—so sombre-bright are they, dropped in golden chequer-work beneath the tangles of old forests—

"The nodding horror of whose shady brows"

had else been threatening—so dark, on the abyss of cataracts, flashing as they leap, that even the thunder of their fall is awed, and does not wake the ancient silence.

Now again columns of smoke pillar the clouds at far intervals; but they ascend from the fires of another race. By the bed of the great Missouri, and along its many arms, the Arabs of the South have planted their tents of buffalo-hide, and from their blazing fires ascend the streams of incense to HIM they worship as Manitou—the Great Spirit and essence of all things!

There they are!—half-naked, decked with dyed horse-hair, and feathers, bearing long lances, quivers, and short bows! They go scudding to and fro, like swallows on the wing, upon their swift and mottled horses—wild and tameless knights are they! Ho! for the Prairie Chivalry!

This is towards the south; but on the northern side of the terrible river the smokes of a different race ascend. They live in villages, and are wholly clothed in garments of dressed skins, and these are made most picturesque by long fringes and figures, worked with a rude art by the fingers of their swarthy maidens. Then their frightful necklaces of the claws of grizzly bears, their plucked crowns, with the long scalp-lock tufted in eagle feathers, and their paint-begrimed faces, remind us of the sterner and more ferocious North.

They, too, have quivers, bows, and lances, like their neighbours with the darker skins, but each is on a larger, heavier scale; and then they have the ugly war-club of the North.

They, too, have the white man's most terrible weapon, the rifle, here and there among them. They are horsemen, too

—-but not such Centaurs as their southern neighbours are; for with them horse and man are one—alike agile, tireless, and fleet.

Here the Kansas river, after a long and weary way from out the sterile country of the Arapahoes, comes bounding on to meet the wild Missouri; and farther yet above, the cold and swift Nebraska is hurled, like a shining lance, down from the strange and snow-capped mountain tangles of the "Three Parks," into that remorseless bourn.

Amidst these wilds we find a group of wanderers. It is composed of six in all, four of whom are rude, athletic men, who reveal at once that they are frontiersmen, hunters, and guides, by the incessant and restless habit of turning their heads to look in all directions as they advance. They, as usual, are armed in the old-fashioned manner, with the long-barrelled rifle and single-barrelled pistols; for, as a class, they have an unconquerable aversion to innovations of whatever kind in arms or equipment.

The other two, like men of sense coming out from civilization, had brought with them its most important improvements in weapons. Each carried a pair of Colt's revolving pistols at his belt, and a short steel-barrelled rifle, that told at nearly a quarter of a mile with fatal accuracy. This they bore before them, across the pummel of their saddles. The heavy and terrible bowie-knife, with its keen, broad, polished blade, hung, too, at their sides, in a leathern sheath.

Their dress was a strange commingling of the two extremes of civilized and savage costume. It consisted of the ordinary buckskin hunting-shirt, and trousers of gray cloth, but faced, or "foxed," as the frontier term is, with the same material as the shirt—that is, those portions of it which were particularly liable to abrasion in the circumstances of their rough life, were covered by this stout defence, stitched on to the cloth.

They carried long lariats of plaited raw-hide, coiled and

hung by a slight thong to the horn of their Mexican saddles —across the deep seats of which the blankets that covered the riders at night were folded. A small bag of provisions was slung beneath them, pannier-like, on either side, and behind were tied a tin-cup and water-gourd. They were all well mounted, but he who led the party seemed superlatively so. The airy-necked and light-limbed mare that carried him stepped as if she were shod with wings.

The person at his side was a smaller figure, yet there was something exceedingly springy and cat-like in his alert bearing and gray, glittering eye. The face was what sentimental young ladies would call "plain," for there was nothing peculiar about it, except the mouth and eyes. The former was something wide for the size of the face, with thin lips, the upper one of which, even in profound repose, was curved in a perpetual sneer. The square under-jaw expressed immense and inexorable energy of will. Over all the face there was an expression that irresistibly attracted, while it left you uneasy and dissatisfied with the fascination.

"Carter, I am heartily tired of this whim of yours!" said he, pettishly.

"I am sorry for it, Newnon! But it is certainly a whim by which we have gained a great deal, for it has filled our veins with healthy blood, and made us stronger in every sense by a hundred-fold than we were before."

. "Pshaw! I am not particularly emulous of the seven labours of Hercules, and do not care to be able to grapple hand to claw with a grizzly bear, or pummel a panther to death with my fists! I was strong enough already—so far as brute strength is concerned."

"Ah! but, Newnon, you are, as usual, uncandid. If we do not have literally to battle in brute strength with the seven labours of Hercules now, we shall have to do it intellectually with a far greater number—and we cannot escape the unfortunate accident, that the spiritual and physical lives are so mutually dependent, that one must be toned by the other. So I shall regard you an ingrate if you do not pronounce, in the solemn presence of this vast prairie-wilderness, your infinite obligations to its free airs and rude accidents, which have renewed your lungs, your digestion, and your nerves, far beyond any previous capacity of either!"

"I do not need the lungs of a Camanche, the digestion of an alligator, or the nerves of a horse; for I only set up for a simple gentleman, and had, as I conceive, quite enough of all these before."

"But, Newnon, you must confess to having had the opportunity of letting off your spleen in several hearty fights, which I thought at the time you seemed to relish very much."

"Why, my good fellow, how you mistake me! I am no warrior, any more than I am an alligator. I consider the idea of chivalry to be most broadly burlesqued, in our firing at these poor naked rascals with our terrible and resistless weapons. I should never have brought myself to do murder upon them, but that I found, in the first camp we sacked, that they only carried parched wheat with them on their expeditions. I accordingly set them down as the primitive originators of all those Grahamitish sins of light diet which sent you out here an aimless wanderer, and, therefore, gave them my pistol-balls with peculiar relish. It is a ludicrous mistake, though, to suppose that there is knighthood or valour in fighting, at any odds, such a pitiable foe. It is vastly chivalric—first to see your enemy enfeebled by starvation, and then strike him because he is too weak to lift his arm!"

"I judge you will find out, before we are done with these 'naked rascals,' as you call them, that there is something sufficiently formidable and annoying in their enmity, to make them, if not 'foemen worthy of your steel' in the chivalric sense, at least worthy extermination in the common sense."

"Not a bit of it; I only shudder with apprehension for the poor wretches, since every time we meet them I expect
T 2

to see you 'spiritually moved' to deliver them a homily upon
the sin and consequences of eating beef, and to find the
tawny reprobates so exalted by your apostolic eloquence, that
they will eschew the 'flesh-pots' forthwith, and make such a
descent upon the gardens and granaries of civilization, as
will quite astound your benevolence!"

"My benevolence or philosophy, as you choose, is not so
easily astounded. I have eaten meat myself since we came
out here, and should continue to do so if I had it in my
power to use other food. I shall conform to the conditions
of savage life so long as I have no means or power of elevating it; but what is morally and physically true of the life
here, is not necessarily so of the higher life of civilization.
It may be well enough for the warrior, whose trade is
blood, to live upon the death of red-blooded animals; but for
the philosopher, who deals with the lofty themes of pure
intellection, to congest and fever the clear-eyed calm of his
benignant purpose with such gross and bestial juices, is to
me revolting. I am quite conscious that I live the life of a
brute and a savage now, but that does not decrease my
aspiring veneration for the highest possibilities of our development. The machinery of society is oiled by compromises, and this is one I am willing to make."

"Do you know, Frank, I pity you greatly. You have
evidently been born too late. The time of the lawgivers,
prophets, and reformers is long since past. You are not a
Mohammed or a Moses—therefore you clearly belong to the
modern type of fanatic, and it has so emphatically secured
the derision of civilization, that I am not surprised that you
should take refuge amid the unsophisticated stupidity of this
savage life. You have some chance here, for you can at
least preach to the deer and buffalo, provided they will condescend to stop and listen to you."

"Whether the deer and buffalo pause or not, I feel assured
that 'Humanity' will at some time listen to this thought.

But, however, the dark is coming on, and here, in this green meadow, beside that stream, is a beautiful place for camping."

"Agreed."

Upon a swift and narrow branch of the arrowy Nebraska, this company of wanderers pitched their tents—or rather spread down their blankets—for the night. The shadows settle over them, and darkness rested there.

The night was spent, in many respects, like other nights, but the tired sentinels must have slept at their posts on the last watches, for, when the full morning came, they looked around in vain for their horses, which had been staked out to graze at a little distance about the camp. They gazed over the prairies until their eyes ached—they turned toward the forest, along the banks of the stream, but its dark shadows revealed nothing.

Poor fellows! Could it be! on foot in this vast and remote wilderness? What can they do? How can they ever get back to civilization? Mariners, left by their wrecked vessel on some desert island, would scarcely have. been more desolate than they.

They rubbed their eyes—they stared and stared about them, but it was of no avail—the thing was done! Their horses had been quietly "stampeded" during the night, and were now far enough away, scurrying over the wide prairie before some band of Indian plunderers.

Our friend Clenny rages and fumes. It is an alternative he had never calculated upon. His contempt for "the half-naked rascals" was somewhat ameliorated, when he came to recognise fully the extent and amount of the mischief done by their silent prowess. The hunters had scattered in every direction in the bootless search, and the two young men were left alone in the camp in the chagrin of their solitude. They stood together on the border of the prairie, and looked out upon its blank and vast perspective with a forlorn and hopeless expression that was almost ludicrous.

"Frank, may the devil take you and your scatterbrain projects! Would I had been tied to the bed-post, and you to your grandmother's apron-string, before this silly expedition was undertaken! But for your eccentric babyisms, we should be comfortably secure now in our arm-chairs, with coffee and breakfast before us, instead of having the unrelieved prospect of some thousand miles or so, over valley, hill, and plain, on foot, with the sure alternative of starvation to console us."

"Good! good! I thought just now that these half-clad savages were in every sense too contemptible to interrupt, in the slightest degree, the calm equanimity of your life! The case is bad enough, I must confess, and we have the prospect of trudging back home on foot. But ho! What is that coming toward us, with such directness, out of the vague distance over the prairie?"

"It is some wild animal."

"No, no! It is my gentle and dear Celeste! She has escaped from the rude brutes, and is coming back to me!"

As the young man spoke, the beautiful mare came rushing past Clenny right up to him, and thrust her small head against his bosom.

"Beautiful Celeste," said the young man, as he gently patted the glistening neck of his returned favourite, "you would not stay with the greasy barbarians. Welcome, welcome! Come, thou faithful pet, we will go out into the wilderness again, and search for some means of rescuing our poor, forlorn comrades."

It required but a few moments to equip the willing animal, and then bounding into the saddle, Frank Carter gayly waved adieu to his disheartened friend, and darted off across the plain to search for help in any form.

For hours and hours his gallant mare kept on towards the west with speed that did not flag. The rider was even more weary than she seemed to be, and still they both urged on.

He had seen nothing yet that looked like hope, when out of the wide prairie he rushed beneath the deep shadows' of a heavy forest, skirting a stream.

He now held up the pace of his mare, and as the last rays of the setting sun fell down through the great armed trees, he for the first time realized that he was lost. He had in his hurry become confused as to the direction he had been going, and now was utterly confounded with regard to the course back to camp. All the day he had chased the shadow of a vague hope, and now even that had vanished; not even the thousandth-and-one chance of meeting with some wandering fragment of a friendly Indian tribe remained, as it seemed.

All was unrelieved despondency and gloom to him. The gallant mare dragged her once elastic feet heavily along, as she slowly, and at random, threaded the aisles of the old forest. Here and there the solemn farewell of the day broke through in golden splendour, illumining the huge trunks even up to their summits and most minute twigs, and down to the delicate mosses and flower-bells at their feet. Though the young man was weary and heartsick, yet the glory of the fading evening fell across his spirit with a forlorn smile.

He had no craven fears; for, had he been capable of such, his arms made him secure against prodigious odds; but he was sad because his friends expected him to come back with help to them, and he could not go, since he was now as helpless as if a thousand miles intervened.

His beautiful mare walked with her fine ears drooping, and with an expression of utter weariness that entirely corresponded with his own condition. Ho! Her ears are pricked forward, and she starts with a bound and a clear neigh. Her fine senses have discovered something friendly in the pathless forest. The young man spurs forward. There, beneath a grand old beech-tree, a young girl is mounted on a black and glossy horse, that moves as if inspired with all volatile es-

sences of grace. Our wanderer pauses, for a slight check
will stop even the fresh impulse of his weary Celeste. This
is a strange, extravagant sight to start from out the depths
of the savage wilderness—yet it is real.

A young girl, with golden hair—and it is not less golden
that the mellow sunset mingles with its glistening threads—
sits easily on a shining horse, that goes quickly into shadow,
and comes glancing into light again as it circles round the
tree.

A strange attraction, surely, is that in the great tree,
round which she circles on her horse, snapping her fingers,
singing as she whirls! On a large limb a tawny panther
crouches. Its ears are laid close back upon its head, its long
tail is waving to and fro, and it is ready for the spring.
Still that young girl gallops round and round him, disturbing
the aim of its gathered leap by the swift movements of her
beautiful horse, and taunts the hot glare of those fierce eyes,
snapping her white fingers gayly in their angry gleam, as she
goes by!

CHAPTER II.

THE ADVENTURE.

IT was strange enough how that young creature came here
—thus illumining the savage wilderness. Her presence, too,
would have been strange enough anywhere, for it expressed,
at a glance, all the wilful and bright tenderness of the young
imbodied April.

But by what spell, yet stranger and more powerful, had
such a being been made to start forth from this blank barbaric wild—mounted, too, like some oriental princess coming
out of Dream-land, on a sleek steed, that glistened as if new
sprung from a young poet's brain!

And then that strange, fantastic whim of hers! To circle round and round on her fleet horse, the spotted cougar crouching on the limb, taunting his heated eyes as she went by, with snapping fingers and her mocking song! No dreamer ever dreamed a dream of such wild, subtile daring, and yet our poor, forlorn Frank Carter looked upon the real from beneath drooping lids.

Hah! They drooped but for a moment with the overcoming weariness of his long ride and hopeless mood, but when he saw to realize the happy gay, audacity of that bright creature, his eyes flew open wide, and the gleam that lit them shot through all his frame, and caused Celeste to bound forward, sympathetically with all her morning springiness.

The young girl, who was intent upon her perilous sport, did not perceive him, even, although very near—when her black steed pricked his ears forward sharply, and gave her warning that either friend or foe was coming.

She did not turn her eyes from off those of the dangerous brute she was teasing, but, watching her chance, quickly urged her fiery animal, lifting him by the rein at the same time—one tremendous leap!—the circle was broken, and she was far beyond the reach of the cougar's spring.

She does not pause, but the black steed darts off with much longer and swifter bounds through the trees.

Poor Carter, whose life has suddenly been inspired, now perceives the beamy source of the inspiration to be vanishing through the shadows.

With her flying form goes all the hope of many things as dear or dearer even to him than life—the prospect of finding his friend and comrades again—of rescuing them from their painful position, and worse than even this—of losing from his sight the clearest, brightest gleam of beauty that has ever crossed his path!

He is utterly maddened by the thought, and wildly urges his exhausted mare. But Celeste has caught the fire of his eager will—for her instinct teaches her that to follow that flying steed must lead her to food and rest, and so she bounds away as if with renewed wings, and needs not the hot urgings of his impatience.

Away they go, pursuer and pursued, down long aisles of the old forest, flying with speed across the deepening shadows. Now and then he perceives, far ahead of him, a glimpse of fluttering drapery between the trees, and this is enough to lead him.

It was vain for him to shout after her—for, in the stupor of his surprise, he had forgotten to do this until she was far enough beyond the reach of his voice.

Now she is gone—she has disappeared utterly—the last flutter of the drapery that guided him has met his aching eye—alas! poor Frank, how his heart beats!

The forest has suddenly grown more close with thickets of underbrush, and among these she has quickly glided, disappearing like some fleet white-footed vision through the gates of sleep.

" Curses! curses!" muttered the young man, from out the depths of his despair, as he checked up to look for the trail of her horse; "I have overrun her trail far enough by this time! Oh! accursed luck—or stupidity, rather! What shall I do?"

Then acting under a sudden impulse, he gave the reins to his mare, while he muttered—

" Her astonishing instinct has often befriended me before, perhaps it may now."

The sagacious creature instantly understood, and turned abruptly to the left of the course he was pursuing. Her pace for the last few moments had greatly fagged, as if she was discouraged by the knowledge that they were going wrong; but now she bounded on as buoyantly as at the beginning of the day.

Frank Carter had so often tested the sagacity of horses

under such circumstances of bewilderment to the rider, and felt such entire confidence in that of the high-bred creature he now rode, that the blood rushed back to his temples with a warm flush of reviving hope, and raising himself in the stirrup, he laughed aloud—

"Ha! ha! my vagabond Sprite of the woods!—we will catch you yet!"

A clear, musical laugh rang out in silvery gladness, close to his side. Celeste gave a desperate shy, that nearly threw him from the saddle.

He turned his head as quickly as he could recover his seat, and just in time to see the strange object of his wild pursuit vaulting her black horse in a tremendous leap across the deep, wide fissure cut down into the alluvion by a small stream which passed a few paces to the right of his course.

She drew up on the other side and turned, still laughing merrily.

"Your vagabond Wood-Sprite is not so easily caught, sir! Now follow my Black Hawk across that gap, if you can?"

"If I only had wings, I might; but my poor Celeste is leg-weary."

"Pity, for she seems a beautiful creature! But you, sir! —who are you? As you can't get at me, I will hold a parley with you, and want a few questions answered; you had as well be docile, and answer me in downright honesty—for if you displease me, I shall leave you to your fate—since I judge you to be lost, and it will be impossible for you to get across the deep cut of that stream, this night, to follow me; and besides, Black Hawk can beat your Celeste running, clear out of sight."

"Not so sure of that, my pretty chatterbox!" said Frank Carter, with a slight laugh, while his heart beat high,—for there was a musical freshness in that voice and in those bantering words that started his blood in career, though he could see her form very indistinctly through the deepening

U

shadows. "Give Celeste a few days to rest, and I will try
the truth of your boast. But, to answer your first question,
—I am a Southern planter, and, I hope, a gentleman! If
that satisfies you, let us have your next question."

"You Southern planters, I suspect, are quaint gentlemen,
then; see how you have illustrated them! First, you come
suddenly and without warning, to interrupt the private amusements of an innocent young maiden; then, you chase her
timid flight through the forest as furiously as if she had been
some savage wild beast, upon whose thick hide you were
emulous to wreak your chivalry; then, to crown all, you insult her by calling her a vagabond Wood-Sprite! Do you
Southern gentlemen habitually deal in such hard names about
young maidens?"

"Southern gentlemen are not frequently, I must confess,
honoured, as I have been, by an introduction to such mysterious characters as Wood-Sprites—or yourself; therefore, I
cannot undertake to say how their language would be guarded
in speaking of them—particularly if they did not expect to
be heard. But recollect, most merciless mystery! that you
can be quite as witty at my expense when we are a little
nearer together. I fear that sweet voice will catch cold, if
you persist in sending it out on the night-air so far, and over
this water, too!"

"Most tender solicitude, that of yours, my gallant Southerner! But you must first tell me how it happens, that you
are here in this wild, dangerous region, alone; and then, if I
am satisfied, I will take the case of your immediate relief
from 'durance vile' into consideration."

"The tale is soon told. The horses of our party were
stampeded last night, and every one carried off; but my
faithful Celeste here would not stay stampeded, but made
her escape, and came back at full speed to rub her head
against my bosom. I came off on her to look for help at
random, and got lost, as you conjectured; you know the rest,

for you can best explain how fate has made this dark day bright to me!"

"A very touching story, that—particularly the portion of it relating to the conduct of your gentle Celeste—for whose bright sake I must relent towards her saucy master. She must have comfortable quarters this night, and of course may bring you along—in spite of the sentimental twang you gave to the close of your piteous tale!"

"Any way!" said he, laughing; "I am willing to accept such patronage on any terms—only let me be nearer you, and I am content."

"Fie! fie! Hush! or I shall be compelled to make you carry Celeste instead of she you. But come on, and I will show you a crossing-place some distance farther up."

She started off at a gallop, waving him to follow with her hand, the whiteness of which showed through the dark which had now fairly set in.

He kept along the stream parallel with her for about a mile, in perfect silence, when she suddenly halted and exclaimed—

"Here, my chivalric friend! Here you can get across, if you are careful. It is a crossing-place for deer and elk, but its ups and downs are very abrupt and narrow. Look sharp for the path, and leave the rest to Celeste!"

This last caution he was by this time, if not before, wise enough to profit by. Horses see better in the dark than men, as he was aware, and after getting into the deep trace, he gave up the reins passively. The sagacious animal descended with great caution, and before she reached the bottom gathered her feet together after the fashion of mules in descending steep places, and steadily slid the rest of the way. When the water was reached, and Celeste paused to slake her thirst in the shallow but singularly rapid stream, he looked up, and perceived that it had cut the banks square

down some twenty feet.   This would have been an ugly pit-
fall to stumble into in the dark !

Now, by a desperate struggle of the gallant mare the
ascent was gained, and he stood side by side with the enchantress who had led him so wild a chase.

"Gallantly done, my brave Celeste!" and she stooped
forward to caress, with her white hand, the slight neck of
the gentle animal.   "You shall have a good night's lodging
for that same feat !   How silky her hair is !" she exclaimed,
with a childlike expression of astonishment, as she ran her
fingers through the wavy mane of the panting Celeste.

"The mare is well enough, but I, too, have silken hair;
may I not claim some slight recognition as well?" said he,
in a tone of affected pettishness.

"Upon my word, I did not know, sir, that your hair was
silken—it is too dark for me to see; consider yourself, then,
if you please, as recognised through the coincidence !"

"Accept my gratitude for the large honour."

"With pleasure, sir !   But come ! come ! it is time this
dear Celeste was stabled, and I suppose she must bring you,
whether or no !   Come, Celeste ! Black Hawk and I are off !
—bring him with you—you may !" and with a gay laugh she
darted along the old trace, followed by Celeste whom she
had so coquettishly dignified, and her laughing burden, our
philosophical friend, Frank Carter.

For some distance, the trace was too narrow for them to
approach sufficiently near for conversation—but then it
widened rapidly, so that before they had passed from beneath the heavy gloom of the forest, the emulous Celeste had
closed up alongside of the light-heeled Black Hawk—for she,
too, had been inspired by the soft touch of those white hands—
and of course brought along her depreciated burden with her
"into position."

Frank Carter felt the strange, delicious thrill of a new joy
passing into his life.   His voice trembled slightly, with a

tender eagerness he could not control, but endeavoured to conceal under the affectation of humorous bantering.

"Ha! it becomes you, most wicked and incomprehensible of sprites, to remember that you are now in my power; and confess to me, on penalty of losing your wings, what sort of resting-place you expect to find in this wild and gloomy forest, to-night. I suspect it will prove to be some mighty Druidical work, amid the moss-draped boughs of which your light hammock swings—while Black Hawk is stabled at the hollow root! Will there be room, think you, for poor Celeste, in such narrow quarters?"

"Never mind, inquisitive sir, whether my house be on the earth, under the earth, or above the earth, so that Celeste be properly provided for; and, besides, supposing your supposition to be true, Black Hawk, I can tell you, sir, is a gallant gentleman—for I have not heard him call Celeste a single hard name yet, or threaten to cut her ears off with his teeth, as my wings were threatened once by somebody under the moon!—Black Hawk would surrender his stall, and neigh with delight at the opportunity of so honouring himself."

"Fortunate Celeste! you shall surely be embalmed, in honour of the interest you have excited, if I do not have the misfortune to die first of envy!" said the young man, in a dolorous voice, stooping to pat the animal's neck.

The merry girl bent forward, too, over her saddle-bow, in an ecstasy of laughter,—but it was subdued, like the soft twittering of an oriole singing in its dreams.

Now they emerged from beneath the deep shadows of the forest into the open prairie, and, as she raised her delicate face, the cold moon shone upon its white, laughing beauty, and was warmed amid the golden tangles of the curls that fell about it from beneath her close riding-cap.

"Well! well! be comforted, poor gentleman. I will

U 2

undertake, with the most disinterested pleasure, to officiate for you in the same capacity, provided such an event occurs. I should like myself to have you preserved as an extraordinary specimen of sentimental melancholy, and should label you, for the warning of future ages, 'Died of a broken heart.' "

And indeed, to have witnessed the rapt, ecstatic trance of gazing wonder into which our friend the enthusiast had fallen since the upturning of that face in the clear moonlight, one would have been justified in fearing some sentimental catastrophe.

If the partial glimpse he had obtained of that face at the tree had been sufficient to thrill the core of his life and urge him on through the desperate pursuit which followed, this clear unveiling of it held him in a sort of trembling awe that lulled his whole being into the mute reverence of worship of a God-revealed beauty, the presence of which was even now at his side!

His nature, electrically convulsed, was changed—utterly changed in one wild instant. The strong spell was on him. He had lived a century in the time of a few hushed breathings. The world was the same world, and went around on its old axle at the same appointed speed—but now, it had hurled its shadowy garments off through the dark space, and let in a new light, flashing over it—revealing itself to him so calmly glorious, that he marvelled whether he was not standing in a dream upon some starry paradise.

This glorifying light was in himself, though not the less real to him. The smouldering fires upon that sacred altar in the centre of his life, which he had so long and jealously guarded, had, at last, been lit by the searching spark, which, alone, could rouse them; and they had flamed up through all the senses, illumining the outer world through every portal.

Before the end of her last speech, the young girl had been

arrested by the strange intensity of his look. Her face
sobered in an instant, while her voice, too, sobered with the
conclusion. A bright light, that had shone from out her
whole face, seemed to gather towards her eyes, leaving the
rest of the face at once solemnly cold, and centring in them
with a keen and glittering brilliancy that was almost blinding,
dwelt steadily with those of the young man through some
moments of profound and mutual silence.

That look! that look! as their swift horses sped on beneath
the brilliant moonlight, and they with faces turned gazed in
a flashing, still communion, into each other's eyes! One
soul, at least, was born again!

Ah! that was a fearful moment—pregnant with all the
purpose and the joy of one life, or of both! We shall see.

Frank Carter was mute; he forgot to make any reply, or
that any was necessary. His life was stilled within itself,
striving to realize the bliss of the new birth.

The strange, bright creature by his side was silent, too, as
if she felt her being had been strangely startled; but then
she urged her horse impatiently, until he had bounded many
paces ahead of the weary Celeste. It seemed as if she were
rushing away, utterly to leave them.

Poor Carter was stupified, and had not realized the danger,
when Celeste neighed with such an agonizing, shrill, peculiar
neigh, as can only come from out the chest of a noble horse,
weary and starving, who trumpets the despairing alarm for
help.

Black Hawk heard it and stopped. The young girl passed
her hand quickly—as if confused—across her brow, and then
wheeled the eager animal to return. She galloped back, and
reining up close to the side of Carter, she leaned forward
towards his ear, and said, with a musical shout—

"Ho! Hilloa! Dreamer, wake up! The lights of my
father's rancho are in sight. We shall be there in a few

moments, and I would not have him imagine I have picked
up some vagabond," and she lifted her finger, archly—"What
shall I say—lunatic or genius? So wake up, and make yourself presentable, by self-possession, before a pair of eyes that
read men mathematically!"

The trance was over with him for the time, for her levity
shocked him out of it.

"Bah!" said he, "I have a contempt in general for minds
which call themselves mathematical—those which are really
so, never know it, and only express it in results—those who
feel the want of this great poising central element of thought,
always manage to get the reputation for it, through the noise
they make to conceal their great want. However," said he,
with a laugh, "understand that I shall be entirely prepared
in meeting this mathematical father of yours to recognise
him through the 'coincidence!'"

Frank Carter said this with more bitterness than he himself could have accounted for.

These young people were now farther apart than when
they first spoke together, and yet neither could tell the reason
why. It is one of the mysteries of the grand passion, which
time may explain.

The lights which were in the distance now seemed close at
hand, and as they came from the prairie into the edge of the
skirting forest, all the sounds and sights peculiar to a rancho
of the extreme frontier greeted them at once.

They dismounted amid the barbarous hubbub in which
the lowing of cows, bleating of sheep and goats, the neighing
of horses, the baying of dogs, and the jargon of Indians of
all ages collected before the gates of the high, strong picketing, which surrounded the rancho, were mingled.

The arrival of their bright mistress was greeted with shouts
by all the Indians, of every age, who were collected as if
awaiting her coming. They gave up their horses to these

willing servants, though not until the young girl had given an imperative injunction to several with regard to the treatment of Celeste.

Turning now, they mounted the high blocks leading to the top of the picketing which surrounded the rancho.

CHAPTER III.

THE QUARREL AND THE BREAKFAST.

FRANK CARTER and his fair guide, on descending the stiles of the picketing, found themselves in the wide court of the rancho.

On the two sides of the square, as they advanced, were low ranges of huts, composed of smaller picket-posts, the interstices of which were filled with moss and mud. A buffalo-robe hung across each entrance, and served for a door—while the flat roofs were thatched with bulrushes.

The opposite side of the square towards which they were moving, presented a higher front, the upright posts of which were larger, while there appeared to be but a single entrance in the centre, which was closed by a wide, strong door.

The light streamed out from a part of its length, through small, square openings, like the port-holes in the sides of a man-of-war. The noise which heralded their approach, had evidently caused some commotion inside, and the lights were seen glancing to and fro behind the port-holes, passing rapidly along the whole length of the front. The lights shone for an instant through the port-holes of that portion of it which had been heretofore obscured, and then it was left again in darkness. All this Frank Carter observed before they reached the great door in the centre, for their way was absolutely impeded by the crowd of dogs composed of

"Mongrel 'grim,
Hound or spaniel, brach or lym,
Or bobtail tike or trundle-tail,"

which came thronging about them, smelling at the stranger,
or bounding in rude gambols around the feet of their young
mistress.

When they reached the great door, the young girl seized
a string which hung outside, and jerking it sharply, caused a
loud rattling within.

After the delay of a few moments, the bolts within were
sprung, and as the heavy door swung slowly back, a mellow,
manly voice exclaimed—

"What has kept you out so late?—this is dangerous, my
daughter!"

A stout man, dressed in fringed buckskins, with a brace
of pistols at his belt, stood in the doorway.

"Papa, I have brought my excuse for the delay along
with me—here he is!" and she made way for Frank Carter,
who had been standing in the shade behind her, to come
forward and present himself.

The man lifted the large iron lamp he carried, above his
head, and as Carter stepped boldly and quickly forward, he
fell back with a gliding movement, while his hand, as it
seemed, involuntarily moved towards his pistol, though it
dropped quickly again.

There was no appearance of startle, or even surprise, in
the face of this man, upon which the habitual smile about the
facile mouth was unbroken. The gesture seemed to be rather
one of habitual caution than of fear. His hair was as white
as the driven snow, and but for the extraordinary contrast
of heavy eyebrows, which were as black as midnight, and
compelled the eye to dwell on them, it would never have been
observed that a slight shade of vexation crossed them the
moment his glance took in the whole figure of Frank.

The men stood facing each other, with steady regard, without speaking, for several moments.

The young girl came forward with a very demure look, and said—

"Papa, I found this *person* lost and wandering through the dangerous forest of the Black Walnut Bottom. His beautiful mare, Celeste, was nearly exhausted, and I knew they would both break their necks by stumbling through the dark into some of the deep cuts which cross it, so I took them under my patronage, and piloted them here for safety."

"You did right, my child," said the gray-haired man; and, bowing with a bland, benevolent smile, to Frank Carter, said, "You are welcome to the rude shelter and hospitalities of my rancho, sir. Walk in."

"Thank you, sir," said Carter, somewhat stiffly, and still pausing at the threshold. "The horses of my party were stampeded this morning by the Indians, and I was on the look-out for help for my comrades, when I was fortunate enough to meet this young lady."

"A very common accident in this region. But come, sir, walk in, if you please. We will first see to your own comfort, and then to-morrow we will concert measures for the relief of your friends;" and he turned, holding the lamp courteously, so as to show the way, and led the young man back through a passage formed of stout stockading, like the outside. At the farther extremity there was a door on either side, opposite. He threw open the door on the left, and handing the lamp to the young girl, said—"See to the gentleman's comfort, while I return to refasten the entrance." Then he bowed to Carter—"Enter, sir; and please excuse me for an instant. We find the precaution of bolts and bars is not to be neglected here."

He retired, and Carter followed the young girl into a square apartment, the sides of which were roughly plastered over the logs.

A fire blazed merrily upon the broad hearth at the farther extremity, and though Carter had not realized that the night was somewhat chilly, he now found its heat very pleasant as he approached.

The young girl placed the lamp upon a rough board table, and pointing to a side of the room along which a number of guns were ranged in racks, formed of buck's horns nailed against the logs, said—

"See, there is my father's armory. You can dispose of your rifle somewhere amid that array of antlered pride, and then be seated."

The young man obeyed, and deposited his rifle and other equipments, except his pistols, which he retained at his belt, as he had perceived that his host wore them within doors. The young girl, who was divesting herself of her riding-cap, said, with something like her former gayety—

"I hope, sir, although you may not find this home of mine quite so airy as the one you supposed me to occupy in the old Druidical oak, that it will nevertheless prove to be substantially comfortable after your exhausting ride!"

"Yes, I find all the difference to be in favour of the substantial reality. This place is singularly cosy, and promises, from the odours of the kitchen, something more than a 'sop of moonshine' for supper."

He turned as he spoke, and for the first time these young people confronted each other with heads uncovered, and in the blaze of a broad light, too. It was a decisive moment with them both.

A necessary consequence of the mutual revulsion which we have described as occurring directly after that extraordinary interchange of electrical sympathy during the moonlight ride, had been distrust of themselves and distrust of each other. They felt as if the astonishing and romantic circumstances of their meeting had unduly excited their senses and imaginations. That possibly the object of this excitement would appear, under other conditions, to be a very commonplace and unattractive person; then these riding-caps had obscured that portion of the face, or rather head, which is instinctively felt to be the most significant of power, sentiment, and truth.

They now faced each other with those white fronts unveiled, which are the tablets upon which God's own hand has placed his immortal signet of the Spiritual.

It is beyond measure surprising what a difference in our first recognition of persons is sometimes caused by the simple act of lifting a hat or bonnet from the face. Both remembered this fact in their experience, and were, from the causes we have given, prepared to be shocked in some degree.

But, whatever the effect, there was but a moment left for its expression.

The young man saw her golden hair fall down, from its release, upon her neck like a shower of summer sunshine upon a bank of snow—he saw that in breadth and height her head expressed as much of dignity as her face had of gentleness, sentiment, and wit—and then the inexpressible presence of joy and beauty which had charmed and arrested his whole life!—it seemed now to be glorified by the strong light.

The young man had only time to see this in one timid glance, and to meet her downcast eye as it flashed on him for a moment from beneath the drooping lids—and then she turned away hastily.

They knew each other now, and had no more time for, or thought of, bantering that night again: at least Frank Carter supposed this to be so, and that her sudden turning off was caused by the sound of the quick approaching steps of her father.

The gray-haired man entered the room.

"Of course, sir, you are hungry. Child, see that the gentleman has enough of substantial comfort to-night, to make him realize that we do not intend to starve him, after all his fatigue and fasting since the morning."

V   16

"Yes, papa!" and she glided out through an opening beside the fire-place.

"Be seated, sir; our chairs are, as you perceive, constructed after a primitive model. The green raw-hide, stretched upon this frame, when once dried, holds it together like iron—and that, too, without nails."

"Yes," said Frank, as he seated himself, "I have observed that the Southern Indians make great use of the same material; their saddles are constructed in a like manner with your chairs, and are as firm as iron could make them, except under a long soaking in the water. But this is an extraordinary position of yours, so remote from civilization that I am surprised to find even common comforts around you."

"Oh! comforts, in the common sense of civilization, we have none of, but we dare to live here as boldly as men *dream* they can live—that is, amid plenty and without fear."

Frank Carter turned suddenly to look in the face of the man who could pronounce himself one of those who were wild enough to hope so much for the future of humanity.

"What!" said he, earnestly, "are you Utopian, and at your age, too? I thought young poets only had such visions. I should hardly expect to be forgiven, myself, for being guilty of the audacity of supposing that the time might come when every man would have enough to eat, and no one be compelled to wear pistols at his belt."

"What you say of 'pistols at his belt' would be witty enough in New York, but here it is too much an inconvenient necessity to be joked about. For certainly, if a prodigal Nature yields us a profuse abundance, the ingenuity of Colt has guaranteed us, in his revolvers, a secure possession thereof. I can only control the savage herd about me by the terror which the constant presence of this, to them, mysterious and really formidable weapon inspires."

"You seem to have been singularly successful in taming these wild Ishmaelites?"

"Yes! I have been a sort of providence to these you see gathered around me. I found them the forlorn fragment of a tribe that had been cut to pieces in a mortal and desperate feud with their distant neighbours, the Pawnees. I discovered they were remarkable, even among Indians, for their skill in trailing; and, as this is a very useful trait in the life of a frontiersman, I secured them to my service by presents, and have gathered them about me in the double capacity of herdsmen and scouts."

"Do you think they can find my friends, to-morrow?" said Carter, eagerly.

"Not a doubt of it. They can take your trail back from where you dismounted this night, and follow it up through every turn of your wanderings, to-day, to the spot from which you started; and if your friends have been patient or sagacious enough to remain where you left them, we shall find them before sundown."

"You greatly delight and reassure me. But, if I may not be deemed intrusive, what do you propose to accomplish by a settlement so remote as this?"

"Oh! as to that, I propose to accomplish my own purposes, and to be out of the way of curiosity."

"A thousand pardons, sir!" said Carter, flushing up to the roots of his hair. "The question was idly asked. I mistook you for a philosopher, and supposed that your purposes here were beneficent and candid. I hope you will forgive the impertinence."

"Hold up, my young friend!" said the gray-haired man, laughingly. "The question was natural and pertinent enough, without being christened im-pertinent; my position here is sufficiently novel to excite curiosity in any one. I did not mean my answer to apply to you in particular—but merely to express that I came out here to live as I pleased, apart from the insolent comments and saucy prying peculiar to the haunts of men. You evidently have enough of philosophy and a knowledge of the world in you to understand all this, without offence."

"Yes; I hope so. But pardon me, for I did not understand—but"—

Here the young girl came back, bearing the supper on a wooden tray.

Frank Carter was unsentimental enough to rather rejoice in the steams of the fat venison, though in her divinest presence.

She set the food on the table before him, and withdrew without a word.

Soon after a meal, which was enjoyed not the less for the fact that it appeared to have been prepared by *her*, Carter lay down upon a pile of buffalo-robes, at the invitation of his host, and slept, as only men who are profoundly weary can sleep.

When morning came, the first thought of the young man was, after the image of his enchantress, of course, that of purchasing horses and going to the relief of his friends. He rose soon after daybreak, and was promptly joined by his gray-haired host.

"You have horses for sale, sir, I judge, from the general character of your establishment?"

"Oh, yes; plenty of them; come with me, and look at them."

They went out into the fresh morning air, and passing through the picketing by a small gate behind the house, came into the "horse-pen."

Here were fifteen or twenty animals, sleepily leaning against each other.

Frank Carter instantly recognised, among them, the horses that had been carried off in the stampede from his camp, and turned upon his host with an inquiring look of startled astonishment.

The gray-haired man smiled mischievously, and said, with a slight laugh—

"You know those fellows, do you?"

"Yes!" said Carter, haughtily drawing up his person, and flashing his wide open eyes in interrogation, while his hand sought the handle of his pistol. "What den of common robbers or horse-thieves is this I have fallen into?"

"Hold! hold! my impulsive friend! I am not a horse-thief, nor do you understand, from what you see, half of what I have to explain to you."

But our impulsive friend, as the gray-haired man facetiously designated him, was not to be so easily restrained.

The fact, that the horses stolen from him in the morning were here openly exposed in the horse-pen of the rancho of his host, was instantly, in the mind of Frank Carter, associated with what had fallen from him during the conversation of the preceding night, with regard to the uses to which his Indians were applied, with all their remarkable skill in trailing.

Then, too, he remembered the pistols worn inside the fortress-like building—the cautious stepping back as he entered—the care with which the strong door was bolted and barred when he and the young girl had passed in—and now the cool and smiling impudence with which he had been shown into the horse-pen to look upon his own wrong. All combined to flash through the brain of Frank Carter the startling conviction that he had stumbled or been decoyed into the den of an audacious frontier robber, whose *sang froid* was probably proportioned to the sense of absolute impunity in crime which his remote position secured him.

This was a terrible blow to poor Frank! His first impulse was one of fierce indignation—and even a deadly resentment would have been the immediate consequence, but that the image of the singular enchantress of the preceding evening's adventure crossed his brain, from heart-wise, at this moment,

V 2

restraining his quick hand, to pause and listen for an instant.

"The facts speak for themselves—of what possible explanation can they admit? For, if not a robber or horse-thief, what are you?" said he, sternly, with his hand still resting on the handle of his pistol.

"Why," said the gray-haired man, smiling blandly, "I am simply an honest man, so circumstanced and surrounded that I cannot help the occasional dishonesty of those in my employ!"

"Pah! I should think your honesty might find a very effectual mode of protection from such little accidents as this, in not keeping thieves about you. How do you account for the complacency with which you offered me horses for sale as your property, of the mode of acquiring which you knew nothing?"

This was said with such a manner of lofty and insulting scorn, that it seemed as if it should have aroused rage in the breast of a canonized saint. But our acquaintance of the black eyebrows only elevated them with a more benevolent and friendly look than ever.

There was no exaggeration of kindliness or friendliness—not even the shadow of a shade of what might be termed insincerity, much less derision, that could be apparent to an uninterested observer of the acutest discernment, in that look, or in the mild, open smile which accompanied it—yet it aroused to the utmost degree the already angry mood of Frank Carter.

He had been abominably outraged—had expressed with proper emphasis his sense of it—had even assumed an aggressive posture, and yet this insolent bandit, as he now thought him, presumed to smile in the face of his wrathful common sense, or rather of a deep instinct of aversion, which now possessed him entirely.

"Insolent wretch!" said he, furiously, interrupting the

other as he was proceeding in a deprecatory tone of mildness with the explanation he had promised. "You shall not add the personal indignity of a taunt to every other outrage. I have unfortunately partaken of your hospitality, and must for the present hold my hand from chastising you as you deserve." (Here the man laughed derisively, while Frank, with a deepening flush upon his face, continued)—"But, sir, you shall not treat my just anger with levity, for if I have not my horse-whip in reach to scourge you as you deserve, I at least wear my boots conveniently enough for your enlightenment on the spot," and he advanced, as he spoke, into a sort of threatening proximity to the person of the gray-haired man.

The man stepped back with that gliding serpent-like movement, of which we have before spoken. The smile upon his face had not changed a line. It was the same smile, except that suddenly it became a white smile, and a fiercer glitter leaped from out his still eyes, about which his black brows contracted strangely.

Frank Carter did not know fear, but there was something so appallingly deadly and remarkable in the face before him, that he forgot his rage in wonder at the psychological phenomenon, and paused for an instant to stare, dropping his hand to his side.

The man muttered, as if to himself, "The wrong-headed young fool won't listen! He's given me trouble enough already. Ha! he will have it!" and at the same moment whipped a revolver from his belt.

Carter was as quick as he—sprang forward—knocked up his arm, and the weapon exploded into the air. He then closed in, grasping the arm which yet held the still deadly weapon with one hand, while he clutched the throat of his murderous antagonist with the other.

The struggle was a desperate one; for the gray-haired man was stouter and heavier, while the other was more agile.

Several moments of darkened and furious wrestling, which seemed as many centuries to Carter, had elapsed, when the man, one of whose arms was free, snatched one of Frank's own pistols from his belt, and placed it against his side.

Before he could fire the pistol, it was jerked away—the shrill scream of a woman's voice in terror accompanying the act.

Frank released his desperate grasp, and staggered back.

" Father ! father ! In the good God's name, forbear. He is our guest ;" and the young girl threw her arms about him in such a way as to prevent his using the remaining pistol, had he been disposed.

The man of the dark eyebrows did not struggle in this embrace, and passively dropped his pistol. Frank Carter stepped back yet farther, and for the first time turned ashy pale, while he folded his arms across his breast.

The man's face remained still, and seemed shrunken in a white and terrible collapse. The young girl shuddered visibly through all her frame, and, reaching up, kissed his blanched lips.

"Dear papa, do not look so. You always do what you repent of, when your face looks this way."

" Child, be still !" he muttered, in a singularly solemn undertone—" The boy is a heady fool. He will not listen !"

" But, dear papa, will you remember that he is my guest, and pardon him for my sake. He is sacred to us both, whatever he may have done, so long as he is here," and she kissed him again.

" What *could* he have done, papa, to bring you into this dreadful mood we both fear so much ?" and she turned back her head as she clung about her father's neck, towards the marble-like figure of Frank Carter, with a look in which reproach and a wild, eager curiosity were strangely blended—

" What did you do, sir ?"

"Ask him!" said Carter, in a smothered, difficult voice, as if he were choking.

"Dearest papa, tell me. I am sure I can make peace between you." And she renewed her caresses with a sort of clinging, frantic tenderness, that produced its immediate effect—for that singularly shrunken, white expression, rapidly gave way to the glow of life returning to the surface.

She looked up inquiringly into his face. In a moment it had resumed its habitual expression of settled and calm benignity.

"Father, dearest father, all will be right now!" and with a warm kiss, she struggled from his now embracing arms, and turned, with eyes glancing joy, upon Frank Carter, and with a laugh as gay as that which first saluted him, said—

"Come, my chivalric friend, you have no excuse. Tell me what it is that has frozen you so suddenly into such a sombre model of living statuary?"

Frank Carter smiled faintly at first, but the penetrating power of purity had gone out like a subtile aroma from the life of this strange, bright creature, illumining, with a soft light, that of both these persons.

Upon her father, we have seen its effect, or rather, felt it glance like sun's rays into and from the ice. Into the soul of the young man it shot with a keen, living flame that vitalized the now smouldering fires upon that sacred central altar, and sent them blazing up with the old fierceness through vein, muscle, nerve, and sense.

His arms were unfolded as if he had been galvanized—the chill dropped from his person, like accumulated snow from the drooped cedar that had been kissed by the warm sun of spring, and as the freezing burden slided off, his keenest sensations sprang back to the topmost reach of their aspiring, more lithe and vigorous than ever.

He said, laughingly—"Ah, my guardian Sprite! the whole of it is, that there was to me some slight mystery growing out of the peculiar circumstances of your father's life—which, as I did not understand at first glance, I was stupid enough to fly into a passion about. I hope he and yourself may forgive me for my haste—for now I am satisfied of my mistake, and that every thing will prove to be correct!"

In the mean time, the Indians of the rancho had come crowding around the scene, attracted by the ominous sound of the pistol-shot.

The gray-haired man turned to them with an imperious wave of the hand, and spoke a few words in their own language. They dispersed instantly, almost, with a seeming of affright.

"You had better go in, my child; the explanation between this gentleman and. myself can as well be made while you superintend the preparation of our morning's meal."

"Yes, papa; I am so sure that all is understood between you two now, that I go with entire cheerfulness—don't be too long!"

And she bounded away, glancing her bright face back with a beaming look at Frank Carter as she went.

The father watched her until she disappeared, and then turning, said, with a kindly voice—

"Now, young sir, permit me to say, that had you only waited a little for me to proceed, you would have been satisfied."

"Possibly so, sir! But pardon my impatient hastiness, and proceed now."

"You are young—your blood is quick and warm, and therefore you are to be forgiven. I am anxious to satisfy you that you have done me injustice.

"Now look at the probabilities of the case! You think or thought me a robber and horse-thief, because you find the horses stolen from your camp in the horse-pen of my rancho. Pretty strong circumstantial evidence to begin with! Now suppose I should tell you that I knew the horses to be in the pen when I brought you here—that I knew them to be stolen, and suspected they had been stolen from you the moment I heard your story—what would you think?"

"Proceed, sir! I would rather hear you fully, before I hazard an opinion again."

"Discretion comes better late than never, young sir! Now hear how I will unravel all this vexed tangle for you. I spoke to you, last night, of my Indians, and gave you some idea of the uses to which their peculiar modes and habits are applied by me to the necessities of my remote and isolated position here."

"Yes—you spoke of having used them as herdsmen and scouts."

"This is their primary use to me. My daughter, as you are probably by this time aware, is something bold and eccentric, so far as her out-goings and in-comings are concerned. Her life here is companionless, and she seeks and will have, in distant and solitary excursions, at nearly all hours, through the forest and prairies in the neighbourhood, a dreamy fellowship with all the external forms of being presented by the rude nature amid which we live."

Frank Carter stepped forward nearer to the gray-haired man; his form relaxed from the stately rigidity which had heretofore characterized his bearing, and in an instant he seemed like an eager child, listening to some fairy tale. He had entirely forgotten his wrath, his suspicions, and every thing else that was unpleasant now, and asked, with the unconscious simplicity of some boy whose big eyes glistened with curiosity—

"What can she find out there to love, sir?"

The answer was accompanied by a slight inflexion of the presiding smile—

"Oh! she has the faculty of finding things to love, and it is necessary for me to see that her wilful humour is protected on these amatory excursions; I, therefore, send a portion of

my Indian scouts, each day, to make the circuit of the range
usually travelled by her, to see that there are no trails coming in which indicate the approach of dangerous intruders
upon her play-ground. Others are employed to herd my
cattle and horses—others are sent off as hunters, and these
must necessarily have a license with regard to horses, which
I cannot well control—for, since I pay them a certain price
a head, it is impossible for me to tell whether they have stolen
them from a wandering party of Indians or adventurers, as
they always represent to me that they catch them with the
lasso from a drove of mustangs. I can only have my suspicions from the appearance of the horses, as in the case
of"——

"Never mind any further explanation," said Frank, with
eager impatience. "But tell me who are her playfellows,
and what are the objects of her love?"

His tormenter, with a mischievous turning down of the
corners of the mouth, proceeded—

"Oh! she has playmates in plenty, and seems to find things
enough to love,—for, to my certain knowledge, she holds
tryst in the forest every morning, mounted on her favourite
Black Hawk. Do not blanch so quickly, my young friend,
for I think that there has been enough of that between us
this morning."

"Sir!" said Carter, bracing himself up and flushing very
much, "I was not aware that you added a connoisseurship
of complexions to the many accomplishments you have already exhibited. However, it occurs to me, from my recol-
lections of the morning, that this should be rather a sore
subject with you!"

The other went on, without appearing to notice the petulant
bitterness of this speech.

"Yes; I am informed by my scouts, who, among other
duties, are sometimes called to attend her wilful progress,
that she has quite as many love affairs as that old, diabolical

witch, Circe. For instance, she calls upon a favourite to accompany her to tryst, before the sun has risen. Away they go!—perhaps to the deep and heavy forest of the Black Walnut Bottom—the scout following at a respectful distance. In a deep glen, or may be on a sunny knoll, she will pause quickly at the foot of some huge hollow oak, and rapping on its side with her riding-switch, her cautious lover will come timidly forth, whisking"—

"Papa, breakfast is ready!"

"Yes, dear! Come, sir, let us walk in!"

Frank Carter followed, laughing an internal laughter, that made the chambers of his heart to ring again with joyous echoes; yet he could not help biting his lips, too, with petty vexation, for he felt that he had been most gracefully and ingeniously quizzed in the first place, and in the next, that he had been brutally hasty that morning.

It was with a half-abashed look that he seated himself at the rude table.

How was the young man surprised at that meal!

Before his host and himself were placed two large pewter dishes, on one of which steamed venison, and on the other a delicate hump-steak of buffalo; between these was a dish of hommony, as it is prepared by the Indians, out of the unbroken grain of Indian corn, and a plate of nicely-browned cakes, composed of the same grain coarsely pounded.

But what caused his "special wonder" was the character of the food placed before the young girl, who sat opposite to them.

On one side of her was a square, shallow basket, fancifully woven of coloured grasses. This was heaped with a variety of nuts, ready cracked—as the walnut, chestnut, hickory-nut, beach-nut, pecan, etc., with a flavorous representative of the family of acorns in a chincupin peculiar to that region.

On the other side were two smaller baskets of the same shape and material, one heaped with pungent wild herbs,

W

small, ruddy grapes, and plums, fresh with the dew upon them, and the other filled with the white, flower-like grains of parched or "popped" corn.

Our enthusiast stared, and was silent with the mute communings of his surprise and wonder. He now remembered what he had not noticed before, because he was too tired and hungry then—that she had not eaten with him the night before.

He took and tasted mechanically of the food her father placed upon his plate, but he watched her with breathless interest.

He answered, mechanically, the bantering questions of his host, while he watched her. Was that intended merely as a dessert to their breakfast? But the father never offered to help her to the dishes before him, nor did she seem to suppose it at all necessary to invite him or her guest to partake of her simple food.

He watched her! He saw her take the kernels from those delicate nuts nearly whole, with the skill which showed a life-habit, and then she would turn to the young herbs and grapes —new births of the "bedabbled morn"—to freshen her glowing lips with their cool, dewy aromas.

Ah! this seemed so chaste to him.

The wonder in his eyes grew warmer, and he saw, as she placidly ate, what he had not observed before, but only felt, which was the crystalline clearness of her complexion. It seemed as if all the body was a window to the heart—as if you looked down through the perfect symmetries of some large precious gem, wrought out by the spell of some weird sculptor, that glowed of its own beauty in welcome to any curious eye that sought to read that throbbing mystery in its centre.

"Beautiful! beautiful!" thought the young man, while he stammered incoherently, in answer to the father: "Here, at last, I have found life to burn with a pure flame! Here we have no murky smoke arising from fatty fuel, to darken and begrim the chambers of its royal palace! Beautiful! beautiful reality!"

The food of which he was partaking became utterly distasteful now, and he asked her, with a pleading look, almost of reverence, while he drew his chair nearer to her,—"May I not share with you your simple breakfast? You seem to have enough for both." The young girl opened her eyes in astonishment, and pushing her baskets towards him quietly, said—

"Why, sir, you surprise me! How does it happen, that a man from civilization can have any taste for acorns, fruits, nuts, and herbs? Surely, you do not mean to cajole me?"

"No; not cajole, but honour you. You have adopted the regimen of daily life out of that pure and holy instinct which comes straight to us from the fresh Eden of innocent and primitive humanity. There God and his good angels walked with the young children of an infant earth, and partook with them of the fruits that were ruddied by sunbeams and inspired by the stars and the calm moon with keener and milder essences, that constituted the fit nutriment of immortal natures!"

The young girl looked at the speaker as if she thought that he came from a new sphere, and said, with an expression of utter amazement on her face—

"What! you don't think it extraordinary that I should love such natural things? Who but men, that struggle with the ruder exigencies of life, could think of accepting as food any thing else than what drops down from towards heaven, as nuts and fruits do from the trees, like manna in a cloudless rain, which only warns us in the pattering voice of its fall, that it *has come to be eaten!* And then vegetables, herbs, flowers, and all humble plants that are not noxious— they seem to me to look up to us with a wise pleading, supplicating through their eloquent colours and odours that they may rather be absorbed by *me* through either sense, and thus passed up into a life more high, than, being browsed by some coarse brute, to go back to nearly utter nothingness. Every herb we rescue from such a downward fate, every flower whose odours we inhale, becomes as much an angel as we do when we too are absorbed or inhaled by a life as much higher than ours as ours than theirs"—

"Why, I am *afraid* that you, too, are an enthusiast!" said Frank, with a look in which his life seemed shot through his eyes; "but your wise and inspired rhapsody will not satisfy the common mind. Where is the limit you would place and define clearly, between the two extremes of vegetable and meat diet?"

CHAPTER IV.

FANNY AND THE RIDE.

THE final adjustment of the nice question we left at issue between these two young people was deferred by an interruption of a somewhat unique character.

Frank had for some moments heard, without noticing it in particular, amid the novel excitement by which he was filled, that there was a distant cry of hounds in pursuit, which every moment seemed to bring nearer.

At once the cry burst upon the startled group as if inside the picket-court, and coming directly towards them; but now it was commingled with the most terrific yells of curs and Indian papooses, the whoopings of the men, and the shrill screeches of the squaws outside.

The party at the breakfast-table had scarcely time to raise their heads and look with startled inquiry into each other's eyes, when there was a quick clattering sound along the passage from the great door, and at once a fine doe burst into

the room, and with a swift bound cleared the table—which
was in the middle—brushing the hair of Carter with its hoofs,
as it passed over.

The creature had a wreath of flowers, withered, amid ever-
greens, about its neck, and paused for a moment, and shivered
so all over with affright, that you could scarcely see how deep
its pantings were. The doe listened for an instant, with neck
stretched high and wildly-glistening eyes, then lowering its
fine head, ran to its mistress and hid it in her embrace.

In the mean time, the gray-haired man sprang to his feet,
and, assisted by Carter, drove out the fierce, clamorous pack
that were rushing after in pursuit.

The hubbub outside was indescribable; for, between quell-
ing the dogs and quieting the excited Indians of the rancho
—who were crowding with eager curiosity in the passage,
and gathered outside of the great door—the two men had
enough to occupy them for several minutes.

When they turned to go back to the breakfast-room, Frank
Carter, who was in advance, saw distinctly the faces of two
men withdrawn quickly from the partly-opened door at the
end of the passage, of which we have spoken as being opposite to that which led into the breakfast-room. The door was
hastily closed, and he heard the sound of a bolt. Frank was
terribly shocked at this sight. All those suspicions which
led to the ugly scene before breakfast, came back upon him
with redoubled force.

It could be no mistake! There were two faces—one of
them was hairy, and seemed to intimate a cross between the
mastiff and wire-haired Scotch terrier; the other one, which
was thin and fox-like, and white, he did not see so distinctly.
There had been but a moment for him to see, yet that moment
was enough. Frank felt that he should know either face, if
he saw it again anywhere—for they were of distinct types
of character, and could by no possibility be mistaken. Then
he recollected instantly how, as they approached the house

W 2   17

the night before, that end of it into which he had been introduced was lighted, and how, at the noise of their coming,
the lights passed hastily by the dark port-holes of the other
wing, before his host came to the door. He muttered to
himself—

"The men were passing into concealment, then! They
have betrayed themselves, by looking out to ascertain the
cause of the unusual hubbub. As I suspected—a robber's
stronghold! Ah! can it be *she* knows of this?" he groaned,
in the silent agony of his heart's inmost depths.

All this passed with the rapidity of light through the brain
of Frank Carter, for there were a few steps intervening before he reached the door of the breakfast-room ; but with all
the startle and commotion within himself, there was not the
slightest variation in the manner of his gait or tread, which
could indicate that he had perceived any thing unusual; for
he felt sure that sharp eyes were upon him from behind, the
astuteness of which he now swore to baffle, will with will.

He entered, with brows contracted like one suffering the
sharp wrench of a mortal pain. He was unconscious of this,
and that all his face was death-like, as that of a swooning
man, and that curses—bitter curses of *her* were hissing
through his teeth. He paused though, as he entered the
door, irresistibly arrested by the scene.

The young girl had not heard him. She had turned her
seat a little aside from the table, and, in entire forgetfulness
of every thing else, was stooping over her pet doe.

The bright, gentle creature had forgotten its fright already,
and, at the moment Frank entered, was reaching up to caress
the bowed cheek of its mistress with its small tongue, and
breathe on her the sweetly-scented breath of its gratitude
for her protection, and for the fresh herbs she held to it from
her basket. She was speaking quaint words of childlike, soft
endearment to the creature, as if to allay its fright and reassure it of its safety, now that it was with her.

There was too much of touching and unconscious innocence in this scene, not to dissipate even the hideous gloom of the latest shadow suspicion had thrown across the brain of Frank. He moved towards her slightly, to the impulse of a swift joy that sprang forward out of the darkness of his heart to lead him.

Now that the noises outside were somewhat stilled, the creature's fine senses detected the movement, and pricking forward sharply its long and beautifully rounded ears, regarded him with lifted head and glistening stare, while it stamped petulantly with its fine hoofs upon the earthen floor. The young girl, who had a presentiment of the comer, said, as she turned her head slowly, while she still continued to caress the creature—

"You see, sir, my pet is impatient because our love-scene has been interrupted!"

"Sorry to interrupt so pleasant a scene!" said he, in a very low voice, that shook, in spite of him, with a slight tremor.

"Oh, never mind! Fanny and I have plenty of time to make love! Sir, you look unwell! have you been hurt?" and she rose in haste, with a look that glowed in the eagerness of alert sympathy, while her pet bounded forward, lowering its delicate head with a ludicrously threatening shake, as if to frighten back the intruder.

Frank, whose face had not quite recovered from its pallor, now laughed outright. He merely said, in answer to her question, "Oh, nothing—nothing!" and then advanced with playful gesture; but the doe commenced a retrograde movement, still shaking its lowered head at him, until it had backed against the side of the room.

"Take care, sir! she will strike you!" said the young girl, nervously.

"Never mind; I know them!"

As he spoke, the creature struck quickly at him with its

snarp forefoot or hoof, as is their formidable manner of defence. Frank avoided the blow, and before it could be repeated merely touched it slightly on the point of the nose,
and stroked it softly up the face and along the neck.

The creature struck out once more, but not so vehemently
this time ; and now it stood for some moments sullenly, with
head to the ground and hair set forward, and submitted to be
stroked by him.   Then it raised its head gradually, smoothed
its hair, and commenced licking his hand.

"You see, I have conquered your jealous pet?" said he,
turning to the young girl, who was looking on in smiling
wonder.

"Yes; you must carry a spell, for such creatures, in your
touch! Fanny has always been incorrigibly combative towards every one but myself, before.   How did you manage?"

"Oh, easily and naturally enough! Let the magnetism
of the human touch be accompanied by a gentleness that
soothes the blindness of brute impulse long enough for that
powerful illumination to wake their dumb senses, and then
they recognise their God-appointed liege, and submit in humble joy to gambol at his feet.   It is because we have been
their bloody and brutal tyrants, that these simple creatures
fear us.   The wildest and most savage brute can be tamed in
a few hours, by a gentle and wisely graduated application of
this supreme law of love, which is represented by the magnetic power—as it is called—indwelling in the human, who is
the highest earthly type of that God whose essence is love.
This is the secret of all those mysterious spells which men
have pretended to cast upon wild animals.   They must be
controlled by one of the two extremes—fear or love.   Fear
is most usually resorted to, and works morbid wonders, which
sometimes react fearfully upon those who trifle with them.
But the conquest of love is like that of the sun upon the
mute and sheathed seed : it springs forth in joy, and lives to
do worship in its green luxuriance to its conqueror, and

render up the incense of its flowering-time to rejoice his nostrils!''

"This is the spell you have unconsciously exerted upon this creature, and, as I should judge, upon many others as well."

"Quite a profound exposition, that!" said the laughing voice of the gray-haired man, who had been for some moments standing in the doorway, attentively observing the manner and language of Frank. He now came forward, watching the expression of his face with a sharp scrutiny, while he smiled a very pleasant smile.

He had not witnessed the first part of the scene we have described, for he had lingered behind a little while, probably for the purpose of passing into the next apartment.

"I should like to know if you can tame men and women as effectually, by this apostolic ceremony of ' the laying on of hands,' my young friend? For I have a great many rude people about me, of both sexes, who require to be tamed by some stronger spell than any I know of."

"Oh, no," said Frank, looking up from caressing the deer, and meeting that shrewd questioning glance with one of the most entire and smiling unconsciousness. "I know no spells but gold and fear, that will tame the human brute!"

"Sit down, and let us finish breakfast." They drew once more about the table. "You do not compliment the humble human, particularly, as contrasted with your four-footed friends?"

"There is no room for compliment or comparison in the case. Man is the most hideously perverted from his natural instincts, and the human brute is the most remorseless of all. Gold falls faster, flashing down an abyss, than the loose clod of common earth, and requires a stronger hand to draw it up again. We are at present gods to the brute; but our God is out of sight, and acts through the representatives of power he has appointed among us!"

"Ah, my young friend," said the gray-haired man, bending forward with a placid look and a smile of benevolent reproof, "I fear you either sneer captiously, or are strangely infidel for one so young! Does not that love which you spoke of as constituting the representative presence of God in humanity, also imply justice and wisdom? Are these, then, more likely to fail in enlightening the blindness of sense in the highest and purest forms of its organization, than in those which are lower and more gross? Confess, then, that you rather sneered than thought when you spoke?"

Frank flushed a little, and stared in the confusion of blank surprise into the bland face of this extraordinary man. Was the wretch mocking, with the insolent mockery of a devilish intellection, or had all those circumstances, which so strongly aroused his suspicions, been illusory? Could it be he was the mild and gentle philosopher he seemed! "Surely, I must be mistaken, for he is *her* father!" he muttered to himself, and said aloud, with a faint effort at a smile—

"Perhaps you are right, sir, and I spoke with the foolish affectation of an incredulity I did not feel. But you must admit that the two extremes easily occur in contrast. Lucifer fell from heaven—the brute, at the worst, can only tumble down a precipice."

"Yes, but fortunate Lucifer had wings to break his fall," laughed the gray-haired man pleasantly, as he rose from the table. "You two must amuse yourselves as you can, until dinner. I will see to despatching a party of my scouts to the relief of your comrades, sir."

"Ah, I shall go with them," said Frank, rising quickly.

"You can, of course, do as you please, but I assure you there is not the slightest necessity for your going. My Indians will find them more readily without your aid or presence, than with it—you will only embarrass their movements. If you persist in going, let me warn you that to keep up with them will be the most difficult, vexatious, and fatiguing feat of horsemanship that you have ever undertaken. If I might assume the privilege of a host, I would advise that you simply write a few lines to one of your friends, stating where you are, and requesting them to join you. The fact that my Indians will bring their horses back to them, will be a sufficient guaranty of honest intention on their part. I engage they will accept such guidance without hesitation, and will probably reach here by to-morrow night. In the mean time, my daughter will cheerfully undertake to amuse you by showing you the country around, and introducing you to those mysterious lovers of hers. If you tire of this, we will get up a grand hunt to-morrow, and give you a practical illustration of the uses of my Indians."

During this frank and hospitable speech, Carter was walking hurriedly up and down the room. His brain was in a confused whirl of uncertainty. "How much was this strange man to be trusted? How much real cause for the vague, but almost shuddering aversion and distrust he felt for him, was there in the circumstances thus far? Was he doing justice to his comrades in permitting them to come here—even inviting them into the midst of such suspicious surroundings? But then he remembered their revolvers, their devotion to him, and their personal prowess. With them ever at his side, if this place proved to be what he had some reason to suspect, he could and would at once destroy the den. But suppose this man does not intend they shall ever reach here! A sure ambush might be an easy thing! But then, if I went, I should most assuredly come back. I feel that the game of my life must be played here. The time has come at last! I will not give up this young girl until I understand more of all this, and of her, though I die for it. This man, if he be a villain, is an astonishing one, and I like to study such characters; it excites and charms me to play around the viper's coil, and then baffle its spring. As yet this man confounds me. He invites all my friends to his rancho, in the face of ω most hostile avowal of my suspicions. This does not look like guilt or fear. One of two things is sure—he is acting with the most direct and straightforward honesty, or with the most diabolical purpose. Pshaw! I am here alone—if he had any foul designs, what interest could he have in slaughtering my friends? They could never find him or me, of course. He has all our horses—what more can he want? I have been made childish by this singular instinct of aversion and distrust which has possessed me since I first met this man's eye! The course he advises is entirely sensible; and then that reproof he gave me at table just now!—oh, I have done the man injustice! I don't care for the mystery of the two faces that shocked me so. He is *her* father!—*nevertheless I will warn Clenny to be on his guard!*" He looked up.

While this vehement struggle—which we have endeavoured to furnish some idea of in expression—had been passing swiftly through his mind, the gray-haired man had ceased to speak, and stood regarding his restless and abstracted movements for a moment with a curious smile.

Frank saw it, and said promptly—

"You are right, sir. I shall do as you advise. I perceive that you are amused at the degree of uncertainty as to the proper course for me to pursue, apparent in my manner; but you must remember, sir, that the tie of companionship in danger is a very sacred one; and I could not but feel that my less fortunate comrades would have good reason to consider me selfish in remaining here, surrounded by comforts, while I merely send to them a troop of half-naked Indian scouts, with orders to escort them to me! I need not remind you that such a course would hardly be in the spirit of good-fellowship demanded by such relations—this was the cause of my doubts. But I am now convinced that my going will probably do them more harm than good, as you suggested. I will have the note ready by the time your scouts are mounted You have writing materials?"

"My daughter will furnish you. I understand and respect your feeling, which was a very natural and proper one. My fellows will be ready for you in a little while."

He passed out, while the young girl sprang up, followed by Fanny, and passed through the small door we have before mentioned as near the fireplace.

She was gone for a moment or two, and returned with a small rose-wood *escretoire*, which she placed before Frank. The presence of this elegant article in so rude a place, tended not a little to heighten the curiosity with which he had continued occasionally, during the morning, to regard that narrow door through which he had first seen her bright form disappear.

Every thing about this little article was feminine and delicate—there was to his sense even an indescribable fragrance which it seemed to have brought along with it, and he forgot to finish his note while his erratic fancy wandered through that door to breathe the air made fragrant by her dreams, or conjure many a graceful object, the creation of her own fresh taste and daring humours, or hallowed by the caressing of her touch.

She noticed his abstraction, and with a joyous laugh, exclaimed—

"What ho!—out of the land of shadows, there!—my father will want your note in a few minutes."

"Yes, yes—I will be ready in a minute;" and he wrote on eagerly, bending low over the paper to conceal the flush upon his face.

They soon after went out to the great gate of the rancho, to see the Indian scouts set off. They seemed to be a sort of transition race, occupying a middle ground between the characteristics of the two great races north and south of the Missouri.

In a word, there was an insolent look of savage and cunning ferocity about them, the formidable character of which

X

was not a little increased by the superior finish of their
weapons and the assured ease and familiarity with which
they handled them.

They numbered eight warriors. When Frank handed his
note to the leader of the party, the fellow, whose complexion
was much fairer than that of his followers, smiled cunningly,
and by a significant gesture betrayed the "itching palm."

Frank threw him a dollar, and with a broad, obsequious
grin and cringing bow he darted away, followed by his warriors.

"That fellow has all the vices of a mongrel, if he be not
one," said Frank, as they turned back to enter the rancho.

"Yes!" said the young girl, somewhat hastily. "He is a
half-breed, and father thinks him faithful!"

"Of what tribe are these ruffians?"

"I believe they are an off-shoot of the Kansas. My
father never explained to me particularly; and as I am not
very curious about such matters, I cannot tell you more than
this. But shall we not ride this morning? I hear the impatient stamp of Black Hawk, and no doubt Celeste is by
this time thoroughly refreshed. Papa has left us with the
day before us, to make it out between ourselves as best we
may!"

"Let us ride, certainly!" said Frank, with eagerness.

She called an Indian and gave the necessary orders. In
a short time the horses were equipped, when they mounted,
and were off in a brisk, emulous gallop, the fine animals they
rode neighing their joy upon the morning, and looking out
from the skirting forest towards the wide prairie, with ears
pricked forward and eagerly, as if they meant to take wing
and fly across its green and flowering expanse.

Their riders, too, seemed quite elate enough to enjoy such
a proceeding wonderfully—perhaps with the proviso that
they and their horses should keep together in the flight.

The riders were long silent. Frank was too full to speak.

He could not see the forest, the prairie with its multitudinous flowers—the white fantastic islands sailing through the blue and shoreless sea—the blessed sun that smiled a benediction over all!

There was but for him one light, and *she* was its source! The glory of the outward world was felt—not seen—for he was looking upon her as she rode by his side with downcast, averted eyes, and face that glowed consciously beneath his gaze.

What a marvellous being she seemed to him! It was as if the fluent summer had been wooed to stay and curl its yellow warmth all peacefully in clinging play about the young roses of the fresh-cheeked April—for her prodigal hair shook such perfume off to the rude breeze that he felt the flowering time of all the year had now come together in his life.

She rode with loose reins, as if her beautiful horse moved of her permission. She seemed as reposeful and abstracted as though she saw through his eyes and guided his movements by an unconscious exercise of will.

Frank thought, if she had only willed that her black steed should

> "Paw up the light,
> And do strange deeds upon the clouds!"

—that forthwith he would have climbed the beams—and, poor fellow!—blessed himself that no such freak happened to possess her for the time—since, left alone, he would have felt unutterably desolate.

He broke the silence at last.

"But—I thought you were to introduce me to your wilderness friends? What are they?—'of what substance are they made?' I am beginning to be quite jealous!"

At this moment both their horses shyed, quite violently, and on looking round, they saw Fanny—with all the withered flowers torn from out the wreath upon her neck—coming in long leaps close after them—with tail drooped, as if she had

been shot, and shaking her lowered head with every bound,
as if in rage at her desertion!

They reined up, and she came alongside her mistress.
The first petulant movement was to strike viciously at Black
Hawk, as if he were responsible for carrying off her mistress.

The horse seemed to be familiar with such demonstrations,
and merely jerked up his leg to avoid the blow, and then
with ears playfully laid back, turned to bite at his assailant.
Fanny dodged him as if it were an old play between them—
and then she rose—as if on the leap, to caress with her
tongue the hand of her mistress.

" You see my pretty Fanny has come to guide us—come!
The jealous witch has found out all my secrets—and as she
made peace with you, maybe she will condescend to be our
guide !"

Fanny now went frisking and anticking before them—
pausing now and then to look behind, as if to invite them to
follow.

" Come !" said the young girl, starting into a swift gallop.
—" We will follow Fanny, and see my people of the wilderness."

CHAPTER V.

THE RIDE.

AWAY! away over the bending grass of the prairie these
two young riders sped, with a swiftness that caused their
nerves to tingle, and made the great beds of sunflowers, over
which they trampled, to run together as though a swift stream
of molten gold went by on either hand—while Fanny, whom
their speed had overtaken, seemed, as she gambolled by the
side of her mistress, a strange dolphin sporting on a wave as
strange !

Even the gentle breeze they met was roused by their wild
speed, and went roaring in a gale of rollicking laughter past
their ears—while, as for their exulting horses!—

"Through mane and tail the high wind sighs,
Fanning the hairs, which wave like feathered wings!"

Away! away! with their hearts on fire, their blood bounds
faster than fleet-footed steeds can go. They do not look
upon each other now. They touch occasionally, and one
sphere encircles them. They feel that if they pause, their
hearts will pale to ashes in that fierce, consuming flame—
that they must on! and shake off the keen ardour that has
gathered there, through motion, outwardly upon the cool wind,
that it may go to warm the soul of nature, and relieve them
of a present death of too much joy.

On! on they go! The yellow flowers have been passed,
and now they come to great beds of the pink sweet-william;
and the swift stream on either hand grows paler suddenly
with a delicate flush, till they seem to be careering down
some roseate river, rippling through the gates of dawn.

On! on! The pink flowers have been passed, and now
come great beds of blue; and the swift stream on either hand
seem like a liquid sky fallen in, with here and there a fleecy
flake of cloud-foam on it, where some white flower swings its
delicate plume along the wave.

But then this mad motion cannot last for ever. For several
miles they had thus gone, when the cool winds and the calm
of the blessed sun drew forth the burning fever of that overcoming ecstasy from their throbbing brains; and now their
pulses could gradually subside to the full but slower beat of
a less tempestuous happiness.

They reined up their reeking horses to a gentle canter;
and then the subtle and more soothing influence of the scene
through which they passed had time to interpenetrate their
beings, and they were hushed in voiceless awe!

X 2

These wonderful prairies!—How gorgeously strange they seemed to them through their love-illumined senses!

Even to their accustomed eyes, they still were a wonder and a miracle—for they combine many of the most picturesque characteristics of both the ocean and the sky.

Here it lay skirted in the vast circumference of a sky-bounded sea, while the stilled undulations rise and dip with the regular sweep of waves. Had the shadow of God's presence passed upon the waters just while they rose and fell in the long swells after a storm, and they had grown afraid, and paused, to wait through all time for his mandate of release—then would that enchanted sea have been like the prairie.

And then, if on the green, glassy mirror of those quiet billows the gorgeous sunset of a day of summer storms threw down the glorious reflex of its cloud-capped splendours, they might see in it the flowering robes the grand prairie wears.

And then all the living creatures that they see upon it—each one, whether deer, mustang, or tall white crane, standing so still as they approach—amid the solemn silence of that primeval solitude—

"As idle as a painted ship
Upon a painted ocean!"

that when one moves it makes them start to see it, as if that were a kind of miracle.

The only sounds they hear are the loud, sweet thrill of the yellow meadow-lark, which, bounding from the grass before them, turns its head as it goes off, to show them the black shield on its breast, and leaves a sigh of timid music, like a perfume, behind it, on their ears.

Or else the little grass-sparrow, with a shrill, affrighted chirp, darts from near their very feet, and dips quickly into covert again. Or when they approach too near the tall, stately cranes, and they begin to stalk majestically to and fro with ludicrous gesticulations of their long, shifting necks

—their hoarse, sudden croak will strike thumping on their ears, like a pistol shot at midnight.

Scattered motts of timber begin to loom upon the blue distance, like islands in the sea. They approach them more slowly. Soon, from banks of haze, they become more distinct; and first the outlines of tree-tops, and then that of each trunk, is clearly defined.

"Come!" said the young girl, breaking the silence at last, as she urged Black Hawk to a renewal of his speed. "Here are some of my wilderness loves, in this little valley."

As she spoke, they commenced descending a gentle slope from the prairie level, the sides of which were covered with a scattering growth of noble oaks. A stream, narrow and glistening with the speed it made, held its way down the centre of the valley, and lit the dark trunks and foliage above with the golden shimmer thrown up by its ripples.

Here the grass seemed greener than elsewhere, for the tint was fresher; and as they passed down below the general level, the roar of the opposing breeze ceased upon their ears, and it was as if they had come suddenly upon the pulseless, sleepy silence of the fenced valley of the Lotus Eatus!

Before Carter could realize how strange this transition was, the young girl had bounded from her horse, throwing the reins upon his neck, and turned to him with a flushed cheek and joyous laugh—

"Dismount, sir! if you would see and know my Lilliputian people!"

Carter had already obeyed, and was approaching her hastily, when she stooped forward, spreading out her arms as if to protect something which he was crushing beneath his tread, and exclaimed, in a voice of tender entreaty—

"Oh! beware, sir! Step more carefully! See! see my gentle flowers."

Frank paused and looked down for the first time, since all

his eyes had been for her.   He saw that the sod about him was enameled with small flowers of the most rarely delicate forms, and of colours as various as they were strange.

He paused, in blank astonishment!   He had never seen any thing so chastely beautiful!

She laughed merrily—

"Oh, you need not look so wild, sir!   I have done no work of enchantment here!   Spring tarries in this sheltered valley nearly all the year—and spring, you know, possesses a refining necromancy.   All flowers that I bring here become gentle people, soon!"

"Ah!" said Frank, with an impulse of tenderness he could not resist, "there need be no idealization to account for all, since the imbodied Spring is here!—But how have you managed to bring together so many curious and delicate flowers upon this remote spot?   I am puzzled!—the groups seem too rich for unassisted nature, and yet they follow her order perfectly!   What is it you have done, and how have you done it?"

"Nothing wonderful!" said she, with a mischievous twinkle in her eye.   "Nothing, at least, which entitles me to assert myself to be an imbodiment of Spring.   The greater number of the flowers you see clustered along this slope down to the water's edge, are the growth of this valley.   Here, the grass is finer, the soil more loose and better irrigated, and the protection from the wind is perfect.   The shade of these few scattering trees is just sufficient to preserve the cool, spring temperature.   Here, therefore, all the most delicate flowers grow best and flourish longest; and wherever I have found them, during my rides, I have taken them up carefully, to be transplanted to this natural garden."

"But do you not cultivate them?—I see no evidence that you have done so."

"It is not what you would call cultivation, in the cities. I merely observe carefully the location, the character of the soil and surroundings in which I find them originally; and when the time for transfer comes, I bring each flower here, and place it, as nearly as I can remember, in a similar location and amid like surroundings. I then pluck away the grass and weeds from immediately about it, that it may have a fair chance for a start; after that it must take care of itself—and usually does."

"I see you have none of those prairie-flowers here, through such enormous beds of which we galloped so ruthlessly, on our way here?"

"Oh, no! I have no use for such coarse flowers, in those vast and firmly matted beds; presenting, with but little variation, a single colour at a time. They suit well to the extent and grandeur of the scene they are intended to diversify. They are like those singular changes in the colour of the water of the ocean, with the indications of which mariners are so familiar; but they are all alike—the individuality of each is lost and merged in the general effect!"

"Ah! I see!" said Frank, eagerly. "The great sea-like plain of the prairie furnishes, in its broad contrasts and garish tints, a rude type of earth's epic or heroic poetry, in colours; while, in this sheltered nook, where each of the elements is tempered as the wind to the shorn lamb, and all

> '—— the blest infusions
> That dwell in vegatives, metals, stones,'

co-operate harmoniously with them—the higher forms of this poetry are produced in more delicate shapes, and far intenser, more varied and glorious colours. It is much like the contrast of the vague splendours of Milton's great epic, with the chisseled, gem-like, and exquisite perfection of particular beauties of the Mask of Comus, and others of his minor poems."

She bent with a fond, caressing gesture, over a strange, frail little flower, the three petals of which were shaped like
18

the wings of a small butterfly—but were of such a new, peculiar, and unearthly tint of blue, that it seemed as if, in fluttering down from heaven, it must have brushed the colour off from farthest space!—it looked so unfamiliar and so unlike all other tints we know.

"Yes; it would seem quite as sacrilegious to me, to hear this rare, blue stranger—which is born only beneath the most beneficent smiles of God—profaned by the association of a vulgar name, as to find the common metre ballad-mongers aiming at the glowing, chaste, yet infinite simplicity of such an image as—

> 'The holy dew—'tis like a pearl
> Dropt from the opening eyelids of the morn
> Upon the bashful rose!'

Milton said that; and in doing so, conveyed an image to my mind that comes, whenever memory brings it up, with scarcely less of the recurring charm of strangeness, than does the presence of this wonderful little flower!"

"They are very like—with the distinction that one is the creation of God, and the other of a godlike humanity. But I suppose you have the type, in colours and in odours, of many a rare thought of highest poetry?"

"Surely; for nature's inspiration is more sure than that of any madman of them all, with 'eyes in fine frenzy rolling.' These creatures are my mute familiars, and I have always thought they seemed to know me when I came. These are my gentle nurslings of the wilderness."

"But you are far from home, here. I wonder at your audacity!"

"It must be a fleet and wary foe that can surprise me, with two such quick-sensed watchers as Black Hawk and Fanny. They run to me instantly, on the slightest indication of the approach of any thing that has danger in it, and leaping with one bound into the saddle, I am safe,—for Black Hawk can defy in speed all the marauders, of whatever colour. from whom I am in danger out here. See; I will show you!"

She gave a shrill whistle, by placing her two fingers in her mouth, and the noble horse, who was feeding a hundred paces off, with his head half-buried in the tall grass, wheeled instantly and dashed to her side, with the last tuft he had plucked still in his mouth. She placed her hand .on the saddle-bow and sprang quickly into the seat.

Frank called Celeste, who came, though not quite so quickly: and away they went once more. Fanny looked after them a moment, then shook her head, and, with a gay frisk, followed.

They followed down the valley, which led them through the open grove, amid a maze of timber-islands. Through these they soon came to a vast and magnificent old forest—like an English park—with a cheerful greensward underneath, and the mighty trees standing far apart.

Now, his strange guide seemed to have almost forgotten poor Frank, who became jealous. Here a bird's nest had to be visited, the winged people of which seemed half a mind not to be frightened; she would look into it, without touching, then drop some food near, and gallop on. Then she made Frank pause in sight of a great old oak. She rode up to it alone, and, tapping on it with her switch right sharply, she waited some moments for her summons to be obeyed. Soon, to his infinite amazement and delight, Frank saw a small head put forth from a round hole some distance up the trunk: a gray squirrel came forth cautiously, and, with widespread tail, making a low chattering sound, commenced descending towards her white, outstretched hand.

Soon came another forth, which was smaller, and seemed to be a young one. Others followed, until there were four of them upon the trunk, beside the old one. These were more timid, and did not come down quite to her hand; but the mother did, and, snatching from it a small ear of pop-corn,

darted up the trunk again, and disappeared in the bole, followed by her young.

She laughed gayly, and turning towards Frank said, as she
joined him—

"You see, sir, that you are a formidable person, for my timid
Bunny would not stay to be caressed as usual, for her quick
senses had perceived that there was a stranger near.   I called
to her—Bunny! Bunny!—without avail, for she had caught
a glimpse of you, and would not stay to thank me."

"But how, in the name of all miracles and wonders, have
you managed to tame this wild creature so?"

"Oh! naturally enough!   Bunny was an old pet of mine,
and lived in my room with me for two years; and then I took
a fancy to bring her out here into the neighbourhood of my
flowers!   I found that old oak without any tenants in its
chambers, and I brought her here, leaving a sufficient supply
of food at the foot of the tree to last her for some days, until
she became accustomed to the new circumstances, and learned
to provide for herself.   She took possession of the tree, and,
as I came to visit her every day, our friendship has never
fallen through!

"I have almost made a conquest, too, of the wild lover she
has found out here: and shall certainly make friends with
her little folks—one of which frequently comes down to eat
from my hand.   So you see, sir, I am not quite a witch,
after all!"

"I do not know that I am any the less convinced of that,
now!" said Frank, with a meaning smile.

They rode on slowly through the forest.   She had a thousand things to show him, for her sharp observation and solitary wanderings had made her quite as familiar with the
homes and habits of the creatures of that forest, as if it had
been a city of humanity, in exploring the haunts and characters of which, her life had been spent.

Now, she would tell him of some peculiar shrub or tree,

remarkable for beauty or for rareness, and then she would dart away to lead him to see it with her.

Then Frank would murmur in her ear—

" Confess that my suspicions are well grounded; repeat, now, the confessional after me :—

'I am the power
Of this fair wood; to live in open bower,
To nurse the saplings tall, and curl the grove
With ringlets quaint and wanton windings,
And all my plants to save from nightly ill
Of noisome winds and blasting vapours chill;
And from the boughs brush off the evil dew,
And heal the harms of thwarting thunder blue;
Or, what the cross, dire-looking planet smites,
Or hurtful worm, with canker'd venom, bites!' "

"Pshaw! pshaw! You are even more sadly beset than the lost lady in the enchanted wood; for, though I found you lost—a gloomy wanderer, and have been doing all since that I could to open your eyes to the real world about you, still you will hear the 'airy tongues.' "

"No; you cannot dodge my implication so—for what is your mission now, but to

'Number your ranks, and visit every sprout
With puissant words and murmurs, made to bless!'—

Answer me this?"

" Oh, never mind! Come on !" and away she would lead again, to show him the fox's den; and when they came near it, she would rein up, and approach with a slow, cautious tread, and point out to him the young cubs gambolling in the sun before a hole which had been dug beneath the upturned roots of some huge forest Titan, that had been thrown in wrestling with the storm.

When they took the alarm, and hurried in, she was off again with a merry laugh.

Now, she would stop her horse suddenly beside the decaying stump of a small tree, into which the woodpeckers had hollowed for themselves a chamber once upon a time; but now, when she touched it, a flying-squirrel would rush out, with its large and meek black eyes glistening in affright, and from the top would dart away, with its rich-furred membrane spread like wings—all white beneath—and sail to some neighbouring trunk.

Then she would take the soft young ones from their warm bed and caress them tenderly, and show Frank their bright, gentle eyes, and talk to them in a quaint, rippling tongue, which she seemed to have learned from the waters, the winds, and the trees.

They were placed back all gingerly and snug again, and some food left for the mother, which Frank now, for the first time, observed was taken from a pouch which she carried at her saddle-bow.

Now they were off again, for she had always some new pet or wonder that he must see; and so the day went swiftly by.

The dinner was forgotten by them both, for they were too happy to think of eating.

As the evening came on, the character of the forest they were travelling became changed. From the open glades, which it seemed as if the most careful cultivation could not have improved, they had gradually come into a more rank and denser growth.

Frank had an idea that they had been skirting the edge of the great prairie round towards the rancho again, and were entering the dense and formidable forest of the Black Walnut Bottom, concerning which we have already heard something. They had been happy all day—too happy for words to tell! Like unheeding children, they had gone out to play, and through hours had gambolled on the lap of Nature—that ancient mother, who yet is ever young.

They had rather felt each other, and been meekly joyous, as they went side by side, than talked much, except in a fragmentary way. This was too much happiness. It could not be real! There must be some wild delusion here! He had struggled so forlornly all his life with that ever present yet treacherous *Shadow of the Ideal*, that he could not realize this the embodied Real found at last.

The reaction of the bewildering joy—the glorified beatitude of all that day—was now distrust. Every thing he had yet found to lavish the garnered tenderness of his whole life upon, had somehow played him false!

Could it be that this was any higher, purer than the rest? Certainly he had never met a being that seemed to nestle with such sublime faith right close to the heart of Nature, where her pulses might be felt to guide a life by—but yet! but yet! there was too much joy in all this for him to realize at once!

There were dark suspicions gathered around the life of this fair young creature. Her father was a wonderfully acute, and, may be, bad man. She evidently loved him with an entire devotion. It might be, if this gray-haired man was vicious—as he instinctively felt him to be—that he still had enough of sacredness left in him to guard *her* from a knowledge of his vices and his crimes, and felt that he pro-pitiated Heaven in permitting her to live, in unconscious ignorance of all this, happily with Nature.

With such gloomy and distrustful thoughts as these, the life of Frank Carter had been hushed for some time, and his brows grown unconsciously contracted. The shadow, too, had fallen on the girl, and she rode mutely by his side, in timid consciousness ; but what it meant she knew not. That she was all at once unhappy, she knew.

They were penetrating more deeply into the sombre forest, and the lengthened shadows, as they fell across his form, seemed to darken his heart yet more.

But there was *that* in this primitive Nature, wearing her century-calms upon her front, which could not fail to over-

come him with a spell—to sink a nameless awe into his being
—brooding in shadowy peace upon the tumult of excitement
the passions had been subjected to during the late incidents.

Nowhere does this invisible power make itself so palpably
felt as in the deep-tangled aisles of an old Southern forest;
when the sun is near setting, too, as it was then, and strikes
its levelled rays square athwart the gloom, glorifying in lines
and angles the stout, rugged boles and gnarled arms over-
head, leaving the severed shades sharply defined beneath and
between the sheeted gold.

High up, sitting in the halo, the roseate-headed Caracara
eagle screams to its mate—the black-squirrel sputters and
barks, whisking its dusky brush, and saucily stamping on the
pecan bark—the long whoo-oose of the bull-bat sighs hoarsely
through the air—the paroquet, with its shrill, waspish chattering, in a glimmer of lit emeralds, goes by—the far tocsin
tolled from out the swamp-lake by the wood-ibis, or dropped
smiting suddenly from the clouds, as the great snowy crane
sails over—the low, quavering wail of the dotted ocelot—the
hack-hack, and quick, prolonged rattle of the ivory-billed
woodpecker's hammer—the smothered shriek of the prowling
wild-cat, impatient for the night—the chirr! chirr! of the
active little creeper—the cracked gong of the distant bittern
—these were the sights and sounds that gradually lulled and
charmed him into utter abstraction—and of course into entire
forgetfulness of every other purpose and object than the
passion in his heart, and the being at his side who had thus
led him in reach of their enchantment.

His heedless pace had gradually slackened—for the mood
of dreams was on him. The unpleasant realities of the wild,
unnatural life he had been leading disappeared, and in delicious revelations the ideal life of calm and holy peace came
around him; and in the hushed quiet of that lull, the bewildered fancy danced with its own airy creatures to the merry
click of the castanet a bright-eyed woodchuck was sounding,

as it sat familiarly on the other end of a log by which they paused.

Doubts, anger, suffering, suspicions, all were as things that had been and were not, while his heart was made blissful of its latest memories amid these evening choristers!

Now his trance was broken, and he turned to her with a bright, meaning look, and her life answered to the summons joyously, for she knew that his spirit had struggled into freedom now.

During the hour's gallop which it required to reach home, they rode with clasped hands, without speaking a word. When they reached the rancho, the young girl found that her father was not at home; and, with a bewitching air of confidence, invited the young man to pass with her that narrow door beside the fireplace, which he had regarded with such curious envy.

Here he found every thing as pure as he had dreamed it should be in the penetralia of such a life.

There were many books, a harp, and a guitar. The rude walls were hung about with quaint, but wild and graceful ornaments. Beside these, *her* ingenious fingers had plaited of flowers inwreathed with coloured quills and natural grasses, there were paintings, in water-colours, of scenes and faces which indicated the highest order of talent.

After the evening meal, she sang to him many songs, with the accompaniment of one or the other instrument. Most of these airs were old familiar friends to him; but many of them seemed to be improvised, as if she had caught the strathspey that the wild winds make when they go echoing amid cliffs, whispering through the deep, mysterious woods, or moaning off through vast prairies into silence!

Frank went to bed that night, and could not tell, for a long time, whether it was that he dreamed or was afloat upon a strange, gleaming sea, that lulled him on its waves of light, as they rocked to and fro harmoniously. It was enough that,

Y 2

sleeping or waking, the cup of joy was filled up for him, until even with

"Beaded bubbles winking at the brim."

The next day was much a repetition of the last, so far as these young people were willing actors.

There had been no word of love spoken between them, and why was this necessary? They felt each other, saw each other, heard each other, lived through each other, and what more?

It seemed to Frank as if the sun was bright because her cheek was to shine upon, and he grew savagely jealous of

"The common-kissing Titan."

The earth rejoiced because of her, and the birds sang to do her praise!

They went forth again to visit the sweet valley of wild flowers, to see the squirrels, and many another wild thing that she knew and loved.

As they skirted the forest, on their return, they saw a long-winged hawk swoop from the clouds and disappear in the deep grass of the prairie. In a moment, it came flapping heavily up again, bearing a hare in its claws. The creature cried out, as it was borne up, with that plaintive, melancholy wail peculiar to the species when captured and in pain.

It was quite close to them that it had been struck; for the hawk had, as is their custom on the prairies, been poised for some time above the heads of the riders, watching to strike whatever small game they should scare up in their progress.

The wail of the poor creature was so touching, that they urged their horses forward with one impulse, in the hope to rescue it. They did not succeed, but were close enough to see the bright, inexorable eye of the winged marauder.

Frank raised his gun, and was about to fire, when she touched his arm.

"No, no! do not shoot—let him go!" He lowered his

gun, and turned to her in surprise, which was heightened when
he saw that tears were streaming from her eyes.

"Why not shoot? You are weeping for the poor hare!"

"Yes; because its plaintive cry was eloquent to me, for
help and mercy! Yet to the hawk, that same cry was only
an appetizer, whetting the raven in its maw! The hawk was
hungry, and the hare must die!"

"But suppose I was hungry; should the hare die then?"
And Frank gazed into her face with curious eagerness.

"Yes; surely! if there was absolutely nothing else for
you to eat. I do not reason—I only feel! But it seems to
me, that even if you seized the hare with the clutch of famish-
ing eagerness, you would feel that such a piteous moan as we
just heard, would move you to weep before you could devour
the creature with flesh and blood so like your own!"

"Thank you! thank you a thousand times!" said Frank,
joyously. "Your beautiful instincts clearly confirm my own
theory. You feel a profound truth, without reasoning upon
it. The power of articulating sound—which is, of course,
the most perfect mode of conveying sensation—constitutes
the dividing line between a monstrous cannibalism and a legitimate diet. Man is the highest type of the Divine—the most
immediate representative of God upon the earth. All articu-
lated sounds are significant to him; and, wherever the power
of producing these sounds exists, it evidently places the creature in intelligent communion with its loyal liege—for it
enables it to appeal to him for mercy, for protection, and for
help! It is well enough for hawks, wild-cats, and all other
creatures, who are, on the ascending scale, merely birds and
beasts of prey, to be dumb to this sort of appeal; but for us,
who should be angels unto them, with a compelling splendour
on our brows—who walk among them with a higher sense,
and know the mournful language of their agony, to devour
them, groans, shrieks, yells, moans, red blood, and all, is one
of the worst forms of cannibalism! You will observe that it

is only the red-blooded animals which are capable of producing sounds the meaning of which our senses can comprehend. The evening song of the mocking-bird teems with inspiration, and is a joy and a glory to us, while that of the katydid contains about as much, significant of the desires and passions of the creature itself, as the rasping sound of two dry sticks rubbed together."

So the day passed, while they looked love, but discoursed of curious truths. They reached the rancho about dark, and found there all the bustle and confusion which indicated a new arrival.

There were many horses grouped outside the picketing, and the Indians of the rancho were busy in hospitable cares among them.

"Ha! they have come!" said Frank, eagerly springing to the ground. He almost forgot to offer his hand to assist the young girl in dismounting, so full was he of joy. But she saved him the trouble, and led the way over the picketing.

He found all his friends in the room where he had first been received. Then congratulations were warmly exchanged, and he even embraced Clenny in his rapture. The gray-haired man was there, and formally presented his daughter to *Mr.* Clenny.

Frank was not so far blinded by his happiness that he failed to observe how pale she turned, as she recognised his friend most formally, after an involuntary start, either when she heard his name, or saw his features fully, he could not tell which. But he remembered the fact for many a day after.

She continued to be pale, abstracted, and constrained during the remainder of the evening, and Frank was greatly troubled. It was a relief to him when their host proposed they should retire to sleep.

Frank noticed, too—for his watchful eye let nothing pass —that although himself and the four men were invited to sleep upon the floor of the same room, still his friend Clenny was invited to sleep elsewhere—perhaps in that mysterious room—a vision through the half-open door of which had already cost him so much of pain.

That night, when Carter was fast enough asleep, dreaming of love and joy, four men were awake—wide awake, in that mysterious chamber, plotting of many things which would not have quite comported with the tenor of his dreams.

There were three pallets of buffalo-robes upon the floor of this room, and when the gray-haired man entered, bearing a shaded lamp in his hand, the three men sprang to their feet as they had lain down, fully dressed, and with their arms about them.

He set the lamp down on the small, rude table, and they gathered about it.

"What the d——l is the meaning, my honoured uncle Cedric, of this last most inconvenient and most ridiculous stratagem of yours—the stampede of all the horses belonging to our party? You left me in a nice position, sucking my thumbs like a bear or a zaney."

"Pshaw! Newnon, do not be impertinent. You know that my scheme was well devised. You should have known the topography of the country better than to have permitted him to come this way. My spies told me that your general course would bring you directly into this neighbourhood. This was to be prevented. I did not wish him to see Freta, and you were likely to cross her eccentric track any moment. My Indians carried off your horses, but that cursed Celeste broke away and went back, only to bring about the very meeting that I dreaded. They met in the woods, and she brought him here. I knew the youngster at a glance, though I wondered utterly how you could have let him go. I found him to be just the fiery, impracticable fool you had represented; for when he saw the horses of your party in my horse-pen, the next morning, he was so savagely indignant and insulting, that he raised the devil *even in me!* Freta interposed in time to prevent my getting rid of the troublesome yonker. I had one of my white fits on me, which, as you know, do not often occur for nothing!—but when the girl interposed, a new idea flashed upon me. I saw that he was already in love, and I determined to encourage the thing to the utmost."

"Why did you not have him shot at once?" said Clenny, with a spasmodic gesture.

"Keep cool, my gentle Newnon," said Cedric, with a sneering smile.

"I see clearly how we are to manage this incorrigible youth, without the necessity of resorting to any such extremities. We have only to disgust him with his ideal here, and he will go back to Myra Haynes again! So you need not grow any whiter, if you can help it. This child you seem to have cultivated an insane passion for since her infancy, is quite as astute as you. She is only to be won through her intellect. I have given her sympathies the proper direction to insure this. This boy cannot touch her life, for she has learned to love and expend her overflowing sentiment and sympathies upon another class of objects, and now she is only to be *commanded.*

"This is a stern word, Newnon; but you are just the man to live up to its condition. Make her respect your intellect —impose her life with the results you shall accomplish, and she will give to you the love she has to spare from her flowers, birds, trees, and indeed all the wild creatures of the natural world, with whom she is now in strict communion."

"I like the peril of the game, my good uncle!—there is something exciting in it to me. But what are we to do with that person for the present? I recall my hasty speech just now. I have a respect for him personally, for he has a great deal in him; and when he can be scourged out of the sphere of this childish sentimentalism, which has given me so much trouble, he will be a great acquisition to us—for even if he lives merely upon the memory of that daring enthusiasm of his, he would be the subtlest agent of our purpose we have ever had—for, of a surety, it would impose upon Lucifer himself! How do you propose to get rid of him?"

"Never mind! I shall get rid of him to-morrow! But let us proceed to other business."

The two men whose faces Frank had seen for a moment, and who had appeared to be impassive spectators during all this scene, now drew up closely around the table, and at once the four persons went into a close discussion of other matters, which, however far-reaching, we must leave to be developed in their future results.

The morning has come, and Frank has gone forth again upon his gay Celeste, with the young girl on her glossy steed—and they are full of love as yesterday.

Away! away they go, asking of Nature only joy—and leaving the gray Cedric to scheme with his apt nephew of "stratagems and spoils." They were unconscious of every thing but of the sunshine and of happiness.

The day had gone by with them as the others—they looked love into each other's eyes, as they had done since they first met, and now felt it more, because the passion had grown stilled within them, and warmed them with a quiet glow, like that which the sun sinks down into the earth, in spring, to come up again in such an odorous beaming silence through young flowers.

They were riding through a narrow path which led from out the dark tangles of the forest of the Black Walnut Bottom —Frank was speaking to her of the gentle themes which had absorbed their lives, and she clung upon his words with looks, when all at once Celeste and Black Hawk shied together, and darted away in a panic of affright, and on the instant poor Frank found himself constrained and dragged powerless from his saddle, with a lasso about his neck, while several

Indians rushed upon him from the thicket. With fading vision he last saw the young girl going off at speed, as if unconscious he had disappeared from her side.

The latest sound he heard, too, was the shrill neigh of Celeste, and then a choking sensation darkened on his life—and all was black to him!

DREAMS come to dreamers out on the waste ways and in the wilderness, as well as in narrow walls amid crowded streets. The ideal is pursued in both, and is as fleeting here as there. Should it seem strange, then, that our hunter-poet has dreamed a short dream beneath the deep shadows of that old forest by the far and swift Nebraska? His awakening into darkness is but the common way. Does not black night follow the rosy-tinted morn? Even the bird, with most aspiring pinion, flashes not the sunlight off it always; he too must sink from his exulting, and crouch beneath the overcoming shadows, where the prowling owl goes hooting with the moaning wolf, and all foul things shine upon the dark, with their green, phosphorescent eyes. We have no new paradise as yet on earth, all fenced about against its evils; we have no dove-cotes of the ideal where hungry kites forget to swoop. It is all alike—the flowers grow in wilderness as well as city—and though the winds may make them wilder, as our Freta was, yet not less delicate are they. Young, manly hearts beat fast and warm, and yearn upon the amorous air, though may be with a swifter beat, out-doors upon the sea-like plain, and through the mighty aisles of " perplexed wood."

We shall see—we shall see! Perhaps the wild flower wilts within the city. Perhaps the dreams forsake the dreamer where the dust of strife is thickened. The ideal may not live in a sooty, stifling air. We shall see!

A just knowledge of life requires a degree of familiarity with its two extremes. The madness and crime of the one may be the joy or justice of the other. These extremes reflect upon and are interwoven with each other, far more clearly and intimately than fireside philosophy can usually realize.

It is our business to give the realities of the Border, to be sure; but then these realities are by no means confined to the wilderness. They may leave their footprints as plainly upon Broadway or Chestnut street, as upon the war-path or buffalo-trace. Such brief and sudden episodes as this we have just given in the adventures of our friend Frank Carter, are by no means peculiar to either condition of life, savage or civilized, since we have daily examples that, let it begin in whichever extreme it may, it frequently ends in the opposite. Nor is it any more true that cut-throats and desperadoes, spitfires and viragoes are the only characters to be found on the frontiers of civilization or in the hearts of the wilderness, than it is true that burglars and sharpers, the murderess and the shrew, are the sole and peculiar denizens of the city. Each has its contrasts—and concerning these I shall proceed to "speak that I do know."

Z   19

THE FIGHT OF THE PINTO TRACE.

But while these sentimental and mysterious affairs, mentioned in our last chapters were being enacted, the author, who, it will be found, has been in one way or another mixed up with the whole apparently disconnected train of events heretofore given in this series, was engaged, a little farther south, in a rougher and somewhat different amusement. I was still with the Rangers, who had lately enjoyed a longer period of idleness than was usual; and although we had quite fallen into listless and loaferish habits, the news that the Camanches were down in considerable force, and ravaging the settlements, was sufficient to drive us to the saddle in double-quick time. The dusky marauders of the mountains had been unusually audacious on this new foray, and we heard, from all the settlements within fifty miles, alarms of their bloody visitation.

They move from point to point with such surprising rapidity, that a long line of frontier is frequently swept by them before the alarm can be spread sufficiently to permit a rally of its defenders in time to intercept the mischief. They can then only pursue; and as these robber horsemen are, though laden down with plunder, often as prompt and cunning in their return as in the descent, the pursuit is frequently bootless.

We had usually been quick enough for them—since our Ranger organization had been perfected by Hays in view of immediate efficiency in these very emergencies—but this time we somehow missed the figure. We were promptly enough under way when we heard the news—perhaps in fifteen minutes we were all mounted and off! But the reports which came in were confused and vague, which caused us to lose a great deal of time in finding the true seat of operations.

We started wrong, and lost a whole day in finding the trail of the plunderers. When we at last found it, we saw that they must have passed nearly twelve hours before. With such a start, it was useless to hope that we could overtake them by following up the windings of the trail.

Our only chance was to intercept them by some short cut before they reached the mountains. Hays judged from their general course that they would make for the head waters of the Guadaloupe; and trusting to his sagacity, we crossed the trail and struck off over the plains in that direction.

We were fifteen men in all, and now that our course had been determined, we moved on at a spanking pace, like men who had something certain to accomplish before them. The outset of a pursuit of this kind is always a merry time with the Rangers. They have had a rest, and are flushed with animal spirits, if not with spirits of another sort, and rush forth whooping in ungovernable delight at the prospect of any new excitement. Their horses are fresh, too, and drink the strong breeze against which they breast as fuel to their headlong speed. Accordingly, very hard riding, laughter, shouts, and merry jokes, constitute the order of the first day. Then fatigue and disappointment have somewhat taken the wire-edge off, and the second is more subdued, but still earnest and impetuous.

But the third day of suspense is almost uniformly too much for such volatile temperaments to get through with on an uncertainty. They become impatient, listless, and careless to an unmanageable degree, and unless some trace of the enemy be found to enliven them, the pursuit had as well be given up.

So Hays found it to be, on the third evening of this pursuit. We had failed again to cross the trail of the Indians, as he had calculated; the first blush of excited animal spirits had been dissipated in the weariness consequent upon excessive hard riding. The men had laughed at each other's old jokes in the jolly *abandon* of the start, but now the attempted repetition of them was a serious matter, and the laughter such attempts called forth any thing but jocose.

As evening closed in, there was an anxious consultation held by Hays with the most spirited and experienced of our Rangers, while we still continued slowly to advance in careless, straggling order. Nothing satisfactory was elicited except the mutual conclusion that unless we found some traces of the Indians early in the day to-morrow, it would be as well for us to give up in despair.

We felt assured that we had come too fast for them to have passed up the valley of the Guadaloupe, without our crossing their trail soon, if they were ahead. If we were ahead of them, the best thing we could possibly do would be to wait for them at a place some distance farther up, where the valley branched in several directions. Hays had been quite certain that they would attempt to reach the mountains by this route, because it was not only the most direct, but the most practicable.

On this route they were sure of firm, open ground to run upon—of good grazing and plenty of water. These were advantages which our astute captain felt assured they would and could not overlook in a retreat. Indeed they had scarcely ever been known to fail of selecting this valley to get out by, when they had come in upon the settlements north of Bahai.

During the greater part of the day we had found ourselves surrounded by quite novel and peculiar features of scenery. Although the ground was tolerably level in the valley, yet in

Z 2

the early part of the day we could easily perceive a low, broken and irregular line of hills undulating the horizon on either side.

Gradually with the evening these distant lines closed in, and as the shadows lengthened in the setting sun, they almost lay across the valley. Now that we were near them, we could perceive that these hills were quite unlike any others we had seen; for instead of occurring in a chain, with something like regularity, they were isolated, and appeared as if they had been sown broadcast over the plain. What had seemed to us in the distance to be a line of hills, was only the nearer edge of this singular formation.

We rode in among them, and it reminded me most of a huge forest, the mighty tops of which had been torn off by the wrench of a whirlwind. They stood at irregular distances apart, and each hill or mound was of a shape peculiar to itself, and of a size for which none of its neighbours were even indirectly accountable, except in contrast. The river here broke up into a number of smaller head-streams, which wound away by the feet of these curious hills, and we could look up their several valleys from nearly the same point of view. A heavy forest of several miles in extent skirted the opposite bank of the largest of these streams. It was at once resolved that we should cross and camp in the forest— or on the edge of it, rather—for the night. We passed around a steep and long-backed hill, which stood along the water's edge on this side; a little beyond it we found a buffalo-crossing, which we knew to be always safe. We crossed, and, following up the buffalo-trace through a sort of meadow-break, or opening in the forest, we found that in a few hundred yards it intersected another very wide and deep trace, which led off up the valley towards the north-west, through a continuation of this prairie opening in the forest.

Hays and the spies examined this trace very carefully for any signs of the Indians having passed, but none were apparent. He said this was the Pinto Trace, and that as it was greatly trampled by buffalo, he expected that the Indians would endeavour to lose their trail on its hard and confused surface. But the sharpest eyes of our trailers could discover nothing which indicated that they had passed.

It was, therefore, concluded that we must be ahead of them, or else have missed them entirely. We found a small thread-like stream running through this meadow, or strip of prairie, beside which we camped, just under the shadow of the forest.

We had by this time given up all hopes of finding the Indians, and accordingly all the ordinary precautions of the scout were neglected. We turned our horses on the luxuriant meadow to graze their fill, while we in the mean time were not disposed to be behind them in gratifying our appetites, which had for three days been stinted upon jerked beef, eaten without cooking, since the smoke of a fire is considered quite too significant a telegraph to be carelessly used upon the prairies while in pursuit of an enemy, or while in his possible neighbourhood.

We determined to have a full meal this night, in amends, and thought of or cared for nothing else but how to secure what we desired. The stringent requisitions of our early march were laughed at now, and recklessly contrasted with the devil-may-care method—or rather want of method—in our proceedings.

We built an enormous fire, while the most skilful hunters scattered in every direction to search for game. They came straggling in until some time after dark, and brought with them quite a sufficient complement of game to satisfy even our cravings. The greater part of a fat buck and of a young bear were basted before the blazing fire, while several wild-geese, and a turkey or two, gave variety to our feast.

Before the feast was over, a belated hunter came in, who announced that he had discovered a bee-tree, not far from the camp, and it was determined by a party of us that wo would go and cut it down, the first thing in the morning, and get the honey in time for breakfast, to eat with the remainder of our bear-steaks. The announcement and the proposition were received with great glee by the Rangers; for there is no higher luxury known to frontier life than bear-steaks and wild honey.

After indulging their appetites to the full, with the intention of waiting for the more delicate feast promised in the morning, one after another stretched himself upon his blanket and dropped off to sleep.

Nothing especial occurred during the night, and with the earliest morning a party of five or six of us were up and equipping ourselves for taking the bee-tree. We took our arms, of course, but, as well, carried with us a hatchet and several coils of lariat, which were to answer for ropes, should they be needed. We left our horses behind. Sam Walker and G—— went with us on horseback, to keep a look-out for *possibilities!* Walker, who has since made himself so illustrious by his extraordinary feats in the opening of the war with Mexico, and whose renowned death, as a Captain of the Rifles, thrilled the country lately to its heart's core, was then a subordinate Ranger, like the rest of us, and under the command of Hays.

G——, too, was a gallant fellow, distinguished for his skill in trailing—he had, since we set out, been acting as the associate of Walker in spying. We proceeded about a half mile through the forest to the bee-tree, which we found to be barely in sight of the long-backed hill on the opposite side of the river, and around the end of which we had been compelled to turn before we found the crossing. Our spies went on to reconnoitre, while we proceeded to attack the bee-tree.

It was a very large post-oak; and we soon perceived that the bees had hived in a limb of great size, the hollow entrance to which was some ten feet out from the main branch.

The tree was too thick through to be cut down in any reasonable time, and the readiest expedient seemed to be that it should be climbed by some one who should cut off the limb from the trunk.

No one appeared to be inclined to undertake this operation; for climbing trees, however pleasant an amusement it may be to us as boys, is never particularly agreeable to men. So general was this disinclination, that our designs upon the beehive seemed to be in a fair way to be relinquished utterly, when one of the men who had lately joined us, and who was a big, fat, and clumsy greenhorn, laughed out with a sort of wheezing chuckle, and said that we were "pretty fellows, not to be able to climb sich a tree as that."

The unfortunate sucker! no one had thought of him before; but now, so soon as he had spoken and attracted attention to himself, the determination to victimize him flashed simultaneously upon the minds of all, and we accordingly beset him. He had made himself ridiculous, ever since he joined us, by boasting, after the most loud-mouthed and bombastic fashion, of his surprising feats in every possible department of human prowess. But the deeds of valour which he described, and of which he was the modest hero, were always only just surpassed by the incomprehensible feats of personal agility which accompanied them—incomprehensible when we looked upon the fat, unwielding personalities of the panting boaster.

Every one now slyly assailed him upon the weak side—his stupendous vanity; and between us we finally coaxed, wheedled, flattered, or bullied poor Lynn into undertaking the very thing, of all others, he was precisely most unfitted for accomplishing.

The tree was not very difficult to climb after the first limbs had been reached, and we were all emulously officious to boust the heavy fellow upon our shoulders, until he reached the lower limbs and got a footing. Then we threw up the coil of a lariat to him, that he might at his leisure draw after him the hatchet which we attached to the other end.

Now that he was fairly started on his way up, we threw ourselves upon the earth at the foot of the tree, and rolled over, and with bursts and roars of unrestrained laughter, as we watched his awkward and timid ascent. Now we would applaud him with cheers for some suspiciously insignificant step in his upward progress—then we would taunt him when he faltered to take breath, until the poor fellow seemed to be scarcely sure whether he were not performing some unheard of labour, worthy to enlist the applause and enthusiasm of assembled nations. Indeed, his round face glowed down upon us in the pauses of his ascent, like the red disc of the harvest moon just rising, and its general expression of doubt, triumph, and vexation was so blended with his sweaty pantings, that we fairly roared again with laughter whenever this occurred.

At last, however, he succeeded in reaching the limb, and according to our directions, proceeded to tie one end of the lariat about it, as far out as he could reach, and then passing the other over a smaller limb, dropped the lariat down to us, that we might ease the limb to the ground, when he had severed it from the trunk. This he now proceeded to do, and at last succeeded in cutting it through.

As it swung off, and we were easing it down by the lariat, out came the whole swarm of bees, and attacked the poor fellow furiously. He had cut it too far out, and blundered into the hollow.

He now steadied himself as best he could, and was fighting blindly with both hands to protect his face, and in his agony had even forgot to cry out, while we were convulsed and rocking with cruel laughter below, when suddenly Walker and G—— shouted, "Indians! Indians!"

This ominous cry was sufficient to sober us in a hurry. We let go the lariat, and dropped our coveted honey very suddenly; for though we could not see the Indians, we knew too well that no false alarm could come through such men as our spies were.

The alarm caused something of a panic; for the contrast was too broad between our reckless hilarity and the immediate danger threatened.

Some of the men at the foot of the tree took up the cry, "Indians!" Poor Lynn, who was already half-maddened and blinded by the bee-stings, heard it, and gave a yell of such agonized, despairing terror as would have stampeded a drove of broken-down pack-mules.

The pain of the bee-stings seemed to be forgotten in a moment, and he dropped himself, with the agility of a monkey, from the limb on which he stood. He was about forty feet from the ground, and taking every thing together, it was no special wonder that he miscalculated his momentum somewhat.

Although we were all thoroughly startled by the alarm, yet I do not think two men budged while we watched the ludicrous descent of our frightened victim. He had clearly forgotten all about the bees, and was dropping hastily from limb to limb, with a constantly increasing momentum, until at last, when something like twenty feet from the ground, he let go all holds, and came crushing down, with the agonizing cry, as he thumped against it his helpless, mushy form,—

"O J—s!—them Indians! Wait, boys!"

But we did not choose to wait now, and with one long burst of laughter, which sent us staggering off, we hurried back to the camp. We saw that Lynn had no bones or limbs broken, and he was certainly of as much use as he lay there grunting and frightened at the foot of that tree, as he could be under any other possible condition of things; so we left him to pluck the bee-stings out of his face, and dream of new prodigies of individual valour.

We found G—— already in camp with the news, and nearly all the horses caught up, in readiness. While we were mounting, G—— returned to join Walker, and we followed in the shortest possible time.

We passed out of the forest along the buffalo trail, and as we came out of the narrow meadow, in sight of the crossing we had used, we saw Walker and G—— already mounting the other bank of the river. Our course was thus indicated, though we as yet saw no enemy.

We hurried on, and when we reached the ford we saw them. They were slowly and deliberately ascending the steep and long-backed hill of which I have spoken, while our two spies rode slowly out into the plain they had left, and seemed to be looking up curiously after them.

We were urging on in the mean time; for though we were in sight, we were still a considerable distance off. It was a large body of warriors!—at least it seemed so to us, as we saw them slowly mounting the steep hill in a long compact line, from which the gaudy feathers flaunted bravely from their heads and from the tops of their long lance-handles.

The two spies followed them slowly in advance of us. When we reached the ford, they had mounted to the crest of the hill, and clustering along its brow, had begun to make insulting and defying gestures to us. But these gestures seemed to be particularly addressed to Walker and G——, who were far in advance of us, and in full view of them, while we were concealed somewhat in crossing the river.

Their position was so favourable, and their numbers so immensely superior, that Hays, reckless and daring as he was, hesitated about charging upon them. Indeed, he would and could never have been rash enough to make deliberately an up-hill onset upon four or five times his number; but the thing was precipitated. There was among them a person who spoke imperfect English, and he roared out insulting taunts to Walker and G——, defying them to come on, with the most filthy and opprobrious epithets.

These fiery and chivalric men had never been in the habit

of counting noses when they were insulted—and accordingly, without turning their heads to see whether we were at hand or not, they urged their horses alone up the hill in the face of nearly a hundred insolent savages.

So soon as we saw this movement, all hesitation—which at any rate had been but momentary—was gone, and we urged our horses up the steeps at their best speed. It was a rough and precipitous ascent, and with all our eagerness, we made slow work of it. We saw the gallant and reckless Walker break into their insolent front, and a warrior tumble as his pistol went off. The throng fell back before him as he gave another shot from his revolver, and then G—— closed in with quick successive shots from his deadly repeater.

But though the panic might be for an instant, yet it was too much to suppose that two men, even with so much audacity, backed even by repeaters, could rout a force of eighty insolent and defying warriors.

We saw them close about our rash and beloved comrades. We urged our horses like madmen up the steep. We saw Walker go down, and with a frantic cry—which was most like the ferocious wail of a pantheress for her young—we burst into the fray with drawn revolvers.

They made terrible work, and although the Indians fought like men possessed to maintain their vantage ground, we drove them back along the ridge with ruthless slaughter. They could not stand before our murderous revolvers.

I remember, as it were yesterday, seeing, as we swept past, poor Walker lying on his face with a lance through him! I considered him as done for, and never expected to see him on his feet again. Poor G—— was writhing near him, with a dozen lance-wounds. The Indians retreated before our furious charge, and, leaving their dead behind, they started off in the most extraordinary panic along the ridge of the hill.

Before long they rallied, and met us again in full shock.

2 A

The collision lasted only for a moment, when they broke again, leaving their dead as before. Thus this terrible fight continued for nearly six miles—they pausing every now and then to fight a moment, and then breaking up before our resistless charge, to fly a few miles farther and make a new stand, to be routed as before. We drew up at last, absolutely weary of slaughter, and permitted them to escape into some timber, with more than one-half their whole number killed or wounded.

This was the most bloody and ferocious fight which ever occurred between our race and the Camanches. We were about fourteen men to eighty stout and well-armed warriors. We routed them from their chosen position on the hill, and with the loss of three men and four wounded, literally cut them to pieces—killing nearly half of their whole number. But for our revolvers, the attack would never have been made; and had it been, we should only have been awfully whipped.

When we returned to the camp, we found that Walker, whom we had supposed to be slain, had drawn the lance out, which had been driven into him from behind, and crawled down to the water to drink. It had missed the vitals, and he lived to render his name illustrious and die at last right gloriously!

G—— was stone dead, with fatal wounds enough on his body to have killed half our whole number. We buried him decently; and, on the examination of the papers on his person by Hays, in the presence of us all, there came to light a small parchment, which was no sooner looked at by Hays, than he hastened to conceal it in his bosom, turning slightly pale as he glanced eagerly around at our faces. It was too late! The signature was in bold, large letters, and many of us saw it—it was " Regulus!" Not a word was spoken.

As for the man of the bee-tree, we found him with his eyes so bunged that he was never able to see double any more.

BACK FROM THE WILDERNESS.

TALES OF THE SOUTHERN BORDER.

BACK FROM THE WILDERNESS.

CHAPTER I.

Six months have elapsed. We have seen Frank Carter, the vague dreamer, the boyish enthusiast, and haughty Quixote of the Ideal, dragged down, almost from the very embraces of the Dulcinea of his wilderness-errantry, and choked into obliviousness by the lasso of a dirty Indian tightened about his throat.

Ah, what a fall! Poor Frank! Only six months since, what an heroic ascetic thou wast, in thy young champion-ship!

The allurements of women, wealth, position,—every thing, indeed, that the cities of civilization had to offer of excite-ment and bewildering enchantment to the senses of fire-hearted youth,—had been passed through calmly, and he had come forth from all unscathed.

But the wilderness!—the weird and shadow-peopled wil-derness!—alas! that Frank Carter ever should have ven-tured to penetrate those haunted depths.

Alas! alas! for the haunted wilderness. Ho! for the cities of men again! We are back in New York city!

Facing St. John's Square, on the east side, stands a large,

plain brick building, the only peculiarity of the external of which is that it is somewhat taller than the other residences of the block.

Lately, this building had seemed to be occupied in a manner so peculiar, as to attract a great deal of attention to it in the neighbourhood, which was a remarkably quiet and staid one.

At all hours, from about noon until three or four in the morning, well-dressed men—principally young men—were to be seen apparently making calls.

The popularity of this house attracted first curiosity, and then suspicion. The drowsy neighbours thought it could be for no good that their rest was so broken in upon at all hours by the clattering hoofs of reckless riders, dashing up to the door; particularly as these sounds were not unfrequently accompanied by shouts of gay laughter when the parties came forth late.

Few vehicles of any kind came; but at least one, and often four or five, and sometimes more saddle-horses of the finest blood and action usually stood before the door, pawing the pavement impatiently, under the charge of several negro grooms, who seemed to belong to the establishment.

The neighbours had in vain questioned the servants, all of whom were negroes or mulattoes. What follows would be about all the satisfaction they could obtain in answer to their inquiries, beginning—

" Whose house is that ?"

" Dat's massa's house, to be sure !"

" Who is your ' massa,' as you call him ?"

" Massa is a gemman !"

" Where's he from ?"

" He a'n't no red-mouph Yankee—dat's sartain !"

" Are you all his slaves ?"

" We waits on him !"

" Where were you born ?"

"Not in dis city, tank de Lord!"

"Where then were you born?"

"Whar Aunt Dinah live!"

"What's your master's name, then?"

"Massa's friends know he name!"

"What does he do?"

"Minds he's own business! Here, Pomp, yonder comes anudder gemman! Be spry, here, you nigger, to hold dat horse!"

And the baffled meddler would be obliged to sneak away as wise as he came, for his pains.

About eleven o'clock of a still winter evening, with a brilliantly clear moonlight, quite a cluster of horses stood before the door of this house. All at once the darkies opened their eyes and rolled up the whites in astonishment, as a light cabriolet whirled round the nearest corner at a great pace, and dashed headlong into the midst of the group they were in charge of, causing great confusion and affright.

Before they had time to think or speak, the tall slim form of the driver, which was enveloped in a long cloak, had bounded to the pavement, and throwing the reins towards one of the grooms, sprang hastily up the steps.

"Gor A'mighty, but dat gemman in a hurry! Whew!" whistled Pompey, as he stooped to catch up the reins.

But great as the hurry of the gentleman seemed to have been, he paused for a moment at the door, as if to compose himself, and then turning the latch, entered without ringing the bell. A negro servant stood in the hall. He sprang forward with a low bow.

"Berry fine evening, Massa Tinkink. Me take de cloak, massa."

"There, my dark-browed thunderer," said the gentleman, dismantling himself with great deliberation, and revealing a lithe, elegant figure, and dark, shining, restless eyes.

"Jupiter, I suppose your master has more company than usual, to-night?"

"Yes, massa; dar is some more gemman dan ɔb usual, on dis night."

"They are at supper?"

"Yes, massa!"

"Show me in!"

"Dis way, massa!"

Jupiter threw open the door of the parlour, and, with a deep salaam, announced—

"Massa Tinkink!"

The clinking din and joyous clamour of a convivial supper burst upon his ears, as the door flew open, while it was almost impossible, between the sudden glare of lights and the brooding haze of cigar-smoke, to distinguish faces at all, for the moment.

There was a momentary lull, and a voice from the fog said—

"Jupiter, what sort of a name is that you have given my friend? Tynenck! Tyn-enck is the name, next time, you thick-tongued rascal!—not Tinker, or any other such plebeian cognomen."

The speaker sits at the foot of the table; and, as he rises to greet the new comer, we cannot fail to recognise the face of our friend, Frank Carter, though he is looking ten years older, with sunken cheeks, sharpened features, and eyes that gleam with an unnatural fire! He stretches out a thin, bony hand—

"Come! Tynenck; I have kept a seat for you. You see, I have not been able to drill that fellow of mine into the pronunciation of that Gotham-honoured name of yours. Sit down when you get ready—but first order what you will have; for you perceive that we have the start of you, and have got somewhat along into the night."

"Resume your seat, Carter; I shall take care of myself!" and he passed down the table, exchanging greetings. When his eye met that of the person seated at the head, there was a scarcely perceptible start, a significant interchange of glances, and Tynenck turned suddenly, and said—

"Carter, I did not observe, before, that you had resigned your seat as host. Hope you are not reduced to dodge the hammer already? You should have let me know, before it came to this extremity. I would have taken your place myself."

"Not if you mean the presiding hammer! I have already so much honoured myself, in the resignation thereof to 'mine ancient comrade and tried' Newnon Clenny, to whom I beg to introduce you,"—the gentlemen bowed formally,—"that I thought there was no other honour left me, in that line. But your offer to take my place overwhelmed me, Tynenck. Though my place is now that of a guest to my friend, I hope you will feel no hesitation in sharing it with me. By the way"—and he looked sharply from one face to the other—"my friend Newnon is an old resident of New York! I should have thought it probable that you two would have met."

"Never as personal acquaintances, though I have long recognised Mr. Clenny by sight and reputation, and desired to know him."

"Curious!" said the clear, shrill, commanding voice of Clenny. "We have almost jostled each other a thousand times, with a mutual recognition and desire of acquaintance, and yet the accident of 'pray know my friend' had never yet occurred, before! But better late than never. Have you ordered any thing, Mr. Tynenck?"

"Yes; some oysters on the shell. I have not heard of you, in the city, for some years past, Mr. Clenny?" ·

"No; my friend Carter can best account for my absence. I have been with him adventuring, at the South-West."

"Ah! here are the oysters! Some pale Sherry now, Sam!" said Tynenck, as he seated himself.

"I say, Tynenck!" said a florid-looking person, in a some-what loud voice, as he leaned forward over the table, several seats above, "what's the news from the bridge, to-night? You always know."

"My dear fellow, how can I know any more than you your-self know? The boats are not in from Albany; none of the expresses can arrive for several hours. Ah! these delicious oysters!"

"Pshaw!" said a young man from the opposite side of the table, and upon whose white, effeminate hand gleamed a large diamond, as he stretched it forth. "Pass on that cham-pagne, Tom! You need be in no hurry to hear from 'the bridge;' your miserable party is already defunct, and I ex-pect, in my morning dream, to hear your sweet voices in chorus with the last, melancholy shriek of that long bray we have been hearing from —— since the late convention. Here's to the lungs of your chief chorister—Tom!"

The young aristocrat raised the foaming glass to his lips, with a sneer upon them; while Tom Durfee flushed a yet deeper scarlet, and, instead of lifting his glass, began to fumble confusedly in his pockets, while he glanced furtively towards Tynenck and Clenny.

Tynenck was just taking a large oyster; and, as he laid down the shell, he looked up archly, and said, with a distinct, emphatic intonation—

"Mr. Catesby, what is that morning dream of your's worth to you?"

"Why, Tynenck, have you turned plebeian, too?" The young man looked surprised, but quietly proceeded, after laying down the cigar he was about to light, to draw forth his pocket-book. "It is worth whatever you are disposed to cover, Mr. Tynenck!"

"I'll bet you five hundred that the Democratic candidate is elected!" said Tom Durfee, eagerly.

"Good! Friend Thomas, you are booked! I am sorry

for you," and Catesby proceeded to make the entry on a fly-leaf.

"Pshaw! Tom, you must be drunk, or else you are a fool," said one of his neighbours.

"No; let Tom alone—he'll win it," said another, a tall man, who sat next, and whose hair was as black as midnight, and whose eyes shone strangely out of a saturnine and ghastly face. He leaned forward and whispered, "He's got his cue! He knows what he is about—let him alone."

Frank heard this whisper, and marked the man.

"I have five thousand at your service, Mr. Catesby," said Tynenck, as he stooped to take another oyster.

"You are up in the figures to-night, Tynenck. You came in last. Pray, how old is your faith in your candidate?"

The buzz around the table was hushed.

Tynenck took another oyster, and laying down the shell deliberately, he looked up with an expression of surprise.

"Why, what's the matter, friend Catesby? Are you frightened at five thousand? Make it a hundred, then, or even fifty, if that will suit you better."

Catesby flushed a little. His suspicions might have been correct enough, but the cool tact of this man had placed him in a false position. He had spoken from an instinctive impulse rather than from judgment. He now saw that Tynenck had placed himself right, in his answer to the first question, with regard to the news from the bridge, in saying that it was yet impossible that any news could have arrived. He had tact, and made the most of an awkward predicament.

"I will see you," he said, "and something more. But a man who has just come in from the fresh air to a party already four hours gone, should not be surprised that we show wonder whether he has not heard from 'farthest Ind' in that time."

"Ay! But you will see me and something more," said Tynenck, with a scarcely perceptible smile. "All that is

right enough. I am satisfied with regard to every thing except the amount you are willing to stake to-night upon the
result of this election."

"Do you propose to bet on the State of New York, as will
be decided by the news of the morning, or on the general
result?"

"You may take either."

"Then I will take the result."

"At what figure?"

"Any, from five to ten."

"Then let it be ten."

With a slight increase of paleness, but a perfectly firm
hand, Catesby wrote out a draft for the amount, while Tynenck did the same.

Tynenck was about to hand them to Carter, but something
in his look forbade. He turned toward Clenny for a moment, and then rising, handed him the draft. Catesby did
the same, and Clenny deposited them in his pocket-book.

The roysterers had forgotten their merriment for the time,
while the formalities of this heavy bet were settled. Frank
Carter looked on with his sepulchral, hollow eyes, and said,
with a quiet sneer, which it seemed as if he could not control—

"I congratulate you, gentlemen, upon the accession of self-
complacency the morning will bring to the one or the other
of you. One will be just ten thousand times better pleased
with himself, his principles, and his party. Happy man!
Happy party! with such a formidable accession to its suc-
cesses. Devil take the hindmost!"

"Hear him! Hear him! Our host from the South is
spiritually moved to sermonize," said Tynenck, with a
laugh.

"Will you take some champagne now, Mr. Tynenck?"

"Yes. Those were glorious oysters, and the sherry seems
flat after them!"

Frank drained the long-necked glass at a draught, and said—

"A truce to politics—it is a stupid game of knave to fool. Boy, place a bottle before every man, and let no time be lost in circulation."

The order was executed with a surprising promptness, and in less than a minute a bottle of champagne was placed before each guest. The wires, with great nicety, had been so nearly severed, that it only required a slight wrench with the thumb to start the cork, and in a moment they were popping all along the table, amid merry laughter and quaint witticisms.

"I say, Carter, do you intend to get us all tipsy again to-night, as usual?"

"I should feel that I was doing a good and disinterested service, Catesby, to drink you under the table; for then, at least, you would be incapable of playing the fool and betting your fine fortune away."

"Pray, Mr. Ascetic, how much better use are you making of yours?"

"Far better! I choose to seek relief from the satieties in convivialities; but in this I am at least unselfish. I do not ask men to do or to suffer what I am not willing to share. If they wake up with a headache after a night with me, they have at least the consolation that I have a headache too, and am sharing with them the wages of sin. But the gambler who has lost, wakes with hatred in his heart—and the gambler who has won, with a pitiless exultation!"

"Pshaw! Frank, stop your preaching, and fill up your glass!" said Clenny, jeeringly.

"Let him alone!" said Tynenck, laughing; "our friend belongs to a common type of fanatic. He hugs his favourite sin to his heart with his left hand, and does battle with the sins of all the world with his right. He loves the excitement of wine and rich feeding, but shrinks from the more refined and intellectual stimulus of gambling."

2 B

"Because it revolts my taste !"

"No," said the dark-haired, saturnine man, with the gleaming eyes, whose whisper we have mentioned Frank had heard and noted. "No, sir; there is, perhaps, a higher reason for all this : Mr. Carter is too honourable to bet upon a certainty !"

"What do you mean, sir ?" said Tynenck, looking startled.

"I mean what I say !"

Every glass was arrested midway, and all the buzz around the table stilled in an instant.

"But what do you mean to say ?" asked Tynenck, blanching somewhat, and looking towards Clenny, as if in appeal. The brows of Clenny were contracting, and his eyes growing large and shining underneath.

"I mean to say that the heavy bet you made just now with Mr. Catesby was made upon a certainty."

"How upon a certainty ?"

The man with the shining eyes went on as calmly and coolly as if he were demonstrating a problem in mathematics.

"You run a private express, in connection with other swindling gamblers, and have the news from the bridge several hours ahead of the mails. You are in a fair way to make a clean percentage to-night, in that bet of ten thousand you made just now."

"Carter, who is this insolent fellow ?" said Tynenck, with a rigid and pale, though somewhat flurried air.

Carter answered coolly, as he sipped from his champagne glass—"That gentleman is my friend, or he would not have been here. It is Captain Yeiger, late of the United States navy."

"Ah ! he has been a captain, has he ? Then he ought to know how to take care of himself; and must be aware of the consequences of his vulgar impudence to-night."

"Captain Yeiger has been so long in the habit of taking care of himself, that it has grown to be quite an unconscious thing with him," said the man with the glittering eyes, very slowly. "Captain Yeiger can even now afford a sort of half-pay conscience, which impels him to warn honourable young men, when he finds them compromised to the tune of ten thousand by a cool and subtle swindler."

The convivialists looked all aghast, and, with one accord, drew their chairs back from the table.

"Pshaw! Carter, this is some low fanatic, who has imposed upon your philosophic tendencies."

Carter said nothing. But the captain rose from his seat, and deliberately dashed his glass, wine and all, into the face of Tynenck.

"Pray, is that a philosophic tendency, sir?"

CHAPTER II.

THE bolt had fallen! The astounding shock of unexpected defeat had stunned into almost death-like stillness the warm hearts of many thousand earnest, chivalric friends of Mr. Clay, in New York city.

Would that so many otherwise faultless citizens and still nobler men had not been hurried, amid the sanguine heat and dusty turmoil of that strife, into fatal compromises by the gambling spirit, and then, through the breathless stillness of that pause, the snapping of so many heart-chords would not have been heard to fill it—twanging in a low, mournful cadence, as they died away.

Ah! that was a terrible day to New York, when the certainty of Mr. Clay's defeat became known! For hours and hours, long after the cool heads of the party had resigned themselves and given up all for lost, the great body of the Whigs continued to struggle against conviction. They could not realize it—they would not realize it; they almost gasped for breath, to shout till the last, "It cannot be so!"

But the obstinate refusal to be convinced could not help them; and when those millions which had been so rashly staked upon the result, changed hands, then came the realization, tangible and palpable—crushing through brain and sense in an awful collapse of purses and patriotism!

It would have been well enough had these tremendous losses been confined to the gamblers of the Whig party. But, alas! it was chiefly the true-hearted, unsuspecting members of the party, who, with an honourable enthusiasm, went for principle, upon the faith of a long-tried confidence in Mr. Clay, that suffered deepest, and were plucked most bare, by the wary sharpers on the other sides.

These were mostly men of character, substance, and position, who, whatever caution they might exhibit towards an opponent, were too frank ‘and just to themselves to imagine such a crime as treason in the camp. They would never dream—when betting on a certain result on the strength of hints from a leading spirit of their party, who was known to be most frequently sure of his ground—that the very sums they lost to seeming opponents, would go into the pockets of their astute adviser.

Still less could they dream that the heavy sum, by staking which this said oily adviser had demonstrated substantially to them his own faith with regard to the question at issue, was in no danger of ever leaving his note-book—let what might turn up!

That in a word, it was a mere stool-pigeon operation—the pluckings from which were shared between their distinguished Whig friend and his perhaps equally distinguished Democratic friend, in a cool, private settlement afterward.

Plucker and Pluckee would meet in a few hours to exchange condolences, and Pluckee would be so melted by the ugubrious melancholy expressed upon the hopeless face of his friend Plucker, that his honest, sympathetic heart could not but be moved by the remembrance of old friendships, and, if not ruined already, the pathetic interview would probably be concluded by an offer on his part of a loan to assist the impudent swindler in redeeming his position.

So the game went. Perhaps never before in the history of our somewhat remarkable country did so large a body of men pay such heavy penalties for the misfortune of being honest, as on the issue of this extraordinary election.

It was like to prove a fatal accident to poor Mark Catesby, that he enjoyed the enviable reputation of being extremely rich. His father inherited an immense fortune and proud rank in England, and had, for some unexplained cause, come over to sink both, in a great measure, among the pale-haired Manhattanese.

He was fiercely aristocratic, and yet dissipated, though magnificent, in his habits. He had invested, by the merest accident, a comparatively small sum in vacant property around Union Square.

He was unfortunately a victim of the demon of chance, although he scorned the common gambler. In his time, men had not outlived the chivalric though melancholy delusion that there was such a thing as honour among gamblers. He was the knightly soul of honour himself, and lived and died in the blind, yet generous faith that his noble fortune had been honourably squandered among honourable men.

He left his two children, Mark and Ruth, the mere fragment of his estate—his wife was dead before he came over. Mark, who was then nearly a man, managed, through the counsel of his family lawyer, with great tact, to keep up appearances and retain for a while the old mansion, which was lower down town, until the unregarded investment in Union Square had so far appreciated in value as to make it desirable for him to resign the old house to his father's creditors, and move upon this property.

2 B 2

He had nothing left him in the world to love but his sister Ruth—this tie had been unboundedly sufficient for him. They loved each other with the beautiful holiness of that chaste, unselfish relation.

The house he now had built for their home expressed the perfect and refined taste of each in its different departments, and was as well the wonder and admiration of the square.

But yet Mark Catesby was not rich—not near so rich as society gave him credit for being.

The reputation of unlimited wealth which the extravagant habits of his father had impressed upon society, had, through his docile and cautious observance of the conduct and procedure laid down by the old and honoured lawyer of his family, been sufficient in preserving that reputation and consequent credit intact. Now this reputation and credit was worth more to Catesby than even his beautiful house and somewhat valuable property.

He had guarded it with the most jealous care for the sake of his dear Ruth—for the fact of his father's bankruptcy had been as carefully concealed from her as from the public.

Enormously wealthy as he was conceived to be, the loss of ten thousand dollars last night was utterly crushing to him. All his property would have to be sacrificed, unless his fictitious credit could be promptly sustained. With the certainty of success before him, he had bet upon his credit, which he well knew to be beyond the limit of his bank account. Yet he had liabilities to nearly the same amount in other quarters, which would come due at the same hour, which fact he had overlooked in the flush of that excitement which was as well hereditary as accidental.

What was he to do to save himself and his dear Ruth from utter ruin? This was the agonizing question which caused a strange collapse in the features of the young man when he came down to breakfast, about noon on that eventful day, after having read all the fatal news of the morning, before he rose.

His sister was at the table. She was very frail and fair, this same sister Ruth of his; but her fairness was not the unnatural bleach of confinement, nor that general seeming of physical frailty, the result of wasting disease. Her complexion was perfectly fresh, and there was a suggestive transparency in its whiteness that reminded one of the outside petals of a blush rosebud, which, though blanched by the sunlight on its surface, seemed to sink, in a delicate, deepening glow, through every fold, as if it would invite the eye to follow it down to the warm, red heart.

The frailty of her figure was rather apparent than real; for when you saw her close at hand, it was evidently caused by that fineness of bone and texture which is the result of high breeding and a great purity of genealogy through many generations; for slight as her limbs seemed, they were firmly knit, and she rather appeared to bound than walk, with an exceeding airiness of movement.

Her features were almost of the pure Grecian, except that the nose turned up slightly, and the chin was somewhat advanced from the true line of that classic profile, which gave to their expression a certain degree of haughtiness, that was not a little heightened by the crisp, beautiful curl of her short upper lip.

This face would have been unpleasantly proud, and even savagely fastidious, but for the surprising tenderness of those meek, blue eyes, that seemed all brimming up to overflow in a quick sympathy, and then they could in an instant freeze the warm tears in which they swam, and glisten coldly on you, if her nice and imperious taste were outraged in the smallest degree.

She sat with her back to the door as he entered, and recognising his beloved step as he advanced, she pouted her budding lips in expectation of the morning kiss. As he stooped over her, she raised her eyes to his face, and for the first time caught a glimpse of the expression there.

She sprang up as if she had been shot, and with a faint scream upon her lips, threw her arms about his neck—her quick instinct had divined it all in the instant of that one glance.

"Mark! Mark! my brother, what has happened?"

He shook in her arms as one stricken with a palsy. She knew his whole soul far more thoroughly than he did himself. She knew the fatal passion he had inherited, and had long prepared herself for this result—and now his deep emotion confirmed her fears. The blow had come at last!

"Dearest brother, never mind it. Let it go. We are sufficient unto each other and unto ourselves. You can sell this house, and you know you say I am such a good artist now," and she kissed him fondly. "Oh, do not look so, Mark! You will kill me! I can bear any thing but that white agony!"

The wretched young man staggered to a chair. He drew her to his breast.

"Sweet Ruth," he moaned.

She kissed him again.

"Dear brother, why should you be so sad? You know that it has always been a favourite whim of mine to take a room on Broadway, and have up on the side of the door a nice little shingle, with 'Ruth Catesby, Artist,' on it in gold letters. Oh, I shall be so proud and strong then! It must be such a glorious thing to live by one's own labour! Then old Mr. Kenyon says you are a first-rate lawyer, and have remarkable talents as a pleader. You have only to stick up your little shingle, too, and you will soon get into practice. Won't it be beautiful then, when we get together at night, after a hard day's work, in my snug little back-room?"

"You are a dear, brave girl, Ruth," said the young man, mournfully, and with quivering lips. "Ah, what a besotted wretch I have been!"

"Do not talk so, Mark. You have only done what thousands of the best men in the land have done during the fearful excitement of this election. Had I been a man, no doubt I would have done so too."

"No, Ruth, you would never have done this," said he, with an expression of bitter self-reproach. "You would never have compromised a gentle, loving sister, in your madness, and driven her to face the ignominious alternative of labouring with her white, delicate hands, for the very bread she puts into her mouth. It can never be, Ruth. I am not quite so far degraded yet, that I will consent to see the last daughter of our honourable house become a menial of the vulgar public—'dancing attendance' on its brutal patronage. I"——

"Brother! brother!"

"Do not interrupt me, Ruth," he continued, while his face flushed through its pallor and assumed somewhat of the haughty air habitual to it.

"It can never be, I say. I have thrown away your fortune and my own; squandered it shamefully, as I have reason to believe, upon infamous swindlers; and I owe you a great reparation. You must let me make it. I know I can succeed in the law. What is done cannot be mended; but after saving my honour, by giving up all, I can borrow money enough among the old friends of my father for us to live upon genteelly, and as Catesbys should, until I get into practice, which will not be long. It shall then be the joy and charm of my life to make you comfortable, and surround you soon again with all the elegances to which you have been accustomed. The law is an honourable profession, and it is honourable for any man to win distinction in it; but the idea of a daughter of a Catesby offering, nay, advertising her rare and graceful accomplishment in art for sale to the highest bidder, to be criticised by a plebeian taste—to be rated, cheapened, and trafficked for by rich, retired grocers, as they

had once trafficked for a side of bacon or a string of onions—
is rather more than even this dark misfortune has prepared
me to face. It cannot be, dear Ruth. Your spiritual genius
would not long survive this desecration of its gentle craft.
Your art would be vulgarized!"

During this speech, the young girl had gradually released
herself from the arms of her brother, and now stood before
him, her form unconsciously drawn proudly up, and her meek
blue eyes lit with a solemn fire. She said slowly, and in a
low voice—

"My brother, Art is too high to be vulgarized! It is the
apostle of the beautiful, and preaches to the masses of 'THE
UNKNOWN GOD!' They cannot touch its austere life by
praise or blame, because it is self-derived, and consciousness is its highest reward. Art does not ask the masses to
come to it; it simply commands them by the yearnings for
higher life instinctive in them—and of which it is the in-
terpreter, through form. The 'raiment of camel's hair' and
the 'food of locusts and wild honey' better becomes those
who aspire to be even the voices in the wilderness that announce the coming of Art to tranquillize, ameliorate, and
ennoble our race, than the silken security of luxurious homes.
Art has nothing to fear of desecration, through me, my brother; for I know that I am a true artist, and I fear nothing
for it from the modest contact—for Art has been the great
compeller of refinement, through all time. As for the degradation of labouring with my own hands, it is a degradation I
have long aspired to; and I tell you that the name of which
you are so sensitively proud will be far more honoured by
such a dedication of what talents I have to boast, and high-
purposed labour, than by the vain, childish, and unfruitful
life of luxurious and stately etiquette! I am determined to
be an artist, brother! and to live by art,—for the labourer is
worthy of his hire!"

"Remember you are a woman, Ruth!" said Mark somewhat impatiently.

"Woman has as much right to work as you have, for she was doomed to live by the sweat of her brow."

"Ah! dear Ruth, you are, and always have been, a strange, wilful creature—but never unkind, though. I am sure you will let me persuade you out of these extraordinary opinions and purposes, before the time shall arrive for carrying them into execution;" and he drew her to him, and kissed her fondly.

"I fear you will not, Mark!" said she quietly, as she struggled free of his embrace; and then turning to him with a pleasant smile, as she resumed her place at the breakfast table, she said—"Come, brother! let us take one more happy meal together, at least."

We leave these young people now, for a time, and the question at issue by themselves to be settled, from the firm conviction that the truest purpose makes the strongest will in such contests, and that right will govern might between them.

About this same hour, two persons are at breakfast in the easy and luxurious back-parlour of the mysterious house in St. John's Square.

The conversation of these two persons, which has been long and confidential, has just now turned upon the affairs and interests of the individuals we have just left. We will listen for awhile.

Captain Yeiger has finished his toast, and is sipping his claret, taking a grape now and then from his plate.

"There can be no doubt, Mr. Carter, that Catesby is ruined —utterly and irredeemably ruined! I knew his father intimately, and have watched this young man closely. He has never been a gambler, except as a losing one, as his father was—and for the same reason—that he is strictly honourable, and will not know the wretched knaves of the profession. He loses to-day much more than he is worth, as I have ascertained since the scene last night. The passion he inherited rose up in the form of a monomania, and he had bet wildly, as his father used to do, during all the day, and the fever was still raging in his blood when that subtle scoundrel, Tynenck, who thinks him to be richer than he really is, tempted him into that last ruinous bet. Catesby was not really a sane man then; and as soon as Tynenck entered the room, I felt what he came for. He knew Catesby would be here; he had received the necessary intelligence, through means concerning which I have given you some general hints, which really are all I have to order now, though I think I am on the track of a certainty, 'sure as proof of holy writ,' which, when I have further elaborated, you shall have the benefit of. He thought him immensely rich—and heard of his bold bets during the day, and came post-haste, as I ascertained from your negro groom, Pompey, for the purpose of securing a heavy bet with him, which he accomplished. I could not contain my indignation, since I knew that Catesby was not to be the only sufferer. Had that been the case, I should have held my peace, for I felt that the lesson would be good for him! But I knew that there was a fair, gentle girl, as gentle as she was strong, who would be most injured by this terrible imprudence of his."

"Was or is this girl his mistress?" interposed Carter, coldly.

"No! no! His sister, man!"

"I beg pardon! Proceed—I am interested now!"

"This young girl has no particular provision made for her in the will of her father. He clung to the old idea of the right of primogeniture, and left her an entire dependant upon the older brother. The old Catesby had little to will; for his immense property was so involved and cut up with mortgages and debts of honour, that he did not know himself what he might legitimately call his own, and so willed to his only son all his unembarrassed estate. This spirited and charming girl is, therefore, left without provision of any sort, except what a spotless name and highly cultivated talents can afford."

"Is she really talented?" said Carter, eagerly.

"Yes. I am consummately skilled in the use of the pistol, and feel strangely disposed to visit upon him a righteous retribution for the wrong, the cold, merciless wrong, he has deliberately done to this young girl, in swindling her infatuated, but honourable brother, out of the last fragment of the magnificent estate their father left them. It was a swindle—base and cold-blooded swindle—and you will see, when I wing the uncertain-eyed scoundrel to-morrow, that he will confess it before he is carried off the ground."

"I hope you may do it, Yeiger; but this man has been in the field before successfully."

"Pshaw! he has never met an eye before. I know my man!"

"Well, well, look out. He knows how to take you at an advantage, as he did poor Catesby. Five o'clock to-morrow morning!"

<hr>

CHAPTER III.

As the day broke, there were three men standing at the row-boat stairs on the North River side of the Battery, foot of Pier No. 1. It was too early even for the habits of that most tenacious, wide-awake, fare-abiding animal—the Battery oarsman.

They have to wait—and we can see, first, that they all have on large, heavy cloaks; second, that two of them carry

2 C

a mahogany case under the right arm, and that said cases have a very suspicious look.

A handsome carriage, which appears to have brought them down, stands in waiting a short distance off.

They soon enter a boat, and are pushed off.

The oarsman seemed to understand his course perfectly; for, without a word of direction, he passed among the vessels of war that were anchored off the castle, and struck out boldly across the bay, in a south-westerly direction, for the Jersey shore.

No word was spoken until they had reached the open water, when Jack, who had been eying suspiciously those mahogany cases, which were deposited carefully in the bottom of the boat, said, after squirting an immense mouthful of tobacco-juice over the side, which was sufficient to have made a shoal of porpoises drunk, had there been any near—

"Capt'en, I've seen them things afore."

"I suppose you have, Jack. What then?"

"Only I wanted to know if it was you this time?"

"Well, supposing it is me, Jack—what have you to say in such a case?"

"Nothing, Capt'en, nothing—only I hope you won't forget that famous line-shot of yourn, that anchored that saucy Englisher so safe on the beach of the Mediterranean, the last time I took you out with them things at daybreak. Just under the pit of the right arm it was, Capt'en."

"Yes, I remember."

"The Britishers said that was too trim betwixt wind and water for them, though it was one of their own people, and they gave us a wide berth afterwards on that station."

"Never fear, Jack. I shall take care about my line-shot, and have it all right, if you will only get me to the ground. Lay to your oars, my man—it is late."

"Ay, ay," and Jack pulled away now as if for dear life. The party had been perfectly silent for some time, and the boat was rapidly nearing the Jersey shore, when Captain Yeiger looked up suddenly and said—

"Ah! Carter, there is one thing I had as well mention to you, now I think of it. In my rooms at the Astor House, there is a small portable writing-desk, which is filled with sheets of manuscript, containing notes of information I have collected during several years of close observation. You will find it all bears upon a certain dangerous mystery, which was yesterday the subject of interesting conversation between us. Should any thing happen to me at any time suddenly, I desire you to take charge of that desk and of the manuscript, and make what use you deem proper of the facts you will find it to contain. They may be of great importance to yourself individually, and of some to the world. You will find the key in the left pocket of my vest: it is in a small leather pouch, which also contains directions how to use it, for the lock is very peculiar. You will remember this for me, will you not?"

"Certainly, captain—I will not fail you. But I hope I shall not be called upon soon to fulfil such a duty."

"Oh, there is little probability of that, this morning at least. It was merely a suggestion which happened to occur to me, with no more particular reference to the business in hand than to any other ordinary contingency."

This was said so very quietly, that Carter was considerably relieved; for he feared his friend had been overtaken by one of those prophetic threatening shadows of doom which sometimes fall mysteriously across the sunlight of the souls of the bravest men, to unnerve them in the moments of their greatest peril.

They had now reached the shore a few miles below Jersey city. They landed near a narrow slip of woods which came down close to the water. A boat like their own was moored a hundred yards off, and they could see the rower leaning back in it, apparently fast asleep. No other human being was in sight.

"They are here, and waiting for us!" said Captain Yeiger, with an expression of vexation, as he looked at his watch.

Carter smiled.

"Never mind, captain. They will have no reason to complain, since they have had just fifteen minutes the advantage of us to grow cool in and survey the ground."

"They are welcome to all the advantage that will afford, for I know that one glance of your eye over the field will be sufficient to baffle all their tactics."

"Yes; my eyes are usually open."

They had now reached the narrow point or tongue of timber. The growth was very thick, but they could hear the sound of voices beyond. They now paused, and Frank turned towards the third person of the party, who had not heretofore spoken at all.

"Doctor, you had better stop here. You are close enough to hear the pistols; but you will please wait my personal summons before making your appearance on the field. There is no reason why you, who came out professionally, should be annoyed, in case of criminal prosecution, by being in any way implicated as an accessory or summoned as a witness."

The person thus addressed had a hard, sharp, professional face, and merely said, in a dry tone—

"Right; perfectly right, Mr. Carter. I am more interested for the bones of your friend than for his honour! I shall be comfortable enough, provided you are not too long in getting them broken for him!"

And placing his case of instruments upon the sand, at the foot of a small tree, he sat down upon it very deliberately, and leaning back, folded his cloak about him as if he were going to take a nap in the mean time.

Frank could not help smiling; but, as he was turning off, he saw, to his great surprise, the oarsman hobbling towards them across the sands. He was about to wave him back impatiently to his boat, when Yeiger arrested his arm.

"Let him alone, Carter! Jack knows what he is about. He has been with me too often on such occasions to compromise us in any degree."

"Well, well, you know the man. Come, let's go round the point."

A few steps brought them around the sharp angle of the wood. Here there seemed to have been a sort of inlet or arm of the bay, which had once run up some distance into the old wood, but as the waters receded, a white and sterile bed of sand had been left, which was yet quite firm to the tread, like that along the beach.

It was a singular nook; and the woods on both sides of it shut out the probabilities of observation, although there were four houses within less than a quarter of a mile, on both sides.

Some fifty paces distant a tall figure was walking impatiently to and fro, holding a watch in his hand: two other persons were seated on a log at the edge of the wood. The tall man paused, returned the watch to his pocket, and the others rose as the two came in sight. One of them advanced, and, to the infinite and inexpressible horror of Frank Carter, he recognised in this person Newnon Clenny.

Poor fellow! He nearly fainted, although not given to the melting mood. It seemed to him as if the sky had fallen in upon his soul!

"Great God!" he exclaimed, "Freta false; and this man, whom I have loved so much, a traitor to our long friendship— to all truth and friendship!"

He griped the arm of Yeiger convulsively, as if to keep him from falling. This singular person seemed to understand the mood of Frank and its causes, as if he read an illuminated scroll. He merely said in a loud whisper, the emphasis of which was hissed into his ear—

2 C 2

"Be a man, Carter! I KNOW this person to be ONE OF THEM!"

"Hah!" said Frank, in the same tone, but with a sort of choked convulsiveness. "What a fool I have been not to suspect this before! How infamously the purest, highest, and noblest instincts of my nature have been trifled with and speculated upon!"

The experience of twenty years of pain and wrong could hardly have congealed a warm heart so utterly as that of Frank became in one instant now. The mild arch of his brows sunk down square above his eyes, with a painful wrinkle between them, which seemed chiselled and fixed in a marble and sphinx-like eternity of suffering.

He greeted Clenny coldly, and as an utter stranger, in reply to his formal salutation.

"We have been accidentally detained in getting over this morning. I hope, sir, we have not kept you waiting long?"

"No, no, sir! My friend is very patient. Our cloaks are something heavier for the mist, but we shall only be the lighter when we throw them off. You have no surgeon, I perceive?"

"I am gratified to relieve your apprehension—we have a skilful and proper person within call."

"Why not bring him forward, as we have done our surgeon?"

"Because I do not perceive the necessity of implicating persons who come out in a professional capacity, in the civil or criminal consequences of our acts."

"Then, sir, I will send our surgeon to join yours."

"If he turns that point of timber, he will not fail to find him, and, most probably, sound asleep, too."

"I will send him."

Clenny walked back rapidly, and soon returned with his surgeon, instrument case, and all.

"Go around the point," said Frank, "and you will probably find him sound asleep behind a tree. You will both please to wait there until we call for you."

The surgeon obeyed; and, taking his case of instruments under his arm, walked off without a word.

They now walked forward to the ground, which seemed to have been selected by the party which came first. It was flanked on either side by the wood, and opened toward the bay. Frank Carter saw all the capabilities of the spot, and quietly waited the demonstration of the other party.

They now approached each other, and Tynenck and Yeiger lifted their hats in formal and frigid greeting. It was out of the question to talk or think of compromise and concession in a case like this, so the business of the morning proceeded in a most methodical manner.

The distance was ten paces, and Clenny commenced to measure the ground. Carter watched him in cold silence, and did not attempt to interfere, as was his duty and right. He had a purpose in this passiveness. The mist had now risen, and the sun was nearly above the horizon.

Clenny marked the places of the combatants, and Tynenck rather hastily stepped forward toward his own. The sun would be up in a few moments. Neither Carter nor Yeiger had yet thrown off their cloaks, and both stood with folded arms and without speaking. We have mentioned that the inlet opened toward the bay, and east.

"Mr. Carter, will you please to measure this ground?"

"Yes, sir," said Carter suddenly; and, dropping his cloak, proceeded formally to step it between the marks that Clenny had made.

"You have measured correctly, sir—this is just ten paces."

He said this as he reached the spot which Clenny had evidently assigned to Tynenck. His back was towards Clenny, and we have mentioned that Tynenck had advanced somewhat prematurely towards his position.

Carter regarded him with a blank, inexpressive look, while, without turning his head, he said in a careless tone—

"Your friend seems to be somewhat in'a hurry to assume his position, Mr. Clenny, which is a pity, when it is evident that the advantage it gives him, will be so much heightened as the sun rises!"

Tynenck was near enough to hear this distinctly, and turned very pale, while Carter proceeded, almost playfully, as he faced about—

"It probably did not occur to you, Mr. Clenny, in selecting this ground, that it would require an extraordinary power of vision on the part of my friend to see his opponent at all with the rising sun in his face. You have unconsciously paid him a singular and poetical compliment in thus taking it for granted that his is an eagle's eye!"

"The sun is not yet up, Mr. Carter."

"It will be," and he pulled out his watch, "according to the almanac, up in five minutes. Besides, Mr. Clenny, a dark background is understood, in art, to bring forward the lights and shades in a picture. You have set the person of my friend quite artistically against the dark background of those trees."

"Your humorous vein is out of place, Mr. Carter. We are not here on your habitual debauch."

"Evidently not; for ' *in vino veritas*,' and I might tell you some unpleasant truths."

Frank looked him steadily in the eye, and could not subdue an involuntary shudder as he recognised the serpent-like malignity which crept into the face of Clenny.

For the first time he read this bad, malicious man, through and through, and saw clear down into the yawning hell of hate and evil in his heart. His manner changed instantly, and his voice became cold and severe.

"Mr. Clenny, I cannot consent to place my friend in the unfair position you have so officiously chosen. Alter their position—let us have it across this inlet, and then your common sense will show you that, with small trees behind each, they are on an equal footing."

"Very good, sir; very good. My choice of positions, out of which you have managed to extract matter for grandiloquent heroics, was entirely accidental. Let it be as you propose."

The ground was accordingly measured, and now the parties took their places. But, since the altercation which we have given, a sort of pitiless gloom had settled down upon the faces of these four persons, which was only the more ominous from its stillness.

Captain Yeiger had been standing with folded arms during all this scene; and now, with a sneering smile, threw off his cloak and came forward to his place. His eyes were strangely enlarged, and glittered with a deadly fierceness as they met those of his foe. In Tynenck's eye there was the cold, dangerous look of the assassin, which could not dwell upon, but played around this angry splendour.

They cast up a coin, and the word fell to Clenny. Just before it was given, Yeiger whispered to Carter—

"I told you, yesterday morning, I meant to 'wing' him. I have changed my mind—I mean to wing him now for the other world. Look for my shot under the pit of the right arm."

"Are you ready, gentlemen? Fire, one, two, three."

Yeiger fired at the word with singular quickness. The form of Tynenck swayed slightly, and then, as it swung round, he fired at "three." Yeiger shuddered down to his very feet, but stood firm.

Frank sprang forward eagerly.

"Are you hit, captain?"

"Only touched, Carter; but I must have another shot. I hit that man!"

Tynenck was leaning in the arms of Clenny, and his face

had assumed a sick and chalk-like whiteness. He rallied as Carter approached, and in a faint voice expressed his readi-- ness for another shot.

Clenny at first protested that his friend was too badly hurt to continue the combat; but Tynenck, with a feeble smile, assured him that he was not hurt, and was anxious that there should be another fire.

The pistols were quickly loaded. Yeiger had, in the mean time, been standing like a stiffened corpse, without having moved a limb. His face was terribly ghastly, and his black eyes scintillated a still, concentrated wrath.

Had Frank Carter been less excited or engrossed, he would have seen there was a pool of blood about the feet of this stern, strong man.

His shoes had run over, and he stood in the ebbing current of his own life.

He snatched eagerly at the pistol which Carter handed him. This time Tynenck fired flurriedly as soon as the word "fire" was pronounced by Clenny; but Yeiger waited with an immovable tension of nerve—then fired at "three."

Tynenck dropped instantly with a ball through his forehead. Yeiger sank down gradually, with the blood gushing from his mouth. He muttered, while his eyes were glazing—

"There is no mail there—I hit him at first—he wears mail about his body!"

Frank rushed forward toward the body of Tynenck, and tore open his vest. Clenny interposed.

"What do you mean, sir?"

"I mean, sir," said Frank, with a savage look, "to ascertain whether this friend of yours wears mail or not."

"Stand back, sir," said Clenny, with a wild gesture, stretching his hand over the still body of Tynenck.

"I will not stand back! I mean to see what he wears next his skin."

Frank clutched the vest and shirt of the dead man, when

Clenny sprang at him, with a sort of shriek, but Frank met him with a blow which stunned him. Clenny fell, and Frank tore open the bosom, and thus revealed beneath, not a steel-linked shirt, as the romances have it, but a close-stitched quilting of silk.

It was only necessary to turn over the coat and vest to see that the ball had struck the fatal line, and been glanced off by this most effective coat of mail. The man had been stunned by the force of the ball, though it had not penetrated the silk.

Yeiger had stiffened as he sank down, and the last words he spoke were, "REMEMBER THE KEY!"

The surgeons now made their appearance, coming hastily forward; and Jack, the sailor, rushed out of the wood and fell upon his knees by the body of his old captain.

"Gentlemen," said Carter, solemnly pointing to the body of Tynenck, "please examine the body of that assassin, and bear me witness that he deserved his fate—and that this wretch!" pointing scornfully at Clenny, who was sitting with an ashy face, "has been accessary to the fact of a deliberate murder upon the body of my friend!"

"The bloody villain!" said Jack, looking up with streaming eyes. "It's a murder he's done, is it?" and he began to finger his knife, while he looked viciously at Clenny.

Frank saw that more mischief was threatened, and stepped hastily between the sailor and Clenny.

"No more blood! no more blood! Enough has been shed this morning!"

"You have no use for me here any longer. These bones are past my skill." And the technical surgeon turned away.

CHAPTER IV.

POOR Frank Carter! It did seem, literally, as if the vials of all wrath had been poured upon his head. He had fortune, but what of that? He had walked over the fresh graves of all that were nearest and dearest to him, into its possession.

Mother, father, brother, and sister, one after another, the whole family group of precious ones—so beautifully elevated in the tender memories of his boyhood, as the mythology of that young time of holy peace and trusting worship—he had seen swept away by the terrible fevers of the South.

When the last went—oh! how desolate, in the mighty bereavement, that tall, lithe youth stood up like a young tree, the last of the forest, which only held erect for pride, although "the cross, quick lightning" had as well touched to the core its life.

But then that life was very vigorous, and responded quickly to the blessing of the sun, and through the healing influence was aroused to spread its arms and reach with upward yearnings once again. And now there had come to him a weird, new Presence, which filled the "valley and the shadow" where his soul stood, with a warm, strange light, but a light no other eyes could see. It was the light of dreams, which entereth the dark gates of sense to make the earthly tabernacle glow through all its chambers, as if an angel had come in to rest. But it was an angel all too mild to hurt with "the destroying splendour," and seemed to plead with his soul for room, while with a meek command it glided in without his answer, and nestled down beside his heart, turning the starshine calm eyes upon it, as if to watch the throbbings.

This was the Ideal, yet he did not worship it consciously, but rather the soul within him lay down beside it peacefully— splendour to splendour—and watched with it how his own heart went.

But sometimes the "elemental rack" of wrath or lust would smite upon that heart, from outward, through the roused and maddened senses, until it bounded wild, and then the Presence and the starshine would go away and leave his forlorn soul to struggle with the tempest through deep night— but it would as surely come back again as the moon does to the storm-lashed sea, through the first rift of clouds.

This was his time to worship it; for he prayed through the dark waves that it would come to his agony, and when he felt its warm light back again, ah! felt what worship his be- wildered joy made out of gratitude, until his heart grew calm once more, and then his soul lay happily down beside it, splendour to splendour—all assured as before.

But these storms returned less frequently after this Pre- sence came, and gradually he grew watchful that his life should be kept still and his heart-pulse regular, lest the bright inmate, with the starshine in its eyes that watched it, should be frightened, and go away again. He grew steady upon this poise, and lived so through years of transition from youth to manhood.

Often, for a time, he was shaken as if an earthquake urged and worked within him, when he saw a vague some- thing in the eyes of a young girl which reminded of that star- shine near his heart—but then the REALITY went suddenly away from its close nestle by that centre of the sensuous life, and he was left to struggle through the dim red haze of a voluptuous mist, like a blind man feeling through "outer darkness" until his fingers waked him from the gross delu- sion,—pah!

2 D   22

Then, after a while, the starshine would creep back through the gloom of sultry moodings, and the Presence would lie down again in peace and joy on its old couch of light, to watch his heart grow calm once more. So his life had flowed with ebbing alternations, passion, gloom, and peace contending, until the time when we first knew him, an adventurer of the wilderness, when the starshine was in the ascendant, though he had substituted friendship, just then, as he supposed, for this ideal passion, because it was more like its deep calm, that shone about his heart, and could not disturb its repose.

This man Clenny had come to him with the surest guaranties, through letters from faithful and time-honoured correspondents of his father, and he had embraced him at once as a brother.

Carter had before known many friends with whom he warmly sympathized, as participating with him to a certain interior degree in the conditions of his life just then ; but in meeting Clenny, he first found " THE SOCIAL SKEPTIC"—the unbeliever in the hope and future of humanity—the shrewd and biting sneerer at all the sacredness of its tameless and undying aspirations.

The character was a novelty to him, and attracted him strongly, at once, as a novelty. He could not believe that any being born beneath God's sunshine, who had ever seen the young flowers grow, could live, and not have felt his soul swell pregnant, not alone to the kiss of spring, and blossom through his brain in fragrant thoughts of tender joy, which deepened on to the summer of opened roses and all glorious flowers into the autumn of hope's fruition.

He could not realize, and would not realize such ungentle skepticism. He could realize that such faith should be wanting to the heavy boor, who woke to eat, as the wild beast does, to absolute engorgement, and of the same bloody food—that he should work, work, plod drowsily through all the day, without any other presence in his congested brain than the thought of his next meal; but that a man of refined cultivation should level his faith to that of the dull-eyed boor, was beyond his comprehension.

The one could see the stars through a clear empyrean above him—the other, with his "downward eye," see them but in their reflex in the puddle at his feet.

He did not believe the sneers of Clenny to be real expressions of his inmost life and thought. He belived that, like many proud and sensitive men, this one had unconsciously fallen into the habit of jeering at the sacredness of others, as a sort of petulant and skin-deep disguise for his own, which he shrank from revealing.

He saw that Clenny was as brave as a lion, and took all the rest for granted; for with quite characteristic impulsiveness, he did not understand how a brave man could be any thing else than generous, true, and honourable.

Indeed, Clenny well understood how to sustain an illusion of this kind, for with him it was quite an indifferent matter whether he did a princely and generous thing, on your behalf, mathematically, or ruined you utterly, body and soul, through the same process of cold calculation. The power of numbers was the power of conscience with him, and ruled a will as patient and inexorable as death.

He was witty and intellectual as he was caustic, and Frank was charmed by the contrast. Though very reserved and cautious in forming such ties, he had yet thrown himself with all his enthusiasm into this friendship of Clenny.

As for Myra Haynes—with whom Clenny had seemed, with strange pertinacity, to be endeavouring to entangle him into a match, through the several years of their intercourse—she had never for a moment by her presence stirred the starshine by his heart.

But ah, when he met Freta, his angel guest rose up and went forth with all its glory on, and disappeared within her form for ever. Then he saw, with his outward vision, that same star-shine appear in her eyes, and felt it upon his heart as of old—through the walls of the tabernacle now, rather than from within its chambers. His IDEAL had gone forth and been embodied.

A few brief days, and rapture had been agony—a bright storm now raged within him, and shook his life with a joy so tameless and intense, that it could be only uttered in electric flashes down the nerves.

But ah, the desolating and terrific gloom which followed— lassoed, and borne away all helpless—while SHE, too, seemed going off all cold and unregardful, without even turning her head for a farewell look. Then his IDEAL had gone out in horror and in gloom.

Months of delirium and nearly fatal illness followed, and he awoke in deep night and went forth a stumbling, stricken man. He yet went groping, plunging on, always through thick darkness, with only one pale star—his passionate friend- ship for Clenny—before him; and now even that had gone out in bloody wrath—in the shame of unutterable dishonour and the gloomy mystery of concerted and premeditated crime.

What wonder, then, that "the Enthusiast" became wild now! He was too strong to die—too fiercely proud to ac- knowledge himself utterly crushed, even to himself.

Despair had no funeral gloom so fearful, or so blind to him, as that his own conscious self-respect would bring in the awful shadows of a ruthless wrath upon him, should he prove recreant to his CENTRAL WILL, against the combined universe of sentiment and action.

He had blinded and stunned and made a beast of himself, in his excesses, and yet through all his strong individuality was asserted, and could not be degraded by the wildest extremes. Though plunged into the most extravagant dissipation, still in its gloomiest disguises he preserved this central consciousness and firmness of will.

Had he been brought up to what he then considered the prejudiced bar of "public opinion," to answer for his acts, he would have haughtily plead guilty, without any excuse—deliberately guilty, with eyes wide open—guilty, because he chose to be so. He was outraging the truth in himself, rather than any truth in the social organization, and asked no mercy at its hands.

Thus he thought, felt, and acted; and had he been some poor man, who only managed to decently compromise between honour and poverty, he would have been hunted down by the hue and cry of drunkard, ruffian, etc.; but as his great wealth was well known, all these things were politely termed the eccentricities of a young Southerner.

Unconscious Frank, had they outlawed him a hundred times, he would have come back, though it had been from the gloomiest depths of poverty, with such a calm and steadfast assurance of a right to place his feet where he willed to place them, that the silly, clamorous crowd of denunciators would have been stilled to ask respectfully, "Who is it?" He did not care—the possession of wealth made no difference with him—the question between himself and society was a paltry one—too paltry to be regarded by him for a moment but with scorn.

The only issue he recognised, was that between himself, his own central consciousness, and God—the God of justice, righteousness, and truth. He was under an awful cloud now, for his IDEAL was gone with the vanished starshine, and his friendship had been fatally outraged, and he was struggling towards the sunlight as best he could through the darkness. What did he care what men said about the mode and moods of this struggle?

It was his business—a private matter between God and himself—and he utterly scorned and contemned the senti-

2 D 2

ment of a public which pronounced upon him ignorantly, out of an unreasoning prejudice.

Had he been ever so poor, his indomitable CONSCIENTIOUS-NESS was strong enough to have outlived the clamour of accident and occasion, and come up out of the shadow with calm, commanding eyes, which would have wrested a place for him out of their vulgar hate.

Since that bloody duel, he had been what the charitable world would call a madman.   That is, he was sober enough to see discreetly to the private burial of Yeiger; and furthermore, to get possession of the mysterious desk and key; and again had prudence enough not to denounce Clenny, and to hush the whole affair, so far as money could go, and then to lock up both desk and key in his own room.

But yet he went into the wildest excesses, and threw off all restraint, except those which his own will regulated.   His brain was too much congested, now, to open or read the curious manuscript which Yeiger had told him was contained in that small desk.

The weekly suppers at his rooms had heretofore been attended by persons representing one or the other phase of a more polished development.   But now, they had assumed rather a quaint character, since, alongside of recognised gentlemen, clothed in all the proprieties of elegant costume, the flash sporting-characters about town, even ruffians, were to be seen—squalid, wretched, and threadbare—as they came from the lowest dens of brutal vice.

Rough, with their tatters on, they sat beside the varnished gentlemen, and made a rude, ribald wit from out their degradation.

Some of these scenes, if we had time, we would look in upon more curiously; but at present we can only follow to others, which are their consequences!

The winding up of these parties almost invariably found Frank partially intoxicated; and frequently, after all were gone, he would go forth disguised, and, in the haunted wretchedness of his life, wander through the great city, stopping here and there amid its gloomiest alleys and low-portalled dens, to relieve the congestion of agony gathering upon his heart and brain—from out those passionate, mournful memories—by looking upon a degree of suffering and depth of degradation which was, in its physical expression at least, more profound and hideous than his own. He gained relief therefrom, and that dumb wail within his heart was often shocked into profoundest torpor by the contrast: he felt almost a savage joy, that there were others more profoundly accursed than himself!

In all this we recognise the war going on in Frank's mind. He had set out in life frank and confiding, believing the world as noble, as generous as himself; and he had been bitterly disappointed!

The result had been a common one—though one none the less wrong: he had lost all faith in humanity; he had become a scorner of the show-virtue, because having, in his recklessness, committed vices, he abhorred the hypocrisy of concealing them. His nature, in fact, was passing through a bitter ordeal. Ah! would that his angel Freta would arise, would rescue him from himself, would restore him to faith, to virtue, and to society!

In this world of mixed good and evil, the great lesson to be learned is, that the cant of others is no excuse for our own excesses. The perfidy of some ought not to teach us to despise all.

This was the lesson that our hero was now learning. His soul is like a volcano in eruption—lurid, fiery, scattering ruin around; but time will exhaust the torrent, the lava will cool, fertile fields will spring up, and the whole landscape smile.

It was now several months since the duel, and the life of Frank continued, in the general features of its eccentricities, to be much the same as that we have disclosed before.

He had taken the precaution, lately, to carry arms on h. person whenever he went out at night—because he had good reason to believe that his house was watched, and that his steps were dogged from place to place.

At first he paid no attention to the fact—which his indomitable habits of observation had never failed to note, in spite of the wine he drank—that there were always persons in sight, loitering about the Park, when he came out from his house.   At first this made no impression upon him, from a feeling of recklessness; yet gradually the recollection of it took hold upon him, in spite of himself.

He found that, go where he might, into alleys and dens however obscure, he would always, when he came forth, detect that there was somebody on the alert in the neighbourhood; and he came finally to suspect that surveillance was carried on even from within the railings of the Park, although that was well known to be exclusive ground, and could only be entered by members of such families who held keys.   And he frequently thought of using his own key for examination.

Then, if he went off, even at full speed, through the streets— as he sometimes did—there seemed to follow him a sort of faint, ghost-like sound of pursuing steps.

He came at last to notice this fact with a degree of nervous apprehension which he could scarcely account for. From what quarter could this sort of insolent surveillance come?

He tried to escape from this haunting sound of steps pursuing.   He would run on for several streets, and then dodge behind the columns of some public edifice, or crouch beneath the vestibule of some private building, and wait for the pursuing step to come on, but always without success; for when he stopped, all was silent as death.

At last, one night he armed himself, changed his ordinary disguise, and thrust a pair of India-rubber shoes into the large pockets of his rough overcoat, and came forth at the usual time, with the determination to find out, at all risks, who this was, and what all these presumptuous dodgings meant.

He walked off with his boot-heels clattering along the pavement; and, after turning down two or three streets and around several squares, he became convinced that he was followed as usual.

He now ran on at full speed until he turned a corner, and then quickly slipping on his India-rubber shoes, glided back with noiseless footfall, keeping as much within the shadow of the lamp as possible. The night was dark, and in a little time he heard the faint pattering of coming feet. He hid behind the columns of a church.

He had scarcely concealed himself, when a man came up with a cautious, gliding step, as if in fear that the sound of his own footfall would prevent him from hearing something for which he listened ahead.

His body was stooped, and his ear turned towards the ground, or pavement rather. Frank at once recognised the posture of an Indian pursuing his enemy, or his game, by the nice sense of hearing, which detects the flying tread in reverberations along the earth.

He sprang out at once from his concealment to grapple with him. With all the angry eagerness of his spring, Frank was not quick enough to secure the person of his pursuer.

The man seemed to have felt him coming, so alert was he in escaping from his clutch; and Frank only succeeded in tearing out a fragment of the rough overcoat which he wore, which remained in his hand.

The man had succeeded in wresting himself from his imperfect grasp by a movement as serpent-like as it was vigorous; but in the momentary struggle, which occurred under one of the street-lamps, Frank thought he recognised, in the pale, copper face there revealed, one which he had good cause to remember.

IIe stood still, looking at the fragment he held in his hand, in blank confusion and amaze, for some moments, while the receding footsteps throbbed upon his startled ear.

"Great God!" he muttered, "is SHE here?"

CHAPTER V.

THE INDIAN.

'THE discovery last made left Frank in a condition of bewilderment which it would be difficult to realize. The man's brain was literally stunned by the detonation of this surprise, and the smothered heart-fires within him moiled and raged anew in the blinded tumult of old tenderness. All was chaos with him for a while—chaos darkened indeed—but storm-like, and wildly illuminated here and there with keen and fiercely vivid flashes of electric joy from out the Past—that would show as well the dreary void yawning in the Present of his desperate and aimless life. For a long period of gross and self-inflicted degradation, his inner consciousness had stretched forth the arms of sense, feeling dumbly for a soul within the gloom, and yet there had been no response until now— and now was ecstasy that only did not swoon! Doubt, joy, hope, shame!—how or by which was he dizzied? Was it a mere vision, or had the ineffable returned within his sphere? He had no tongue to ask, no thought to reason—he could merely feel!

IIe had discovered a trace—however dim—of Freta. It mattered not to him how vague, it yet was real—how fleeting, its palpability was still assured. The good angel had returned to his life, and hovered invisible about his steps! The starshine had arisen once more to glimmer from its dark bed beside his heart—faint—however faintly, yet he felt the light!

The recognition of the face of the Indian beneath the lamp, instantaneous as it was, had yet been perfect. He had had good reason for remembering those strange, wan features, and dark, ghastly, hollow eyes. They had been the first that shone upon him when he aroused from the death-like stupor which followed upon his being choked down with the lasso, as he rode joyously beside Freta.

He had found himself on board a steamboat descending the Missouri River, with this Indian face bending over him, and he remembered well this man as a favourite serviteur of Freta's, who had always accompanied her on her wild rides at a respectful distance, to guard her from impending dangers. He remembered as well, too, the tumult of rage and tenderness commingled which this recognition had caused him; for, regarding Freta as in someway a party to the foul treachery of which he had been the victim, his heart had struggled desperately within him to forswear its faith, and curse her in his wrath; yet the presence of this man, whom he knew to have been much trusted by her, had suggested vague and happy doubts as to her wilful agency in the grievous wrong he had endured;—and then his sudden reappearance here in the great city—his close haunting upon his track which he had detected —had called up, ah, a world of blissful mysteries, to which he dared not give a name, even within himself! He now remembered, too, that there had been in the face of this Indian an expression of settled and yearning melancholy, expressive of sentiment more refined and spiritualized than he had ever supposed the coarse organization of the race permitted. This unusual character had therefore been strongly impressed upon his mind, apart from the fact of the Indian having been his close and constant nurse during a considerable period of illness which had followed. And then there was another characteristic which he vividly remembered, which was, that this man had always, and with marked pertinacity, refused, in seeming at least—to understand a single phrase of the English

tongue; in regard to the most common terms, he remained
inexorably mute—and would only afford apparent recognition,
when addressed in his own tongue or by gestures, which constituted his favourite mode of communication with others.

Frank could not help thinking it strange that this young
Indian, who had for years been in constant intercourse with
Freta and her father, should yet refuse any recognition of
the sounds of the tongue in which they habitually spoke. He
had, however, marked it as a proud and sulky peculiarity of
the Indian race, rather than in any suspicious light. Although
the man had watched over him until his complete recovery,
at New Orleans, with a zeal and carefulness which seemed
almost religious, yet he had there suddenly disappeared, leaving with Frank not even the slightest trace of the means or
manner of his exit. Since that time, even amid the wildest
excesses of his debauched life, the image of this singular Indian had frequently occurred to him, as constituting the con-
necting link between him and the troubled though delicious
Past. That glancing recognition could not therefore now
have failed him.

He was sure, and his heart made the assurance doubly sure,
that it was Freta's closest serviteur he had seen, and that, by
some indescribable process of sympathy, Freta must be near
—near! near!

And why near?—Watching over him?—through her agent
—or, it might be—tumult of tenderness!—through her own
eyes. It might be that from some window that overlooked
his daily life, she even saw him now and then, and in her
proper flesh.

Oh, ecstasy!—might it be so? Might it be, that all the
yearnings of his inner life would yet find their reality—that
treachery, gloom, and hate had not yet overcome the beautiful
within him? He became instantly a new man—the trammels
of habit were thrown off; and the aimless energies he had
been dissipating were concentrated upon a single purpose—to

find Freta—to look once more upon that face that had so thrilled and charmed his life!

This Indian must be watched in turn, until some clue to the locality of Freta's dwelling might be obtained through his movements. Days and nights of sleepless vigilance were at length so far rewarded as to have enabled him to trace this man to the back entrance of a large dwelling near his own. He saw him approach it cautiously, and with a bounding heart assured himself that he had entered noiselessly. Here at least seemed a discovery—a great point of certainty gained. Here must be the home of Freta, and, as he had at first wildly conjectured—near his own! Ah, joyful reality!—and then it might all be true!—he had not been demented quite! His soul had indeed been electrified into a seer-like vision; and now his fate was within those walls—it had been upon him ever, a vague but mighty and resistless shadow; and now it was to take incarnate form again—become a substance of reality, and he had found for it "a local habitation." Only those walls divided them—he should see her to-morrow face to face, and all mysteries and doubts should banish before the radiant beamings of that face! He held down his heart for joy, and mused dreamily beneath the moon.

All that Frank previously knew of this house amounted to nothing more than that it was known to be occupied, though the inmates were seldom seen, and were supposed to be foreigners. It had not once occurred to him that there might be any difficulty in obtaining entrance. Why should he? Walls and doors were no barriers to be thought of now! His life was up—his will aroused—why should he think of physical obstructions, or forms and customs, as between him and his joy? His feet were scarce on earth now, and why should he regard the more earthly obstructions in his way? His first attempt, however, sufficed to wake him promptly enough from this momentary delusion. To be sure, when gruffly informed by a burly and insolent servant, who slammed

2 E

the door in his face at the same time, that he "knowed no
such 'oman" as she whom he named, he felt for an instant as
if making a breathless descent to the common globe again;
yet, when the jolt was over, he smiled, though his heart felt
deadly sick, and, choking down the upheaving within him, he
walked leisurely away; coolly bethinking him of the absurdity
he had committed, and of the new measures to secure him
against failure in the future.

Ridiculous!—how could he have expected it to be otherwise!—of course she was under restraint! How could he
have expected that any message from himself would be permitted to reach her! He would seek out this ruffian jailor of
hers—Thomson was said to be his name, and he was called
an Englishman—and find out something first from him, if
possible—if not, demand an interview, which if he also refused, should finally be compelled by the intervention of the
police, from which he should obtain a search-warrant for her
rescue. In the mean time, he would address her through the
post, and watch the house continually. These and a thousand other resolutions Frank endeavoured to carry into effect
—but, with all his vigilance and energy, with about like success in each. He could obtain no satisfaction whatever from
the stolid or astonished Englishman—he could not well judge
which. His letters remained unanswered—his vigils brought
no result; and, therefore, he was compelled to perceive that
any attempt at forcible entry upon the premises would be regarded by the very police whose intervention he had thought
to seek, as absurdly quixotic, if not criminal.

Baffled in these directions, but by no means discouraged
or convinced withal, Frank at once determined, if possible,
to out-general the young Indian, who had kept himself as invisible during all these efforts as if those silent walls through
which he had beheld him disappear had been sealed upon him
for ever. The Indian had somehow obtained the advantage
of position of him, and warily kept himself out of view. Re-

solved to throw him off his guard, Frank suddenly and secretly disappeared from the city, first closing up his house, and sending off his servants, as if the chase had either been given up in despair, or he had departed upon some false scent.

This cost him a sufficiently severe struggle indeed, but he heroically stood it out until, as he thought, the certainty of his absence had become sufficiently assured to throw even the Indian off his guard: he, in the mean time, through an un-suspected agent, kept himself informed of the general move-ments of the household.   When things were fully ripe, Frank entered the city carefully disguised, one night, and approach-ing with circumspection the scene, discovered the Indian at his old accustomed post, within the privileged railings of St. John's Park.   Provided with his own key, Frank cautiously entered, and concealing himself within the abounding shrub-bery, he glided in noiseless movement upon the man, who, with body cowering in an attitude singularly expressive of dejection, sat with face turned toward his closed mansion. Frank stood watching this motionless form for a few moments with feelings indescribably agitated by curiosity in regard to the meaning of what he had seen and now saw in the ex-pression of this strange being—together with eagerness to hold him once fairly within his grasp, and wrest from him, by force if it must be, the secret which he felt assured was held by him.

Thus trembling on tiptoe he stood, then sprang upon the man, clasping him about with an embrace that not all the startled strength of savage energies could break—for though the stern and breathless struggle held long in silent fury, yet the Indian, who seemed to be somewhat emaciated, appeared finally sinking from exhaustion, as his chin fell upon his breast, and his whole frame quivered as in an ague-fit.   His hands dropped listlessly to his side as Frank slowly released his terrible grasp, and the two men, panting for breath, stood re-garding each other with cold, dilated gaze.   There was nei-

ther hate nor rage in the expression: they simply bore themselves as two old gladiators would, who paused to rest for a
moment in the arena.   But the struggle which now commenced was not again of physical forces, but of will.   The
Indian made no further effort to escape, but stood sullenly
obdurate; while Frank, with the fiery eagerness of the conqueror, demanded, through gestures, the truth as to the resi-
dence of Freta.

The Indian, with folded arms, made no reply, but continued
to watch his eyes with steady gaze.   Frank threatened and
raved—but all in vain.   The man's face and figure were like
marble.   At last the young lover, rendered wild by the agony
of these continued delays—this last and most harrowing baffle,
sobbed aloud, beating his breast for the wo.   Then seizing
the Indian, shook him as if he would have annihilated him—
while, with streaming eyes, and passionate, imploring gestures,
he pointed mutely toward the suspected house.

The Indian shuddered through his whole frame—while for
an instant his dry eyes glared upon Frank a sultry look of
furious hate, then melting into softness, he suddenly, as if his
tongue were now by some miracle first loosed—

"She thar!"

Frank could scarcely restrain the shout of exultation—
forgetting in his excitement the strangeness of the fact, that
the Indian had just now for the first time found his tongue—

"She is there!   Oh, you will make me to see her?   I will
give you much money—I will make you rich!"

The Indian with a sudden gesture threw off Frank's grasp,
drew himself proudly up, and regarded him with that peculiar
deadly look which we have already noticed.   Frank saw he
had made a mistake, and it instantly recalled all that he had
observed in this man's remarkable bearing; and now it came
upon him like a flash—that this unusual expression, which he
had so often observed, might have a direction similar to that
with which his own life was filled.   Fool! not to have thought

of this before! How could it be otherwise? How could any living thing approach her but with the same results. Had not the very creatures of the wilderness where he had found her, loved her? Had not the very wild-flowers bowed their heads in adoration as she passed? Had not the stars been "sicklied o'er" that she came not forth, when the moon paled for her sweet presence? Could this free child of nature then escape the pure enthralment? Could he, day by day, live within the sphere that radiated only love and holy joy, and not have yielded to the soft enchantment? It could not be! He now first realized this being with whom he strove! Theirs was one common bond!—and, without one jealous pang, his heart yearned toward him in this new fraternity of worship.

His whole manner changed at once, and, grasping the man's hand, he exclaimed—

"Indian love Freta! Indian my brother!"

The man crouched for a moment, and bent himself nearly double, as if shot through the heart!—his secret had been discovered!—but with a deep groan he now lifted himself, and stood erect—his face beaming with an expression Frank had never seen upon it. It now expressed all of frankness, eagerness, and tenderness combined—while, with vehemence almost incoherent, he proceeded to inform Frank that Freta was actually under durance in the house which he had suspected to contain her—that he was the only person with whom she was permitted to communicate freely—that he had only been permitted to approach her thus under the pretence on his part of acting as a spy on her movements—that, playing this part, he had kept her constantly informed of Frank's outgoings and incomings—that, learning of his reckless life in New York, she had only been content while she knew that the Indian followed close upon him, watching his every step. To Frank's vehement questioning as to who they were who held her under this rigid surveillance, the In-

2 E 2   23

dian only shook his head mournfully, but made no reply; at once seemingly overwhelmed by a sudden influx of feeling— the Indian exhorted Frank, in his broken tongue, to go to her—expressing in his picturesque gesticulation, "that she was dying! dying of a broken heart—and that he alone could rescue her!"

The Indian now again sank into a brooding silence, from which Frank laboured, for a long time in vain, to arouse him. For, by no means yet satisfied, he wished to arrange with him the proper and necessary expedients for obtaining the so much desired interview with Freta. The Indian would only shake his head, and repeat she had forbidden it!—until at last, roused again by Frank's imploring despair, he resumed his late bearing and energies. Again he proceeded, frequently interrupting himself with the exclamation—" She die—must be done!"—to explain to Frank the difficulties which beset any attempts at ingress, and to arrange with him a plan by which they might all be set aside, and an interview be obtained for him in the morning at eleven o'clock. Having made himself fully understood, the Indian darted suddenly away beneath the shadows, and in another moment Frank heard the iron clank of a door of the park.

His heart and brain were too full—and when silence had returned he sank upon the grass, where he lay for hours pressing his throbbing temples against the dewy sod.

CHAPTER VI.

THE INTERVIEW.

THE next morning the plan of the interview succeeds, and at eleven o'clock Frank has passed the hitherto invincible portals, and finds himself, with a heart that fluttered—ah, how wildly!—in the presence of Freta herself. He was all dishevelled as he came from his night-watch under the heavy dews of the park. His hair, damp and dark, hung elf-wise about his ashen cheeks, and his great hollow eyes glowed with an illumination that seemed almost madness. He threw off the rough outer garb of his disguise as the Indian threw open the door of a large darkened room and retired. He trembled a moment with faintness on the threshold, then entered the deep silence on tiptoe, lest an echo of the sacred stillness that reigned there should be disturbed. The room at first seemed unoccupied save by a few articles of costly furniture—when in the most shaded extremity, he detected a pure and delicately small, white hand, that seemed to lie upon the folds of a dove-coloured silk drapery that lay upon an ottoman. His heart bounded convulsively, and stealing softly across the room, in another moment he knelt and pressed his trembling lips thereon. The hand was slowly withdrawn, and with a calm and listless movement, the figure arose to a sitting posture. Her eyes were half closed, and she was wan as death. She gradually opened them as her gaze met his where he knelt there with lips half parted. Like the sun's arrows, the devouring splendour struck her to the heart, for she knew not of his coming, and, with a faint cry of childlike ecstasy, she swooned upon his neck, her cold cheek nestled against his, and her arm wound about his neck in a convulsive clasp. Bewildered with the burden of a single sense, Frank thought not of other relief but kissing her back to life. When it came at last, and those great blue eyes, swimming in tenderness, trembled to full opening upon him, and became fixed in one large, liquid, steadfast gaze, he felt his inmost soul go up into them, and light and life transferred into those still orbs. Long they gazed thus, while the Present seemed lost to both. Together they were all unconscious of the Past, and a soft smile would flit—ah, how sweetly!—across the wan transparency of her face, as some gay bright image would arise:—Black Hawk and the panther, her wild-wood pets—Fanny, the fawn—the gallop across the rainbow-hued prairie, the wild-flower beds, and back again upon the circle—that strange moment when their souls leaped and flamed to meet each other as they rode beneath the moon on the night of their first meeting. Then came the dark shadow of that sudden and frightful separation by the lasso, when Black Hawk, who had been first purposely wounded from the thicket by an arrow, ran away with her,—when the shudder from the trance into which she had fallen recalled her with a cry of terror to the present, as at the same moment a door of the apartment swung rudely open.

Frank sprang to his feet, and the blood rushed fiercely to his brow, as he saw Clenny, in his white cravat, dressed in the utmost precision of fashion, advancing directly toward them. There had been a slight corrugation of this man's brow, and the slightest perceptible flush had darted across his smooth fair cheek, as the scene presented itself to him on his opening the door. But now his brow was as impassive as marble, and his smile as bland as ever, while he proceeded in formal terms to apologize for interrupting what he termed a pleasing scene.

"A renewal of your acquaintance with—my betrothed, Mr. Carter! Ah, I remember you were then quite like very young people will be together—affectionate—very! You had both of you nothing else to do out there in the wilderness. Let me see you seated, Mr. Carter! The health of my betrothed is rather delicate at present!" And placing a chair for Frank, he was proceeding to push himself between him and Freta.

Frank listened to the cool effrontery of this speech: at the word betrothed his eye sought that of Freta, who had sunk back, with her head upon the pillow of the lounge. The reply to his appeal was a look of such utter and hopeless despair, that Frank felt that the pretensions of this man could not be entirely groundless: however it came about, she was clearly in this man's power. He had not once taken his eye from hers, and as Clenny made this last movement, as if to interpose himself between them, Frank's frame, although his face remained unmoved, suddenly dilated with such an expression of resistless passion, that Freta, with a mingled expression of tenderness and terror, lifted her hand and exclaimed—

"No! no! Do not touch him! It is so!"

"Ah!" uttered Frank with a deep exhalation from his oppressed lungs—then turning to Clenny, who had taken his position nearest Freta, and now faced him with a cold half smile, he bowed, and with perfect ease, saying—

"I was not at first aware, sir, of your relations to this lady, you will therefore pardon my very natural surprise at meeting you here. You will, no doubt, however, my dear sir, permit me the pleasure of renewing, at an early date, the long interrupted intercourse with my old friend, Newnon Clenny!"

"With pleasure, sir!" said Clenny; "I shall be delighted at the opportunity of such renewal! Shall it be this evening, at three?"

"At three, at our old rendezvous," said Frank, bowing himself toward the door. For one moment he looked back at Freta—she had raised her head! the wild and mournful tenderness of that last gaze, darkened as it was by the shadow of a mortal terror—could he ever forget it? Alas, poor Frank!

CHAPTER VII.

ARRANGEMENTS FOR A VOYAGE.

AT three o'clock, according to appointment, the young men met; and as it was yet too early for the Battery to be much occupied, they sauntered carelessly down Broadway toward that famous promenade, conversing indifferently as they went upon the passing scenes. Arrived there, and selecting the most unfrequented walk, they turned in. They were now alone. "Clenny," said Frank quietly, "you remember our conversation one night at the St. Charles' Hotel, just before we set off on that hunting excursion to the West."

"Yes, I remember it well—and that you talked a great deal of nonsense, too !"

"No doubt ! I merely wish to recall it to you, however. I happened, by some amazing combinations of chance, or the resistless attraction of some law of affinities, to have been led directly through the vicissitudes of our adventure, to the forest home of her who was the incarnation of that ideal of which I spoke—and whom I had vainly sought through life, as one blindly seeketh for his flitting angel through his dream."

"Yes, yes !" said Clenny, somewhat pettishly. "I know, as a very romantic young gentleman knight-errant, seeking for his Dulcinea among buffaloes and greasy Indian squaws, you chanced to meet with a very young and silly girl, whom you, in your chivalric honour, were bound to recognise as neither more nor less than the veritable Lady Del Toboso, and to adore accordingly. But it won't do, friend Frank! Such nonsense"——

"Hark ye, friend Newnon! No prosing, if you please! There have been certain passages between I and you, since the time when I could afford to listen to such. For one thing, there is a certain unavenged blow! Hey? You attempted to stop my hand when I was stripping the body of your traitorous confederate, to exhibit the chain-mail which he wore next his skin!"

"Well, sir—what then?" drawled Clenny in a deliberate tone, turning his eye with a quick, keen flash upon Frank.

"Oh, nothing, nothing," said Frank with a smile, and looking carelessly about. "I only wanted you too hold this in mind, when you feel good-natured enough to commence with your confounded and perpetual snarling at my acts, sayings, and opinions."

"Never fear, Frank, that the account will ever lose any thing in my keeping!"

"Ah! that's the way to talk! Now I love you, 'mine ancient.' But this last item, Newnon, makes it rather heavy to run longer, does it not?"

"Pray explain!"

"With pleasure, sir. You have, by 'treason and stratagem,' or what not device of your black spirit, robbed me of my young love—of Freta—or, if you have not already done so, it is your fixed purpose so to do!—Is it not?"

"It is my purpose to marry Freta, most certainly—call it robbery or what not!"

"Yes! Well, it is equally my purpose that marry Freta you shall not! I shall require her at your hands, at your peril!"

"Pooh, boy! I am no driveller of La Mancha, whatever you may imagine yourself to be. At my peril, forsooth!"

"Look you, Newnon—my blow has already branded you as a caitiff and an assassin—and I will at once here, and on the spot, hide you as a hound, if your language to me is not more measured!"

Here Frank stopped, while the big veins knotted on his

temples. The eyes of the two men met, ánd glinted against each other for one steadfast minute. At length Frank said in a low tone—

"It's no use, Newnon, we've got to fight. Death alone can decide this issue between us. I feel that you have no purpose to give her up—and *you* feel as well that I have no purpose of relinquishing her to you!"

"But suppose I will not fight? The game is in my own hands—I should be a fool to do so! I have other modes of securing my ends. No wise man risks his life for what can be secured without it!"

"Yes, you will fight, Newnon—and by this sign I tell you, I know that you will fight! She loves me—and hates you! While you love her, and, as you know, hopelessly while I live. You will, therefore, never brook my living!"

"Ay! if I only knew what you say to be true, I might oblige you, my friend!" muttered Clenny, grinding his teeth. "Bah! it was only a girlish romance!—Is it not so?"

"Console yourself!" continued Frank quietly. "But all was renewed between us in that interview which you so opportunely interrupted with your villanous politeness!"

Clenny stamped his foot upon the ground, and his teeth clanked as they came together.

"Yes, it is vain to console yourself. I know you for a villain, Clenny, as you are very well aware—that you would take a man's life by treachery as coolly as you would rub out a decimal from your infernal mathematics. I know that you have a secret power—that you wield a terrible, and even mysterious force, that could at any time be brought to bear upon my extermination—and I might fear you—but that I know you better than your confederates, perhaps. I know you to be brave as steel—game to the very backbone—and proud as Lucifer. With all your cunning, you are more of the wolf than the fox! There are passions in which you will know no fear, and can brook no rival——

"Sagacious!"

"Yes, sagacious. It is by this sign of personal courage, which redeems you from utter monstrosity back to common humanity—that I do not fear your secret power—and that I know you will fight."

"Upon my word, Master Frank, you are appreciative! You reason cogently. I have half a mind to admire your logic! But, pray, how can what you seem to think such reasonable expectations be realized without entailing a degree of notoriety which would be disagreeably enhanced by the late incident to which you are pleased to refer, and in which we were both conspicuously prominent?"

"My little yacht lies here at the wharf, and is equipped for a voyage. There is, as you say, quite enough notoriety connected with us already, concerning late events. Come on board to-morrow. A short and pleasant voyage to the Gulf will take us to a country you wot of—where they are used to these things."

"Ah, I understand! just the thing—I will be with you. We manage this matter between ourselves?"

"Of course!—of course! We go alone—no necessity for any parade between old friends. Come on board at two o'clock precisely." And Frank turned upon his heel as if to leave.

"Ha! no treachery, now, Frank!" said Clenny with a raised voice, smiling strangely at the same time.

"No fear of you, at any rate! I know you, Newnon! Remember the time!—two o'clock! I must send my crew on board." And then the two young men parted.

CHAPTER VIII.

THE CONVERSATION.

In order to the full comprehension of the occurrences and characters of our narrative, it becomes necessary to turn back upon the track of years.

Long prior to the scene last given between Frank and Newnon Clenny, the two young men were sitting one night in a room of the St. Charles' Hotel, smoking. It was late, for they had already been conversing long and earnestly. They had come to a dead pause, and for at least five minutes had been puffing away most industriously, and staring absently through the window, in front of which a wan, struggling moon seemed to have much ado to keep the track amidst the ugly, black masses rapidly driving against its keen, shining prow. At last Clenny, the elder of the two, tipped the white ashes from the end of his segar on the point of his boot, which rested on the window-sill, nearly as high as his head, and broke the silence.

"The fact of the business is, Frank Carter, that this fastidiousness of yours amounts to nothing but a miserable affectation."

"Affectation! the deuse! Clenny, are you demented. You call it affectation, do you?—to be disgusted with a woman who eats beef heavily twice a day, and at a lunch, too, for all I know?"

"I do; and the most egregious affectation, too. This is a mere morbid whim. You have more common sense than to be in earnest about breaking off an affair which has progressed so far and promises so well as this, simply because the wo-

man has an appetite. This is namby-pamby stuff, and might
do for some open-collared Byron-struck sop o' moonshine of
a country village, who flourishes a whalebone cane, and fills
a corner in the country paper with rhymes of breezes, tresses,
wooing, cooing, loves and doves, and signs himself Alonzo;
but for you, who pretend to some calibre, it is utterly pre-
posterous."

"But be reasonable, man. I actually see her habitually
eat more beefsteak for breakfast than you—and you are no
mincer."

"Pish! Frank, this is coarse as well as ridiculous. What
business have you with what the woman eats? Does that
prevent her from being pretty, witty, and rich?"

"Yes! it prevents her being pretty and witty at least."

"What are you talking about? Isn't she the belle unrivalled of New Orleans—the scourge and terror of all bores—
more feared and famous for her wit and satire than any woman of the day? Besides, what connection is there between
beauty and wit, and beefsteak for breakfast?"

"A much greater affinity than between the true state of
the case and that which you have described. She is not a
wit or a satirist; but in good honest English, she is coarse
and unfeeling, as every other woman is who is so given to
strong meats, and plumes herself upon the reputation of being
sarcastic. Any one whose social backers—family and wealth
—are strong enough, and who has impudence and petty cruelty enough, can make a reputation with the mob of society
for sarcasm. It is only necessary to say mean and malicious
things, and sneer at all that is exquisite and sacred, to have
a herd of tinselled small fry—'cap-and-knee slaves'—haw!
haw! to any degree. When a really silly woman does this,
it is all well enough; she is living out the purpose of her
being, and there is no harm done: but when a woman like
Myra Haynes, who has naturally a good heart and a fine,
nay, even brilliant intellect, has so far fallen from the high

estate of womanly delicacy as to permit, much less glory in,
a reputation of this kind, I set it down that there is a
strong constitutional obesity at the bottom of it—that her
nervous susceptibility—that gossamer network vibrating to
the faintest airs from dream-land, which should guard about
the heart of a pure woman—has been actually drowned,
smothered in animal oils.   Willie Shakspeare says, 'When
the mind is free the body's delicate,' and I believe him, too.
It is as much impossible that a woman—the ducts and con-
duits of whose body are turgid with unctuous humours—
can buoy herself steadily in the rare empyrean of the
beautiful and true, as that a goose fatted for the spit can
play the humming-bird, and suck nectar from the woodbine's
coral trumpet on the wing.   She may flutter along the earth,
pounding up the dust with sufficient strength of pinion to
show that she might make a glorious air-voyage but for the
too great ballast of essential oils on hand—that is all.   There
is nothing like the pungent subtlety of the Attic, smarting
while it cures, in her wit; this could not live upon "breath
rank with gross diet.'"

"Carter, such *thoughts* are rank of grossness, connected
with the name of Myra Haynes.   Pray, my transcendental
coxcomb, would you have her sip dew from cups of violets
for breakfast; dine on fricasseed larkspurs and butterflies,
and take moon-sop for supper?   Such whimsicalities are
undignified and unmanly, when they lead to serious results.
Why, a pale dyspeptic miss of fifteen, sighing at the stars
from the garret attic of a convent, would blush to disclose
them to her "soul's sister" in earnest; and yet for such
splenetic fantasies of a cloyed taste, you talk of sacrificing
the just expectations of your father, friends, and the lady
herself.   It is only people who have gormandized themselves
into an indigestion whose brains generate such weak vapours.
Your favourite Willie says—

'Who can speak broader than he that has no house
To put his head in—such may rail against great buildings.'

So with those who have no stomach—they fret their irritable souls into whinings, and speaking broad against those who have. Such may rail against the pleasures of the table, talk of coarseness, stupidity—want of just sentiment being the necessary concomitants of an indulgence in them, but who will give them credit for either discrimination or sincerity? Besides, your own authority is expressly against you. Recollect—

'The veins unfill'd, our blood is cold, and then
We pout upon the morning——
——But when we've stuff'd
These pipes, and these conveyances of our blood,
With wine and feeding, we have suppler souls.'

And Cæsar says, 'Let me have men about me who are fat.' And furthermore, Mr. Frank, I am astonished that you haven't the good taste to admire her independence. She scorns the finicking, contemptible affectation of those would-be zephyr misses, who are horrified at the idea of eating honest, substantial food 'before folk,' but nibble puffs and sip flummery at balls most daintily, with the determination to make up for it on 'hog's foot and hominy,' or some other such delicacy, when they get home. I am afraid you are losing your balance and becoming a regular new-light Grahamite, or some other sort of fanatic."

"No, sir! I am neither a dyspeptic, a Grahamite, or any ite else. But I know enough of the moral and physical anatomy of our being to be convinced that the law of self-control is the stern law of the higher life, and that the unconstrained indulgence of appetite in man or woman, whether strong or weak, is inaccordant with the spiritual harmonies, unfriendly to physical as well as moral and intellectual symmetry—to that consistent repose and balance of at-

2 F 2

tributes which makes the powerful unity.   For my part, I'd
rather die as Icarus, suddenly, of a fall from the clouds,
than sink, as the gourmand does, inch by inch, into the
greasy slough of sensuality.   The diseases, the intellectual
and physical monstrosities, the low-browed ferocious super-
stitions, the hopeless, rayless, animal-eyed ignorance, as well
as the small swarm of captious jealousies, feverish malignities,
hatreds and fears—with all uncleanly lusts—which make
hideous, poison and convulse the social organism, are one
and all the venomous spawn of this monster vice.   Science
has demonstrated it—common sense tells us it is so, yet it is
fanatical to denounce it, indelicate to speak of it, even when
you mark its ravages in the wilted skin, the suffused cheek,
the hollow eyes, with their unnatural flashes of fantastic and
capricious humours, on the person of the woman you are expected to love.   By all that is blissful! I have no fancy for
the ingenious purgatory, the cross-grained and perverted
energies of such a woman would be expended in inventing
for my benefit!"

"Hold up, Frank, for Heaven' ssake!   Are you going to.
elocutionize even on till daybreak?   Give me another segar!
I see you have been taking a sagacious peep into the mill-
stone as well as the transcendentalists, and are grown quite
Orphic.   I suppose this misty revelation of yours, 'being
interpreted,' means that you intend to measure female at-
tractions by a scale of dietetics, and that the nearer they
come to starving themselves into the 'second sight'—seeing
visions, dreaming dreams, and hearing 'airy tongues that
syllable men's names,' and such like ghostly accomplishments—the nearer will they approach to victimizing you.
Shade of Cupid! but you have found a new road to the
heart, through the stomach.   You are clearly a 'New-
Light,' Frank!"

"It is a light as old as time, that the stomach has a great
deal to do with the sentiments.   I won't quote Records upon

you, to show that it was once considered the seat of them; but your own experience, if you will be candid, will suffice to convince you that there can be no delicate truthfulness of sentiment—no clear, concise thinking, where the laws of life have been outraged systematically—as is the case three times a day with those given to table excess. I tell you, sir, I had rather be assured of the habitual self-command of a woman in this particular, which is founded either on an unviolated instinct, which we all have, and which a proper education might keep intact, or a sense of duty, than to be familiar with any or every other of her habitudes. I mean the woman I should think of as my wife; for were I satisfied on this point, I should feel there was every thing to hope, since what she lacked in elevation and refinement, she would acquire naturally, as the flower drinks splendour in the beam-lit dew; but, in the other case, however much of fitful brilliancy she might display, I should only look forward through a painful perspective of 'fading still fading!'"

"But what does all this monody amount to, more than that you saw your lady-love honestly eat a beefsteak for breakfast in your presence, and thereat you are hugely indignant, seeing that from what you know of spirit-land the young ladies there who wear wings never carry such heavy ballast! I warrant you, if these shadowy damsels took a long gallop on horseback every day, or danced three or four hours every night, as Myra Haynes does, they would find something more substantial quite comfortable."

"Beefsteak is strong food for a labouring man—not stopping to discuss whether it isn't grosser than is needful for him—but for the delicate organization of such a woman, it is rank poison. During the riding party this morning, I could see its effects in the rather boisterous gayety, which would have been charming in you; in the spiteful, malignant abuse heaped upon every thing and every body, except your humble servant, remember! and which you call wit and sar-

casm—in her love of headlong, rapid motion. It had precisely the effect upon her a stiff glass of brandy would have
had upon me. Her blood was evidently burning in her
veins; there was no repose, no natural dignity of sentiment
drawn from her own healthful and happy emotions; no calm
appreciation, and clear-souled mirroring the charmed quiet
and wonders of apparelled Earth. She seemed restless as
one fever-stricken; her eye rested nowhere; she talked high-
flown sentiment, but it was by rote; she borrowed it from
Bulwer, who borrowed it from Byron, so that it was but the
ghost of an echo indeed! and yet the Thing-a-mys who
made up the party sighed and rolled up their eyes, or haw-
haw'd like mad, as they took their cue from her expression
—and she looked triumphant—and such triumphs! She may
have them all to herself hereafter for me; and yet the woman is capable of higher things! It is fortunate that the
effect of such indulgences and excesses is as legible as the
blossoms on a toper's nose; so that the honesty you boast
of her displaying amounts to nothing. The man who goes
with his eyes open can detect these things just as readily as
you can detect the 'three sheets in the wind' of your boon
companion."

"Frank, all this hyperbole of criticism sounds superbly
ridiculous, when you remember that it is applied to a peer-
less beauty, universally toasted as the most fascinating woman of the South!"

"That very fact of her being a universal toast is another
link in the chain of effects I have been tracing. That any
whipster who can sport 'rooms' and a cab, does not feel it
is presumption to take her name in vain on his unhallowed
lips, but swaggers over wine to his brother ape of his last
real or imaginary passage at wits with the famous Belle,
Myra Haynes, and swears she is 'a dem foin girl!' is proof
conclusive enough that she herself has authorized this by
the reckless exhibition of an inordinate passion for display—

in perfect keeping with the exaggerated, garish taste I remarked in the morning ride. It is always a woman's own
fault, when such tailor-advertisements as these dare to take
liberties with her name—she has licensed them, you may
be sure. There is a reverence of exalted Womanhood living
in the minds of men, which does not easily give way; and
untrue to that standard she must have been whose name,
whether for praise or censure, is a common topic. I tell you
there is a fence of awful dignity about the clear innocent Nature, which pert vulgarity would sooner attempt to scale the
blue walls of heaven than to break through. Why, I have seen
a Whiskerando—in comparison of whom a forked winter-tur-
nip, with its bunch of frosted greens, was a respectable entity
—look about him in consternation, as if he expected the earth
to gape, and sink his voice to a whisper, when it was necessary for his polluted lips to pronounce the powerful name
of a pure Woman."

"All *à la transcendentale,* and very fine! But, Master
Frank, I think your prayer had better be, 'Give me an
ounce of civet, good apothecary, to sweeten my imagination,'
if you can't make a better use of it, in the presence of a
beautiful woman, than tracing the effects of her digestion
in all sorts of incongruities. It strikes me it would be
more gallantly employed, at all events, in robing her in azure
and evening beams, and sprouting zephyr pinions on her
shoulders !"

"Bah! If the world choose to be hoodwinked, well and
good. I want the use of my eyes, and I should not stretch
the courtesy of conventional blindness quite so far as not to
see the bloat of debauchery on the person of a man addressing my sister; or, if my sweetheart took opium, refuse
to mark its ravages upon her cheek; or if, as in the instance
we discuss, she be guilty of other excesses which, equally
with these, unharmonize the exquisite Ideal I demand, be
mole-eyed and dumb, because a flippant delicacy bans the

24

topic. I can only afford to be blind when I meet a reality so dazzlingly like the radiant Seraph which is haunting me, as to make it a luxury to close my eyes and take the rest on faith ; but I can never be dumb or blind because a selfish and stupid fashion requires it. These things, upon which I insist so much, no doubt appear to you mere specks in the sun; but to me, who thirst only for the Pure and Perfect, they seem monstrous blotches !"

" Vastly complimentary to my taste ! But I can stand the contrast with a frigid acumen which so ingeniously inverts the common instincts of gallantry !"

" ' Still harping on my daughter !' But I insist, my dear fellow, it is a woman's own fault when these cruelly unsweetened imaginings you complain of, run riot in a man's brain. Why, sir, the clear eyes of a True Woman are the windows of heaven to me—in their unfathomable depths I see infinite beauties—the glancing of embodied Joys and Hopes, soft-plumed and sunny browed, beckoning me to bliss. My whole being is transformed by the enchantment—low gushes from the rills and fountains of the Better Land—odours, like whispered symphonies, of starry flowers and pleasant airs— they burden all my sense with ecstasy, until I feel what Angels hymn about, and adoration goes exulting up in praise to God—that he has blest us so—has sent this Living Beam of his own Love to throw its shining track across the desolation and the wastes of life, leading our aspirations right to him. My heart brims up with calmest happiness— flows out in faith and charity through all the world ; for I have seen the sure Promise in a Daughter of our race, and know the white feet of Angels to be yet upon our hills."

" A precious specimen of rhapsodizing that ! But, my foaming Pythian, I fear our poor belles would be sadly taken aback should they be required by the fiat of etiquette to make every young fellow who looked into their eyes, see sights so wondrous in them, and smell and hear at the same time odours so ravishing! I should be dreadfully alarmed lest, to dodge the letter of the law, they would hide all the windows of heaven behind goggles!"

"Newnon, you would strangle a Peri singing among flowers, if you could get your rude fingers on its throat. It does not follow that in such a case the emotions of every man must be identical with mine; but that they must be ennobling and elevating to the height of his susceptibilities under the influence of a pure woman's eye, is very certain; and I thank God that unless all is right within, this power over our holiest impulses fades from out her glance. I tell you, sir, Woman floats in a rarer atmosphere above us, and between us and the light of Heaven—and all the sacred rays from the Eternal throne which reach us, must be first refracted through her heart; if that be dark, then is earth dark to us; if that be clear, then do we see Heaven and Earth are filled with beams. My reverence of her in this high place—the sense of my dependence on her as, under God, the medium of all Good, is too profound to permit me, as a patient witness, to look on while she of her own accord deliberately will, for 'the mess of pottage,' to cast her wings and sink unutterably! I glory in this dependence though, and however often I may be disappointed, yet will I be strong in faith. One fleeting glimpse through the crystal bars of Paradise, half lifted, is sufficient to last a mortal life, and that I have had! and cheerily I'll plod onward in the pilgrimage before me. When heart-sick, as now, I'll go aside to open the gem-lettered scroll of memory, and feed my spirit with refreshing on its light—still elate in hope that Earth has yet another Wanderer of the Skies hid somewhere in its green nooks, awaiting me! Woman can never make me worse than my own passions have—but she can make me better, immeasurably far, and happier; her power ceases when our course is prone, she lends strength only to the wings!"

"I think you would immortalize yourself as the champion of Woman's Rights, and be feasted the round of the cities on sugar-plums! Hadn't you better try it, Frank?"

"Woman's rights! They can be fanatics as well as we. Her rights, are to be true to herself, and elevate man, and she will have nothing to complain of. The truth is, I am sick of the flat, stale, common-place, and vapid cant of the Society-Woman, and as to Men, I care nothing for them. I am determined that I will plunge beneath the mighty shadows of the great West—where the wild Daughters and flowers of Earth spring together—the nurslings of the mountain-winds amid ocean plains and cloud-aspiring forests, with torrent rivers thundering past for lullabies—they will, at least, be free and strong, and fresh, as prodigal nature made them; and my lungs and heart which, in this sickly air of hot-house faint perfumes, have almost wearied in their vocations, will learn again to play boldly and free as theirs!"

"Yonder's the morning star! let us at least take a nap before you set out!"

CHAPTER IX.

THE CHILD FRETA.

AGAIN we must revert yet farther back than this memorable conversation, from which those adventurings of Frank Carter we have previously traced, took origin; to show how fate had already prepared for him those surprises and startling realizations which so enthralled his life in the heart of that deep wilderness toward which we have seen his vague yearnings urging him.

Ho! presto! The parlour of one of the magnificent homes

of the "Merchant Princes" of New York in 1836 is open to
our view.

This palace is in Waverly Place.   It is large and very
imposing, with its granite front—but the interior, which has
been thus suddenly revealed, is far more extraordinary.
The subtlest refinements of luxury seem to have been lavished
in perfecting its splendid comfort.   The most learned and
exacting taste in upholstery can ask nothing more delicate
in drapery or richly massive in furniture.   The travelled
connoisseur would be astounded to recognise upon its walls
pictures of such value as he had thought only the galleries
of foreign princes might aspire to contain.   The gorgeous
chandelier throws down a soft shaded light like moon-rays,
and the white figures of grouped statuary start forth beneath
it from the niches and corners of the great room, seeming to
hold the silence pulseless by the awe of their immortal gestures.   Though the silence is very profound, you may detect
in the most shaded corner, the figure of a man almost buried
between the silken swell of purple cushions, amid which it is
listlessly reclined.   The shadow of a bust of Talleyrand, by
David, falls across the head of this man.   The broad white
calm of the marble brow, and the chill, yet honeyed sweetness of the subtly sculptured mouth above, seem to smile
that shadow down in congenial coldness upon a brow as
slumberously powerful, and mouth of much the same dangerous beauty.   But there are yet differences not easily detected
between the marble bust and that breathing bust.   The calm
of the first is unutterably inscrutable.   The face of Talley·
rand lives in marble as it lived in flesh—the illumination in
it as cold and sweet as the sun-light falling through the
petals of a frozen lily.   The face of this man upon which
that frore shadow falls, is stamped with much the same
character, and is now very still and marble-like, yet it be-
trays something.   There are two slight lines between the
eyebrows, and one still fainter slanting upward from each

2 G

corner of the ever-smiling mouth, which hint at the "lurking devil." It seems as if in striving to attain the consummate art

"To speak and purpose not,"

a passion had overflown its aim and left the marks of rude brushing wings behind upon that face. He is not an old man, for though his hair is white as snow, yet it is as luxuriant as ever, and falls back behind his ears in massive flakes. He is clearly not over fifty, since his eyebrows are as black as a crow's wing, and the bronzed flesh of his lean face has a singularly firm look. There is "speculation in his eye" —those clear gray eyes, that look off into the distance steadily as if that dead wall before them were not seen, and far beyond they traced some grave majestic dream, uplifting airy battlements and wondrous shapes against the sky.

It almost oppresses you that this man should be so very still that you cannot hear him breathing—should look as if in body and in soul he had been frozen!

Suddenly there is a loud, harsh scream, and then a shout of tiny laughter, as if a dozen little silver bells had all gone mad together—a clumsy mulatto servant-girl bursts into the parlour, screaming yet louder with genuine fright, as the golden-haired little elf in chase seizes her dress. With one hand this little creature strives to arrest the flight of her frightened maid—while at the same time she advances the other, which is gloved to the elbow, closer and closer toward the face of the shrinking slave. The mulatto tumbles headlong to the floor, shrieking in an agony of terror. "Massa! De snake! de snake! Miss Freta make he bite me!"

"Freta, my child, what have you there!" and the frozen, gray-haired man springs forward quickly.

Seizing the little hand, as she was almost sinking to the floor, beside her victim, in the muscular convulsions of her laughter, he saw that she held in it, firmly grasped between forefinger and thumb, the neck of a small "house-snake," while the striped length of the reptile was coiled about her arm.

"Freta! Freta! what a whim is this! Where did you get that loathsome thing?"

She sprang quickly to her feet, and stroked its shuddering back lightly with the other hand.

" Papa, it is not a loathsome thing; it is pretty, very pretty!"

" Where did you find it, dear?"

"In the conservatory! Oh, papa! it was under my beautiful Luxembürg rose, and Sylvy there was frightened!" She pointed with a scornful gesture toward the girl, who was crouched and creeping off on her hands and knees over the carpet.

"I was not scared though, papa, for I never was afraid of any thing beautiful. Its little black diamond eyes were *so* pretty! and its forked tongue made such a funny light— flash! flash! flash!"

"But how did you catch it, child?"

"Oh, right easy, papa! I knew that some snakes were poisonous, but I did not think this little fellow was, he looked so bright and innocent! I put on my gloves, and that not because I was afraid, pa, but because I thought that the *feel* of creeping things is not pleasant to people; then I seized it by the back of the head, and chased Sylvy with it. But don't you think it is pretty, papa?"

"Pretty for a snake, child; but you know that such creatures have a bad name in the world."

"No, that was a serpent, pa! not a snake that made Eve do wrong. But I don't care! If I had been Eve, I would have strangled it for saying naughty things to me—that's all!"

"Well! well! you little heretic! throw your snake out into the street now—it is not a suitable pet for little girls to have."

"But, papa, it has made me happy; and it is cold out of doors! I do not like to! It was the warm air in the conservatory that made it come out to see the roses and me, and now you want me to pay it by throwing it out to freeze in the street!"

"But, Freta, it is a base reptile. What would you do with it? You cannot love it!"

"I should not kill it if I can't love it, papa; for if our conservatory had not been warm it would not have come out from his hole until summer-time, and then it could have taken care of itself—now I ought to take care of it."

"Well, well! you wilful imp, go; warm it anywhere but in your heart or bed, and I will be satisfied, for the creature is entirely innocuous!" and stooping by her side, this hard and subtle-seeming man smiles tenderly, as with gentle touch he parts those dishevelled curls of "paly gold" from off that fair sweet forehead, and presses a soft kiss upon it.

Those large, blue, jutting eyes flash against his frigid face, and warm it for an instant with the light of love, which sparkles through a momentary suffusion of tears. The bright creature bounds away, followed shyly and at a distance by the still terror-stricken Sylvy. That strange, smooth man looks after the bounding step of the child for a moment, as he stands erect where she left him, and then smiling proudly as he turns toward the sofa, again mutters—

"Daring witch! she knows nothing of vulgar fears—she will be invaluable to me!" and he sinks down heavily amid the silken pile of cushions.

In a little while his face resumes the cold, placid, and abstracted expression we first observed: then "silence comes heavily again" in that great gorgeous room. All is still once more, and the statues become eloquent as his own figure. Now, you cannot hear him breathe;—but there comes the gay tintinnabula of low, melodious shouts and laughter! Again the sprite-like Freta bounds into the room!

Her arms about his neck, and she nestles gently in his lap.

"Father! father! I let go the pretty snake beneath my rose, and do you think it would not stay! It glided off, shining as it went, and then I did not see it any more. Wasn't it a naughty snake to run away so?"

"So you will find many bright things to glide from beneath your grasp, my child."

"But then I will love them, papa, because they were bright and gave me pleasure! Kiss me, won't you? You do not look happy to-night!"

She turned up her delicately pouting lips with such a bewitching sweetness, that the hard man could but melt, and he bent over to kiss her, while a tear fell upon her cheek. The beautiful child laid her face in his bosom for a moment, and then looked up through her brimming eyes, and said tremulously, "Papa is not happy to-night?"

At once she dashes the moisture from her eyes, and springing away from his arms, says gayly, " O papa, I will play for you that merry reel you love so much. Listen, listen!"

She took her place before the open piano opposite, and, with a skill most extraordinary in so young a creature, launched into the wild cadences of Scottish music.

A furious ring at the door-bell interrupts—there is a pause. The tones of the stammering Sylvy, commingling with those of a clear, commanding voice, are heard for a moment, and then a young man enters the parlour, somewhat hastily, hat in hand. The gray-haired man almost might be said to spring to his feet, so quickly does he rise to meet the new-comer.

"Hah! my venerable uncle Cedric!" said the young man as he stepped rapidly forward and placed his hat on the centre-table, "it is all up with us. But here is little Freta! Kiss me, little witch and cousin mine."

He catches the struggling little one in his arms, and only
2 G 2

succeeds in kissing her white forehead, when she escapes
from the room with the flushed haste of aversion apparent
on her face.

"Now, Newnon, what have you to say—what news do
you bring me?" said the gray-haired man, whose life seemed
thoroughly startled out of its deep stillness since the new
arrival. "I have expected your coming this hour."

"Well, good uncle, I am too much a pupil of your own
ever to permit myself to be either hurried or flurried by
any thing. I stayed just long enough down-town to hear all
that it was necessary for you and me to know."

"That was right. Well, what is the result?"

"Why, in the first place, the failure of your house this
morning was the sole topic upon Wall-street, and of course
it made the bulls and bears stare more wildly than they have
ever done through all the 'lets down' and 'crashes' that
have occurred during the last disastrous six weeks."

"That I expected, of course; but have they discovered
any thing with regard to my operations?"

"Ah, my good uncle, that's the question—'To be or
not,' &c.—you understand?" and the young dandy sinks
listlessly upon the cushioned sofa, and, stretching out his
legs, looks admiringly at his delicate boots.

"Pshaw, coxcomb! what do these antics mean? They
have got wind of it, have they?"

The gray-haired man stands up before the dandy, smiling
placidly, yet impatience is apparent in the slight twitchings
of the muscles—not of his *face*—but of his body.

"Y-a-w!"—a long gape, and the young gentleman
switches the point of his exquisite boot with his frail cane.
"Yes, my good uncle, as usual, you divine rightly! They
have got wind of your operations—or *our* operations, if
you insist upon implicating me, an innocent victim. And
the plain English of it is, that you must make me your executor, and be found *minus* to-morrow morning, or else the

Tombs will be *plus* a distinguished character, on charge of
sundry—you best know what—little peccadilloes !''

"That white-livered scoundrel, Nevers, has betrayed all !''

"Yes, yes ! we'll take care of him—so do not fret yourself on that score. I have brought you all the gold and
available notes I could raise.''

He lazily drew from beneath his clothes several fat,
heavy-looking packages, which he placed upon the table.

"You will probably not get out of the reach of the hue
and cry this side of the bounds of civilization. The schooner
Grattan sails to-night for New Orleans; I have secured
passage for yourself, Freta, and Sylvy; so you see every
thing is ready to your hand. For a person of my easy
habits, you must admit that I have done well, since all these
preparations have been made within three hours.''

"You have done well,'' said the other coolly. "Have
you seen any of our people in the mean time?''

"Yes, they are all true as steel. They are somewhat
indignant, to be sure; and we expect to feel prodigiously
the absence of your controlling influence—but you will be
obeyed as implicitly a thousand miles distant as if you were
here.''

"I have rather anticipated this result for several days;
but I think, on the whole, that it may not prove so unfortunate for us. I shall extend the limits of our operations, as
I pass through the South—where I shall take occasion to
see, personally, to this affair of the Haynes estate, which we
have so much at heart. Perhaps I may find it best to give
over the entire management of it into your hands. You
have known one of the parties, at least, since boyhood; and
if I find that you retain the strong hold that I suspect upon
his memory, I shall probably send for you to take him in
hand. In the mean time, try and keep this nestling-place
intact for me, for I have spent too much in adorning it to
my taste, to relish the idea of having these rare gems of art

profaned by the vulgar mob of New York soap-boilers, who have come to wear purses!"

"Set your mind at ease upon that point as well, my most admirable and venerated uncle; for this is a very clever establishment which your rare and restless genius has elaborated for my peculiar benefit. I can occupy it for several years quite pleasantly, greatly to my own glorification and comfort. If you have got the deed we spoke of—in anticipation—made out in due form, I think I can promise myself an unquestioned occupancy."

"All is prepared in due form—here is the deed!"

He pressed a spring beneath the lid of the centre-table, a segment flew up, and the papers were revealed.

"You perceive I have been as careful of you, as you have this night proven yourself to have been of me and mine. Take that package!"

The young man obeyed, rising at the same time and grasping his hat. Cedric shut down the lid of the table, and the two stood face to face in silence. He extended his hand—the young man took it without speaking. There was no passion in their clear and cool gray eyes that met each other steadfastly for a few moments—not as if in search of regrets at parting—of memories of the past or hopes of the future—of any sympathies indeed, or even Faith—but as if two diamonds came quietly together, point with point, between the tremendous pressure of great wills that tried if either could be made to crumble one fine atom of its spiritual edge! Then the young man turned, leaving the parlour with a sauntering, listless air. Cedric, the gray-haired man, stands alone in that magnificent room; but now, when he relapses quickly into that old air of frozen abstraction, we are not so much surprised, and we can see before the distant gaze of those calm eyes, new schemes of grand and subtle villany, rising beyond the wreck amid which he stands so dauntlessly.

CHAPTER X.

REGULUS.

TEN years, which would again bring us back to about the period of the conversation at the St. Charles', have now elapsed since the unceremonious exodus of Cedric with Freta described in our last chapter took place, and yet we must now return again to the mansion in Waverley Place. Its ex terior is not changed since we saw it first, though such a period has intervened. Even less change is apparent in the interior of that magnificent parlour. The chandelier, the drapery, the pictures, the statuary, the sofas, all, indeed, look the same. It seems as if the presence of the gray-haired Cedric, though he is far enough away, still holds that room, and all that it contains—even to its very atmosphere —frozen motionless as he left it.

Out of doors the night was very gloomy, and the neighbourhood was badly lighted. The clock of St. John's gave out that one melancholy stroke, which sounds so like a wailing cry of the young day breaking upon the dark silence of its mournful birth, and then, one after another, the different quarters of the great city took it up, until it died away, sobbing in the distance.

You will perceive two figures glide into that silent parlor noiselessly. The doors and windows are all closed, and you will observe that they must have found some other mode of entrance, since they advance from behind a group of statuary in one corner. They stop beside the centre-table, and beneath the softened light of the chandelier. The man who comes forward with a light, quick step, as if he trod upon eggs, has a very pleasant face, for though the cut of his eyebrows be sharp and square, and that of his eyes be sharp and hard, yet you feel that the mellifluous mouth "overcomes" the face with sweetness like a summer-cloud. You cannot well realize now the comparative and superlative degrees of sharpness expressed in the nose and chin, which neighbour that placid nectary of smiles. The smooth forehead is so disproportionably expanded above the temples that you cannot but think the outline of the face resembles that of a fox —but that it is all so delicately blanched, it is impossible to associate an image of gross animality with it—especially since that acute chin rests upon a snowy neckcloth, which is duly relieved by a full suit of irreproachable black.

This person might readily be placed in the calendar of the Saints; but whether among those who have been sanctified by their devotion to the Christian's God, or to that Pagan deity of Wall street—the god Mammon—might, perhaps, be cautiously doubted. He has a quick, imperative manner about him, as if accustomed to command. If there are no wrinkles on his brow, the spirit of them so rested there, that you thought in mathematics—from magnetic sympathy—in his presence, and were not surprised to see the slave behind him look, act, and speak like a machine. This man pressed the same concealed spring that we have seen the gray-haired Cedric press, and up flew a segment of the table. He took out sundry packages of sealed letters, which, from the diversity of the postmarks, seemed to have come from all quarters of the Union, and even the distant extremes of the continent. The negro placed a chair behind him and retreated to a respectful distance—standing as though on drill. The man sat down, and stooping low over the table, as if near-sighted, broke seal after seal in quick succession, and glancing rapidly down the sheets, laid the letters aside. It was impossible to perceive any thing in his expression as he read, until at last he came to one which was greatly soiled.

and had several post-marks upon it. This one he opened with a nervous eagerness, which was quite perceptible, and bent lower than ever while he read.

He had finished and rose quickly. "Dick, it is time they were coming—go and unbolt the basement door into the back alley?"

"Yes, Massa!" said the negro, and wheeled about mechanically to execute his mission.

"Stop there, Dick! are you sure *our* Captain of Police is on duty to-night?"

"B'lieve him is, Massa."

"There must be no doubt about it. Run back into Washington Place and see if he is on the look-out. Tell him to count the men who enter the alley, carefully, and look sharp for lurkers in the neighbourhood."

"Yes, Massa."

"And look you, Master Dick!—be very sure of *The Word* before you let any man in below!"

"Yes, Massa;" and the negro marched off alertly.

When he disappeared behind the group of statuary, you might have heard a slight sound as of sliding panels, and then all was still again. For fifteen minutes this man walked back and forth restlessly, still holding that soiled letter in his hand. Now and then he would pause by the heap of opened letters on the table, take one from it, stoop, glance over it, and lay it down to resume his walk. A slight sound had reached his acute ear, and he reseats himself quickly, and appears to be absorbed with the letters. A tall man, whose face and figure is completely shrouded in a long black cloak, enters with a noiseless step from behind the group of statuary. When this new comer had approached the table, the man seated at it merely nods in recognition, as he looks up from his labour for a moment. The new comer acknowledges the recognition in the same business-like manner, and proceeds to divest himself of his large cloak and broad

brimmed hat in a very leisurely manner. This proceeding
revealed the tall slim figure of a very intellectual-seeming
man, whose bright unsteady eye expressed a quick and volatile nature entirely in unison with that lithe and supple
frame.   He was dressed in the last degree of rich and elegant fashion.   He said, as he sank down listlessly upon a
sofa, "You seem to have a heavy mail before you, to-night,
Mr. Secretary.   I hope there is something from our nomadic
President, for it is full time we heard from him!"

"There is—and something of importance, too—as you
shall hear when the rest arrive!"

"Glad of it, we want something to stir us up!   What is
it now—Financial, Commercial, Political, or what?"

"Political!"

"I thought so, for it is high time—high time!" and he
gave a long yawn, and threw himself back upon the sofa.

At this moment another person entered by the same way,
and in the same noiseless manner we have described.   Before
he had divested himself of his cloak, another followed, and
then soon another, until in a short time there were ten men
lounging or standing in scattered groups through that
magnificent parlour.   There could be no mistake as to the
social rank of these men.   It was stamped upon their pale,
intellectual faces, expressed in their calm, possessed and
purposeful bearing, and advertised in their faultless costume.   It requires "no ghost come from the grave to tell"
that they are all men of the world—men of position and
refined cultivation, who know perfectly well what they are
about, whether it be for evil or for good.   There was one
prevailing trait which characterized the expression of this
company—not so much individually as collectively—and that
was intellectual daring—a cutting, cold, calculating audacity
of purpose and will.   There was no attempt at disguise beyond that they had worn from the street.   They all seemed
to know each other well, both personally and socially, and

out-door titles and designations were used with the familiarity and freedom that would have characterized a meeting "on 'Change." The banker, merchant, politician, lawyer, doctor, gentleman, poet, editor, and priest, had evidently met there in that gorgeous room to hear something of importance from the mellifluous lips of that fair, sharp-faced gentleman in black, who sat beside the centre-table still bending over his letters. This person looked up at last, and glancing his eye quickly around the room, said in a clear, formal tone, "I believe all are here. Gentlemen, shall we proceed to business?"

There was a general rustling through the room as those who stood seated themselves, and those who were seated at a distance drew nearer the centre table.

"I am prepared, as usual, gentlemen, with a full synopsis of our correspondence since we met last night. It is more than usually voluminous, and brings us many items of interesting intelligence. First, we have news from our commercial agent at New Orleans, which has been sent through at an expense of over a thousand dollars, and which is twenty-four hours ahead of the mail, and twelve ahead of any other express. He says, that up to the moment of despatch, cotton had risen two cents, with a steady upward determination —thinks it will reach three, on account of heavy orders from England."

While the sensation caused by this intelligence was yet buzzing through the room in a low-voiced commentary, the technical secretary, in his clear, formal tones and sweetly placid manner, went on with his synopsis.

"Another from our trusty agent of manufactures in Massachusetts, who speaks in glowing terms of the spread of our system of industrial monopoly in that state; and says that our mills are becoming the sole and central arbiters of Labour, and are rapidly absorbing every form of production on a small scale, and that even independent agriculture had begun to

2 H   25

acknowledge the power of our combinations. He mentions that the wool-growing districts are at our feet already, and thinks that our system of espionage and individual denunciation, if inexorably persevered in, will awe these small farmers and the operatives of our mills into subjection, and that we shall soon control the value of produce and prices of labour as we proposed. He mentions the name of several of our agents whose conduct should be inquired into, as they exhibit a faint-hearted disinclination to push our great idea, and are beginning to cant about the cruelty of crushing the poor operatives. You perceive that it is necessary they should be attended to promptly, since the third section of our constitution expressly provides that all disaffected, opinionative and fanatical persons, who may be discovered among our employées in, this as well as some other departments of our operations, must be dismissed and provided for."

"Yes! Yes!"   "Down with them!"   "They must be seen to at once!"   "We will ballot to-night for who shall go to see to this matter!" And such like expressions ran around the room, while the pale secretary paused.

"Here are several other letters from our New England agents, with regard to improvements in labour-saving machinery, which require our careful supervision, for they contain unusually important suggestions. They develop several important agents of monopoly in manufactures, which cannot be passed by without our careful regard—but these must lie over for action till to-morrow, as we have more pressing business on hand to-night."

"That will do. Put them aside."

"Here is a letter with regard to the Dickson property, in Apalachicola, Florida. Our agent writes that the widow has been frightened by the costs of the suit with which he has threatened her, and desires a compromise. She will take ten thousand dollars in hand, and surrender her right to us. Shall we make the appropriation, gentlemen?"

There was a pause, then a few hurried words of consultation. The whole party rose to their feet. The secretary glanced coldly around upon them, and muttered as he made a note upon the sheet before him,—

"Unanimous! That's done with."

They sat down and he resumed.

"Here are some thirty letters from various quarters of the Union and adjacent territories, mostly of minor importance, considering the business we have yet before us; their contents are generally satisfactory as to the success of our operations. Specially does our old-established system of transplanting ruined adventurers into the new countries of the South-West, at the successive occupation and annexation of which we aim, seems to be working well. We hear of new concessions obtained everywhere, discipline seems perfect, and the spell of our formidable signature, 'Regulus,' seems to be potent as ever. We must continue to use it with the greatest discretion. Any abuse of it would be fearful to us!"

Putting this correspondence aside, the secretary took up another paper from the table, and shaking it slightly in his hand toward them, he went on.

"Here we have an interesting report from *our* chief of police in this city. We have first, as usual, all the crimes of the month, with the names, characters, residences, and haunts of the criminals. I observe that there is quite a number of *suspected* persons, who have been 'spotted' as such by the city police, who are in our employ. This only calls for greater watchfulness on our part. There are several names presented which particularly demand our attention. They are those of persons most of whom have been, or ought to have been, sent to the Tombs and to Sing-Sing, for sundry crimes, and are now at large. They are Free-soilers, Abolitionists, and Professors, both male and female, of new sciences and isms; expounders of Woman's rights, Amalgamation, &c. But our report represents them as persons of indomitable energy, extraordinary recklessness and daring; who have a rude eloquence, which can impress the mob. These people have clutched the Agrarian ideas of reform, and as all their tendencies are disorganizing and subversive, as they are wielding an immense power with the labouring classes, they require encouragement. They have already organized extensively. They have clubs and newspapers, and are prepared to exert a very formidable influence in this city, and through the country, upon the coming Presidential election. We must see to, and propitiate these persons, as you will clearly perceive. The estimated cost of that substantial aid and comfort which should be extended by us at the present crisis toward these incendiaries, is fifty thousand dollars. Here are the names. You will perceive that this expenditure refers only to their leaders—for the people must have a magical watchword, if we expect to lead them; even all our enormous capital will not bribe the masses, while a simple *word* will arm them to follow us as trustingly as sheep to the shambles, at the heels of their shepherd. I think, however, that the vote with regard to expenditure had better not be taken until our next meeting, as I have yet some most important matter in this connection to submit in reference to the greater encouragement to be offered to a class of restless, flippant, and fanatical women, who are rapidly becoming prominent at the North. The sickly sympathies, the clap-trap cant, and termagant vituperation of this disaffected sisterhood of virginity, promise a most decided and practical availability for our general purposes of corruption and disorganization of the Republican in favour of Oligarchical tendencies! Their babble will do much toward increasing the wordy dust of disaffection between the North and the South, under the cloud of which we operate successfully This is to be looked to."

The report was rapidly glanced over by the most curious

of these men; and, as the names were read, the idea that these persons—whom they all knew—were to be secured, seemed to be unanimously recognised; but it was hastily laid by, for it was now late, and all knew that the secretary had reserved the most important communication for the last. He drew the soiled letter from his pocket, and with great deliberation proceeded to unfold it. "That must be from *our* President!"

"What has he to say?"

"Let us hear!"

The secretary read out in the same tone.

"He writes from the remote home he established as a place of refuge a number of years since. He has just returned from an extended excursion through the valley of the Mississippi, including all the principal States and towns of the great South-West. He has been remarkably successful generally, and sends a long list of agents who will co-operate with us, and correspond regularly. But what is of far more importance, he thinks that he has at last consummated the great purpose for which we have so long and patiently laboured. He pronounces the South-West to be fully prepared for a war of conquest with Mexico. The secret society organized by him so many years ago, has spread and prospered wonderfully. This resurrection of the grand scheme of his patron and master, Burr—which he effected so long ago, and has worked at with such indomitable purpose ever since—has, after including among its sworn supporters, two Presidents and four great popular leaders, resulted in the annexation of Texas. Now, he says, the people have grappled in earnest the magnificent idea, with all its vast sequences, and nothing can stay their resistless will. At the coming Baltimore Convention it has been determined that we shall throw aside the old 'King of Trumps' on both sides, and take up that new 'Ace of Spades,' which will open our way to the mines of Mexico. Who he is to be,

2 H 2

depends upon his availability; but an apt pupil of Jackson and the old *regime* of Democracy, is to be preferred. This is determined upon, and no power upon earth can prevent its consummation. It is our old purpose, and the whole strength of our immense capital and extended chain of influence is to be cast in its favour! Now, gentlemen, what do you think?"

The sharp-eyed secretary looked around with a keen, unimpassioned glance into the faces of those about him. The proposition was tremendously startling, and some of the well-schooled faces there betrayed that they felt it to be so. The smooth-tongued, placid secretary continued in the same tone, as he handed over the letter to them.

"You perceive that he furnishes a list of names from the North, South, East, and West, who are solemnly sworn to support this movement and this nomination. If you look at the list carefully you will recognise them as veritable signatures; and it presents an array of names, powerful enough, if united, to tear to pieces and utterly subvert the Federal constitution. The movement is evidently matured; we have but to resolve, and it is consummated!"

The paper was passed around, and carefully examined by every one. No one seemed to be taken entirely by surprise, though all were somewhat astounded by the suddenness with which the question, involving such great consequences, had been presented for their adjudication. But these were prompt men—prepared, by their previous training and thought, to act in any emergency.

There was a pause of some fifteen minutes, during which the letter and list were examined, and some consultation in an undertone went on, and then one of them said in a sharp, impatient voice,—

"We are ready for a vote, Mr. Secretary, upon this letter; go on!"

"Gentlemen approving, will rise."

They all rose simultaneously, and then there was a general movement toward cloaks and hats, as for a breaking up— when the secretary said, in a shrill, loud voice,—

"Gentlemen, there is yet another letter to which I would direct your attention. It is from our Vice President, Newnon Clenny, who dates from the St. Charles' Hotel, New Orleans."

"Well, what does he say—in short! Let us hear!"

"It is that Frank Carter proves to be a dreamy enthusiast, and he fears is an incorrigible fool, of whom we can make nothing. For some silly whim he has broken his engagement with the daughter of old Haynes, and is about pushing off to the Rocky Mountains on a vague and boyish adventure. I fear that our schemes with regard to those two enormous estates are to be greatly compromised by the eccentricities of this unripe whipster. Clenny thinks there is something available in him yet, and proposes to keep by him through this new enterprise."

"Clenny is in earnest, and the boy is safe enough in his hands. If I had any designs upon the morals of Lucifer himself, I should send Clenny to him with his subtle sneer. But it is late—let us go."

This was said by the tall, elegant man, as he threw on his cloak, and they all started toward the group of statuary.

"One moment more, gentlemen," said the secretary, rising. "What do you say to the appropriation spoken of in the report of our Chief of Police?"

"You must have it!"

"You must have it, of course!" said several, while all nodded assent.

"Certainly," said the tall man; "we have just resolved to bait the Bear of Conservatism, and we must find our bulldogs in butcher's meat!"

With a slight laugh they all disappeared. In a few moments that large parlour was left alone with the silence and its statues.

CHAPTER XI.

THE ESCRITOIRE.

THE author, being a resident of New York during the period of the principal incidents narrated as occurring in that city, had formed the acquaintance of the principal personages. Himself a Southerner, he had, from the natural affinities of origin, inevitably been attracted toward Carter. The intercourse between them, at first reserved, had imperceptibly warmed into a degree of intimacy, which, however, had by no means been such as to render him at all cognisant, beyond the merest generalities, of the progress of his private affairs. He was not a little surprised, therefore, at finding, one day, an elegant escritoire of dark, rich wood, heavily banded in the old-fashioned style with silver, which had been placed, in his absence, on the table of his sanctum. A note, in a sealed envelope, lay upon it. He instantly recognised the hand-writing of the address as that of Mr. Carter, and broke the envelope.

It was evidently written in great haste, but without any sign of trepidation. It ran thus:—

"MY DEAR FRIEND:

"I have no time for explanations, as I am in the midst of hurried preparations for an unexpected yacht-voyage—upon which I set sail in a few minutes. I send you the escritoire, which was left in my charge by a highly valued friend. He was an extraordinary man; and its contents are, I doubt not, of great value to the world.

It was given me, with the injunction that it should not be opened until six months after his death. The six months were up some weeks since, but I have lately been too much otherwise absorbed to think of making use of the privilege of the key. I now therefore transfer to you this bequest in full, with the proviso that you will not open it for six months. If at the end of that time I have not been heard from, please open, and without reserve make what use of it your excellent sense may justify. Please take charge of whatever correspondence may arrive to my address for the same length of time, at the expiration of which time you will also please to consider yourself as my executor—open my correspondence and proceed as you may think best. Pardon this unceremonious intrusion of responsibilities upon an intimacy, the terms of which I hardly feel would strictly justify me; but the plea that I know no one else whom I can trust, and have no time for further explanations, will I am sure justify me in the eyes of a brother Southron.

"Yours truly,
FRANK CARTER."

Six months having elapsed, and still no news of my singular friend Carter, the fulfilment of the important duties of executor, thus unexpectedly devolved upon him, were deferred by the narrator as long his sense of duty would possibly admit. At last, when longer delay would have seemed to assume almost the aspect of criminality, the duty of opening the correspondence was unwillingly entered upon. As little that was there revealed was specially germain to the purposes of this book, the writer will be excused for using his discretion so far as to reveal the contents of but a single letter. It was from Freta, and was dated on the morning of the day on which Carter sailed on his mysterious yacht voyage.

"*St. John's Square.*

"Oh, my friend, do not believe, when I wrote you yesterday eve, that I meant you should never think of me again on earth: when I said that we must never meet again, that I was leaving the city for ever, and that it would be in vain that you attempted to trace me. I said what was right— for I am betrothed to another. That promise was forced from me as the actual price of my father's life, and unwearied assiduities, extending from my childhood up through my whole life, and sanctioned by my father. Yet, though my heart was never given, my word has been wrested from me, and my honour is pledged. He will never release me. I know his inexorable temper well, therefore have I resolved to face this issue. I have long known that its consummation must be instant death to me—and with prayers and tears I have won respite from time to time, hoping always that I might see you once again on earth. I have been favoured —I have watched over you long through my faithful Indian —and I was happy, though I felt myself to be dying fast. I beheld you at length for the first time since our horrid separation, and my frame yet quivers with the ecstasy. Oh! the joy, the joy I felt that I had swooned into heaven on your shoulder. Again and again the interminable thrills yet cleave through my soul. If this be love, it shall die free with me, as it came—as pure in its warm flood that seemeth ever gushing down the boundaries of sense, as when in single drops of dew, through flowers and all the forms of beauty in the natural world, it freshened my still life in that far wilderness. Aye, all thoughts, all shapes, all aromas of the beautiful, gather like drops in this wild glowing tide of love on which I am born aërially elate, where wings could never bear me. I'll know no other existence! Life, that has given me this, lifted me to the fair beatification of Death through which Nature exalts her soul to transcendent realities. I would not say to you—do not die! but strive to be ever near me in soul. Do not come near me on earth, but be with me always!

"FRETA."

This letter had missed Frank, and who can say what effect upon his destiny its reaching him would have had. Our paths here are sometimes inscrutably darkened.

Nearly two years had now passed, and still not a syllable of news from the yatch voyage. The escritoire had been opened, and found to contain many valuable and strangely interesting papers, the startling character of which (the writer would mention incidentally) would justify him in giving them hereafter in form of a sequel to the present. The escritoire will, of course, be recognised as that left in the hands of Frank by the murdered Yerga, who fell in the treacherous duel to which Clenny was a party, and which has been previously described.

Accident at last threw in our way one of those methodical, matter-of-fact, quiet sort of personages, who seem to have been born nowhere—to have never had a home; who are always penniless, but whose lives appear to have been as constantly spent in adventuring as they most probably originated in an adventure. One of those warps and estrays of love which seem to have taken

"More composition and fierce equality,"

in "the lusty stealth of nature," than enters into the organization of a dozen common citizens.

This man gave me an account of an extraordinary scene, to which he was accidentally an eye-witness, which may throw some light upon the fate of the persons in whom we are interested.

CHAPTER XII.

THE DUEL BY MOONLIGHT.

HE relates that on one occasion he had crossed over from the mainland of Texas—some distance south of the entrance to Matagorda Bay, to a curiously insulated beach, which stretches for many miles parallel with the coast. There is a wide channel of deep water between the coast and this narrow beach, or breakwater, as it might most properly be called. Here the turtles resort in incredible numbers to deposit their eggs in the sand; and, as he had been in from the Frontier idling about Matagorda for some time, he bethought him of turtle-egging by the way of a small adventure and by way of passing the time. He had gone over alone, with the purpose of spending the night, which was very pleasant, and watching the turtles deposit their eggs, preparatory to the morning operations. The moon did not rise until late, so he threw himself down upon the sand for an early nap—intending to rise with the moon. He waked as he thought, about eleven o'clock; the red disk of the moon was just then showing itself above the waters. When he had raised himself upon his elbow, he was not a little startled at perceiving the broad, white sails, and slender spars of a small schooner-rigged vessel lying between him and the mainland. In a moment his ear caught the creaking of pulleys, as the sail went down, and she swung round as if she had just reached her mooring. He was startled at this unexpected appearance, and with excellent reason. He knew that this beach had long been famous as the resort of smugglers, who were in the habit of gliding into the channel during the night, to land their goods here, when they buried them in the loose sand, and then stole out again before daybreak— leaving them to be carried across to the mainland, in small boats, by accomplices, at their leisure.

He knew well that if this were a smuggling vessel with such an object in view, his presence there would be very dangerous to him. He, therefore, in no inconsiderable tre- pidation, crouched close upon the sand, and began to look about him to discover whether the inequalities of the ground were such as to enable him, by crawling, to place a greater distance between him and such unwelcome neighbours. There was clearly no hope for him; the surface of the beach presented few undulations, and the only chance for a hiding place seemed to be an old drift log, that lay in rather un- comfortable proximity to low-water mark. He crawled to this with all possible speed, and having ensconced himself behind, felt considerably more comfortable, although every dash of the waves drenched half his body. The fact that the little vessel bore no light at her bows, had increased his suspicions of her character from the first. But now little time was left him for further speculation, for a splash at her side announced the launching of a small boat, and in another moment a small lantern appeared over the side, and he could distinguish the sound of adjusting oars, and men taking their places in the boat. In a moment afterward it shot from under the shadow of the vessel, and he could distinguish, though faintly, for the moon was behind him then, there were four persons in the boat. The oarsmen, whose general appearance was that—so far as he could distinguish it—of man-of-war's men, and two passengers, who wore glazed caps, and what appeared to be a sort of undress Navy uni- form. He had thought, as they entered the boat, that he could distinguish the flash and clatter of weapons being de- posited in the bottom. He heard no sound of voices, while the boat was pulled rapidly to the beach. The two passen-

2 I

gers were landed within two hundred paces of his hiding place. There was only a moment's delay, when the boat returned in profound silence to the vessel, which received it —and then in an instant every thing was dumb and dark as death on board.

The two men who had landed, stood watching the boat, and then turning, they walked a little higher up on the beach. There were but few words spoken, the sound of which faintly reached the watcher's ear, when they suddenly stopped, and stood facing each other. Directly, he saw a quick flash—a sudden movement of both men, and the steely clank of meeting blades shocked upon his shuddering ear.

So great was his horror and astonishment that he had almost sprung erect. But with a returning sense of caution he again crouched, though not so low as to deprive him of a full clear view of this singular combat—for combat it now surely was—as the swift blades flashed and gleamed with fearful rapidity; while the forms of the two men, beneath the now full splendour of the moon, seemed endowed with a supernatural activity as they flitted to and fro, shifting position with the various changes of the fight. The men had thrown off their caps. The taller of the two, who wore his hair in lovely curls, seemed the most impetuous—while the other, with close locks, stood most on the defensive, and seemed wary and cold, but active as a panther.

The combatants were singularly well matched, and for several moments the sparks fell in heavy showers from the rapid collision of their short Roman blades. Suddenly the taller and more impetuous staggered and seemed struck. His opponent bounded quickly in upon him, and for a moment they writhed as in one embrace—when at once the taller man, shaking himself as if to get free, sprang backward, when the other fell forward upon his face and was still. There was now no weapon in the tall man's hand, and he folded his arms and stood still, looking down upon the body of his foe as he lay. There was the gleam of the sword-blade that came up through his back as he lay upon his face. The survivor did not touch him again, but shaking his hair he sounded three calls upon a whistle, and then picking up his cap, walked with an unsteady step along the beach straight to the driftwood, behind which our trembling watcher lay. He did not seem to observe him, however, but sat down upon the log with his back toward him. He groaned once, as if in deep pain, as he pressed his hands upon his side. The man saw he was pale as death, had a very high forehead, and said he thought he was remarkably handsome.

The boat had been instantly lowered, and when it ran upon the beach, he rose with difficulty; the men came forward and helped him into the boat. He simply ordered them back to the vessel, and they asked no explanation, although they could plainly see the other man lying dead upon the beach. After putting him on board, two men came back with them, and they now rowed directly toward where the dead man lay. They landed, and after digging a hole, higher up on the beach, and returning to the body, my informer plainly saw them draw the blade from the breast of the corpse. They then took it up to the hole and buried it, first placing the cap upon its head.

As they returned by the place where the combat occurred they picked up the bloody sword, which had no doubt passed through the heart of the dead man, pushed off the boat, and returned to their vessel, which immediately set sail, and when day-light came was out of sight.

The young man, when he arose and shook his stiffened limbs, found it difficult to realize that all had not been a terrible and solemn drama. But there were the unmistakable traces of the struggle in the sand; there was a black stain where the dead man had fallen; there was the blood upon

the log, where the survivor had sat down so close to him—
and last of all, there was the new-made grave! You may be
sure our young adventurer did not gather many turtle eggs
that morning.

Some eighteen months from this time, while promenading
Broadway one fine morning, the author's attention, in common with a thousand other pedestrians, was attracted to a
stand-still of admiration, at the elegant horsewomanship
of what all would judge to be a Southern woman, who,
mounted upon an airy-limbed and magnificently spirited
black horse, swept along the pave at a bounding gallop, accompanied by a gentleman, who was also splendidly mounted.

A strange thrill passed through me as I recognised the
striking features of this man, whose long dark hair fell about
his shoulders. It was undoubtedly my old friend Frank Carter; and if one had risen from the grave, it could not have
caused me greater astound. And that superbly etherial beauty
by his side, with her translucent complexion, and great miraculous eyes, must be Freta!

I found Frank considerably sobered and cured of many
ultraisms of opinion in regard to dietetics, &c. But the man
seemed walking in such a trance of assured bliss, that he
continually appeared as one who knew not that this was
the old common Earth he yet tarried upon, so did his soul
overflow toward all things in love!

Sylva is still the favourite waiting-maid of Freta; who
tells me that her faithful Indian, after having brought
Frank and her together, again disappeared strangely, on the
morning of their marriage.

Concerning the fate of Cedric I could hear nothing
Thomson, the Englishman, was a mere minion of Clenny's.
Concerning the mysterious and omnipresent "Regulus," we
may yet learn something more.

THE END.